INVASION OF THE SEA

THE WESLEYAN
EARLY CLASSICS OF
SCIENCE FICTION
SERIES
GENERAL EDITOR
ARTHUR B. EVANS

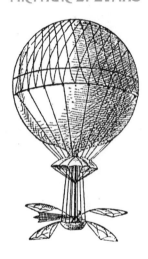

INVASION OF THE SEA

JULES VERNE

TRANSLATED BY EDWARD BAXTER
EDITED BY ARTHUR B. EVANS
INTRODUCTION AND CRITICAL MATERIAL
BY ARTHUR B. EVANS

Wesleyan University Press *Middletown, Connecticut*

Published by
Wesleyan University Press,
Middletown, CT 06459
Translation copyright © 2001
by Edward Baxter.
Introduction and notes © 2001
Arthur B. Evans

Printed in the United States
of America on acid-free paper

Designed by Rich Hendel
and set into Cochin and
Metropolitaine type by
B. Williams & Associates

ISBN 0-8195-6545-8 paper
ISBN 0-8195-6465-6 cloth

CIP data appear at the back
of the book

5 4 3 2 1

Contents

 Introduction

Closing the Circle: Jules Verne's *Invasion of the Sea*

As the first title to be published in Wesleyan University Press's new book series Early Classics of Science Fiction, this volume of Jules Verne's *Invasion of the Sea* is historically significant for many reasons. It is the first English translation of this important work,[1] and the first complete, unabridged, and fully illustrated scholarly edition of any late Verne novel ever to appear in print. Its original French counterpart, *L'Invasion de la mer,* was the last of Verne's *Voyages Extraordinaires* to be published before the author's death in 1905[2] and, as such, the last novel that can be attributed to Verne's hand alone.[3] In many ways, both thematically and narratologically, *Invasion of the Sea* completes Jules Verne's fictional odyssey where it began. And it closes the circle on nearly a half-century of "extraordinary" contributions to world literature that, rightly or wrongly, have immortalized him as the "Father of Science Fiction."[4]

Publishing History

L'Invasion de la mer (1905, Invasion of the Sea) is one of four late novels by Jules Verne that have previously never been translated into English. The other untranslated titles from Verne's *Voyages Extraordinaires*—a series comprising over sixty novels published from 1863 to 1919—include *Le Superbe Orénoque* (1898, The Mighty Orinoco), *Les Frères Kip* (1902, The Kip Brothers), and *Bourses de voyage* (1903, Travel Scholarships). Unlike the recent "discovery" of his early unpublished manuscript of *Paris au XXe siècle* (1994, Paris in the Twentieth Century), these late works by Verne were never "lost." Following their original French publication in the familiar octavo red-and-gold Hetzel editions, they soon appeared in translation in dozens of other languages, from Spanish to Slovak.[5] Yet, to date, they have never been available in English. Why?

The reasons for this perplexing lacuna have less to do with the quality of the novels themselves than with certain trends in the reading and publishing market of the late 1890s and early 1900s. In one sense, Verne was the victim of his own success. With the unparalleled triumph of his early best-selling novels—*Cinq semaines en ballon* (1863, Five Weeks in a Balloon), *Voyage au centre de la terre* (1864, Journey to the Center of the Earth), *De la terre à la lune* and *Autour de la lune* (1865 and 1870, From the Earth to the Moon and Around the Moon), *Vingt mille lieues sous les mers* (1870, Twenty Thousand Leagues under the Sea), and *Le Tour du monde en quatre-vingts jours* (1873, Around the World in Eighty Days)—Verne achieved what no writer before him had succeeded in doing: he popularized a new brand of literature that mixed fiction with real science. This new literary genre, a forerunner of what would become known as "scientifiction" and then as "science fiction" in America during the 1920s, might be accurately described as "scientifically didactic Industrial Age epic" or, more simply (as the author himself chose to label it), *le roman scientifique*—the "scientific novel." With the worldwide success of his early romans scientifiques, Verne established a strong tradition for this innovative literary form, finally providing it with a socially acceptable institutional "landing point" and ideological model.[6] And soon after, spurred on by the public's increasing interest in contemporary discoveries in science and technology, this new genre became all the rage. During the last years of the nineteenth century, a veritable host of "Verne school" writers such as Paul d'Ivoi, Louis Boussenard, Henry de Graffigny, Georges Le Faure, and Maurice Champagne inundated the French market with their fictional spin-offs. Their immediate popularity—in addition to the growing demand for the speculative works of other French writers such as Camille Flammarion, André Laurie, Villiers de l'Ile-Adam, Capitaine Danrit, Albert Robida, and especially J.-H. Rosny Aîné—soon began to chip away at Verne's domestic monopoly on these types of narratives.[7]

Similarly, in Great Britain and America, the English translations of Verne's oeuvre found itself in competition with imaginative works by a host of anglophone authors such as H. Rider Haggard, Percy Greg, Robert Cromie, James De Mille, George Griffith, Edward Bellamy, Mark Twain, Jack London, and Frank Stockton, as well as with scores of inventive (and cheaply produced) "dime-novels" in series such as *The Frank Reade Library*.[8] Finally, the rapidly growing popularity of Verne's primary rival, H. G. Wells, had a major impact on the demand for Verne's fiction.

Undoubtedly, the huge success of H. G. Wells's "scientific romances" most adversely affected the sales of Verne's later works, especially among anglophone readers. After the publication of his 1895 and 1898 masterpieces, *The Time Machine* and *The War of the Worlds*, Wells was promptly acclaimed "the English Jules Verne"[9] (i.e., the "new and improved" version). And his highly conjectural fictions soon began to dominate the Anglo-American marketplace. For fin-de-siècle readers at the dawn of a new millennium, Verne's "hard science" and heavily didactic plots came to be viewed as stodgy and old-fashioned. In contrast, Wells's scientific romances seemed more imaginative, more cosmic in scope, and more provocative in their futuristic extrapolations. In a word, Verne's unique and once-successful formula of "scientific fiction" was progressively losing favor to its younger and more fanciful cousin, "science fiction."[10]

English-language book publishers during the 1890s and early 1900s were unquestionably aware of and very sensitive to these market trends. Even in France, the demand for Verne's books had been slowly but inexorably diminishing during the final decade of his life, as he continued to churn out two or three novels per year. In contrast to the continuously sold-out print runs of thirty thousand to fifty thousand copies per title for Verne's earlier works between 1863 and 1880 (*Le Tour du monde en 80 jours* alone topped a hundred thousand), the first-edition sales of his later novels, from 1880 to his death in 1905, averaged only seven thousand to ten thousand each. The first printing of *Le Superbe Orénoque* in 1898, for example, was limited to a mere five thousand—and unsold copies still remained in Hetzel's stockroom many years later.[11] Given these sales trends, it is understandable why British and American publishers might begin to be wary of offering their readers another new English translation of Verne's *Voyages Extraordinaires*.

But in addition to the factors of decreasing sales and a growing abundance of other Verne-like books in the marketplace, Anglo-American publishers also refused to publish many of Verne's later works on purely ideological grounds. As described by Vernian scholar Brian Taves:

> By 1898, political questions had become the deciding factor in whether the latest Verne books were published in English at all. The tenor of his newer works were less agreeable to English-speaking audiences, or at least their publishers, who were not prepared to faithfully present Verne's views. The censorship grew beyond simply changing or removing controversial passages until eventually entire books were suppressed by simply not translating them into English. British publishers were fearful of offending their readers in the empire, and the anticipated taste of the British market largely governed what appeared on either side of the Atlantic. Although translations had been appearing with regularity to commercial success for a quarter century, a sudden change in policy was made. *The Superb Orinoco* became the first of Verne's annual books not to be translated, and thereafter few of his new works appeared in English.[12]

As a result, of the seventeen *Voyages Extraordinaires* published in France after 1898, more than half were destined to remain untranslated into English until the late 1950s and 1960s (in severely abridged editions), and several have remained untranslated until the present day.

The "Two Jules Vernes"

Brief mention should also be made of the quality (or lack thereof) of the early English translations of Verne's works. It is now recognized that most English-language versions of Verne's *Voyages Extraordinaires* were very badly translated, and some were so bowdlerized that they bear little resemblance to the original French works. In a rush to bring Verne's potentially profitable stories to market, British and American translators often severely abridged them by deleting most of the science and the long descriptive passages (sometimes 20 to 40 percent of the original); they committed thousands of translating errors, both literary and technical; they frequently censored Verne's texts by either removing or "adjusting" passages that might be construed as anti-British or anti-American; and, in many cases, they actually rewrote Verne's novels to suit their own tastes—changing the names of principal characters, adding new scenes and episodes, reordering or relabeling the chapters, and so forth.

In recent decades, Vernian scholar Walter James Miller has probably done the most to call attention to the shockingly poor quality of some of the English translations of Verne—both in his 1965 introduction to a new translation of *Twenty Thousand Leagues under the Sea* and, more importantly, in his two-volume translation series entitled *The Annotated Jules Verne* (1976–78). Miller's conclusions are concise and categorical: "The English-speaking world has never had a fair chance to know the real Jules Verne."[13]

It is also useful to understand how these English translations were originally published because, at least in Verne's case, *how* his novels were published often determined *what* was published. Verne's French publisher, Pierre-Jules Hetzel, was a very shrewd businessman and had great success in marketing his books to French readers both young and old. American and British publishers adopted many of Hetzel's successful strategies but chose to promote Verne's translations almost exclusively to a juvenile audience. And they did so in one of three ways: elegant, cloth-bound luxury editions that could be offered as holiday gifts, collectible editions such as those in the "Every Boy's Library" series by the publisher Routledge, or serials in a magazine such as *The Boy's Own Paper* (a popular periodical for youth begun in the late 1870s, somewhat reminiscent of Hetzel's own *Magasin d'Education et de Récréation*).

Did the editors of the English-language publishing houses purposely shorten, cleanse, and "adapt" Verne's works in order to better suit this youthful public? Or were the translated manuscripts they received for publication judged to be so unsophisticated in content and tone that only adolescents and pre-adolescents were targeted as their potential readers? It is impossible to determine. But whatever the sequence of these events, the outcome was the same: Verne's English translations were marketed primarily to British and American youngsters. As a result, in most anglophone countries until quite recently, Jules Verne's literary reputation among adult readers has suffered.

But all that is now changing. As I have explained in more detail elsewhere,[14] Verne's critical reappraisal began to gain momentum in France during the structuralist and poststructuralist 1960s and 1970s through the influential studies of both academic and nonacademic scholars such as Michel Butor, Michel Carrouges, Jean Chesneaux, Charles-Noël Martin, Roland Barthes, René Escaich, Michel Foucault, Marcel Moré, Michel Serres, Simone Vierne, and Pierre Macherey. By 1978 (the 150th anniversary of the author's birth), the literary stature of Jules Verne and his *Voyages Extraordinaires* had already begun to metamorphose. No longer a paraliterary pariah, Verne was rapidly moving to—as one critic rather hyperbolically mused—"a first-rank position in the history of French literature."[15] And this Verne renaissance has continued through the 1980s and 1990s through the work of Piero Gondolo della Riva, François Raymond, Christian Robin, Olivier Dumas, Jean-Michel Margot, Volker Dehs, Daniel Compère, and Jean-Paul Dekiss.

In America and Great Britain, however, still burdened with the poor English translations described above, a similar reassessment of Verne's place in literary history has lagged far behind.[16] But a glimmer of hope now shows on the horizon. First, new and more accurate English-language versions of a (very) few of Verne's works have begun to appear in the Anglo-American marketplace during the past few years.[17] Second, during the mid- to late 1980s, a handful of American and British university scholars completed their doctoral theses on Verne and subsequently published them as books,[18] paving the way for more advanced study of this French author in academe. And, finally, the 1990s witnessed a variety of developments in Great Britain and America that brought Jules Verne out of oblivion and into the limelight: the discovery and publication of his early futuristic dystopia *Paris in the Twentieth Century*, the birth of the North American Jules Verne Society (along with its informative newsletter *Extraordinary Voyages*), the online presence of Zvi Har'El's excellent Jules Verne website (http://JV.Gilead.org.il/), and a growing number of English-language studies on Verne by British and American scholars such as myself, William Butcher, Andrew Martin, Brian Taves, Stephen Michaluk Jr., George Slusser, Herbert Lottman, Ron Miller, Lawrence Lynch, Peggy Teeters, and Thomas Renzi.

In the three and a half decades since Walter James Miller first remarked that two entirely different Jules Vernes seemed to exist in America and in Europe,[19] a great deal of progress has been made toward familiarizing anglophone readers with the "real" Jules Verne. But much remains to be done. Of highest priority are first-edition printings of all previously untranslated works by this prolific French author. Next in importance are updated and unabridged editions of those many Verne novels that are currently available only in severely bowdlerized English translations. Finally, there continues to be a pressing need for new collections of translated Vernian criticism in order to provide a critical "bridge" for Anglophone researchers to the wealth of extant foreign-language scholarship on Jules Verne. The first step has now been taken. Wesleyan University Press is to be commended for publishing Verne's *Invasion of the Sea* as the inaugural volume in its new Early Classics of Science Fiction series, and additional Verne titles will be forthcoming. It is hoped that these critical editions of Verne's works will serve both as a catalyst to more English-language studies of this important author and as a stepping-stone to a long overdue reassessment of the place of Jules Verne's *Voyages Extraordinaires* in the evolution of this unique literary genre.

Historical Sources for *Invasion of the Sea*

It is not unreasonable to assert that the majority of Jules Verne's *Voyages Extraordinaires* were either inspired by or documented from real scientific discoveries, theories, or debates taking place during the latter half of the nineteenth century. Although not a scientist himself, Verne was an indefatigable documentationalist and spent many hours each day keeping abreast of recent developments in the field. For example, during an 1894 interview, he explained:

> I have never studied science, though in the course of my reading I have picked up a great many odds and ends which have become useful. I may tell you that I am a great reader, and that I always read pencil in hand. I always carry a notebook about with me, and immediately jot down, like that person in Dickens, anything that interests me or may appear to be of possible use in my books. To give you an idea of my reading, I come here every day after lunch and immediately set to work to read through fifteen different papers, always the same fifteen, and I can tell you that very little in any of them escapes my attention. When I see anything of interest, down it goes. Then I read the reviews, such as the "Revue Bleue," the "Revue Rose," the "Revue des Deux Mondes," "Cosmos," Tissandier's "La Nature," Flammarion's "L'Astronomie." I also read through the bulletins of the scientific societies, especially those of the Geographical Society, for, mark, geography is my passion and my study. I have all Reclus's works—I have a great admiration for Élisée Reclus—and the whole of Arago. I also read and re-read, for I am a most careful reader, the collection known as "Le Tour du Monde," which is a series of stories of travel. I have thus amassed many thousands of notes on all subjects, and to date, at home, have at least twenty thousand notes which can be turned to advantage in my work, as yet unused.[20]

It is thus very likely that two reports published in 1874 immediately attracted Verne's attention. The first appeared in the French Geographical Society's March *Bulletin* (for its members) and the second—almost identical in content—was printed in May in the popular journal *Revue des Deux Mondes* (for the public at large). Written by Captain François-Élie Roudaire, geographer in the French army, both articles proposed "une mer intérieure en Algérie" (an inland sea in Algeria) via the construction of a two-hundred-kilometer Suez-like canal linking the Tunisian Gulf of Gabès with the eastern territories of Algeria. Such a waterway would allow the Mediterranean to fill nearly eight thousand square kilometers of semiarid desert and saltflats (the *chotts*), which were below sea level and assumed to have once been covered by an ancient inland sea. This artificially engineered body of water, according to Roudaire, would serve many purposes: it would bring moisture and humidity to this Saharan region, dramatically improving its climate; it would permit marine navigation as far west as Biskra (Algeria), thereby facilitating increased commerce with—and colonial influence on—the peoples of North Africa; and it would create a natural barrier against the troublesome desert Tuareg tribes of the south.

Roudaire's proposal was the result of a geographical and geological survey he had conducted of this area during the previous year. It included specific engineering recommendations for the construction of such a canal, provided details of the various topological obstacles to be overcome, and even suggested an estimated budget (a modest twenty-five million francs). Roudaire's daring yet pragmatic proposition was strongly supported by the famous French engineer Ferdinand de Lesseps, and it immediately sparked widespread interest among the French public. In July 1874, the French Academy of Sciences created a commission to study the question. In the same month, the French government unanimously approved a supplement of thirty-five thousand francs to the annual budget of the Committee of Scientific Missions (of the Ministry of Public Instruction) in order to send a military expedition, led by Roudaire, to North Africa to determine the project's feasibility.

Over the ensuing eight years, Roudaire led several more reconnaissance missions to North Africa, and, with the political and financial backing of de Lesseps, worked tirelessly to materialize his dream of a "Sahara Sea." But despite being promoted to major and then lieutenant colonel during this period, Roudaire's ambitious plan was never adopted. By 1882–83, French scientists and politicians had turned against his project. The scientists cited basic geological and hydrometric errors in Roudaire's reports (e.g., that this region had never contained an inland sea), and the politicians cited both the astronomic cost (over a billion francs) and the enormous social and political ramifications of relocating the indigenous peoples there. Exhausted, embittered, and abandoned by his erstwhile supporters—by this time, de Lesseps was embroiled in his own problems (financial and other) related to his new Panama Canal venture—Roudaire died on January 15, 1885, at age forty-eight, from a fever contracted during his final expedition.[21]

A sad story. But a quite noteworthy one, not only because Roudaire's ill-fated project was the primary historical source for Verne's novel *Invasion of the Sea* but also because it serves as a concrete example of Verne's practice of documenting current events and incorporating them in his fiction.[22] In fact, Verne's first novelistic reference to Roudaire's "Sahara Sea" was not in his 1905 novel *Invasion of the Sea* but, rather, in an earlier novel— *Hector Servadac* (1877)—a work whose composition and publication were contemporary with the French engineer's real-life efforts. Although an interplanetary disaster narrative, the story of *Hector Servadac* takes place mostly in Algeria and Tunisia, and it contains a revealing passage in chapter 11 and an equally revealing footnote in chapter 13:

> The reason that induced the Count and his two colleagues to persevere in their investigations towards the east was that quite recently a long-abandoned project had been revived and, by French influence, the new Sahara Sea had been created. This great achievement, which had refilled the Lake Tritonis that had borne the vessel of the Argonauts, had not only secured to France the monopoly of traffic between Europe and the Soudan, but had materially improved the climate of the country. From the gulf of Cabes [*sic*] in lat. 34° N., a wide channel had been opened for the purpose of giving the waters of the Mediterranean access to the vast depression which comprehended the Shotts of Kebir and of Gharsa; the isthmus existing between an indentation of the Tritonis basin and the sea having been cut asunder, so that the water had once again taken pos-

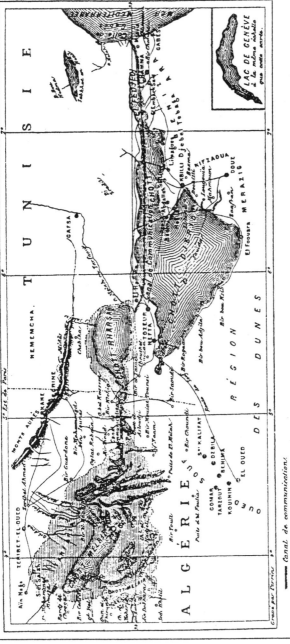

Map of the Proposed Saharan Sea (Duveyrier, 1875).

session of the ancient bed, whence, in default of a continuous supply, it had long ago evaporated under the influence of the Libyan sun. (Chap. 11)

1. . . . England, astonished at the success of the Sahara Sea lately formed by Captain Roudaire, and unwilling to be outdone by France, was occupied in a great scheme for the formation of a similar sea in the centre of Australia. (Footnote in chap. 13)[23]

In other words, as early as 1876–77, Verne was already assuming the successful completion of this historic "Great Works" project in the not-too-distant future—nearly three decades before he would begin writing *Invasion of the Sea* (a narrative whose own fictional setting, incidentally, is nearly three decades into the future from its date of composition). Further, the unqualified success of this Sahara Sea, "lately formed" by the French, provided Verne with a handy means to satirize ongoing Franco-British rivalries (also extrapolated into the future), as England immediately set about constructing its own "inland sea" in its colony of Australia.

Thematic and Ideological Significance of *Invasion of the Sea*

Verne's *Invasion of the Sea* is a novel that "closes the circle" on both the author's life and those *Voyages Extraordinaires* that were by his hand alone. And it does so in a very fitting manner by returning the reader to the continent of Africa—the fictional locale of Verne's first novel in this series, *Five Weeks in a Balloon* (1863). Of course, *Invasion* is not one of Verne's best works, especially if compared to some of his recognized masterpieces like *Twenty Thousand Leagues under the Sea* or *Around the World in Eighty Days*. But it is nevertheless a fascinating one because, when viewed from a thematic and ideological standpoint, *Invasion of the Sea* also "closes the circle" in another important way—it marks the author's unexpected return to the Hetzel-mandated, optimistic, and pro-science positivism that was evident throughout much of his early writing career.[24]

Many works in the latter half of the *Voyages Extraordinaires*, dating roughly from the 1880s, exhibited a growing anti-science pessimism in Verne's outlook, and issues of human morality and social responsibility tended to be foregrounded more often. Consider, for example, the dystopian portrayal of the "City of Steel" (Stahlstadt) constructed by Verne's first truly evil scientist, Herr Schultze, in *Les Cinq Cents millions de la Bégum* (1876, The Begum's Fortune); or the famous "Gun Club" engineers Barbicane and Maston in *Sans dessus dessous* (1889, The Purchase of the North Pole), who, as caricatures of their former selves, are wholly indifferent to the potentially catastrophic effects on the entire world when they attempt to alter the earth's axis with a blast from a gigantic cannon; or, finally, in *Maître du monde* (1904, Master of the World), the once-heroic aeronaut Robur turned crazed megalomaniac, who, with his powerful vehicle *Epouvante*, now seeks to rule all the nations of the earth. In these and many later *Voyages Extraordinaires*, the central "message" of the story seems to echo the dictum of François Rabelais: "Science sans conscience n'est que ruine de l'âme" (science [knowledge] without conscience leads to the ruin of one's soul). Further, in many of these works, it is only through the last-moment intervention of a providential deus ex machina—in the form of a gas leak, a lightning bolt, etc.—that the heroes are saved, the presumptuous scientist(s) punished, the scientific "novum" eliminated, and the status quo safely reestablished.

In contrast, Verne's *Invasion of the Sea* seems astonishingly "politically *in*correct" in its near total inattention to the potential human and environmental consequences of constructing an inland sea in North Africa. And the sudden earthquake that functions as the deus ex machina climax of this novel, rather than destroying the project and causing a return to the status quo, actually completes the French scientists' work-in-progress: the "Sahara Sea" is ultimately created, albeit by natural causes instead of by human design. Finally, suggesting the wrath of a vengeful God, an ensuing tidal wave drowns the rebellious Tuareg and their leader Hadjar, who had fiercely opposed this project from the beginning. The implication is quite clear: both morality and destiny are on the side of Science and Progress.

Although some critics have dismissed Verne's *Invasion of the*

Sea as merely "one more panegyric to the civilizing mission of the Europeans,"[25] its true status within Verne's oeuvre is considerably more complex. What caused the aging and ailing Verne to suddenly revert to the apparent positivistic ideology of his earliest works? Why, for the first time in his *Voyages Extraordinaires*, did he abruptly end his narrative after the completion of the scientific project in question, portraying no fictional follow-up to its realization? Why, after so many late novels in which he had sympathetically portrayed numerous oppressed peoples—for example, Greek freedom fighters in *L'Archipel en feu* (1884, Archipelago on Fire), Hungarian nationalists in *Mathias Sandorf* (1885, Mathias Sandorf), French-Canadians in *Famille-sans-nom* (1889, Family without a Name), and Russian peasants in *Un Drame en Livonie* (1904, A Drama in Livonia)—did Verne apparently turn his back on the fate of the Saharan Tuareg in their fight against French colonialism? And why, instead of *A New Sea in the Sahara*, did Verne choose at the last moment to retitle this work *The Invasion of the Sea*—a title that, ironically, would seem to reflect the perspective of the Tuareg themselves as victims of this twofold "invasion"? There are no definitive answers to these important questions, and scholarly opinion on them continues to be divided.[26] But one fact is certain: this novel is both more polyvalent and less prone to facile reductionism than any one-dimensional reading of it might suggest. If Jules Verne's *Invasion of the Sea* "closes the circle" on his life's work, critical discussion of the book itself remains far from closed.

JULES VERNE

L'INVASION

DE

LA MER

i  The Oasis of Gabès

"How much do you know?"

"I know what I heard in the port."

"Were people talking about the ship that's coming to get—coming to take Hadjar away?"

"Yes, to Tunis, where he will go on trial."

"And be sentenced to death?"

"And be sentenced to death."

"Allah will not allow that to happen, Sohar! No! He won't allow it!"

"Sh!" said Sohar suddenly, listening intently as if he heard footsteps on the sand.

Without standing up, he crawled to the entrance of the abandoned marabout in which this conversation was taking place. It was still daylight, but the sun would soon disappear behind the dunes bordering this side of the coast of the Gulf of Gabès.[1] At the beginning of March, twilight does not last long on the thirty-fourth parallel of the northern hemisphere. The solar orb does not approach the horizon obliquely, but appears to fall vertically, like a body obeying the law of gravity.

Sohar stopped, rose, and took a few steps through the doorway, which was scorched by the heat of the sun's rays. In one brief glance he took in the surrounding plain.

To the north, a kilometer and a half away, swelled the verdant treetops of an oasis. To the south stretched the endless band of yellowish shoreline, fringed with foam flung up by the backwash of the rising tide. To the west, a group of dunes stood out against the sky. To the east was the broad expanse of the sea that forms the Gulf of Gabès and that washes the Tunisian coast as it curves south toward Tripolitania.

The light westerly breeze that had cooled the atmosphere during the day had died down as evening fell. No sound came to Sohar's ears. He had thought he heard someone walking near the marabout, a square structure of old white masonry sheltered by an ancient palm tree, but realized he had been mistaken. There was no one, either in the direction of the dunes or in the direction of the beach. He walked all around the little building. There was no one, and no footprints in the sand, except for the ones he and his mother had left in front of the entrance.

Barely a minute had elapsed after Sohar went out when Djemma appeared at the door, worried because she did not see her son coming back. As he came around the corner of the marabout, he waved to her reassuringly.

Djemma was an African woman of the Tuareg tribe,[2] more than sixty years old, but tall, strong, energetic, and erect in bearing. There was a proud and passionate look in her eyes, which, like those of all women of her ethnic background, were blue. Her white skin appeared yellow under the ochre dye covering her forehead and cheeks. She wore dark clothing, a loose-fitting *haik* made of wool abundantly provided by the flocks kept by the Hammâma who lived near the *sebkha* (salt marshes) and *chott*s (salt lakes) of lower Tunisia.[3] A wide hood covered her thick head of hair, which was only now beginning to turn grey.

Djemma stayed where she was, without moving, until her son joined her. He had seen nothing suspicious nearby, and the silence was broken only by the plaintive song of a few pairs of *bouhabibi*, or Djerid sparrows, flitting about near the dunes.

Djemma and Sohar went back into the marabout to wait for nightfall, when they would be able to reach Gabès without attracting attention.

The conversation continued.

"Has the ship left La Goulette?"

"Yes, mother. It rounded Cap Bon this morning. It's the cruiser *Chanzy*."

"Will it get here tonight?"

"Yes, unless it puts in at Sfax. But it will more likely come and anchor off Gabès, where your son—my brother—will be taken aboard."

"Hadjar, Hadjar," murmured the old woman.

Shaking violently with anger and grief, she cried out, "My

"No, no, Allah will not allow this to happen!"

son, my son! Those foreigners will kill him, and I'll never see him again. And he'll no longer be here to lead the Tuareg in our holy war. No, no, Allah will not allow this to happen!"

As if exhausted by this outburst, Djemma dropped to her knees in a corner of the small room and fell silent.

Sohar had come back and taken up his position at the door, leaning against its frame. He was as still as if he had been made of stone, like one of those statues that sometimes decorate the entrance to a marabout. Not a sound disturbed his immobility. The shadows of the dunes gradually lengthened eastward, as the sun sank lower on the western horizon. To the east of the Gulf of Gabès the first stars were coming out. The slender crescent of the lunar disk, at the beginning of its first quarter, had just slipped behind the last mists of sunset. It would be a calm night, and dark, too, for a curtain of light vapor would hide the stars.

A little after seven, Sohar went back to his mother. "It's time," he said.

"Yes," replied Djemma, "and it's time for Hadjar to be snatched from the hands of those foreigners. He must be out of Gabès prison before sunrise. Tomorrow it will be too late."

"Everything is ready, mother," replied Sohar. "Our comrades are waiting for us. Those in Gabès have planned the escape. Those in the Djerid will act as Hadjar's escort, and before another day dawns they'll be far away in the desert."

"And I'll be with them," declared Djemma. "I won't abandon my son."

"And I'll be with you too," added Sohar. "I won't abandon my brother—or my mother."

Djemma drew him to her and held him close in her arms. Then, adjusting the hood of her haik, she went out.

On their way to Gabès, Sohar walked a few steps ahead of his mother. Instead of following the shoreline, along the swath of sea plants left on the beach by the receding tide, they followed the base of the dunes, where they hoped to cover the kilometer and a half with less likelihood of being seen. The clump of trees at the oasis, almost lost in the deepening gloom, could be seen only vaguely. Not a light shone through the darkness. In those windowless Arab houses, only the inner courtyards receive any daylight, and after nightfall no light escapes from them.

Soon, however, a point of light appeared above the dim silhouette of the town. It was fairly intense, and must have come from the upper part of Gabès, perhaps from the minaret of a mosque, perhaps from the castle that overlooked the town.

But Sohar knew it was coming from the fort. Pointing to the light, he whispered, "The *bordj* (the fort)."[4]

"Is that the place, Sohar?"

"Yes, mother. That's where they've confined him."

The old woman had stopped. It seemed as if the light had established some kind of communication between her and her son. Perhaps it did not come from the very cell where Hadjar was imprisoned, but it certainly came from the fort to which he had been taken. Djemma had not seen her son since the fearsome leader had fallen into the hands of French soldiers, and she would never see him again unless he escaped that very night from the fate that military justice had in store for him. She stood on the spot as if transfixed, and Sohar had to urge her twice, "Come on, mother. Come on."

They went on their way, along the base of the dunes, which curved around toward the oasis of Gabès with its cluster of villages and houses, the largest settlement on the shore of the gulf. Sohar headed for the part that the soldiers called Coquinville, or Roguetown, a collection of wooden huts inhabited by bazaar merchants (hence its well-deserved name). The village was located near the entrance to the wadi, a stream that winds this way and that through the oasis, in the shade of the palm trees. There stood the bordj, Fort Neuf, from which Hadjar would not emerge until the time came for him to be transferred to prison in Tunis.

It was from this fort that his comrades, after taking every precaution and making every preparation for escape, hoped to free him that night. They had gathered together in the huts of Coquinville, and were waiting for Djemma and her son. But extreme caution was called for, and it was better to avoid meeting anyone as they approached the village.

The wadi near Fort Neuf. (Photo by Lt. Rebut)

How anxiously they turned their eyes out to sea, fearful that the cruiser would arrive that evening and take the prisoner aboard before the escape could be carried out. They looked to see whether any white smoke was visible in the gulf, listening for the whinnying sound of a ship's steam engine or the shrill wail of a siren which might mean a ship was coming in to dock. But they saw only the lights of the fishing boats reflected in the Tunisian waters, and no ship's whistle rent the air.

It was not yet eight o'clock when Djemma and her son reached the bank of the wadi. Ten more minutes would bring them to the rendezvous point.

Just as they were about to start out along the right bank, a man, crouching behind the cactuses on the bank, half stood up and asked, "Sohar?"

"Is that you, Ahmet?"

"Yes. And your mother?"

"She's right behind me."

"And we'll follow you," said Djemma.

"Any news?" asked Sohar.

"Nothing," replied Ahmet.

"Are our friends here?"

"They're waiting for you."

"Does anyone in the bordj suspect anything?"

"Not a soul."

"Is Hadjar ready?"

"Yes."

"How did they get to see him?"

"Through Harrig, who was released this morning. He's with our comrades now."

"Let's go," said the old woman, and all three walked up the wadi along its bank.

The direction they were now following made it impossible for them to see the dark mass of the fort through the thick foliage, for the oasis of Gabès is really only a very large palm grove.

Ahmet walked along the path confidently and unerringly. First they would have to pass through Djara, which lies on both sides of the wadi. In this formerly fortified village, which had been in turn Carthaginian, Roman, Byzantine, and Arab, was located the main market of Gabès. At this hour it would still be crowded with people, and Djemma and her son might have some difficulty getting through unnoticed. On the other hand, the streets of these Tunisian oases were not yet lighted by electricity or even by gas. So, except in the vicinity of a few cafés, they would be shrouded in darkness.

Nevertheless, Ahmet was very cautious and circumspect, and he continually reminded Sohar that they could not be too careful. There was a possibility that the prisoner's mother might be known in Gabès, and that her presence might lead to increased vigilance around the fort. Although planned far in advance, carrying out this escape would be difficult, and it was important that nothing arouse the guards' suspicions. For this reason, Ahmet chose to follow roads leading to the area adjacent to the bordj.

Further, there was a great deal of activity in the central part of the oasis as this Sunday evening was drawing to a close. In

Africa, as in Europe, the last day of the week is usually a holiday in garrison towns, and especially in French garrison towns. The soldiers are given leave, sit around in the cafés, and return to their barracks late at night. The local inhabitants take part in the general hustle and bustle, especially around the bazaar with its mixture of Italian and Jewish merchants. And this hubbub goes on far into the night.

It was possible, then, that Djemma might not be unknown to the authorities in Gabès. Indeed, since her son's arrest, she had ventured near the bordj more than once, risking her liberty and perhaps even her life. It was well known that she had had a strong influence on Hadjar, the maternal influence being so strong among the Tuareg people. Since she had urged him to revolt, she was quite capable of touching off another rebellion, either to free the prisoner or to avenge him if the military council sent him to his death. Yes, there was every reason to fear that all the tribes would rise at her call and follow her in a holy war. All attempts to find and capture her had failed, as had the many expeditions sent out through this land of sebkha and chotts. With the protection of her devoted people, Djemma had escaped all attempts to put her in prison along with her son.

And yet, here she was in the middle of this oasis, with so many dangers threatening her. She had insisted on joining her comrades who had met in Gabès to carry out the escape plan. If Hadjar managed to elude his watchful guards and get outside the walls of the fort, he and his mother would go back along the road to the marabout. About a kilometer from there, in the densest part of a palm grove, the fugitive would find horses on which to make good his escape. He would be free again, and—who knows?—perhaps make another attempt to lead an uprising against French rule.

Among the groups of Frenchmen and Arabs that they encountered from time to time as they continued toward the bordj, no one had recognized Hadjar's mother under the haik she was wearing. Moreover, Ahmet did his best to warn them when someone was coming, and all three crouched in some dark corner, behind an isolated hut, or under cover of the trees, and went on again after the passersby had gone.

Gabès, the European quarter and the native quarter.
(Photos by Soler, Tunis)

They were no more than three or four steps from the meeting place when a Targui who seemed to be awaiting someone suddenly rushed up to them.

The street (or rather, the road) that angled off toward the bordj was deserted at this moment, and Djemma and her comrades had only to follow it for a few minutes and go up a narrow side street to reach the *gourbi*, or shack, that was their destination.

The man went straight up to Ahmet and held up his hand to stop them.

"Don't go any farther," he said.

"What's the matter, Horeb?" asked Ahmet, who had recognized the newcomer as a member of his Tuareg tribe.

"Our comrades have left the gourbi."

The old mother stopped, and in a voice filled with anxiety and anger she asked Horeb, "Do those Frenchie dogs suspect something?"

"No, Djemma," he replied, "and neither do the guards at the bordj."

"Then why aren't our comrades still at the gourbi?"

"Because some soldiers on leave came and asked for something to drink, and we didn't want to stay with them. One of them was Nicol, the cavalry sergeant. He knows you, Djemma."

"Yes," she muttered. "He saw me there, at our camp, when my son was captured by his captain. Ah! That captain! If I ever . . ."

And from her throat came a sound like the roar of a wild beast.

"Where will we find our comrades?" asked Ahmet.

"Come with me," replied Horeb. Taking the lead, he slipped through a little palm grove and headed toward the fort.

This thicket was deserted at that hour and came to life only on the days when the main market in Gabès was open. There was every chance, then, that they would not meet anyone else between there and the fort, which of course would be impossible to enter. The fact that members of the garrison had been granted Sunday leave was no reason to assume that there would be no one on sentry duty.

In fact, security would be all the tighter while the rebel Hadjar was a prisoner in the fort and until he had been transferred to the cruiser and handed over to military justice.

Walking under cover of the trees, the little group came to the edge of the palm grove.

There was a cluster of some twenty huts at that spot, and a few beams of light were filtering through their narrow openings. The rendezvous point was now no more than a gunshot away.

But hardly had Horeb started along a winding little street when the sound of footsteps and voices made him stop. A dozen soldiers—spahis—were coming toward them, singing and shouting under the influence of the libations of which they had been partaking, too freely perhaps, in the nearby cabarets.

Ahmet thought it best to avoid meeting them, and drew back with the others into a dark recess near the French-Arab school to let them go past.

There was a well there, with a wooden framework over it to hold the winch that raised and lowered the bucket.

In an instant they had all taken refuge behind the coping of the well, which was high enough to hide them completely.

The soldiers kept coming on, then stopped, and one of them shouted, "My God, I'm thirsty."

"Have a drink, then. There's a well here," said Sergeant Nicol.

"What? Water, Sergeant?" exclaimed Corporal Pistache.

"Pray to Mohammed. Perhaps he'll turn the water into wine."

"Ah! If I could be sure of that!"

"You'd convert to Islam?"

"No, Sergeant, of course not. Anyway, since Allah forbids his followers to drink wine, he would never agree to perform a miracle like that for nonbelievers."

"That's logical, Pistache," said the sergeant. "Now, let's get back to our post."

But just as the soldiers were about to follow him, he stopped them.

Two men were coming up the street, and the sergeant recognized them as a captain and a lieutenant from his own regiment.

"Halt," he ordered, and his men raised their hands to their fezes in a salute.

"Well," said the captain, "if it isn't Nicol."

13

An encounter at the well of Gabès

"Captain Hardigan?" replied the sergeant, with a trace of surprise in his voice.

"It is indeed."

"We've just come from Tunis," added Lieutenant Villette.

"We're leaving shortly on an expedition, and you'll be coming with us, Nicol."

"At your service, sir," replied the sergeant, "and ready to follow you wherever you go."

"Of course, of course," said Captain Hardigan. "And how is your old brother?"

"Just fine. Still walking on his four legs, and I make sure they don't have a chance to get rusty."

"Good for you, Nicol. And how about Ace-of-Hearts? Is he still your brother's friend?"

"As much as ever, sir. I wouldn't be surprised if they were twins."

"That would be strange, a dog and a horse!" replied the officer with a laugh. "But don't worry, Nicol, we won't separate them when we leave."

"It would certainly be the death of them if you did, sir."

Just then, there was the sound of a loud gunshot off shore.

"What was that?" asked Lieutenant Villette.

"Probably a canon from the cruiser anchoring in the gulf."

"Coming to get that rogue Hadjar," added the sergeant. "You really got a prize when you captured him, sir."

"You mean when we all captured him," said Captain Hardigan.

"Yes, and the old brother, and Ace-of-Hearts too," exclaimed the sergeant.

Then the two officers continued their way up toward the fort, while Sergeant Nicol and his men went back down toward the lower town of Gabès.

ii ~~ Hadjar

The Tuareg, who belong to the Berber race, used to live in Icham, the area bounded by Touat to the north (a vast oasis in the Sahara five hundred kilometers southeast of Morocco), Timbuktu to the south, the Niger to the west, and the Fezzan to the east. But at the time of our story, they had been obliged to move to the more easterly regions of the Sahara. At the beginning of the twentieth century, their many tribes, some almost sedentary and others completely nomadic, were to be found in the middle of the flat, sandy plains known in Arabic as *outtâ*, stretching from the Sudan to the area where the Algerian and Tunisian deserts meet.

For a number of years, after work was abandoned on Captain Roudaire's project of creating an inland sea in Arad,[1] the region extending westward from Gabès, the resident-general and the bey[2] of Tunis had persuaded some Tuareg to settle in the oases around the chotts, hoping their warlike nature might make them in a sense the gendarmes of the desert. It was a vain hope. The Imohagh still deserved the insulting nickname of "Tuareg," or "night bandits," which had made them feared throughout the Sudan. Furthermore, if work on the Sahara Sea were to be resumed, there was no doubt that they would be in the forefront of the tribes most hostile to the idea of flooding the chotts.

But while any individual Targui might work, ostensibly at least, as a caravan guide and even as its guard, he was nevertheless a thief by instinct and pirate by nature, and his reputation was too well established not to inspire profound distrust. Several years earlier, Major Laing, while traveling through these dangerous lands of the Dark Continent, ran the risk of being massacred in an attack by these fearsome natives.[3] And in 1881, during an expedition that left Ouargla under the command of Major Flatters, that brave officer and his comrades lost their lives at Bir-el-Gharama.[4] The military authorities in Algeria and Tunisia had to be constantly on their guard, relentlessly pushing back those populous tribes.

Of all the Tuareg tribes, the Ahaggar were considered one of the most warlike. Their leading chieftains were involved in all the attempted uprisings that made it so difficult to maintain French influence over the wide expanse of the desert. The governor of Algeria and the resident-general of Tunisia, always on the alert, had to keep a particularly close watch on the region of sebkha and chotts. This was especially important because of a project that was nearing completion, the flooding of the inland sea, which is the theme of this story. It was an undertaking that would create extreme hardship for the Tuareg tribes and deprive them of their source of livelihood by reducing the volume of caravan traffic. By making it easier to quell them, it would also reduce the number of their attacks and the growing list of names that were still being added to African obituaries.

It was to this Ahaggar tribe, one of the most influential, that Hadjar's family belonged. Enterprising, bold, and ruthless, Djemma's son had always been known as one of the most redoubtable chieftains in the whole region to the south of the Aurès Mountains. During the past few years he had led many attacks against caravans and isolated detachments. His fame grew among the tribes who were gradually drifting back toward the east of the Sahara, as the vast lifeless plain in that part of Africa is called. He moved with disconcerting rapidity, and, although the authorities had ordered the military leaders to capture him at any cost, he had always been able to elude the expeditions sent out after him. When he was reported to be near one oasis, he would suddenly appear in the neighborhood of another. At the head of a band of Tuareg no less fierce than their leader, he scoured the whole country between the Algerian chotts and the Gulf of Gabès. The *kafila*, or caravans, no longer dared to set out across the desert without the protection of a large escort, and the heavy traffic bound for the markets of Tripolitania suffered greatly from this state of affairs.

True, there were several military posts at Nefta, Gafsa, and

Gafsa, the kasbah, and the termil. *(Photos by Dr. Tersen)*

Tozeur, which is the political center of that region, but the expeditions mounted against Hadjar and his band had never had any success. The daring warrior had always managed to escape from them until the day, a few weeks earlier, when he had fallen into the hands of a French detachment.

This part of northern Africa had been the scene of one of those catastrophes that unfortunately are all too common on the Dark Continent. The passion, dedication, and bravery of explorers, successors to Burton, Speke, Livingstone, and Stanley, as they set out over the years across this vast field of discovery, are well known. They number in the hundreds, and many more will be added to the list before the day (far in the future, no doubt) when this third part of the ancient world will give up its secrets. And how many of these perilous expeditions will end in disaster!

The most recent expedition was led by a brave Belgian who ventured out into the least frequented and least known regions of the Touat.

Carl Steinx had organized a caravan in Constantine and headed south. It was not a large caravan, about a dozen men in all, Arabs who had been recruited locally. They used horses and *méharis*, or dromedaries, as mounts and as draft animals to pull the two wagons that carried the expedition's supplies.

The first leg of their journey brought them to Ouargla by way of Biskra, Touggourt, and Negoussia, where Steinx had no difficulty replenishing his supplies. The French authorities living in those towns promptly came to the explorer's assistance.

At Ouargla, which lies on the thirty-second parallel, he was, so to speak, in the very heart of the Sahara.

Until then, the expedition's ordeals had not been too onerous. They had suffered fatigue, even exhaustion, but had encountered no serious dangers. Even in those far-off lands the French influence made itself felt. The Tuareg, outwardly at least, proved to be docile, and the caravans satisfied all the needs of inland commerce without undue risk.

At Ouargla Steinx had to make some changes to his personnel. Some of the Arabs accompanying him refused to go any farther, and he had to pay them off—no easy matter, in view of their insolent demands and ill-tempered squabbles. It was better to get rid

19

of these overtly uncooperative people whom it would have been dangerous to keep as part of the escort.

On the other hand, he could not start out again without hiring replacements, and under the circumstances he clearly had no choice. He thought he had solved this problem by accepting the services of some Tuareg, who offered, for a high price, to accompany his expedition as far as its destination, whether at the west or the east coast of Africa.

Steinx had some reservations about the Tuareg as a people, but how could he have suspected that he was bringing traitors into his caravan, that it had been watched by Hadjar's band ever since it left Biskra, and that the formidable chieftain was only waiting for the right moment to attack? His followers, who were now part of the expedition because they had been hired to guide the caravan through those unknown regions, would be able to lead the explorer to the point where Hadjar was waiting for him.

That is exactly what happened. From Ouargla the caravan headed south, crossed the Tropic of Cancer, and reached the territory of the Ahaggar. From there it veered southeast, intending to head for Lake Chad. But from the fifteenth day after his departure there had been no news of Carl Steinx or his companions. What had happened? Had the kafila been able to get as far as Chad? Was it now on its way back by the eastern or the western route?

Steinx's expedition had aroused keen interest among the many geographical societies whose special area of concern was travel to the African interior. They had been kept informed of its itinerary as far as Ouargla. For the next hundred kilometers or so beyond Ouargla, a few scraps of information had still come through, picked up by desert nomads and passed on to the French authorities. It was thought that within a few weeks, under favorable conditions, the expedition would reach the vicinity of Lake Chad.

But weeks went by, and then months, and no news could be obtained about the daring Belgian explorer. Messengers were sent to the far south and French outposts lent a hand in the search, which spread out in every direction. All efforts proved fruitless, and there was reason to believe that the entire caravan had perished, either in an attack by the nomads of the Touat, or

Gafsa. (Photo by Dr. Tersen)

from exhaustion and disease in the heart of the immense solitude of the Sahara.

The geographical community did not know what to think, and it was beginning to lose hope, not only of ever seeing Steinx again, but of ever hearing any news of him. But three months later there arrived in Ouargla an Arab who shed light on the mystery surrounding this unfortunate expedition.

This Arab was a member of the caravan's personnel who had managed to escape. He reported that the Tuareg who entered the explorer's service had betrayed him. Steinx had been led into an ambush and attacked by a band of Tuareg operating under the leadership of the tribal chieftain Hadjar, already famous for his raids on a number of caravans. Steinx and the loyal members of his escort had defended themselves bravely. For forty-eight hours, entrenched in an abandoned *kouba,* or chapel, he had managed to hold off the attackers, but the numerical inferiority of the little group made it impossible for them to resist any longer, and they fell into the hands of the Tuareg, who massacred them all.[5]

21

Gafʃa, general view. (Photo by M. Brichard)

Needless to say, this news aroused deep emotions. The out-
raged public demanded vengeance and grieved for the death of
this brave explorer; they insisted that the ruthless Tuareg chieftain, whose name was held up to public loathing, pay for this
crime and for his many other attacks on caravans. The French
authorities decided to mount an expedition to capture him, to punish him for his crimes, and, in so doing, to eliminate his nefarious
influence on the native tribes, who were known to be gradually
moving toward the eastern part of the continent and settling in
the southern part of Tunisia and Tripolitania. The heavy commercial traffic that traveled through these regions was in danger
of being disrupted, or even destroyed, if the Tuareg were not
completely subdued. An expedition was therefore ordered. Both
the governor-general of Algeria and the resident-general in
Tunisia commanded that it be supported by the cities in the region of the chotts and sebkha, where military outposts had been
established. For this difficult campaign, which was expected to
yield such important results, the Ministry of War assigned a
squadron of spahis commanded by Captain Hardigan.

A detachment of some sixty men arrived at the port of Sfax aboard the *Chanzy*. A few days after disembarking they left the coast and headed west, with their Arab guides and with their supplies and tents carried on the backs of camels. They would replenish their supplies in the towns and villages of the interior, Tozeur and Gafsa among others, and there was no lack of oases in the Djerid region.

The captain had under his command a junior captain, two lieutenants, and several noncommissioned officers, including Sergeant Nicol.

Since the sergeant was with the expedition, that meant that his old brother Giddup and the faithful Ace-of-Hearts were necessarily part of it as well.

The expedition, pacing its marches regularly so as to ensure the success of its journey, crossed the entire Tunisian Sahel, or grassland region. After passing through Dar el Mehalla and El Quittar, it came to Gafsa, in the Henmara region, to rest for forty-eight hours.

The town of Gafsa occupies a plateau surrounded by hills, on a large bend of the Wadi Bayoeh. Several kilometers beyond the hills rises a formidable range of mountains. Of all the settlements of southern Tunisia, Gafsa has the largest population, which lives in an urban area of houses and shacks. It is dominated by the Kasbah, where Tunisian soldiers used to stand guard, but which is now manned by French and native troops. Gafsa can also boast of being a literate community and has a number of schools where Arabic and French are taught. Industry thrives there also, in the form of cloth weaving and the manufacture of silk haiks and blankets and burnouses made from the wool provided by the Hammâmma tribe's many sheep. One can still see the *termil*, baths built during the Roman period, and thermal springs whose temperature ranges from twenty-nine to thirty-two degrees centigrade.

In Gafsa, Captain Hardigan obtained more precise information about Hadjar. The Tuareg band had been observed in the vicinity of Ferkane, a hundred and thirty kilometers to the west. It was a long distance to cover but, to a spahi, weariness and danger mean nothing.

When the members of the detachment learned how much energy and endurance their leaders expected of them, they could not wait to start out. As Sergeant Nicol put it, "I've spoken to my old brother, and he's ready to do double route marches if need be. And Ace-of-Hearts would like nothing better than to be in the front ranks."

Well supplied with provisions, the captain set out with his men, heading southwest. First they had to go through a forest of no fewer than a hundred thousand palm trees, which contained another composed entirely of fruit trees.

They passed through only one settlement of any size between Gafsa and the Algerian-Tunisian frontier. This was Chebika, where the information they had received about the presence of the Tuareg chieftain was confirmed. He was wreaking havoc among the caravans traveling through the far regions of the province of Constantine, adding new attacks on persons and property to his already long dossier of crimes.

A few days' march from there, when the commandant had crossed the border, he made great haste to reach the village of Négrine, on the banks of Wadi Sokhna.

The day before he arrived, the Tuareg had been spotted a few kilometers to the west, between Négrine and Ferkane, on the banks of Wadi Djerich, which flows toward the large chotts in that region.

Hadjar, who was accompanied by his mother, was reported to have about a hundred men. Captain Hardigan had only about half that number, but he and his spahis would have attacked without hesitation. African troops are not frightened by odds of two to one, and they had often fought under even less favorable conditions.

That was exactly what happened when the detachment reached the neighborhood of Ferkane. Hadjar had been forewarned and was not eager to rush into battle. It would be better, he reasoned, to let the squadron advance farther into this harsh region of large chotts, to harass it with continual attacks, and to send out a call to the nomadic Tuareg, who were moving through the country and would certainly not refuse to join Hadjar, since he was well known to all the Tuareg tribes. Moreover, now that

Captain Hardigan had picked up their trail, he would not abandon it and would no doubt pursue them as far as necessary.

In view of this, Hadjar had decided to slip away. If he could cut off the squadron's retreat after recruiting new partisans, he could probably annihilate the little detachment that had been sent out against him. This would add an even more deplorable catastrophe to the one that had befallen Carl Steinx.

Hadjar's plans were frustrated, however, while his band was trying to move up Wadi Sokhna to reach the base of Djebel Cherchar in the north. A platoon led by Sergeant Nicol, who had been alerted by Ace-of-Hearts, cut off their line of advance. Fighting broke out and the rest of the detachment soon joined in as well. Rifle and musket shots rang out, interspersed with revolver fire. Some of the Tuareg were killed and some of the spahis wounded. Half of the Tuareg forced their way out and managed to escape, but their leader was not among them.

As Hadjar was spurring his horse to its fastest gallop in an attempt to rejoin his comrades, Captain Hardigan was riding in pursuit, also at top speed. Hadjar tried in vain to knock him out of the saddle with a shot from his pistol. The bullet went wide of its mark. Suddenly his horse lunged to the side and Hadjar, slipping from his stirrups, fell to the ground. Before he had time to get up, one of the lieutenants hurled himself upon him. Other spahis hurried to the scene and held him down, despite his desperate efforts to break free.

Djemma rushed forward and would have reached her son if she had not been grabbed by Sergeant Nicol. But half a dozen Tuareg managed to pull her away from him, and the brave dog's attempts to attack them as they dashed away with the old woman were in vain.

"I had the she-wolf," cried the sergeant, "but she slipped through my fingers. Here, Ace-of-Hearts, come here," he repeated, calling the animal back. "Anyway, the wolf cub is a good prize."

Hadjar was now in close custody. If the Tuareg did not manage to rescue him before he got to Gabès, the Djerid would finally be rid of one of its most dreaded felons.

The band would undoubtedly have attempted a rescue and

The capture of Hadjar

Djemma would not have left her son in the hands of the French, if the detachment had not received reinforcements from the military posts at Tozeur and Gafsa.

The expedition then regained the coast. The prisoner was locked up in the fort at Gabès until he could be transported to Tunis and handed over to the military authorities.

These were the events leading up to the present story. After a short trip to Tunis, Captain Hardigan had just returned, on the very evening when the *Chanzy* was dropping anchor in the Gulf of Gabès.

iii ～～ The Escape

After the two officers, the sergeant, and the spahis had left, Horeb crept along the side of the well to a point where he could see up and down the path.

When the sound of footsteps had died out in both directions, the Targui motioned to his companions to follow him.

Djemma, her son, and Ahmet quickly joined him. They went up a narrow, winding street, lined with old, vacant, tumbledown houses, and made their way toward the bordj.

That part of the oasis was deserted, and the din of the more populous quarters could not be heard. It was pitch dark under the dense ceiling of clouds hanging motionless in the still air. The murmur of the surf on the beach, carried by the last breaths of wind off the sea, could barely be heard.

It took only a quarter of an hour for Horeb to reach the new rendezvous point, the lower room of a kind of café or cabaret run by a Levantine bazaar merchant who was part of the escape plot. His loyalty had been ensured by the payment of a substantial sum of money, which was to be doubled if the plan succeeded. His cooperation had already been very useful on this occasion.

Among the Tuareg gathered in the cabaret was Harrig, one of the most devoted and daring of Hadjar's followers. A few days earlier, after a street brawl in Gabès, he had been arrested and imprisoned in the fort. During his time in the prison courtyard, he had been able to communicate freely with his leader. What could be more natural than that two men of the same race should associate with each other? No one knew that Harrig belonged to Hadjar's band. He had managed to escape during the battle and fled with Djemma. Now that he was back in Gabès, according to the plan worked out by Sohar and Ahmet, he took advantage of his imprisonment to work out the details of Hadjar's escape.

Arab homes in Gabès. (Photo by Soler, Tunis)

However, it was important that the Tuareg chieftan be set free before the arrival of the cruiser that would carry him away. And that vessel, which had been seen passing Cap Bon, was now about to drop anchor in the Gulf of Gabès. Hence the necessity for Harrig to get out of the bordj in time to coordinate his activities with those of his friends. The escape had to be carried out that very night. Once morning dawned, it would be too late. By sunrise Hadjar would have been taken aboard the *Chanzy*, and it would no longer be possible to wrest him from the hands of the military authorities.

This is where the bazaar merchant played his role. He knew the head guard of the military prison. The light sentence imposed on Harrig for his part in the street brawl had been served the previous day, but his companions were still waiting impatiently for him to be released. It was unlikely that his sentence had been extended for breaking some prison regulation, but it was nevertheless urgent that they know how things stood, and above all to make sure that Harrig would be released before nightfall.

The merchant decided to go and see the guard, who often relaxed at his café during his free time. That evening he set out for the fort.

Approaching the guard in this way, which might have aroused suspicion after the escape, proved to be unnecessary. As the merchant drew near the rear gate, he met a man in the street.

It was Harrig, and he recognized the Levantine. Since they were alone on the path leading down from the bordj, there was no danger of their being seen or overheard, let alone spied on or followed. Harrig was not an escaped convict, but a prisoner who had served his sentence and been released.

"What news of Hadjar?" was the merchant's first question.

"He's been told," replied Harrig.

"Tonight?"

"Tonight. And Sohar, and Ahmet, and Horeb?"

"They're waiting for you."

Ten minutes later Harrig was with his comrades in the lower room of the café. As an extra precaution, one of them stayed outside to keep an eye on the road.

Less than an hour later, the old Tuareg woman and her son,

with Horeb as their guide, entered the café. Harrig briefed them on the situation.

During his few days in prison, Harrig had spoken with Hadjar. There was nothing suspicious about two Tuareg, confined in the same prison, talking together. In any case, the Tuareg chieftain was to be sent off to Tunis shortly, while Harrig would soon be released.

Sohar was the first to question Harrig after Djemma and her companions had reached the merchant's café.

"What news of my brother?"

"And my son?" added the old woman.

"Hadjar is aware of the situation," replied Harrig. "Just as I was leaving the bordj, we heard the *Chanzy* fire her cannon. Hadjar knows he'll be taken aboard tomorrow morning, and he'll try to escape tonight."

"If he put it off for twelve hours," said Ahmet, "he'd be too late."

"What if he doesn't make it?" whispered Djemma.

"He'll make it, with our help," Harrig replied quickly.

"But how?" asked Sohar.

Harrig explained.

The cell where Hadjar spent his nights was in a part of the fort facing the sea, so close that the water of the gulf lapped at its base. Adjoining this cell was a narrow courtyard, accessible to the prisoner, but surrounded by high, impassable walls.

In one corner of the courtyard was an opening, a sort of drain, leading to the outside and blocked by a metal grating. The other end of the drain was about a dozen feet above sea level.

Hadjar had noticed that the grating was in poor condition and that its bars were rusting from the effect of the salt air. It would not be difficult to pry it loose during the night and crawl through to the outside.

But how could Hadjar make good his escape after that? If he dropped into the sea, would he be able to swim around the edge of the fort to the nearest beach? Was he young and strong enough to take his chances with the powerful gulf currents running out to sea?

The Tuareg chieftain was not yet forty years old. He was a tall man, white-skinned, but tanned by the fiery African sun, lean, strong, accustomed to all forms of physical exertion. Given the general sobriety of his race, whose diet of grain, figs, dates, and dairy products kept them strong and hardy, he would be in good health for many years to come.

It was no accident that Hadjar had acquired a strong influence over the nomadic Tuareg of the Touat and Sahara, who were now confined to the chott region of southern Tunisia. He was as daring as he was intelligent. He had inherited these qualities from his mother, as do all the Tuareg, who trace their ancestry through the maternal line. They regard women as equal, if not superior, to men. In fact, a man whose father was a slave and whose mother was of noble lineage would himself be considered a noble. The opposite never occurs. Djemma's sons had inherited all her energy, and had remained close to her since the death of her husband twenty years earlier. Under her influence, Hadjar had acquired the qualities of a charismatic leader, with his handsome face, black beard, piercing eyes, and resolute demeanor. At a word from him, the tribes would have crossed the vast expanse of the Djerid, if he had wanted to lead them in a holy war against the foreigners.

In short, he was a man in the prime of life, but he could not have succeeded in escaping without some help from the outside. It would not be enough to pry off the grating and crawl through to the other end of the drain. Hadjar knew the gulf, and he was aware of the powerful currents that build up there, even though, as throughout the whole Mediterranean basin, the tide never rises very high. He knew that no swimmer would be able to make his way against those currents and that he would be carried out to sea without being able to set foot on dry land, either above or below the fort.

There had to be a boat waiting for him at the end of that passage in the corner of the prison wall.

When Harrig had finished giving all this information to his companions, the merchant said simply, "I've got a boat over there that you can use."

"Will you take me to it?" asked Sohar.

"When the time comes."

"You'll have kept your part of the bargain, then, and we'll keep ours," added Harrig. "If we succeed, we'll double the sum we promised you."

"You'll succeed," insisted the merchant. Like a typical Levantine, he viewed the entire operation merely as a highly profitable business transaction.[1]

Sohar got to his feet. "What time is Hadjar expecting us?" he asked.

"Between eleven and midnight," replied Harrig.

"The boat will be there well before that," Sohar assured them. "Once my brother is on board, we'll take him to the marabout, where the horses are ready."

"At that spot," the merchant pointed out, "you'll be in no danger of being seen. You can row right up to the beach. There'll be no one there until morning."

"But what about the boat?" asked Horeb.

"All you have to do is pull it up onto the sand, and I'll come and get it."

Only one question remained to be settled.

"Which one of us will go and get Hadjar?" asked Ahmet.

"I will," said Sohar.

"And I'll go with you," said the old Tuareg woman.

"No, mother," Sohar insisted. "It will only take two of us to row the boat to the bordj. If we should meet anyone, your presence might arouse suspicion. You must go to the marabout. Horeb and Ahmet will go with you. Harrig and I will take the boat and bring back my brother."

Realizing that Sohar was right, Djemma simply asked, "When do we leave?"

"Right now," he replied. "In half an hour, you will be at the marabout. It will take us less than half an hour to get to the base of the fort with the boat, at the corner of the wall where there's no danger of being seen. And if my brother doesn't appear by the time we agreed on, I will try—yes, I will try to go in and get him."

"Yes, my son, yes. Because if he doesn't get away tonight, we'll never see him again—never!"

The time had come. With Horeb and Ahmet leading the way,

they went down the narrow road leading to the market. Djemma followed them, hiding in the shadows whenever they came across a group of people. They might have been unlucky enough to meet Sergeant Nicol, and it was crucial that he not recognize her.

After they reached the outskirts of the oasis there would be no more danger, and if they stayed close to the base of the dunes they would not meet a living soul until they came to the marabout.

A little later, Sohar and Harrig left the cabaret. They knew where the bazaar merchant's boat was located and they preferred that he not go with them. He might be noticed by some passerby walking late at night.

It was now about nine o'clock. Sohar and his friend went back up toward the fort and skirted its southern wall.

The bordj seemed quiet both inside and out. Any noise would have been heard, for the air was still, without a breath of wind. It was also dark, for the sky was covered from one horizon to the other with thick, heavy, motionless clouds.

It was not until they reached the beach that Sohar and Harrig encountered any activity. Fishermen were going by, some returning home with their catch, others going back to their boats to head out into the gulf. Here and there, lights pierced the darkness, criss-crossing in all directions. Half a kilometer away, the cruiser *Chanzy* made its presence known by its powerful searchlights, which sent out luminous tracks across the surface of the water.

Taking care to avoid the fishermen, the two Tuareg headed for a breakwater under construction at the end of the port.

The merchant's boat was tied up at the foot of the breakwater. An hour earlier, as planned, Harrig had checked to make sure it was there. There were two oars under the seats, and all they had to do was get on board.

Just as Harrig was about to pull in the grapnel, Sohar put a hand on his arm. Two customs officials, on watch along that part of the shoreline, were coming their way. They might know who the owner of the boat was and be surprised to see Sohar and his comrade taking possession of it. It was better not to arouse suspicion, to keep their project as much in the dark as possible. The customs officials would certainly have asked Sohar what they were doing with a boat that did not belong to them, and since they had no fishing gear they could not have passed themselves off as fishermen.

So they quickly ran back up the beach and crouched against the breakwater, out of sight.

They stayed there a good half hour, and it is not hard to imagine how impatient they felt when they saw that the customs men seemed to be in no hurry to leave. Would they be on duty there all night? No, at last they went on their way.

Sohar walked across the sand, and, as soon as the customs officials had disappeared in the darkness, he called to his friend to join him.

They hauled the boat as far as the beach. Harrig got in first, then Sohar stowed the grapnel in the bow and followed him.

They quickly fitted the two oars into the oarlocks and gently rowed the boat past the pierhead of the breakwater and along the base of the prison wall, where the waters of the gulf lapped against it.

In a quarter of an hour Harrig and Sohar had rounded the corner of the stronghold and stopped directly beneath the opening of the drain through which Hadjar would try to escape.

At that moment the Tuareg chieftain was alone in the cell in which he was to spend his final night. An hour earlier, the prison guard had left him and drawn the heavy bolt, locking the door of the little courtyard adjoining the cell. With the extraordinary patience typical of the Arabs, whose fatalism is combined with complete self-control under all circumstances, Hadjar was waiting for the moment to act. He had heard the *Chanzy* fire her cannon. He knew the cruiser had arrived and that he would be taken on board the next day, never again to see this region of chotts and sebkha, this land of the Djerid! But his Muslim resignation was combined with the hope that he would succeed in his attempt. He was certain he could escape through that narrow passage, but had his friends been able to get a boat? Would they be waiting for him at the base of the wall?

An hour went by. From time to time Hadjar left his cell, went over to the entrance to the drain, and listened. The sound made by a boat scraping against the wall would have come through to him clearly, but he heard nothing. He returned to his cell, where he remained absolutely still.

Sometimes, fearful that he might be taken aboard the cruiser during the night, Hadjar listened at the door of the little courtyard to see if he could hear the footsteps of a prison guard. Complete silence reigned all around the bordj, broken only occasionally by the footsteps of a sentinel walking on the platform of the fort.

But midnight was approaching, and the arrangement with Harrig had been that by half past eleven Hadjar would have removed the grating and made his way to the end of the passage. If the boat was there, he would get in at once. If it had not arrived, he would wait until the first light of dawn, and then—who knows?—perhaps he would try to swim to freedom, even at the risk of being dragged away by the currents into the Gulf of Gabès. It would be his last and only chance to escape a death sentence.

Hadjar went out to make sure no one was approaching the courtyard. Then, wrapping his clothing tightly around his body, he slipped into the passage.

The passageway was about thirty feet long and just wide enough for a man of average size to squeeze into it. As Hadjar crawled along it, some folds of his clothing caught and were torn on its jagged sides. But slowly and with great effort, he finally reached the grating.

This grating, as mentioned, was in very poor condition. The bars had come loose from the stone, which crumbled at a touch. After five or six good tugs, it gave way. Hadjar set it back against the side of the passageway, and the way was clear.

The Tuareg chieftain had only two more meters to crawl to reach the opening. This was the hardest part of all, since the drain became extremely narrow at the end. He managed to push through, however, and did not need to wait long.

Almost at once, these words came to his ears: "We're here, Hadjar."

With one final exertion, Hadjar emerged half way out of the opening, ten feet above the surface of the water.

Harrig and Sohar stood up and reached out to him. But just

Hadjar's escape

as they were about to pull him out, they heard footsteps. Their first thought was that the sound had come from the little courtyard, that a guard had been sent to get the prisoner and take him away earlier than planned. Now that the prisoner was gone, the alarm would be sounded in the fort!

Fortunately, this was not the case. The sound had come from the sentinel, walking on the prison's parapet. Perhaps the approach of the boat had attracted his attention, but he could not see it from where he was standing. And, in any case, such a small boat would be invisible in the darkness.

However, they needed to be very cautious. Sohar and Harrig waited a few moments, then seized Hadjar by the shoulders, gradually pulled him free, and lowered him into the boat with them.

A strong pull on the oars propelled the boat seaward. Wisely, they decided not to row along the walls of the bordj or along the beach, but rather to proceed up the gulf as far as the marabout. In doing so, they could avoid the little boats that were moving in and out of the port, for the calm night made for good fishing. As they passed the *Chanzy* on their beam, Hadjar stood up, crossed his arms, and stared for a long time at the cruiser, his eyes full of hatred. Then, without saying a word, he sat down again in the stern of the boat.

Half an hour later they disembarked on the sand and pulled the boat onto dry land. The Tuareg chieftain and his two comrades headed for the marabout, and reached it without incident.

Djemma came to meet her son, took him in her arms, and spoke only one word: "Come!"

Rounding the corner of the marabout, she rejoined Ahmet and Horeb. Three horses were waiting, ready to dash off into the night with their riders. Hadjar quickly swung up into his saddle, and Harrig and Horeb did as well.

"Come," Djemma had said when she saw her son. Now, with her hand pointing toward the shadowy regions of the Djerid, she again spoke a single word: "Go!"

A moment later, Hadjar, Horeb, and Harrig disappeared into the darkness.[2]

The old Tuareg woman stayed in the marabout with Sohar until morning. She had ordered Ahmet to return to Gabès. Had her

"Go!" said Djemma.

son's escape been discovered? Was the news already spreading through the oasis? Had the authorities sent out detachments in pursuit of the fugitive? In what direction across the Djerid would they go looking for him? And would the campaign against the Tuareg chieftain and his followers, which had earlier led to his capture, now be resumed?

That was what Djemma desperately wanted to know before starting out toward the chotts region. But Ahmet could learn nothing as he prowled around the outskirts of Gabès. He even went within sight of the bordj, stopping at the bazaar merchant's house to tell him that the rescue had succeeded—that Hadjar was free at last and was now fleeing across the solitary wastes of the desert.

The merchant had heard no gossip of the escape and, if there had been any, he would certainly have been one of the first to know.

But the first glimmers of dawn would soon light up the eastern horizon of the gulf, and Ahmet did not wish to tarry any longer. It was important for the old woman to leave the marabout before daybreak. She was well known to the authorities and, next to that of her son, her own capture was of highest priority. While it was still dark, Ahmet returned to her and guided her onto the road to the dunes.

The next day, the cruiser sent a launch to the port to pick up the prisoner and take him back to the ship.

When the prison guard opened the door to Hadjar's cell, all he could report was that the Tuareg chieftain had disappeared. A glance down the drain, from which the grating had been removed, made it only too obvious how the escape had been carried out. Had Hadjar tried to swim to safety? If so, had the current dragged him out into the gulf? Or, rather, did he have accomplices who might have taken him somewhere along the shore in a boat?

There was no way to know for certain. A search of the area near the oasis brought no results. Not a trace of the fugitive, living or dead, was to be found—either on the plains of the Djerid or in the waters of the Gulf of Gabès.

iv ～ The Sahara Sea

r. de Schaller extended a warm welcome to everyone who had accepted his invitation and thanked
the officers, the French and Tunisian officials,
and the leading citizens of Gabès who had hon-
ored the meeting with their presence.

"There is no denying, gentlemen," he began,
"that the progress of science has made it more and more impossible to confuse history and legend. In the final analysis, they are
mutually exclusive. Legend belongs to the poets, history to the
scientists, and each has its own special following. Although I
fully recognize the merits of legend, today I am obliged to rele-
gate it to the realm of the imagination and come back to realities
proven by scientific observation."

The new hall in the Gabès casino could hardly have found an
audience more willing to follow the lecturer in his interesting
demonstrations. Since the project that would be the topic of his
lecture already had their full support, his words were greeted
from the very beginning by a flattering murmur. A few of the natives in the crowd were the only ones who seemed to maintain
a cautious reserve, and that was because the project Mr. de
Schaller was preparing to review had been looked on with dis-
favor for half a century by the sedentary and nomadic tribes of
the Djerid.

"We will readily admit," continued the speaker, "that the people of the ancient world had vivid imaginations, and that historians skillfully catered to their tastes by repeating as history what
was in fact only tradition. The inspiration for these tales was
purely mythological.

"Bear in mind, gentlemen, what Herodotus, Pomponius
Melas, and Ptolemy have to say. In his *History of Peoples*, Herodotus tells of a land that extends as far as the River Triton, which

Mr. de Schaller

empties into the bay of the same name. He recounts an episode in the journey of the Argonauts, when Jason's ship, driven by a storm onto the coast of Libya, was cast back westward as far as the Bay of Triton, whose western shore could not be seen. From this account it must be concluded that the bay in question was at that time connected to the sea. That is, in fact, what Scylax, in his *Journey around the Mediterranean*, says about a large lake whose shores were inhabited by various Libyan peoples. It must have covered the present-day region of the sebkha and chotts, and at that time was connected with the Gulf of Gabès by a narrow canal.

"After Herodotus came Pomponius Melas, near the beginning of the Christian era, who noted the existence of a large lake named Triton (also known as Lake Pallas),[1] whose connection with the Gulf of Petite-Syrte, the present-day Gulf of Gabès, had disappeared as a result of a drop in the water level due to evaporation.

"Finally, according to Ptolemy, as the water level continued to fall, the lake separated into four depressions—Lake Triton, Lake Pallas, Lake Libya, and Turtle Lake—known today as Chott Melrir and Chott Rharsa in Algeria and Chott Djerid and Chott Fedjedj in Tunisia. The latter two are often referred to collectively as the sebkha, or salt marsh, of Faraoun.

"As for these ancient legends, gentlemen, which have nothing to do with precision and modern science, we can take them or leave them—and it is better to leave them. No, Jason's ship was not driven across this inland sea, which was never connected with the Gulf of Petite-Syrte, and he could never have crossed the coastal ridge unless he had been equipped with the powerful wings of Icarus, the venturesome son of Dedalus. Observations taken at the end of the nineteenth century show conclusively that there could never have been a Sahara Sea covering the whole region of chotts and sebkha, since at some points these depressions, especially those nearest the coast, rise fifteen or twenty meters above the level of the Gulf of Gabès. That sea could never, at least during the period of recorded history, have been a hundred leagues in width, as some overactive imaginations claimed.

"Nevertheless, gentlemen, by reducing it to the maximum size permitted by the nature of the terrain surrounding the chotts and sebkha, it would be possible to carry out the project of creating a Sahara Sea, by bringing in water from the Gulf of Gabès.

"This, then, was the plan elaborated by a few bold but practical scientists, a plan which, after many attempts, has yet to be carried out. What I want to do now is review for you the history of this project, as well as the vain struggles and cruel setbacks that have characterized it for so many years."

A movement of approval could be heard in the room, and every eye followed the speaker's hand as it gestured toward a map with large spots, which was hanging on the wall above the platform.

The map showed the part of Tunisia and southern Algeria lying at the thirty-fourth degree of latitude and between the third and eighth degrees of longitude. The large depressions southeast of Biskra were clearly marked. They included all the Algerian chotts lying below the level of the Mediterranean Sea, known as Chott Melrir, Grand Chott, Chott Asloudje, and others, as far as the Tunisian border. Indicated on the map was a canal that joined the end of Chott Melrir with the Gulf of Gabès.

To the north extended the plains inhabited by various tribes, and to the south lay the vast region of dunes. The principal towns and villages of the area were marked in their exact locations: Gabès, on the shore of the gulf of the same name; La Hammâ to the south; Limagnes, Softim, Bou-Abdallah, and Bechia on the strip of land lying between the Fedjedj and the Djerid; Seddada, Kri, Tozeur, Nefta in the space between the Djerid and the Rharsa; Chebika to the north and Bir Klebia to the west of that; and finally, Zeribet-Aïn Naga, Tahir Rassou, Mraïer, and Fagoussa, near the proposed Trans-Sahara Railway to the west of the Algerian chotts.

In one glance, the audience could easily discern on the map all the depressions, including the Rharsa and the Melrir, which, once flooded, would form the new African sea.

"But," continued Mr. de Schaller, "whether or not nature has been kind enough to arrange these depressions in such a way as to receive water from the Gulf of Gabès can only be established after a lengthy surveying operation. In 1872, during an expedition across the Sahara Desert, Mr. Pomel, the senator from Oran, and Mr. Rocard, a mining engineer, claimed that this work could not be carried out because of the nature of the chotts. The study was taken up again in 1874, under better conditions, by Staff Captain Roudaire, in whose mind the idea for this extraordinary project first took shape."

Applause broke out on all sides at the mention of this French officer, who was acclaimed as he had often been already and always would be in the future. To his name, moreover, should be added those of Mr. de Freycinet, chairman of the Council of Ministers, and Ferdinand de Lesseps, who later recommended this gigantic undertaking.

"Gentlemen," continued the speaker, "we must go back to that early date to witness the first exploration of this region, which is bounded on the north by the Aurès Mountains, thirty kilometers south of Biskra. It was in 1874 that this daring officer developed the plan for an inland sea, a plan to which he would devote so much effort. But could he have foreseen the many obstacles that would arise, and which might be beyond his ability to overcome? Nevertheless, it is our duty to give this brave man of science the recognition that he deserves."

After the first studies had been carried out by the minister of public education, who was the sponsor of this undertaking, Captain Roudaire was officially put in charge of several scientific missions having to do with the exploration of the region. Precise geodesic measurements were carried out, which made it possible to map the contours of that part of the Djerid.

As a result, legend had to give way to reality: this region had never been, as was once believed, a sea connected to the Gulf of Gabès. Further, it was discovered that this depression in the earth's surface, which was once viewed as being completely floodable from the Gabès ridge to the farthest chotts of Algeria, could in fact be flooded only over a relatively small part of its total area. But the fact that the Sahara Sea would not be as large as popular belief would have it was no justification for abandoning the project.

"In principle, gentlemen," said Mr. de Schaller, "it was apparently thought that this new sea might cover an area of fifteen thousand square kilometers. From this figure, we have had to subtract five thousand for the Tunisian sebkha, which lie above the level of the Mediterranean. In fact, according to Captain Roudaire's calculations, no more than eight thousand square kilometers of Chott Rharsa and Chott Melrir, which lie some twenty-seven meters below the level of the Gulf of Gabès, can be flooded."

Moving his pointer over the map and explaining each detail of its panoramic view, Mr. de Schaller guided his audience through that part of ancient Libya.

First of all, in the sebkha region, starting at the coast, the area above sea level ranges in height from 15.52 meters to 31.45 meters, the highest point being near the Gabès ridge. Farther inland, the first large depression, some forty kilometers in length, is the basin of Chott Rharsa, two hundred and twenty-seven kilometers from the sea Then the ground rises for a distance of thirty kilometers, as far as the Asloudje ridge, and drops for the next fifty kilometers, as far as Chott Melrir, most of which could be flooded over a distance of fifty-five kilometers. This point, at longitude 3°40', is four hundred and two kilometers from the Gulf of Gabès.

"This, gentlemen," continued Mr. de Schaller, "is the geodesic work that has been carried out in those regions. If the eight thousand square kilometers that lie below sea level are definitely capable of receiving water from the gulf, would it not be beyond the power of man, given the nature of the terrain, to dig a canal two hundred and twenty-seven kilometers long?"

After making many probes, Captain Roudaire did not think so. As Maxime Hélène explained in an excellent article written about this time,[2] it was not a question of digging a canal across a sandy desert, as at Suez, or through limestone mountains, as at Panama and Corinth. Here the terrain is not nearly as solid as that. It would be a matter of digging through a salty crust, and a drainage system would keep the ground dry enough for this work to be carried out. Even on the ridge of land between Gabès and the first sebkha, a distance of twenty kilometers, the pick would encounter only a layer of limestone thirty meters thick. All the rest of the digging would be in soft ground.

The speaker continued, summing up very precisely the advantages which, according to Roudaire and his successors, would result from this gigantic undertaking. In the first place, the climate of Algeria and Tunisia would be appreciably improved. Under the influence of southerly winds, the clouds formed by vapor from the new sea would bring beneficial rain to the whole region and increase its agricultural yield. Moreover, the depressions of Chott Djerid and Chott Fedjedj in Tunisia, and of Chott Rharsa and Chott Melrir in Algeria, which are now swampy, would be made more healthful by this deep, permanent layer of water. After these physical improvements, who knows what commercial gains might ensue once this region was transformed by the hand of man? Captain Roudaire concluded by putting forward, quite legitimately, these final arguments: in the region to the south of the Aurès and Atlas Mountains new roads would be built, where caravans would travel more safely; a merchant fleet would enable trade to develop throughout the whole region, which is now inaccessible because of its low-lying areas; if troops were able to disembark south of Biskra, they would be able to maintain order by increasing the French influence in that part of Africa.

"However," continued the speaker, "although this plan for an inland sea has been studied with scrupulous care, and although the geodesic operations were carried out with the strictest attention to detail, many naysayers tried to deny the advantages that the region would derive from this great work."

One by one, Mr. de Schaller dealt with the arguments, published at the time in various newspapers, which had declared relentless war against Captain Roudaire's undertaking.

First of all, it was argued that the canal intended to carry water from the Gulf of Gabès to Chott Rharsa and Chott Melrir would be so long, and the capacity of the new sea—twenty-eight billion cubic meters—would be so great, that the depressions could never be filled.

Next, it was claimed that the salt water from the Sahara Sea would percolate through the soil of the neighboring oases, rise to the surface by capillary action, and destroy the huge stands of date palms on which the economy of the country depends.

Then, too, there were critics who, quite seriously, predicted that the water from the sea would never reach the depressions, but would evaporate every day on its way through the canal. And yet, in Egypt, under the fiery rays of a sun at least as hot as that of the Sahara, Lake Menzaleth, which some claimed could never be filled, was indeed filled, even though the canal was at that time only one hundred meters wide.

It was also argued that it would be impossible, or at least extremely costly, to dig the canal. But when this was put to the test, it turned out that the soil between the Gabès ridge and the first depressions was so soft that the probe sometimes sank under its own weight.

Then came the most pessimistic of all the prognostications put forward by the critics of the project. Since the margins of the chotts were very flat, they would supposedly soon turn into pestilential breeding grounds, which would infect the area again. The prevailing winds, instead of blowing from the south, as the authors of the project claimed, would come from the north. The rain produced by evaporation from the new sea, instead of falling on the countryside of Algeria and Tunisia, would go to waste on the vast sandy plains of the great desert.[3]

These criticisms marked the beginning of a tragic and fateful period, in this land where fatalism reigns supreme. And its events remain engraved in the memories of everyone who lived in Tunisia at that time.

Captain Roudaire's plans had fired the imaginations of some and aroused the speculative passions of others. Mr. de Lesseps, one of the former, had shown great interest in the matter until he turned his attention to the problem of cutting through the Isthmus of Panama.

However, all this could not fail to affect the attitudes of the local native inhabitants, both nomadic and sedentary. They foresaw all of southern Algeria falling under the control of the French, with the consequent loss of their security, their precarious livelihood, and their independence. If their desert was invaded by the sea, it would put an end to their centuries-old control. And so a widespread but concealed agitation began to grow among the tribes, gripped by the fear that their privileges, or at least those they granted to themselves, would be under attack.

In the meantime, a weakened Captain Roudaire died, more

from disappointment than from illness, and the work he had dreamed of lay dormant for a long period. In 1904 Panama was bought by the Americans, and a few years later a group of foreign engineers and capitalists took up his plan where he had left off. They founded a company known as the France-Overseas Company,[4] which started making preparations to begin the work and to carry it quickly to completion—first for the good of Tunisia and second for the prosperity of Algeria.

The idea of conquering the Sahara had occurred to a number of minds, and the push to carry this out was gathering momentum in the western Algerian city of Oran as Roudaire's abandoned project was fading from view. The national railway had already gone beyond Beni-Ounif, in the oasis of Figuig, and was gradually transforming itself into the railhead for the Trans-Sahara.

"There is no need," continued Mr. de Schaller, "for me to go back over all the operations of the France-Overseas Company, the energy it expended, or the massive projects it undertook—with more boldness than foresight. Its operations, as you know, extended over a vast territory, and since it had not the slightest doubt as to its success, it concerned itself with everything, including the forestry service to which it had assigned the task of stabilizing the dunes to the north of the chotts, using the methods employed in the Landes region of France to protect the seacoast against the twofold threat of sea and sands. Even before completing its projects, the company considered it necessary—indispensable, in fact—to protect existing towns and those still to be built from any unforeseen perils of a future sea that would certainly be no tranquil lake, and against which it would be well to be on their guard from the very beginning.

"At the same time, a whole system of waterworks had to be constructed to bring drinking water from the nearby streams. Surely it would be better not to offend the natives, as regards either their customs or their interests. That was the price of success. And it would be necessary as well to build ports that would quickly give rise to a profitable coastal trade.

"For these operations, which had begun everywhere at once, concentrations of workers and temporary towns sprang up almost overnight where almost complete solitude had reigned shortly before. The nomadic tribes, despite their strong moral resistance to the project, were held in check by the sheer number of workers. The engineers spared no effort, and their inexhaustible store of knowledge won the respect and complete confidence of the hundreds of men under their orders. At that moment, southern Tunisia began to turn into a veritable human beehive, giving no thought to the future. Speculators of all kinds, profiteers, swindlers, etc., did their best to exploit the first pioneers. The latter could not live off the land and were forced to depend for their existence on suppliers of dubious origin, who always appear wherever there are large masses of people.

"And over everything, over all these basic material necessities, hovered the idea of an ever-present but invisible danger—the feeling of an undefined threat, something comparable to the vague anxiety that precedes all atmospheric cataclysms. It troubled many people, surrounded by that vast solitude, a solitude that held a hint of something—no one knew what—but definitely something mysterious, in those almost limitless surroundings, where there was no living creature to be seen, neither man nor beast, and where everything seemed to be hiding from the eyes and ears of the workers.

"Through miscalculation and lack of foresight, gentlemen, the project ended in failure, and the France-Overseas Company was forced into bankruptcy. Since that time, nothing has changed, and what I have come here to speak to you about is the possibility of resuming this interrupted work. The company had tried to do too much at once—projects of the most widely varying kinds and speculations of every sort. Many of you still remember the sad day when it ran out of money before it had completed its overambitious program. The maps I have just shown you illustrate the work begun by the France-Overseas Company.

"But these unfinished works are still there. The climate of Africa, which is essentially protective, has certainly not eroded them, or at least not seriously. Our new Sahara Sea Company will purchase them for a sum to be negotiated, depending on the condition in which we find them. And they will serve as a legitimate stepping-stone to the ultimate success of this enterprise. It is essential, however, that we first closely examine them to see what use can be made of them. That is why I propose to inspect them carefully, first by myself and later with a group of expert engineers. We shall always be under the protection of an escort large enough to ensure our own safety during the journey (which, rest assured, will be as brief as possible) and the safety of the present and future outposts and construction sites.

"I have no serious worries about the native population, despite the complications caused by settling part of the Tuareg tribe in the southern territories. It is possible that this development may even prove to be a very positive one: after all, the desert Bedouins were very cooperative during the digging of the Suez Canal. For the moment, these nomadic tribes appear to be quiet but watchful; it would nevertheless be a mistake to rely too heavily on their seeming inactivity. With a brave and experienced soldier like Captain Hardigan, who has confidence in the men under his command and is thoroughly familiar with the ways and customs of the strange inhabitants of these regions, you may be sure that we will have nothing to fear. Upon our return we will give you a precise account of its status and an exact estimate as to the cost of completing this project. As a result, you will be able to share in the glory (and, I venture to say, the profits) of a 'great work' that is both progressive and patriotic. Although earlier doomed to failure, it will now, thanks to you, be successfully completed. We shall accomplish this for the honor and prosperity of our homeland, which will come to our assistance as needed and, as in the south Oran region, will find a way to transform the hostile tribes into the most loyal and trustworthy guardians of our incomparable conquest over nature.

"Gentlemen, you know who I am, and you also know what strengths, both financial and intellectual, I bring to this great work. These combined strengths overcome all obstacles. Once our new company is organized, I guarantee that we will succeed where our predecessors, less well equipped than we, have failed. That is what I wanted to tell you before I leave for the south. As you well know, confidence and steadfast energy always lead to success. A hundred years after the French flag was raised over the kasbah in Algiers, we will finally see our French fleet sailing over the Sahara Sea, bringing supplies to our desert outposts."[5]

V 〜 The Caravan

As Mr. de Schaller had announced at the meeting in the casino, the work would be resumed in an orderly and energetic fashion after the planned expedition returned, and the Gabès ridge would finally be breached, permitting the waters from the gulf to flow through the new canal. But the first essential step would be to make an on-site investigation of whatever was left of the previous work. The best method to accomplish that seemed to be to follow the route of the first canal through the Djerid to the point where it emptied into Chott Rharsa, and the route of the second from Chott Rharsa to Chott Melrir, through the smaller chotts lying between them, then to travel around Chott Melrir (after making contact with a work party that had been hired at Biskra), and finally to decide on the location of the various ports on the Sahara Sea.

For the exploitation of the two million five hundred thousand hectares granted by the state to the France-Overseas Company,[1] as well as the purchase, as needed, of the latter's existing constructions and available raw materials, a powerful new company had been formed, with a board of directors based in Paris. The stocks and bonds issued by the new company seemed to elicit a favorable response from the public. Their quoted value in the stock exchange was high, mostly because of the financial success the company's directors had previously shown in large business dealings and beneficial public works projects.

The bright future of this undertaking, one of the largest of the mid-twentieth century, seemed to be guaranteed from every standpoint.

The new company's chief engineer was the very speaker who had just outlined the history of the work already completed, and he would be in charge of the expedition that would assess the present state of this work.

Mr. de Schaller was forty years old, of medium height, strong-willed (or, to use the popular expression, bull-headed), with short hair, a reddish-blond moustache, a small mouth, thin lips, sharp eyes, and a piercing gaze. His broad shoulders, his strong limbs, the barrel chest where lungs pumped as smoothly as a high-pressure machine in a large, well-ventilated room, were all signs of a very robust constitution. And he was as perfectly well equipped mentally as he was physically. After graduating near the top of his class from Central,[2] he immediately made a name for himself with his first construction projects and progressed rapidly along the road to fame and fortune. No one ever had a more positive attitude than he. With his reflective and methodical mind—mathematical, if one may use that term—he never let himself be deceived by illusions. It was said of him that he calculated the chances of success or failure of a situation or a business affair with a precision "carried to the tenth decimal place." He reduced everything to figures and summed it up in equations. If ever there was a human being immune to flights of fancy, it was certainly this number-and-algebra man, who had been assigned to complete the vast work of creating the Sahara Sea.

Since Mr. de Schaller, after an objective and meticulous study of Captain Roudaire's plan, had declared it to be feasible, then that clearly meant it was. Under his direction, there would certainly be no miscalculation in either materials or finances. Those who knew the engineer said over and over again, "If de Schaller is involved in the project, it must be a good one!" and there was every reason to assume that they were right.

Mr. de Schaller's plan had been to travel around the perimeter of the future sea, to make sure nothing would prevent the water from flowing through the first canal as far as the Rharsa and through the second as far as the Melrir, and to check on the condition of the banks and shoreline that would contain the twenty-eight billion tons of water.

Since his team of future coworkers would include some members of the France-Overseas Company as well as new engineers and entrepreneurs, some of whom, including senior officials, could not come to Gabès at that time, the chief engineer had decided not to take with him any members of the new company's still incomplete personnel, in order to avoid any subsequent conflict of authority.

He did take with him, however, a servant, or valet—if he had not been a civilian, he could have been called an "orderly." Punctual, methodical, one might say "military," even though he had not seen military service, Mr. François was the ideal man for this task. His robust health enabled him to endure without complaint the many exhausting ordeals he had experienced during his ten years in the engineer's employ. He said little, but though he was short on words, he was long on ideas. He was a thinking man, a perfect precision instrument, for whom Mr. de Schaller had a high regard. He was sober, discreet, and clean, and would never let twenty-four hours go by without shaving. He wore neither sideburns nor moustache, and had never, even under the most difficult conditions, neglected his daily *toilette*.[3]

It goes without saying that the expedition organized by the chief engineer of the French Sahara Sea Company would not accomplish its objectives unless certain precautions were taken. It would have been foolhardy for Mr. de Schaller to set out across the Djerid accompanied only by his servant. Work sites established by the former company were widely separated and lightly guarded, if at all; accordingly, communications were notoriously unreliable, even for caravans, in this land where nomads were constantly on the move. The few military command posts set up previously had been taken out of service many years ago. Further, the attacks of Hadjar and his band must not be forgotten. That fearsome leader, following his capture and imprisonment, had escaped before the just sentence in store for him could rid the country of his presence. It was only too obvious that he would want to resume his thieving activities.

Moreover, the situation was in Hadjar's favor at the moment. It was highly unlikely that the Arabs of southern Algeria and Tunisia, to say nothing of the sedentary and nomadic tribes of the Djerid, would stand by without protest while Captain Roudaire's project was carried out, for it would involve the destruction of several oases in the Rharsa and Melrir regions. The owners would be compensated, of course, but by and large, the compensation would not be to their advantage. Undoubtedly, some interests had been infringed upon, and those owners felt a deep hatred whenever they thought of their fertile *touals* disappearing beneath the waters coming in from the Gulf of Gabès. Those peoples whose way of life would be disrupted by the new "Sahara Sea" now also included the Tuareg, who were still inclined to resume their adventurous life as caravan raiders. What would become of them when there were no more roads among the chotts and sebkha, when the caravans that had been traveling the desert toward Biskra, Touggourt, or Gabès since time immemorial no longer carried on their commerce? Merchandise would be transported in the region south of the Aurès Mountains by a fleet of schooners and tartans, brigs and three-masters, sailing vessels and steamships, to say nothing of a whole native merchant marine. How could the Tuareg ever dream of attacking them? It would mean imminent ruin for these tribes who lived by piracy and pillage.

The undercurrent of unrest among this particular part of the population was quite understandable. Their *imams*[4] were inciting them to revolt. Several times, Arab workers employed in digging the canal were attacked by angry mobs and had to be protected by calling in Algerian troops.

"What right," proclaimed the Muslim holy men, "do these foreigners have to turn our oases and plains into a sea? Why do they try to undo what nature has done? Is the Mediterranean not big enough for them, that they must now add our chotts to it as well? Let the Frenchmen sail around on it as much as they like, if that makes them happy, but we are land dwellers, and the Djerid is meant to be traveled by caravans, not by ships. These foreigners must be wiped out before they drown our land, the land of our forefathers, under the invading sea!"

This growing agitation had played a part in the downfall of the France-Overseas Company. Over time, after the work was abandoned, it had seemed to subside, but the inhabitants of the Djerid were still haunted by the fear that the desert might be invaded by the sea. This fear had been consistently encouraged by the Tuareg ever since they had settled south of the Arad, and by the *hajjis*, or pilgrims, returning from Mecca, who maintained that their brethren in Egypt had lost their independence with the building of the Suez Canal. It continued to be a universal concern, one that was uncharacteristic of Muslim fatalism. These abandoned installations, with their fantastic equipment—enormous dredges with strange levers that looked like monstrous arms, excavators that might well be compared to gigantic land octopuses—had entered into local legend and figured prominently in the tales told by the country's yarn-spinners, tales that those people have eagerly listened to ever since the *Arabian Nights* and the other narratives of countless Arabian, Persian, and Turkish storytellers.

By reviving memories of people of ancient times, these stories kept the native population obsessed with the idea of an invasion by the sea. It is not surprising, then, that Hadjar and his followers had, prior to his arrest, been frequently involved in aggressive actions against this project.

For this reason, the engineer's expedition would be carried out under the protection of an escort of spahis led by Captain Hardigan and Lieutenant Villette. It would have been difficult to find better officers than these two, since they were familiar with the south and had successfully led the difficult campaign against Hadjar and his band. They would study what security measures needed be taken to protect the project's future.

Captain Hardigan was in the prime of life, barely thirty-two years old, intelligent, daring but not rash, accustomed to the rigors of the African climate, and possessed of a stamina that he had demonstrated beyond question during his many campaigns. He was an officer in the fullest sense of the term, a soldier at heart, who could see no other career in the world than the army. Since he was a bachelor and had no close relatives, his regiment was his only family, and his comrades-in-arms were his brothers. He was not only respected in the regiment, but loved. The affection and gratitude of his men showed in their devotion to him, and they would have sacrificed their lives for him. He could expect anything from them, and could ask anything of them.

As for Lieutenant Villette, suffice it to say that he was as brave, energetic, and resolute as his captain, and, like him, a tire-

Captain Hardigan

less and excellent horseman who had proved his worth in previous expeditions. He was a highly trustworthy officer, a member of a rich family of industrialists, with a promising future ahead of him. He stood near the top of his graduating class at the École de Saumur[5] and was in line for an early promotion.

At the time this expedition across the Djerid was decided on, Lieutenant Villette was due to be recalled to France. When he learned that Hardigan was to be in command of it, he went to see him.

"Sir," he said, "I'd really like to be part of your expedition."

"And I'd really like to have you," replied the captain, in the same tone of warm and honest camaraderie.

"I can go back to France just as well two months from now."

"Of course you can, my dear Villette. Even better, in fact, because then you'll be able to take back the latest news about the Sahara Sea."

"So I can, sir, and we'll have seen the Algerian chotts for the last time, before they disappear under water."

"They'll be gone a long time," replied Hardigan, "as long as old Africa lasts, or in other words, as long as there is a moon above the earth."

"There's every reason to think so, sir. So it's settled, then, and I'll have the pleasure of coming with you on this little campaign —just an ordinary outing, no doubt."

"Yes, just an ordinary outing, as you put it, my dear Villette, especially now that we've managed to rid the country of that madman, Hadjar."

"That was a capture that did you honor, sir."

"And you too, Villette."

Needless to say, this conversation between Captain Hardigan and Lieutenant Villette took place before the Tuareg chieftain had made his escape from the bordj at Gabès. But now that he was free, there was reason to fear new attacks. Nothing would be easier for him than to touch off an uprising of the tribes whose way of life would be changed by that inland sea.

The expedition would have to keep an eye on his movements across the Djerid, and to that matter Captain Hardigan would devote his full attention.

It would have been very surprising if Sergeant Nicol had not been a member of the escort. Wherever the captain went, the sergeant inevitably went as well. He had taken part in the action in which Hadjar was captured, and he would be with the expedition that might renew the struggle between his captain and the Tuareg bands.

Now thirty-five years old, the sergeant had already done several tours of duty, always with the same cavalry regiment. The sergeant's stripes on his sleeve fulfilled his ambition. He asked nothing more than to live out a well-deserved retirement, but to postpone it for as long as possible. A soldier of unusual stamina and resourcefulness, Nicol was also a stickler for discipline. He considered it the first law of existence, and would have liked to see it apply in civilian life as well as in the army. However, while he believed that man was created solely to serve his nation's flag, it also seemed to him that man would be incomplete without his natural complement of a horse.

"Giddup and I," he was in the habit of saying, "are a single unit. I am his head and he is my legs, and you will agree that a horse's legs are built differently for marching than a man's legs. Now if only we had four . . . but we have only two . . . although we could use half a dozen!" Obviously, the sergeant envied myriapods. But all the same, he and his horse were perfectly well suited to each other just the way they were.

Nicol was above average height, with broad shoulders and a well-built chest. He had managed to keep his weight down and would have made any sacrifice to avoid getting fat. He would have considered himself the unhappiest creature in the world if he had seen the slightest sign that he was putting on weight. By tightening the buckle of his blue trousers and forcing the buttons of his cape into their buttonholes, he could easily fend off any attack of obesity, if that should ever occur to one with such a spare frame. Nicol was redheaded, a fiery redhead, with short hair, a bushy goatee, a thick moustache, grey eyes that moved around constantly in their sockets, and such amazingly keen sight that he could spot a fly at fifty paces, as a swallow does, much to the admiration of Corporal Pistache.

Pistache was a cheerful sort, always happy, and he would be

as happy at sixty as he was at twenty-five. He never complained of hunger, even when the meals were several hours late, nor of thirst, even when waterholes were scarce on the endless, sun-scorched expanse of the Sahara. He was one of those solid southerners from Provence, always good for a laugh, a man after Sergeant Nicol's own heart. They were usually to be found together, and one would follow the other's footsteps throughout the entire course of the expedition.

Finally, the detachment included a number of spahis and two mule-drawn wagons that carried the squad's camping equipment and food. Such, then, was the entire composition of engineer de Schaller's escort.

Although there is nothing in particular to be said about the horses ridden by the officers and their men, special mention must be made of Sergeant Nicol's horse and of the dog that stayed as close to him as his shadow.

The name "Giddup," which Nicol had given his horse, is self-explanatory. The animal richly deserved its name, for it seemed always on the point of bolting, always trying to get ahead of the others, and only a horseman as skilled as Nicol could keep it in check. As mentioned, horse and rider got on admirably together.

But while Giddup is an acceptable name for a horse, how could a dog ever have come to be called Ace-of-Hearts? Was this dog as talented as Munito,[6] or other celebrities of the canine species? Did he make appearances at local circuses? Did he play cards in public?

No, Nicol and Giddup's companion possessed none of these social talents. He was simply a brave and loyal animal, a credit to the regiment, loved, cherished, and petted by officers and men alike. But his real master was the sergeant, and his closest friend was Giddup.

Now Nicol was passionately fond of the game of *rams*.[7] To tell the truth, it was his one and only passion during his free time when on garrison duty. He could not imagine that there was anything more enticing for ordinary mortals. He was very good at it, and rather proud of the nickname of "Sergeant Ram," which his many victories had earned him.

Two years earlier, as it happened, Nicol had made a singularly lucky play near the end of a game. It was something he enjoyed remembering. He was sitting in a café in Tunis with two of his comrades, in front of the board on which thirty-two cards were laid out. After a long session, his luck and skill had completely run out, much to the satisfaction of his friends. Each of the three players had won three games. It was now time to go back to barracks, and the winner would be decided by a final game. Sergeant Ram felt victory slipping from his grasp; it was not his lucky day. The players were all down to their last card. One of the players threw down the queen of hearts, another the king of hearts. They could assume that the ace of hearts, the final trump card, was among the eleven cards left in the deck.

"Ace of hearts!" bellowed Nicol, pounding the table with his fist so hard that his winning card flew out into the middle of the room.

And who went and carefully picked it up? Who brought it back between his teeth? The dog whose name, until that memorable day, had been Misto.

"Thanks, thanks, old buddy," exclaimed the sergeant, as proud of his double win as if he had captured two flags from the enemy. "The ace of hearts, do you hear? I had the ace of hearts!"

The dog barked out a long expression of satisfaction.

"Yes, the ace of hearts," repeated Nicol. "And your name isn't Misto any more. It's Ace-of-Hearts. How do you like that?"

Obviously the noble animal found the new name very much to his liking, for he pranced around and jumped up onto his master's lap, nearly knocking him over.

Soon Misto had forgotten his old name and answered only to Ace-of-Hearts, the name by which he has been honorably known in the regiment ever since.

There can be no doubt that the proposal for a new expedition was greeted with great satisfaction by Sergeant Nicol and Corporal Pistache, but they made it clear that Giddup and Ace-of-Hearts would be just as happy as they were.

The day before they were to leave, the sergeant and the corporal had a conversation with their two inseparable friends that left no doubt whatever on that score.

"Yes, you good old dog, you'll be coming with us too!"

"Well, my old friend Giddup," said Nicol, patting his horse's neck, "so we're starting out on a new campaign."

Giddup must have understood what his master said, for he whinnied happily.

Ace-of-Hearts answered his whinnying with a series of joyful little barks, whose meaning was unmistakable.

"Yes, you good old dog, you'll be coming with us too," added the sergeant, while Ace-of-Hearts frisked around as if he wanted to jump up on Giddup's back. In fact, he sometimes did take to the saddle, and the horse seemed to enjoy this arrangement as much as the dog did.

"We're leaving Gabès tomorrow," the sergeant went on. "Tomorrow we'll be on our way to the chotts. I hope you'll both be ready and won't lag behind the others."

This admonition was greeted by more whinnying and more barking.

"By the way," continued Nicol, "you know that arch-devil Hadjar, that cursed Targui we all helped to capture, has sneaked away from us."

If Giddup and Ace-of-Hearts did not know it before, they knew it now. Ah! That Tuareg scoundrel had gotten away.

"Well, my friends," declared the sergeant, "there's a good chance we'll meet this Hadjar out there, and we'll have to surround him and trap him again."

Ace-of-Hearts was ready to rush right out, and Giddup was ready to follow as soon as his master was astride him.

"See you tomorrow, then," said the sergeant as he left.

It is safe to say that in the days when animals talked (and no doubt spoke much less nonsense than humans) Giddup and Ace-of-Hearts would have answered, "See you tomorrow, Sergeant, see you tomorrow!"[8]

vi ～ From Gabès to Tozeur

At five o'clock on the morning of March 17, with the vast sandy plains of the chott region twinkling in the light of the sun rising over the gulf, the expedition left Gabès.

The weather was clear. A light northerly breeze was blowing, driving before it a few clouds, which dissipated before they reached the far horizon.

Winter was already coming to an end. In the east African climate, one season follows another with remarkable regularity. The *ech-chta*, or rainy period, is usually confined to the months of January and February. Summer, with its excessive heat, lasts from May until October, with prevailing winds varying from northeast to northwest. Mr. de Schaller and his party were leaving at a propitious time. They would certainly complete their reconnaissance before the onset of the terrible heat that makes it so difficult to travel across the flat, sandy expanse of the Sahara.

As mentioned, there was no port at Gabès. What was once the inlet of Tnoupe was now almost completely filled in with sand and accessible only to vessels of shallow draft. The semicircular gulf between the Kerkenath Islands and the Lotophages Islands has been given the name of Petite-Syrte, and sailors have as much reason to fear it as they do the Grande-Syrte, the scene of so many maritime disasters.

The starting point of the canal would be at the mouth of the Wadi Melah, where facilities for a new port were already being put in place. From this twenty-kilometer-wide Gabès ridge, twenty-two million cubic meters of earth and sand had already been removed, leaving only a narrow strip of land to hold back the waters of the gulf. A few days might be enough to remove that strip, but of course that operation would not be carried out until the last minute, after all the shoring up, cutting through, and deepening in the chotts had been completely finished. Plans also had to be made for building a bridge to carry the extension of the Kairouan-Feriana-Gafsa railway across on its way to Gabès and the Tripolitanian border.

The Gabès ridge, the beginning and shortest part of the first canal, had been very exhausting and very costly, since it rose in some places as high as a hundred meters, with only two gaps fifty or sixty meters high, and the sand was mixed with rock strata that was difficult to remove.

From the mouth of the Wadi Melah, the canal followed a course toward the plains of the Djerid, and the detachment began the first stages of its journey by following it, sometimes on the north bank and sometimes on the south. The second section began at Kilometer 20 and followed as much as possible the north bank, in order to minimize the difficulties and dangers presented by the nature of the terrain in the chott region.

Mr. de Schaller and Captain Hardigan led the way, escorted by a few *spahis*. Next came the convoy carrying provisions and camping equipment, under the command of Sergeant Nicol. Bringing up the rear was a platoon commanded by Lieutenant Villette.

Since the expedition's sole objective was to reconnoiter the route of the canal over its entire length and to assess the conditions of its construction, first as far as Chott Rharsa and then on to Chott Melrir, the group would travel only a short distance each day. While it is true that caravans going from oasis to oasis and keeping to the south of the Algerian and Tunisian mountains can cover as much as four hundred kilometers in ten or twelve days, the engineer planned to travel no more than a dozen kilometers every twenty-four hours, for he had to take into account the poor condition of the trails and former roads along the canal.

"We're not going to make any discoveries," said Mr. de Schaller. "What we're going to do is study the present condition of the work that our predecessors have left us."

"You're quite right, my friend," replied Captain Hardigan. "In any case, there's been nothing left to discover in this part of the Djerid for a long time. But, as for myself, I'm not sorry to visit it

65

Mr. de Schaller and Captain Hardigan,
escorted by a few spahis, *lead the way.*

one last time before it's transformed. Do you think the change will improve it?"

"Definitely, captain, and if you'd care to come back . . ."

"In about fifteen years . . ."

"No, much sooner than that I'm sure you'll find a bustling commercial life where there's nothing now but the solitude of the desert . . ."

"Which has a charm of its own, my dear fellow."

"Yes, if neglect and emptiness have power to charm."

"To a mind like yours, probably not," replied Captain Hardigan. "But who knows? The old stalwart admirers of nature may yet have cause to regret the changes imposed on it by the human race."

"Well, my dear Hardigan, don't complain too much. If the entire Sahara Desert had been below the level of the Mediterranean, you can be sure we would have turned it into an ocean all the way from the Gulf of Gabès to the Atlantic coast, just as it must have been during some geological periods."

"Present-day engineers really have no respect for anything," declared the officer with a smile. "If they had their way, they'd fill the oceans up with mountains and our globe would be nothing more than a smooth, polished ball, like an ostrich egg, with a convenient network of railways!"[1]

It is safe to assume that, during the several weeks of their travels through the Djerid, the engineer and the officer would rarely see things from the same point of view, but they would be good friends nevertheless.

As they crossed the Gabès oasis, they passed through some delightful countryside. Between the sandy seashore and the dunes of the desert, specimens of many kinds of African flora can be found. Botanists have collected five hundred and sixty-three species of plants. The inhabitants of this oasis are fortunate, for nature has showered them with its favors. Although bananas, mulberries, and sugar cane are rare, there is an abundance of figs, almonds, and oranges growing under the tall fans of the countless date palms, not to mention the vine-covered hillsides and the fields of barley stretching as far as the eye can see. The Djerid is date country, with a hundred and fifty varieties of date palms, and more than a million trees. Their fruit, including that of the "light date," with transparent flesh, is of excellent quality.

After passing through this oasis, the caravan traveled up the Wadi Melah and entered the more arid part of the Gabès region, through which the new canal extended. Thousands of hands had been needed to complete the work there. But despite many complications, there had been no shortage of workers, and the France-Overseas Company had been able to hire as many Arabs as it needed at low wages. Only the Tuareg and a few other nomadic tribes that frequented the approaches to the sebkha had refused to take part in digging the canal.

As they went along, Mr. de Schaller took notes. There would still be a few corrections to be made to the slope of the banks and even to the canal bed itself in order to create the grade necessary to obtain a flow of water sufficient, according to Captain Roudaire's calculations, "to fill the basins and maintain them at a constant level, by replacing the water that would evaporate every day."

"But how wide, generally speaking, was the canal going to be?" asked Captain Hardigan.

"Only twenty-five or thirty meters, on average," replied Mr. de Schaller, "and it was to be designed in such a way that it could be widened by the water flowing through it. However, although it meant more work and greater expense, it was considered necessary to increase the width to eighty meters, as you see it today."

"That was probably done with a view to shortening the time required to flood Chott Rharsa and Chott Melrir."

"I'm sure it was, and, as I told you before, we're counting on the strong current to push the sand to the sides, thereby increasing the flow of water from the gulf."

"But at the beginning," continued the captain, "there was talk of waiting at least ten years for the Sahara Sea to reach its normal level."

"I know, I know," replied Mr. de Schaller. "It was even claimed that the water would evaporate on its way through the canal and that not a drop would reach Chott Rharsa. In my opinion, it would have been much better to keep to the width originally decided on and make the canal deeper, at least over the first part of it. That would have been infinitely more practical and less costly. But as you know, that was not the only mistake our predecessors made in their calculations. Besides, these assertions can now be refuted on the basis of more precise studies, and it will certainly not take ten years to flood the depressions in Algeria. Within five years, merchant ships will be sailing the new sea from the Gulf of Gabès to the most distant port on the Melrir."[2]

The two stages of the first day's journey were completed under favorable conditions. The caravan had stopped whenever the engineer had to examine the condition of the trench. Around five o'clock in the afternoon, when they were about fifteen kilometers from Gabès, Captain Hardigan gave the signal to stop for the night.

Camp was set up at once on the north side of the canal, under the shade of a little grove of date palms. The riders dismounted and led their horses to a meadow where there was an ample supply of grass for them. There was a stream winding through the grove, and its water proved to be cool and clear.

The tents, used only for sleeping, were soon set up, and the men ate their meal under the trees. The engineer and the two officers were served by Mr. François, who had prepared a fine dinner from the supplies brought with them from Gabès. In meat and canned vegetables alone, the caravan had food enough for several weeks, and in the settlements and villages of southern Tunisia and Algeria, in the neighborhood of the chotts, it would always be easy to replenish their supplies.

Needless to say, the sergeant and his men, resourceful fellows that they were, had set up their tents in the twinkling of an eye, after first placing the convoy's two wagons at the entrance to the grove. But before attending to his own needs, Nicol had made a point of grooming Giddup. The worthy steed seemed satisfied with this first day's travel across the Djerid, and whinnied long replies to his master's queries while Ace-of-Hearts barked his own.

Captain Hardigan had, of course, taken every precaution for guarding the camp. The silence of the night was broken only by the usual outbursts of shouting by the local nomads. The wild

The wadi Menzel in Gabès. (Photo by Soler, Tunis)

beasts kept their distance, and no unwelcome visitor approached the camp during the night.

By five o'clock everyone was up, and at ten past five Mr. François had already finished shaving in front of a piece of mirror hanging on the tent post. The horses were rounded up, the wagons loaded, and the little group set out once more, in the same order as on the previous day.

The banks of the canal that they were following, sometimes on one side and sometimes on the other, were not as high here as in the part of the Gabès ridge closer to the gulf. They were com-

In the oasis of Gabès. (Photo by Soler, Tunis)

posed entirely of very soft earth or loose sand, and would certainly not resist the pressure of the water if the current gained any force. As had been planned by the engineers and feared by the natives, the canal would widen by itself, thereby shortening the time needed for completely flooding the two chotts. But on the whole, Mr. de Schaller was able to ascertain that the canal bed appeared to be solid. In this part of the canal, running through the great Tunisian sebkha, the layers of earth were soft, and the digging had proceeded more rapidly than in the terrain bordering the Gulf of Gabès.

The land was as solitary and sterile as it had been when they left the Gabès oasis, with occasional stands of date palms and plains covered with tufts of esparto grass, which is the real wealth of the country.

Since its departure, the expedition had been heading west along the canal, in order to reach the depression known as the Fedjedj and the settlement of La Hammâ (not to be confused with another of the same name at the eastern end of the Rharsa, which the expedition would visit after it had passed through the whole extent of the Fedjedj and the Djerid).

At La Hammâ, to the south of the canal, Captain Hardigan went to find billets for the night on the evening of March 18, after completing the day's two regular route marches.

The various settlements of this region are all set in identical locations, each in the middle of a small oasis. Like the villages, they are surrounded by earthen walls, which enable them to resist attacks by nomads and even by the large wild beasts of Africa.

La Hammâ had a population of only a few hundred natives, interspersed at times with a few French colonists. A small detachment of native soldiers occupied the bordj, a small, simple house strategically located in the center of the settlement. The spahis, who were warmly welcomed by the residents, were billeted in Arab homes, while the engineer and the officers accepted the hospitality of one of their countrymen.

When Captain Hardigan made inquiries about the Tuareg chieftain who had escaped from prison in Gabès, the colonist replied that he had heard nothing about him whatsoever. Hadjar had not been reported anywhere in the vicinity of La Hammâ. There was every reason to believe that the fugitive had bypassed the Fedjedj and returned to the chott region of Algeria, where he had taken refuge among the Tuareg tribes in the south. However, a resident of La Hammâ, returning from Tozeur, had heard that

Arab hospitality in La Hammâ

Djemma had been seen in that vicinity, but no one knew which way she had gone from there.

On the morning of March 19, with a slightly overcast sky promising cooler weather, Captain Hardigan gave the signal to move on. They had covered some thirty kilometers from Gabès to La Hammâ, and the distance from there to the Fedjedj was only half of that. They could do it in a day's march and in the evening the little group would camp near the chott.

For the last leg of the march to La Hammâ, the engineer had had to travel at some distance from the canal, but now, early in the day, he had come back to it at the point where it entered the chott. Over a distance of one hundred and eighty-five kilometers, through the long depression of the Fedjedj, between fifteen and twenty-five meters above sea level, the excavation had been carried out without too much difficulty.

During the next few days, the detachment was able to follow the banks of the canal on ground that was not as firm as they might have wished.

In the middle of these depressions, the probes sometimes sank in until they disappeared, and what happened to an instrument could also happen to a man. This Tunisian sebkha is the largest one of all. Beyond Bou-Abdallah Point, the Fedjedj and the Djerid (not to be confused with the part of the desert that bears that name) form a single depression as far as their western end. The canal had been dug through the Fedjedj, starting at the village of Mtocia, north of La Hammâ. It was there that its route had to be followed, traveling in almost a straight line as far as Kilometer 153, then veering southward, parallel to the coast, between Tozeur and Nefta.

The lake basins known as sebkha and chotts are curious phenomena. The ones known to geographers as Djerid and Fedjedj have lost all their water, even in the central part. As they rode along, Mr. de Schaller gave the following explanation to Captain Hardigan and Lieutenant Villette, who had joined them, as he often did.

"The reason why we can't see the groundwater is because it's covered by a hard layer of salt. But there's nothing between it and the surface except that saline crust, which is a real geological curiosity. You'll notice that your horses' footsteps resound, as if they were walking over a vault."

"So they do," replied the lieutenant. "It makes you wonder whether the ground will suddenly give way under them."

"Certain precautions must be taken," added Captain Hardigan, "as I keep telling our men. We've seen places in the lowest part of these depressions where the water came up to the horses' chests."

"That happened before, while Captain Roudaire was reconnoitering this sebkha, and cases have been cited of caravans suddenly getting bogged down on their way to the various settlements in this part of the country."

"This region is neither a sea nor a lake, and not land either, in the true sense of the word," observed Lieutenant Villette.

"Something that doesn't exist in the Djerid can be found in the Rharsa and the Melrir," continued Mr. de Schaller. "In addition to the hidden water, those chotts contain shallow surface water, but still remain below sea level."

"Well, my dear sir," said Captain Hardigan, "it's really a shame that those conditions don't exist in this chott. A thirty-kilometer canal would have been sufficient to bring water from the Gulf of Gabès, and we would have been sailing over the Sahara Sea for several years now."

"Yes, it's a great pity," agreed Mr. de Schaller, "not only because the work would have been less extensive and taken less time, but also, perhaps, because the new sea would have been twice as big. Instead of seven thousand two hundred square kilometers, or seven hundred and twenty thousand hectares, it would have covered about a million and a half! When you look at the map of this area you can see that the Fedjedj and the Djerid have a larger surface area than the Rharsa and the Melrir, and the latter will not be entirely flooded."

"After all," said Lieutenant Villette, "since the ground we're walking on is unstable, mightn't it sink even lower in the more or less distant future, especially after the water from the canal has been flowing into it for a long time? Who knows? A gradual or sudden change in the ground level might turn the whole southern part of Algeria and Tunisia into an ocean bed and allow the Mediterranean to flow into it from east to west."

"Now our friend Villette is really getting carried away," remarked Captain Hardigan. "He's letting himself be taken in by all the phantoms that haunt the imaginations of the Arabs in their tales. He's trying to outrun good old Giddup, our friend Nicol's horse."

"Well, Captain," answered the young officer with a laugh, "I think anything can happen."

"And what's your opinion about that, my dear de Schaller?"

"I don't like to express an opinion unless it's based on well-established facts and precise observations," concluded the engineer. "But, to tell the truth, the more I study the ground in this region, the more I find something abnormal about it. It makes one wonder what changes may occur over time as a result of unpredictable events. But in the meantime, I suggest we leave the future for now and be satisfied with bringing this splendid Sahara Sea project to completion."

After a number of route marches to the settlements of Limagnes, Seftimi, and Bou-Abdallah, on the strip of land lying between the Fedjedj and the Djerid, the expedition completed the exploration of the first canal as far as Tozeur, and stopped there on the evening of March 30.

"Here," said Sergeant Nicol to Corporal Pistache and Mr. François that evening, "we are in superb date country. This is what the captain would call a genuine 'datery,' and my buddies Giddup and Ace-of-Hearts would call it that, too, if they had the gift of speech."

"All right," replied Pistache, "but dates are dates wherever you go. As long as they come from a date palm, it doesn't matter whether you pick them in Gabès or in Tozeur. Isn't that right, Mr. François?"

They always addressed him as "Mr. François." Even his boss never called him by any other name, and Mr. François insisted on it with natural dignity.

"I really couldn't say," he replied in a deep voice, passing his hand over the chin that he would shave first thing the next morning. "I must admit I have no particular liking for that fruit. It's all right for Arabs, but not for Normans like me."

"Well, now, you are being difficult, Mr. François," exclaimed the sergeant. "All right for Arabs indeed! You mean it's too good for them, because they don't appreciate it as it deserves. Dates! I'd give every kind of fruit grown in France for them! Pears, apples, grapes, oranges . . . "

"But French fruit is not to be sneered at," declared Pistache, licking his lips.

"Anyone who talks like that," said Nicol, "has obviously never tasted dates from the Djerid. Look, tomorrow I'll give you a 'deglat-en-nour' date to eat, right off the tree. It's firm and transparent and, as it ripens, it forms a delicious sweet paste. Try it and you'll see. It's a fruit from paradise, pure and simple. It was probably a date, not an apple, that tempted that gourmand who was our first ancestor."

"That's quite possible," added the corporal, willingly accepting the sergeant's authority.

"And don't assume, Mr. François," continued the sergeant, " that I'm the only one who holds that opinion about the dates from the Djerid, especially the ones from the Tozeur oasis. Ask Captain Hardigan. Ask Lieutenant Villette. They both know their dates. You can even ask Giddup and Ace-of-Hearts."

"What?" said Mr. François, great surprise showing on his face. "Your horse and your dog?"

"They're crazy about them, Mr. François. When we were still three kilometers away, their nostrils detected the odor of date palms. Yes, tomorrow they'll have a feast together."

"Very well, Sergeant," replied Mr. François. "If you wish, the corporal and I will be delighted to partake of a few dozen of these highly esteemed products of the Djerid."

The sergeant was not exaggerating by any means. In the whole country, and especially in the vicinity of Tozeur, the dates are of a very high quality. In the oasis there are more than two hundred thousand date palms, producing more than eight million kilograms of dates. They are the region's greatest wealth, and the numerous caravans they attract bring in woolens, rubber, barley, and wheat, and take back with them thousands of sacks of this precious fruit.

It is quite understandable, then, that the inhabitants of these oases might have genuine fears about the creation of an inland sea. If they were to be believed, the humidity brought about by flooding the chotts would ruin the excellent quality of the dates, which, because of the dry air of the Djerid, are the choicest of all. They make up the staple diet of the tribes and can be kept more or less indefinitely. If there were a change of climate, their dates would be no more highly regarded than those harvested near the Gulf of Gabès or the Mediterranean.

But were these concerns well-founded? Differences of opinion on that subject were known, but there is no denying that whenever the natives of southern Algeria and southern Tunisia thought of the irreparable damage Roudaire's project would cause, they protested angrily against the creation of the Sahara Sea.[1]

The dam at Tozeur. (Photo by Soler, Tunis)

At that time, too, an embryonic forestry service had been organized to protect the region against the encroaching sand. The many plantings of fir and eucalyptus trees and the anti-erosion works similar to those in the French Landes region had succeeded quite well. But although the methods of fighting off the invading sand are known and widely practiced, it is essential that this laborious struggle remain ongoing, otherwise the sand will break through the obstacles and continue to destroy and swallow everything in its path.

The travelers were now in the very heart of the Tunisian Djerid, whose chief towns and villages are Gafsa, Tameghza, Mides, Chebika, Nefzaoua, and Tozeur, to which should be added the great oases of Nefta, Oudiane, and La Hammâ. It was a center where the expedition could assess the condition of the work done by the France-Overseas Company, so suddenly interrupted by insurmountable financial difficulties.

Tozeur has a population of about ten thousand and nearly a thousand hectares of land under cultivation. Its only manufactured products are burnouses, blankets, and rugs. But, as mentioned, caravans come there in great numbers and the fruit of the date palm is exported by the millions of kilograms. Perhaps surprisingly, education is held in relatively high regard in this remote village in the Djerid: nearly six hundred children attend eighteen state schools and eleven *zaouia*s, or Muslim schools. There are also many religious orders in the oasis.

Although Tozeur was not a town to arouse Mr. de Schaller's curiosity, for either its trees or its fine oases, he was much interested in the canal, whose channel, only a few kilometers away, led to Nefta. Captain Hardigan and Lieutenant Villette, on the other hand, were making their first visit to this town and thus spent an entire day there—one that would have satisfied the most curious of tourists. Some of the squares and streets were especially charming: the houses were built of colored bricks arranged in designs of surprising originality and they would no doubt catch the eye of an artist much more than the few insignificant vestiges of the ancient Roman occupation located nearby.

Early on the morning of the following day, Captain Hardigan gave his NCOs and men leave to spend their time in the oasis at

An Arab house in Tozeur. (Photo by Soler, Tunis)

whatever suited their fancy, as long as they were all present for the noon and evening roll calls. They were forbidden, however, to venture out beyond the area patroled by the military post in the village, which was under the orders of a senior officer. It was more important than ever to be vigilant because of the extreme tension that the resumption of the work and the imminent flooding of the chotts would arouse among the sedentary and nomadic tribes of the Djerid.

As usual, Sergeant Nicol and Corporal Pistache were out walking together at the crack of dawn. Giddup had not yet left

The central market at Tozeur. (Photo by Soler, Tunis)

the stable, where he was knee-deep in fodder, but Ace-of-Hearts was frisking along by their side. He would undoubtedly report his impressions—those of a curious and inquisitive dog—to his good friend Giddup.

The most frequent meeting place for the engineer, the officers, and the soldiers during that day was the Tozeur market. Most of the local population congregated there, in front of the Dar-el-Bey. This souk, or market, resembles a military camp when the tents sheltering the vendors are set up and hung with matting or light cloth supported by palm branches. In front of the tents is displayed the merchandise carried on camel back from oasis to oasis.

There the sergeant and corporal had an opportunity (one that occurred frequently, as a matter of fact) to imbibe a few glasses of palm wine, a native drink known as *lagmi*. It is distilled from the sap of the palm tree, obtained either by cutting off the top of the tree (which inevitably dies as a result of this decapitation) or by simply making a number of incisions in the trunk, which do not allow the sap to escape in great enough quantity to kill the tree.

"Pistache," said the sergeant to his subordinate, "you know we mustn't overdo a good thing, and this lagmi is devilishly treacherous."

"But not as treacherous as date wine, sergeant," replied the corporal, who had very precise ideas on the subject.

"True. I agree with you there," continued Nicol, "but we have to be very careful with it, because it attacks the legs as well as the head."

"Don't worry, sergeant. But look at those Arabs. They're setting a very bad example for our men."

Two or three natives, obviously in their cups, were staggering this way and that as they crossed the marketplace, in a state of inebriation that was wholly inappropriate, especially for Arabs.

"I thought," the corporal remarked pointedly, "that their Mohammed forbade his followers to get drunk."

"Yes, Pistache," replied the sergeant, "on any kind of wine at all, except this lagmi. The Koran apparently makes an exception for this product of the Djerid."

"And I see the Arabs are making the most of that exception," said the corporal.

It seems that palm wine is not included in the list of alcoholic beverages forbidden to the sons of the Prophet.

The palm is the native tree par excellence of that region, but beautiful flower gardens are also grown in the marvelously fertile soil of the oasis, along with a great variety of vegetables. The Wadi Berkouk brings its life-giving waters to the surrounding countryside through its main stream and the many little side streams that flow from it. Can there be any more admirable sight than that of a tall palm tree sheltering an olive tree of average height, which in turn shelters a fig tree, under which a pomegranate tree gives shelter to a grape vine, whose branches grow among the rows of wheat, vegetables, and garden plants?

At the invitation of the commandant, Mr. de Schaller, Captain Hardigan, and Lieutenant Villette spent an evening in the great hall of the Kasbah. The conversation turned naturally to the current status of the construction project, the imminent opening of the canal, and the advantages that the flooding of the two Tunisian chotts would bring to the region.

"It's only too true," remarked the commandant, "that the natives refuse to recognize the benefits the Djerid will derive from the Sahara Sea. I've had occasion to talk with the Arab chieftains. With few exceptions, they're hostile to the project, and I haven't been able to make them see reason. What they're afraid of is a change in climate that would have a harmful effect on the produce of the oasis, especially the palm groves. And yet, everything points in the opposite direction. The best scientific authorities have no doubts on that score. Along with water from the sea, the canal will bring wealth to this country. But the natives are stubborn and refuse to give in."

"This opposition comes from the nomads rather than from the sedentary tribes, doesn't it?" asked Captain Hardigan.

"Definitely," replied the commandant, "because the nomads' life will be very different from what it has been up to now. Of all the tribes, the Tuareg are clearly the most violent, and understandably so. The number and size of the caravans will decrease. No more kafila to guide along the roads of the Djerid, or to plunder, as still happens. Trade will be carried on entirely by ships on the new sea. So, unless the Tuareg change occupations, and become pirates instead of thieves . . . But, under those conditions, they would soon be rendered powerless. It isn't surprising that they take every opportunity to indoctrinate the more sedentary tribes, telling them that their future will be ruined if they have to give up the kind of life led by their ancestors. What we're up against is not only hostility but a kind of irrational fanaticism. For the moment, it still remains latent, held in check by Islamic fatalism. But at any time it could suddenly erupt into widespread violence. Those people obviously don't understand the effects of a Sahara Sea any more than they understand how the water will be brought in. They see it only as the work of sorcerers, which might lead to a horrible catastrophe."

The commandant was not telling his guests anything they did not already know. Captain Hardigan was well aware that the expedition would meet a hostile reception among the tribes of the Djerid. But the important thing was to find out whether the tension had reached such a level that there was danger of an uprising in the near future among the inhabitants of the Rharsa and Melrir region.

"All I can tell you on that score," replied the commandant, "is that, apart from a few isolated attacks, the Tuareg and other nomads have not yet posed a serious threat to the canal. As far as we can tell, many of them believed that this construction was inspired by Cheytân, the Muslim devil, and said among themselves that a power higher than his would come and restore order. But then, how is it possible to know what goes on in the minds of such secretive people? Perhaps they're biding their time, waiting until construction work starts again and the workers hired by the new company have arrived, in order to make their attack more violent and their pillaging more profitable."

"What kind of violent attack?" asked Mr. de Schaller.

"They might band together, several thousand strong, and try to block the canal over part of its route, throw the sand from the banks back into the canal bed, and by brute strength prevent the gulf's water from passing through at one given point."

"They'd have more difficulty filling it in," replied Mr. de Schaller, "than our predecessors had digging it out. When all is said and done, they wouldn't have much success."

"Time is one thing they'd have plenty of," remarked the commandant. "Haven't we heard that it will take ten years to fill the chotts?"

"No, Commandant, no," declared the engineer. "I've already stated my opinion on this question—an estimate based on exact calculations, not on false data. With the help of a great deal of manual labor, and especially with the powerful machines we possess today, it won't take ten years—or even five—to flood the Rharsa and the Melrir. The water will widen and deepen the bed that has been opened for it. Who knows? Maybe even Tozeur, which is now several kilometers away from the chott, will some day be a seaport, connected with La Hammâ on the Rharsa. And that explains the need for certain defense constructions, which I've already had to give some thought to, as well as for plans for seaports to the north and to the south, which are among the important objectives of our journey."

Given Mr. de Schaller's methodical and serious mind, he was obviously not the type of man to base his calculations on mere hopes and dreams.

Captain Hardigan had a few questions about the Tuareg chieftain who had escaped from the fort at Gabès. Had he been seen in the vicinity of the oasis? Was there any news about the tribe to which he belonged? Did the people of the Djerid know that Hadjar had regained his freedom? Was there reason to suspect that he might try to incite some of the Arabs against the Sahara Sea project?

"I can't give you definite answers to those questions," replied the commandant. "There's no doubt that word of Hadjar's escape has reached the oasis. It created as much of a stir there as did the news of his capture, in which you yourself had a hand, Captain. But while I haven't had any reports of the chieftain being seen in the neighborhood of Tozeur, I have learned that a whole band of Tuareg were heading for the part of the canal joining Chott Rharsa and Chott Melrir."

"Do you have any reason to believe that the report is accurate?" asked Captain Hardigan.

"Yes, Captain, because I heard it from one of the men who stayed behind in the country where they had been working and who consider themselves watchmen or guards of the construction works. They probably hope in this way to curry favor with the new management."

"The construction works are basically finished," added Mr. de Schaller, "but they should be very carefully guarded. If the Tuareg attempt to carry out an attack on the canal, this is the point where they would most likely concentrate their efforts."

"Why is that?" asked the commandant.

"Because the flooding of the Rharsa worries them less than the flooding of the Melrir. There's no oasis of any great value in the first, but the situation is quite different in the second, where some very large oases would disappear beneath the waters of the new sea. It's precisely against the second canal, the one joining the two chotts, that we must expect such an assault. We must have a military force ready in anticipation of such potential attacks."

"In any case," remarked Lieutenant Villette, "our little detachment will have to keep a sharp lookout once we have crossed the Rharsa."

"And that's just what it will do," declared Captain Hardigan.

"We caught this Hadjar once, and we can certainly capture him again. And, this time, we will keep him under closer guard than we did at Gabès, until the War Council has rid the country of him once and for all."

"The sooner that happens the better," added the commandant. "This Hadjar has considerable influence over the nomadic tribes, and he might start an uprising of the whole Djerid. In any case, one of the advantages of the new sea will be to remove from the Melrir some of these criminals' hideouts."

But not all of them. In this vast chott, the leveling done by Captain Roudaire had left a number of zones that would not be submerged, such as the Hinguiz and its main village of Zenfig.

The distance from Tozeur to Nefta is about twenty-five kilometers, and the engineer planned to cover it in two days, camping the next night on the bank of the canal. This section, which did not follow the route Roudaire had marked out, transformed the region of Tozeur and Nefta into a sort of peninsula between the Djerid and the Rharsa, much to the satisfaction of the inhabitants. This part of the work was completely finished and here, too, everything was in good condition.

The little group left Tozeur on the morning of April 1 in unsettled weather that in lower latitudes would have brought heavy showers. In this part of Tunisia, however, there was no danger of rain, and the clouds, although very high, would certainly offer protection against the heat of the sun.

At first they followed the banks of the Wadi Berkouk, crossing several of its branches on bridges that had been constructed out of material taken from the debris of ancient buildings.

Endless grayish-yellow plains stretched westward, and one would have searched in vain for shelter from the sun's rays, whose heat was fortunately greatly reduced. The only vegetation to be seen during the two stages of that day's march was the slender, long-leaved grass known to the natives as *driss* and (fortunately for the Djerid caravans) much enjoyed by the camels.

They marched from dawn until dusk without incident, and the tranquillity of the camp was not disturbed until morning. A few bands of Arabs appeared far to the north of the canal, on their way back up to the Aurès Mountains. But they did not cause

Captain Hardigan any concern, and he made no effort to communicate with them.

On the following day, April 2, the march toward Nefta continued under the same conditions as the day before. The sky was overcast and the heat tolerable. As they neared the oasis, however, the countryside changed and the soil became much less sterile. The plain was green with countless stalks of esparto grass, with little streams winding through it. The artemesias reappeared too, and hedges of Barbary figs stood out on the plateaus, where fields of pale blue flowers and convulvulus delighted the eye. Then clumps of olive and fig trees appeared along the banks of the streams, and finally whole forests of gum acacias, massed together along the horizon.

Almost no game animals lived in this area except for antelopes, which ran off in herds so quickly that they were out of sight in a few moments. Even Giddup himself, no matter what his master believed, would not have been able to run them down. As for Ace-of-Hearts, he confined himself to barking furiously whenever a few Barbary apes, which were numerous in the chott region, began capering among the trees. They also noticed some buffaloes and Barbary sheep, but it would have been pointless to hunt them, since supplies were to be replenished in Nefta.

The most common predators in that part of the Djerid are lions, whose attack can be very dangerous. But after work had been started on the canal, they had been gradually pushed back toward the Algerian border and into the regions adjoining the Melrir.

Although there was no danger of an attack by wild beasts, both men and animals nonetheless had to take great care to protect themselves against scorpions and hissing snakes—known to naturalists as *naja*, or cobras—which are very common in the approaches to the Rharsa. They are so common, in fact, that certain regions are completely uninhabitable, such as the Djerid Teldja, which the Arabs had to abandon. When the expedition made camp that evening, near a thicket of tamarind trees, Mr. de Schaller and his companions could not rest until they had taken the most complete precautions. And while Sergeant Nicol slept with one eye open, Giddup slept with both eyes closed. But Ace-of-Hearts kept watch, and would have sounded the alert if he had seen any suspicious creeping about that might have constituted a threat to the horse or his master.

Nothing untoward happened during the night, and the tents were struck at daybreak. Captain Hardigan was still heading southwest, the direction the canal had been following since Tozeur. At Kilometer 207 it veered toward the north near Nefta, where they arrived that same afternoon and from which their route would take them due north.

The length of the canal might have been reduced by some fifteen kilometers if it had been possible to bring it to a point at the extreme eastern end of the Rharsa, in the direction of Tozeur, but this would have been very difficult to accomplish. In order to reach the chott from this direction, it would have been necessary to cut through some very hard terrain consisting mostly of rock. It would have been more time-consuming and more costly than in some parts of the Gabès ridge, and an altitude of thirty-five meters above sea level would have necessitated considerable work. That was why, after a thorough study of the region, the engineers of the France-Overseas Company had abandoned the original route and chosen a new one, starting at Kilometer 207, to the west of Nefta, where it turned north. This third and last section of the first canal had been completed over most of its length, taking advantage of many depressions. It connected with the Rharsa at the head of a sort of inlet located at one of the lowest points of the chott, almost halfway along its southern edge.

Neither Mr. de Schaller nor Captain Hardigan intended to spend two days in Nefta. They only needed to spend the latter part of the afternoon and the night there, to give the detachment time to rest and replenish its supplies. Besides, neither the men nor the horses had been exhausted by the journey from Gabès, one hundred and ninety kilometers as the crow flies, which they had covered between March 17 and April 3. They could easily make it the next day to Chott Rharsa, where the engineer was determined to arrive on the exact date he had set.

From the standpoint of terrain, soil composition, and vegetation, the oasis of Nefta was not appreciably different from the oasis of Tozeur. There were the same cluster of dwellings among

Nearing the oasis of Nefta

Bridge over the wadi at Nefta. (Photo by Soler, Tunis)

the trees, the same arrangement of the kasbah, and the same military occupation. But the oasis was less densely populated, with no more than eight thousand inhabitants at that time.

Captain Hardigan's little group was warmly welcomed by both the French community and the natives, who made every effort to provide the best possible lodgings for them. They had a personal interest in doing so, which is not surprising in view of the new route to be taken by the canal. Nefta's trade would benefit considerably from the canal's proximity to the oasis. All the business that would have been lost if the canal had gone directly from Tozeur to the chott would now be returned to it. It was almost as if Nefta were about to become a port town on the new sea. Hence the inhabitants were profuse in their congratulations to the engineer of the French Sahara Sea Company.

However, despite pressing invitations for the expedition to remain for a while, even if only for twenty-four hours, the departure was scheduled for the next morning at sunup. Captain Hardigan was still worried, given the news he had received about the unrest among the natives in the region of the Melrir, where the second canal ended. And he was impatient to finish that part of his journey of exploration.

Early the next morning, before the sun was over the horizon, the men were assembled, the horses and wagons were made ready, and the signal to move out was given. They covered the twelve kilometers between Nefta and the bend in the canal in the first march, and the distance from the bend to the Rharsa in the second.

There was no incident along the way, and about six o'clock Captain Hardigan halted the detachment at the point where the completed canal emptied into the chott.

～ Chott Rharsa

On the evening of April 4, camp was set up at the base of the steep dunes surrounding the head of the inlet. The location offered no shelter. The little detachment had passed the last trees in that desolate region three or four kilometers back, between Nefta and the chott. There was nothing now but the sandy desert, with barely a trace of vegetation, the Sahara in all its dryness.

The tents had been pitched. The wagons, refilled with supplies at Nefta, held several days' food for men and horses. While skirting the Rharsa, the engineer would stop at some of the many oases, where there was always an abundance of fresh fodder. In the chott itself no oases were to be found.

That was what Mr. de Schaller was explaining to Captain Hardigan and Lieutenant Villette as they sat together in their tent before sharing in the meal that Mr. François was about to serve. A map of the Rharsa was spread out on the table, so that they could study its outline. This chott, whose southern edge lies close to the thirty-fourth parallel, curves northward across the region bordering the Aurès Mountains, near the village of Chebika. Its greatest length, measured precisely along the thirty-fourth degree of latitude, is sixty kilometers, but its submersible area covers only one thousand three hundred square kilometers or, as the engineer put it, three or four thousand times the area of the Champ de Mars in Paris.

"Well," remarked Lieutenant Villette, "it may be huge for a Champ de Mars, but it doesn't seem like very much for a sea."

"Quite right, lieutenant," replied Mr. de Schaller, "but if you add to that the surface area of the Melrir with its six thousand square kilometers, that gives the Sahara Sea an area of seven hundred and thirty thousand hectares. Besides, it's quite possible that, in time, the Neptunian action of the sea[1] will ultimately connect it with Chott Djerid and Chott Fedjedj."

"So, my friend," said Captain Hardigan, "I see you're still counting on that eventuality. Is that what the future has in store for us?"

"Who can read the future?" countered Mr. de Schaller. "Our planet has certainly seen more extraordinary things than that, and I don't mind telling you that that idea does occupy my attention at times, although it's not an obsession with me. You've surely heard of the lost continent of Atlantis, which is covered today, not by a Sahara Sea, but by the Atlantic Ocean itself, and at definitely established latitudes.[2] There have been many cataclysms of that kind, although on a smaller scale, I grant you. Look at what occurred in the East Indies in the nineteenth century during the terrible eruption of Krakatoa.[3] What happened yesterday could happen again tomorrow, couldn't it?"

"The future is humanity's great surprise package," replied Lieutenant Villette with a laugh.

"Exactly, my dear lieutenant," declared the engineer, "and when the package is empty . . ."

"The world will come to an end," concluded Captain Hardigan.[4]

Placing his finger on the map at the point where the two hundred and twenty-seven kilometers of the first canal ended, he asked, "Shouldn't there be a port here?"

"Right there, on the shore of this inlet," replied Mr. de Schaller, "and everything indicates that it will be one of the busiest ports on the Sahara Sea. Studies are under way, and there's no doubt that houses and shops, warehouses and a bordj will all be built before the Rharsa becomes navigable. Moreover, at the extreme eastern end of the chott, the village of La Hammâ was already undergoing changes when the first route was marked out, in anticipation of the maritime and commercial importance it expected to enjoy. In spite of the change of route, that importance will likely be assured by its position as the advance port of Gafsa."

For this village at the tip of the Rharsa, which the engineer was pointing out on the map, the dream of becoming a commercial port in the very heart of the Djerid had formerly seemed impossible. Now, human genius would make it a reality. The village's only regret would be that the first canal had not led directly to its doorstep. But it is common knowledge why the engineers had had to bring the canal into the chott at the head of this inlet, now known as Roudaire Inlet. No doubt that name will eventually be given to the largest port on the Sahara Sea.

Captain Hardigan asked Mr. de Schaller whether he planned to lead the expedition across the entire length of the Rharsa.

"No," replied the engineer, "I only have to inspect the edges of the chott. I hope I may find some valuable construction materials there that we can put to use somewhere, since it's right on the site. Modern material is certainly superior, but it has to be brought here."

"But didn't caravans at one time cross the chott as a matter of choice?" asked Lieutenant Villette.

"And they still do, my dear lieutenant. It's a rather dangerous route over unstable ground, but it's shorter and less difficult than traveling along the dune-encumbered banks. However, we'll go by the latter route, heading west until we come to the point where the second canal begins. On the way back, after we've determined the extent of the Melrir, we can travel along the southern edge of the Rharsa and return to Gabès more quickly than we came."

This was the plan that had been adopted. By the time he had reconnoitered both canals, the engineer would have traveled all the way around the perimeter of the new sea.

The next day Mr. de Schaller and the two officers set out at the head of the detachment. Ace-of-Hearts was frisking along in front, disturbing flocks of starlings, which flew away with a mournful rustling of wings. Their route followed the inside base of the dunes surrounding the chott. Fears that the waters of the Sahara Sea might spread out and overflow the edges of the depression on this side were groundless. The southern part of the Djerid was completely safe, since the high banks, very similar to the strip of land forming the Gabès ridge, were of such a nature that they would not give way under the pressure of the water.

They had broken camp early in the morning and continued marching in the usual order. No change had been made in the distance to be covered daily. It would still average twelve to fifteen kilometers, in two stages.

Mr. de Schaller was especially eager to find out where the boundaries of the new sea would be, and whether there was any danger that it would overflow its banks and flood the neighboring regions. For this reason, the little groups followed the base of the sand dunes stretching westward in a line along the chott. There certainly seemed to be no need for any human modification of what nature had already done in that respect. Whether or not the Rharsa had ever been a lake previously, it was well situated for becoming one. The water from the Gulf of Gabès, which the first canal would feed into it, would be rigorously contained within the predicted boundaries.

As they were making their way along, they could look over the vast expanse of the depression. The surface of this arid basin of the Rharsa glittered under the sun's rays as if it were lined with a layer of silver, crystal, or camphor. The brilliance was stronger than the eyes could bear, and both officers and men had to protect themselves with smoked glasses to avoid the ophthalmia that occurs so frequently in the blazing light of the Sahara. Sergeant Nicol had even acquired a pair of large spectacles for his horse, but glasses were apparently not to Giddup's liking. Since they made his appearance a bit ridiculous, and since Ace-of-Hearts did not recognize his friend's face behind that optical apparatus, neither Giddup nor any of the other horses was provided with this protective device that was so essential to their masters.

The chott looked like one of those saline lakes that dry up in the summer because of the tropical heat. But when the water is soaked up by the sand, it releases gases and the ground becomes covered with blisters that make it look like a field full of mole tunnels. The bottom of the chott, as the engineer explained to the two officers, was made up of red quartz sand mixed with calcium sulphate and calcium carbonate. This layer was covered with deposits of sodium sulphate and sodium chloride, a crust of real salt. The pliocene terrain where the chotts and sebkha are found also contained an abundance of gypsum and salt.

It should be noted that at this time of year the Rharsa had not yet lost all the water that the wadis bring to it during the winter. The horses occasionally moved away from the *ghourd*, or the surrounding dunes, and stopped at the edge of the hollows filled with stagnant water.

In the distance, Captain Hardigan saw what he thought was a detachment of Arab horsemen moving back and forth across the far reaches of the chott. When his men approached them, the whole troop fled, but instead of galloping away, they took to their wings.

What they had seen was a flock of blue and pink flamingos, whose plumage resembled the colors of a uniform. No matter how quickly Ace-of-Hearts ran after them, he could not catch up with these magnificent wading birds. At the same time, what myriads of birds he disturbed all around him, and what cries filled the air as the boa-habibis, those deafening Djerid sparrows, took flight!

By following the perimeter of the Rharsa, however, the detachment would easily find campsites, which they would not have found in the center of the depression since this chott was almost completely floodable, whereas parts of the Melrir were above sea level and would still be above water after the Mediterranean flowed in. They went from oasis to oasis, each one more or less inhabited, but which together were destined to become the *marsâ*—the ports or inlets—of the new sea. In the Berber language they are called *toua*, and in these oases the soil reassumes its full fertility. Palms and other trees reappeared in great numbers, and pastures were plentiful, so that Giddup and his friends had no reason to complain of a shortage of fodder. But once past these oases, the ground immediately returned to its natural aridity. The grassy *mourdj* suddenly gave way to the *reg*, or flat ground consisting of sand and gravel.

No great difficulty was encountered in reconnoitering this southern edge of the Rharsa. It is true that the heat at the base of the dunes was a severe ordeal for both men and horses when there were no clouds to shield them from the burning sun. But after all, Algerian officers and spahis are already accustomed to these scorching climates, and Mr. de Schaller was also an African, tanned by the sun and by previous expeditions. That

A kafila *in the Djerid. (Photo by M. Brichard)*

was exactly what had qualified him to take charge of the final
work on the Sahara Sea.

The only possible danger might come from crossing the *hofra*,
the deepest depressions, where the ground shifts and provides no
solid support. But on the route the expedition was following
there was little likelihood of their sinking into the ground.

"These dangers are very real," the engineer repeated, "as was
demonstrated on many occasions while the canal was being dug
across the salt marshes of Tunis."

"Yes," added Captain Hardigan, "that was one of the problems
Captain Roudaire foresaw when surveying the Rharsa and the
Melrir. Didn't he tell of sinking down to his knees sometimes in
the salty sand?"

"And he wasn't exaggerating," declared Mr. de Schaller.
"These hollows are covered with holes that the Arabs call 'eyes of
the sea.' No probe has ever found the bottom of them, and there's
still some danger of accidents. While Captain Roudaire was on a
reconnaissance mission, a horse and its rider were swallowed up

in one of these crevasses. Even by tying twenty ramrods together, his comrades couldn't pull him out."

"Well, let's take every possible precaution," recommended Captain Hardigan. "We can't be too careful. My men are under orders not to stray away from the dunes unless we have carefully examined the condition of the ground. I'm always afraid that little devil Ace-of-Hearts, who keeps running across the sebkha where he shouldn't go, may suddenly disappear. Nicol can't keep him in check."

"He'd be heartbroken," said Lieutenant Villette, "if such a misfortune happened to his dog."

"And I'm sure," added the captain, "that Giddup would die of sorrow."

"There certainly is a unique friendship between those two fine animals," remarked the engineer.

"Unique indeed," said the lieutenant. "Orestes and Pylade, Nisus and Euryale, Damon and Pythias, Achilles and Patroclus, Alexander and Ephestion, Hercules and Pirithous, were of the same race, at least, but a horse and a dog . . ."

"You might add, 'and a man,' Lieutenant," concluded Captain Hardigan, "because Nicol, Giddup, and Ace-of-Hearts are an inseparable trio of friends, one man and two animals."

What the engineer had said about the dangers of the shifting ground in the chotts was not an exaggeration. And yet the region of the Rharsa, the Melrir, and the Fedjedj was the preferred route of the caravans. It shortened their journey, and the travelers found it easier going on flat terrain. But they never set out without the help of guides who were thoroughly familiar with the lake regions of the Djerid and able to avoid the dangerous quagmires.

Since leaving Gabès, the detachment had still not met any of the caravans that carry merchandise, in the form of farm produce and manufactured goods, from Biskra to the shore of the Gulf of Gabès, and whose arrival is always impatiently awaited at Nefta, Gafsa, Tozeur, La Hammâ, and all the towns and villages of lower Tunisia. But on the afternoon of April 9 they did make contact with a caravan, under the following circumstances.

It was about three o'clock. After their first march of the day,

Captain Hardigan and his men had resumed their journey under a burning sun. They were heading for the farthest curve in the perimeter of the Rharsa, a few kilometers away at its western extremity. The land rose perceptibly here, and the outline of the dunes stood out more sharply. New water would never be able to make its way into the chott from this direction.

As the road took them higher, they could see over a wider sector to the north and west. The depression sparkled under the rays of the sun. Every little stone on this salty ground became a luminous speck. To the left, the second canal, which would link the Rharsa and the Melrir, was taking shape.

The engineer and the two officers had dismounted. Their escorts followed them, leading the horses by the bridle.

At one point, when they had all stopped on the plateau of the dune, Lieutenant Villette motioned with his hand.

"I think I see a group of people moving at the far end of the chott."

"A group of people," wondered Captain Hardigan, "or a flock of sheep?"

"At this distance," added Mr. de Schaller, "it's hard to tell for sure."

There was no doubt, however, that three or four kilometers away in that direction, a dense cloud of dust was rolling along the surface of the Rharsa. Perhaps it was only a herd of ruminants heading north in the Djerid.

But the dog was showing very definite signs, if not of concern, at least of attention, and the sergeant shouted to him, "Come on, Ace-of-Hearts, use your nose and ears. What's down there?"

The animal barked loudly and stood with his legs rigid and his tail wagging, as if he were about to go racing across the chott.

"Down, boy, down," said Nicol, holding him back.

The movement going on inside the dust storm grew stronger as the swirling dust came closer. But it was difficult to determine what was causing it. No matter how good their eyesight was, neither Mr. de Schaller, nor the officers, nor any member of the detachment could have said for sure whether the disturbance was coming from a moving caravan or from a flock of sheep running across that part of the chott to escape some danger.

Two or three minutes later, all uncertainty disappeared when flashes of light shot out through the cloud, followed by detonations and smoke that mingled with the dust storm. At the same moment, Ace-of-Hearts broke away from his master and barked furiously.

"Gunshots!" exclaimed Lieutenant Villette.

"It's probably a caravan defending itself against an attack by wild beasts," said the engineer.

"Against bandits, more likely," said the lieutenant, "because the shots seemed to answer each other."

"Mount up!" ordered Captain Hardigan.

In an instant the spahis were rounding the edge of the Rharsa, heading for the scene of the fight.

It may have been rash, or at least unwise, to commit the escort's few men to this affair without knowing what had caused it. Probably a band of brigands from the Djerid, and perhaps a large number of them. But Captain Hardigan and his men did not stop to consider the danger. If, as seemed likely, a caravan was under attack by some Tuareg or other local nomads, a soldier's honor demanded that he rush to its assistance. Urging on their horses, they turned away from the edge of the dunes and raced across the chott, led by the dog, which Nicol no longer attempted to call back.

The distance seemed to be no more than three kilometers, and in ten minutes they had covered two-thirds of it. Shots continued to ring out right and left, amid clouds of smoke and dust. But a southeasterly breeze was springing up and beginning to disperse the dust.

Captain Hardigan could finally make out the nature of this violent encounter that was still continuing.

It was indeed, they soon learned, a caravan whose progress had been interrupted in this part of the chott. Five days earlier, it had left the oasis of Zéribet, north of the Melrir, heading toward Tozeur, from which it would go on to Gabès. Its personnel consisted of some twenty Arabs, driving about a hundred camels of all sizes.

They had been moving briskly along, with the animals in the lead carrying their sacks of dates, and the camel drivers walking behind and repeating the cry that one of them shouted out in his hoarse voice to urge the animals forward.

The caravan had found good traveling conditions until then. It had just reached the western end of the Rharsa and was getting ready to move across it to the other end, under the direction of an experienced guide. But as soon as they were well on their way up the first slopes of the rocky desert terrain, misfortune struck. A group of about sixty horsemen suddenly appeared from behind the dunes.

It was a band of brigands, who could easily overcome the personnel of the kafila. They would put the camel drivers to flight, or massacre them if necessary, seize the camels and their loads, and drive them off to some distant oasis in the Djerid. This attack, like so many others, would likely go unpunished, given the impossibility of discovering who was responsible for it.

The people in the caravan put up a futile resistance, firing their guns and pistols, but they were outnumbered by the attackers, who returned fire. After a ten-minute battle the kafila scattered and the terror-stricken animals fled in all directions.

It was just before this that Captain Hardigan had heard the gunshots. The brigands, spotting this little group and seeing these horsemen coming to the caravan's rescue, stopped in their tracks. And at this moment Captain Hardigan shouted, "Charge!"

Their rifles were in good working order. They passed from the spahis' backs to their hands, and then to their shoulders. The whole detachment swooped down like a whirlwind on the bandits, leaving the convoy behind to be guarded by the drivers. The soldiers would return to it after the caravan was rescued.

The brigands did not wait for the attack to come. Perhaps they did not feel strong enough, or brave enough, to stand up to this platoon in their familiar uniforms, advancing so boldly to meet them. Were they motivated by anything other than fear? The fact remains that before Captain Hardigan and his men had come within range, they had fled off to the northwest.

The order to fire was given nevertheless, and several volleys of shots rang out. Some of the fleeing men were hit, but not seriously enough to stop them.

The sergeant proudly insisted that Ace-of-Hearts had re-

The caravan attacked by the Tuareg

Tuareg. (Photo by Lt. Rouss)

ceived his baptism of fire. He had seen the dog shake his head from side to side, and concluded that a bullet had whistled past his ears.

Captain Hardigan did not consider it advisable to pursue the attackers, who were retreating as fast as their horses could take them and soon disappeared behind the screen of a *tell*, or tree-covered knoll, which stood out on the horizon. In this country that they knew so well, they would easily have found some hiding place where it would have been difficult to get at them. They would undoubtedly not come back, and the caravan would have nothing more to fear from them as it made its way eastward through the Rharsa.

But help had arrived just in time. A few minutes later, and the camels would have fallen into the hands of these desert pirates.

The engineer questioned the leader of the kafila to find out what had happened, and under what circumstances he and his camel drivers had been attacked.

"Do you know what tribe this band belongs to?" asked Captain Hardigan.

"Our guide assures me that they are Tuareg," replied the caravan leader.

"The Tuareg were supposed to have gradually abandoned the western oases and moved to the eastern part of the Djerid," said the engineer.

"Oh, as long as there are caravans traveling through it, there will be bandits to attack them," remarked Lieutenant Villette.

"There will be no more danger of that after the chotts are flooded," declared Mr. de Schaller.

Captain Hardigan asked the caravan leader whether anyone in those parts had heard the news of Hadjar's escape.

"Yes, Captain. That rumor has been going around for several days now."

"There are no reports of his having been seen in the neighborhood of the Rharsa or the Melrir?"

"No, Captain."

"And he was not the one in command of this band of robbers?"

"Definitely not," replied the guide. "I know him, and I would have recognized him. It's quite possible that he has led these brigands in the past, and if you hadn't come along, Captain, we would have been robbed and perhaps massacred to the last man."

"But is it safe for you to go on your way now?" asked the engineer.

"I think so. Those scoundrels have probably gone to some village west of here, and in three or four days we'll be in Tozeur."

The leader now gathered all his people together. The camels that had scattered were already coming back to their places, and the caravan regrouped. It had not lost a single man. A few had been wounded, but not seriously, and they were able to continue the journey. After thanking Captain Hardigan and his friends once more, the leader gave the signal to move out, and the whole kafila went on its way again.

In a few minutes, both men and beasts had disappeared around a *tarf*, a sandy point stretching out into the chott, and the shouts of the leader as he urged on his camel drivers gradually faded away in the distance.

When the engineer and the two officers rejoined each other

after this scuffle (which might have had serious consequences), they exchanged their impressions and concerns about the incident. Mr. de Schaller was the first to speak.

"So now Hadjar has turned up again in these parts."

"We might have expected that," replied the captain. "Let's hope the chotts will be flooded as soon as possible. That's the only way we'll be finished with these lawbreakers in the Djerid."

"Unfortunately," remarked Lieutenant Villette, "it will be a few years before the Rharsa and the Melrir are filled with water from the gulf."

"Who knows?" mused Mr. de Schaller.[5]

The Tuareg did not appear again in the vicinity, and the encampment was not disturbed during the night.

The following afternoon, April 10, the detachment halted at the starting point of the second canal, which connected the two chotts.

ix ≈ The Second Canal

The second canal, connecting the Rharsa and the Melrir to Chott Djerid, was only about a third as long as the first. But whereas the terrain between Gabès and the Rharsa varied in elevation from fifteen to forty-six meters, there was no point in the Asloudje ridge, located between these last two chotts, that rose above ten meters.

It is important to note that, in addition to the Rharsa and the Melrir, other depressions several kilometers long had been incorporated into the canal. The largest of them was Chott El Asloudje.

The excavation of the second canal, therefore, had taken less time and involved fewer difficulties than the first, so it had not been undertaken until later. The final stages of the work could now be resumed, using the province of Constantine[1] as a base of operations and a source for supplies. It had been arranged before leaving Gabès that, when Mr. de Schaller reached the Melrir at the end of the second canal, he would find a construction site there, supervised by a highly competent representative of the Ministry of Public Works and staffed by men who would come by train to Biskra and by caravan through the Farfaria. They would get in touch with him as soon as they reached their destination.

Once the work had been evaluated, Mr. de Schaller would only have to follow the edge of the chott back to his point of departure, and his inspection would be finished.

When the detachment reached the end of the Rharsa, the engineer was greatly surprised to find that none of the Arabs and other workers whom the company had sent from Biskra were there.

What could have happened? It was naturally somewhat disturbing, especially after the attack on the caravan and the reappearance of Hadjar.

Had there been some change in the plans about which the engineer had not been informed? Had there been some last-minute change in supervisor?

As Mr. de Schaller was pondering the matter, Captain Hardigan asked him, "Wasn't the work on this section completed?"

"Yes, it was," came the reply, "and according to reports, the ridges between the floodable areas had been dug through, with the required slope, as far as the Melrir, which is entirely below sea level."

"Why does it surprise you that the workers are not here?"

"Because the man in charge of the work was supposed to send some of his men a few days ago, to meet me here. When I think about it, I see no reason why they should have been delayed at Biskra or at the Melrir."

"How do you explain the fact that they aren't here, then?"

"I can't explain it," the engineer admitted, "unless some unforeseen incident has detained them at the main construction site, at the other end of the canal."

"Well, we'll soon get to the bottom of this," said Captain Hardigan.

"Still, as you see, I'm annoyed and very concerned not to find the men here that I needed. Without them, my plans are frustrated."

"While the men are setting up camp," suggested the captain, "shall we go on a bit farther?"

"Yes, by all means," replied Mr. de Schaller.

The sergeant was summoned and ordered to set up camp for the night near a clump of palm trees beside the canal. Green grass was growing in the shade of the trees, and a little stream flowed nearby. There was ample water and pasture, and they could easily replenish their provisions in an oasis at the edge of the Asloudje.

Nicol immediately carried out his captain's orders, and the spahis took all the usual precautions when making camp under such conditions.

Taking advantage of the last hour of daylight, Mr. de Schaller and the two officers followed the north bank, intending to ride along it for a distance of about a kilometer.

This excursion gave the engineer an opportunity to confirm that the excavation had been completely finished at that point, and that the condition of the work was as good as he had expected. The bottom of the trenches between the chotts offered an easy passage for the water that the Rharsa would discharge into them when it arrived from the gulf, and the slope conformed to the engineers' plans.

Mr. de Schaller and his friends did not pursue their inspection any farther than one kilometer from the campsite. As far as the eye could see in the direction of Chott El Asloudje, that section of the canal was deserted. Since they wanted to get back before nightfall, the engineer, Captain Hardigan, and Lieutenant Villette then turned back toward camp.

A tent had been set up, where Mr. François served them with his usual correctness. Guards were posted for the night, and there was nothing left to do but to sleep in order to renew their strength for the next day's journey.

Although Mr. de Schaller and the two officers had not noticed anyone during their inspection of it, this part of the second canal was not as deserted as it appeared to be. True, the work party was definitely not there, and the engineer had found no trace of any recent work. But he and the officers had been observed by two men crouching behind thick clumps of driss, or tall grass, in a gap between the dunes.

If Ace-of-Hearts had been there, he would certainly have spotted the two men, even though they had taken great care not to show themselves. From less than fifty paces away, they watched the three foreigners pass by along the bank, and then they watched them return. Not until the first shadows of dusk fell did they venture near the encampment.

Ace-of-Hearts began to stir as they approached, and uttered a deep growl, but the sergeant, after glancing around outside, calmed him down, and the dog lay down again near his master.

The Arabs had stopped first at the edge of the little thicket. By eight o'clock it was already dark, for twilight is short in these latitudes. No doubt they both intended to get a closer look at this

Harrig and Sohar, hidden in the driss

detachment that had halted at the entrance to the second canal. What was it doing there, and who was in command?

They knew that these horsemen belonged to a regiment of spahis, since they had seen the two officers out riding with the engineer. But how many men were in the detachment, and what material were they bringing to the Melrir?

The two men entered the thicket and crawled between the plants from one tree to the next. Through the darkness they could see the tents standing at the entrance to the grove and the horses lying on the grass.

At this point the growling of the dog put them on their guard, and they returned to the dunes without anyone in the encampment having been aware of their presence.

Once they were no longer afraid of being heard, the following conversation ensued:

"So, is it really him, is it Captain Hardigan?"

"Yes, the same one who took Hadjar prisoner."

"And his junior officer?"

"That's his lieutenant. I recognized them."

"Just as they would have recognized you, no doubt."

"But you—they've never seen you, have they?"

"Never."

"Good! Perhaps it will be possible. There's an opportunity here that we have to take advantage of. We won't have another chance."

"And if this captain and his lieutenant fall into Hadjar's hands . . ."

"They won't escape, as Hadjar did from the bordj."

"There were only three of them when we saw them," continued one of the natives.

"Yes, but the ones who are camped there aren't very many," replied the other.

"Who was the third? He's not an officer."

"No. He's some engineer from that damned company of theirs. He must have come with his escort to make another inspection of the work done on the canal before it fills up with water. They're heading for the Melrir, and when they get there, when they see . . ."

"When they see that they can't flood it now," gloated the more violent of the two men, "and that they'll never be able to create their Sahara Sea, they'll stop. They won't go any farther. And then, a few hundred faithful Tuareg . . ."

"But how can we inform our comrades, so they'll get here in time?"

"The Zenfig oasis is only about twenty leagues away. If the detachment stops at the Melrir, and if we can hold it there for a few days . . ."

"Maybe we can, especially now that they'll have no reason to go any farther."

"And if they wait there for the water from the Gulf to flow into the chott, they can dig their graves in that place, because they'll all be dead before it gets there! Come on, Harrig, come on!"

"I'm with you, Sohar."

These men were the two Tuareg who had helped Hadjar to escape: Harrig, who had planned the escape with the bazaar merchant from Gabès, and Sohar, the Tuareg chieftain's own brother. They now left the scene, and soon disappeared in the direction of the Melrir.

The next morning, an hour after sunrise, Captain Hardigan gave the signal to move out. The horses were saddled and harnessed, the men mounted up, and the little group proceeded in their usual order along the north bank of the canal.

Mr. François, freshly shaven, was in his accustomed place at the front of the convoy, near Corporal Pistache, and the two men chatted as they rode along.

"Well, how are things going, Mr. François?" asked Pistache in his normal good-natured tone of voice.

"Very well," replied Mr. de Schaller's trusty servant.

"This expedition isn't too much trouble or too tiring for you, then?"

"Not at all, Corporal. It's just a little outing through a curious country."

"This chott will look very different after it's been flooded."

"Very different indeed," replied Mr. François in his measured and pedantic voice.

A meticulous and methodical man, he was not one to slur his

words together. He savored them and rolled them around in his mouth as a gourmet does with a fine candy.

"Just think," continued Pistache, "right here, where our horses are walking now, fish will be swimming and boats will be sailing."

"Yes, Corporal, fish of every kind, and porpoises, and dolphins, and sharks."

"And whales," added Pistache.

"No, I don't think so, Corporal. There would certainly not be enough water for them."

"Oh, Mr. François, from what our sergeant says, it will be twenty meters deep in the Rharsa and twenty-five in the Melrir."

"Not everywhere, Corporal, and those underwater giants need plenty of water to frolic about in and blow when they feel like it."

"Do they blow very hard, Mr. François?"

"Hard enough to fill the bellows of a blast furnace, or the organs of all the cathedrals in France."

It must be admitted that Mr. François felt quite pleased with his irrefutable answer, which took Pistache somewhat by surprise.

Sweeping his hand around the perimeter of the new sea, he continued, "I can already see this inland sea with steamers and sailing ships, large and small, plowing its surface, going from port to port, and plying their trade. And do you know what my fondest wish would be, Corporal?"

"Tell me, Mr. François."

"I would like to be on board the first ship to sail across the waters of these former Algerian chotts. And I feel quite sure that our friend the engineer will have booked passage on the same ship, and that he and I will sail together around this new sea that we created with our own hands."

Mr. François almost believed that, in some small way, he was collaborating with his employer in the creation of the future Sahara Sea.

All in all, since the expedition had begun so well, there was every reason to hope that it would finish well also. And it was with that wish that Corporal Pistache brought this interesting conversation to an end.

By maintaining their usual pace—two marches a day of seven or eight kilometers each—Mr. de Schaller expected to reach the end of the second canal without delay. As soon as the detachment reached the edge of the Melrir, a decision would be made whether to go around it to the north or to the south. It made little difference, moreover, since the engineer's plan was to reconnoiter the entire perimeter.

The first part of the canal could be inspected during the first march. This section began at the Rharsa and ended at the small depression of El Asloudje, lying between dunes that rose to a height of seven to ten meters.

Before reaching the Melrir, however, they would have to cross or follow along a number of small chotts spreading out in all directions, forming an almost continuous line of shallower depressions, with low banks, which would inevitably be submerged with the arrival of the water from the Mediterranean. It would be necessary to set out beacons along them to mark the channel through the chotts to be followed by the boats of all kinds that would soon make their appearance on this new sea created by man's science and determination. This was done during the excavation of the Suez Canal, to indicate the channel across the Bitter Lakes, where it would have been impossible to navigate without these precise markers.

There again, everything was well under way. Powerful machines had dug deep trenches as far as the Melrir. There was no limit to what might be endeavored, if the need arose, through the use of these machines—gigantic dredges, drills that could penetrate anything, earth-conveyors traveling along improvised railway tracks—all this formidable equipment of which Captain Roudaire and his successors could not have dreamed. Inventors and builders had designed and constructed them during the many intervening years from the beginning of the Roudaire project, through the more advanced work of the France-Overseas Company (later abandoned), to the present resumption of the project by the French Sahara Sea Company, under the direction of Mr. de Schaller.

All the work that had previously been done was still in fairly good condition, just as the engineer had foreseen in the predic-

The deserted construction site

tions he had so eloquently enunciated during his talk at Gabès. He had spoken then of the essentially preservative nature of the African climate, which seemed to respect even recently excavated ruins that had been buried in the sand. But surrounding all this nearly finished work on the canal, there was now complete solitude. Where only a little while ago a swarm of workmen had been moving about, nothing was left but the gloomy silence of a deserted area, with not a human being to be found. Only the abandoned construction sites remained, mute testimony to the human toil, perseverance, and energy that had once temporarily given these empty regions the appearance of life.

And so it was in solitude that Mr. de Schaller carried out his inspection of these sites, before taking up the construction of new ones that he had every reason to believe would be permanent. But this solitude was disturbing to him, and the engineer felt genuinely disappointed at not seeing any of the men from the Biskra work party coming forward to meet him, as had been arranged.

It was a serious letdown, but as he thought about it, Mr. de Schaller said to himself that going from Biskra to the Rharsa is not the same thing as going from Paris to Saint-Cloud and that, in the course of such a long journey, some accident might have occurred to upset plans and change schedules. But no, that was impossible, because the agent had cabled him at Gabès from Biskra, to say that up to that point everything had gone smoothly and in accordance with the instructions he had been given in Paris. Something unexpected must have happened during the journey, perhaps between Biskra and the Melrir, in the unfamiliar region of Farfaria, which is swampy and often flooded, to delay the people he had expected to find there. Once one begins making suppositions, it is not easy to stop. They follow one another in an obsessive stream, and at that moment they were racking Mr. de Schaller's imagination without giving him the slightest plausible explanation. Little by little, his surprise and disappointment became serious uneasiness, and his face still wore a morose expression when they reached the end of the march. Captain Hardigan thought it wise to scout out the road ahead.

He gave orders for the sergeant and several cavalrymen to take up positions at a distance of one or two kilometers on either side of the canal, while the rest of the detachment went on its way.

The region was deserted or, to be more accurate, appeared to have been recently deserted. Following the second march, the detachment halted for the night, at the end of the little chott. The place was absolutely barren, with no oasis in the vicinity. Until now, they had never made camp under such inadequate conditions. No trees, no pasture, nothing but this reg of mixed sand and gravel, without a single blade of grass growing on it. However, the convoy had brought enough fodder to provide food for the horses, and the little group would easily find fresh provisions as it went from oasis to oasis along the edge of the Melrir.

Fortunately, in the absence of wadis, there were a number of *ras*, or springs, at which both men and beasts could quench their thirst. It seemed as if they would drink them dry, so all-consuming had been the heat of that day.

The night was calm and clear, with a full moon and a star-filled sky. As usual, a watch had been set at the approaches to the camp. In this open country, Sohar and Harrig would not have been able to prowl around the encampment without being spotted. They did not show themselves. It was part of their plan, no doubt, to let the engineer, Captain Hardigan, and his spahis advance farther into the region of the Algerian chotts.

Early the next morning they broke camp. Mr. de Schaller was in a great hurry to reach the end of the canal, where the trench was being opened that would let the water from the Gulf of Gabès flow into Chott Melrir.

But there was still no trace of the work party that had left Biskra, and its whereabouts was still a mystery. What had happened to it? Mr. de Schaller was lost in speculation. He had reached the precise point that had been agreed upon and had found none of the people he was expecting. Their absence struck him as ominous.

"Obviously, something serious has happened," he kept repeating.

"I'm afraid so," admitted Captain Hardigan. "Let's try to get to the Melrir before nightfall."

The noon-hour halt was a short one. The wagons were not unhitched and the horses were not unsaddled; they stopped only long enough to take some nourishment. There would be plenty of time to rest after the second march.

The detachment met no one during its second march and made such good time that by four o'clock in the afternoon they caught sight of the heights of land surrounding the chott. To the right, at Kilometer 347, was the company's last construction site where the work had come to an end. Beyond this point they had only to cross Chott Melrir and Chott Sellem, which leads into it, to reach the high ground.

Lieutenant Villette observed that there was not a wisp of smoke rising above the horizon, and not a sound to be heard.

The horses were urged on, and since the dog took the lead, Nicol could not prevent his horse from dashing after Ace-of-Hearts.

They proceeded at full gallop to the end of the canal, where the spahis halted in a cloud of dust. As at the Rharsa, there was no trace of the party that was to have come from Biskra. To the utter surprise and stupefaction of the engineer and his friends, they found the construction site a shambles! And the trench had been partly filled in, blocked by a barrier of sand that made it impossible for the water to pour into the depths of the Melrir without a complete reexcavation of this part of the canal!

x ⟅⟅⟅ Kilometer 347

The name Roudaire-Ville had been considered for the location where the second canal ended at the Chott Melrir. However, since the real terminus of the canal was the western side of Melrir, it had been suggested that this name be replaced by that of the president of the France-Overseas Company, and the name of Roudaire be reserved for the port that would be built in the vicinity of Mraïer or Sétil, in connection with the Trans-Sahara Railway or a branch line. In the end, since his name had already been given to a cove in the Rharsa, the place continued to be called Kilometer 347.[1]

Of that part of the last section of the canal, not a trace remained. It was filled with sand from one side to the other over a distance of more than a hundred meters. Granted, the excavation had not been completely finished. But at that time, as Mr. de Schaller was well aware, the end of the canal should have been blocked by only a narrow barrier, which could be cleared out in a few days. Obviously, some bands of fanatical nomads had passed that way and had ravaged and destroyed, perhaps in a single day, what time had so carefully preserved.

Standing motionless and silent on a narrow plateau overlooking the canal at the point where it joined the chott, with the two officers beside him and the rest of the detachment at the base of the dune, the engineer sadly contemplated the disaster, unable to believe his eyes.

"There are plenty of nomads in the country who could have done this," said Captain Hardigan. "It might have been tribes stirred up by their leaders, or the Tuareg, or others from the oases in the Melrir. These caravan raiders, who are furiously opposed to the Sahara Sea, undoubtedly made a mass attack on this construction site at Kilometer 347. The whole region would have needed to be guarded by the Maghzen day and night to stop these nomad attacks."

The Maghzen to whom Captain Hardigan referred are an auxiliary body attached to the regular African army. They are troops (both spahis and foot soldiers) responsible for internal policing and limited military actions. They are picked from intelligent and trustworthy men who, for some reason or other, choose not to remain with their tribes. They can be recognized by their blue burnouse. The sheiks wear a brown burnouse, while the red burnouse is part of the spahis' uniform and also the mark of investiture of the great chieftains. There are squads of Maghzen in the larger communities of the Djerid, but an entire regiment would have had to be organized to travel from place to place while the work was in progress, to prevent any uprising by the natives, whose hostile attitude was well known. Once the new sea was navigable and ships were sailing over the flooded chotts, there would be less danger of such assaults. Until then, it was important for the region to be kept under close surveillance. Attacks similar to the one just made on the canal terminus might occur elsewhere if the military authorities did not maintain order.

The engineer and the two officers were discussing the situation at that very moment. What should they do? First of all, they had to start looking for the work party that had come from the north. But how? In what direction should they look? That was of the utmost importance. The first step, said Mr. de Schaller, was to find them without delay, if possible, since under the circumstances their failure to be at the meeting point was becoming more and more worrying. Afterward, they would see. If the workers and foremen were brought back, the damage could be repaired in good time, or so he believed, at least.

"Provided they are protected," said Captain Hardigan, "but watching over them (assuming that we find them) and rescuing them from large bands of marauders is more than I can manage with my handful of spahis."

"In that case, sir," said Lieutenant Villette, "we absolutely must have reinforcements, and we must go and get them from the closest possible place."

"The closest place would be Biskra," said Captain Hardigan.

The town of Biskra is located in the northwestern part of the Melrir, at the entrance to the great desert and the plain of Ziban. It has been part of the province of Constantine since 1845, when the Algerians occupied it. With a population of several thousand and a military post, it has been for a long time the most remote French possession in the Sahara. Its garrison could provide, temporarily at least, a contingent of men who, together with Captain Hardigan's few spahis, would be in a position to give adequate protection to the workers, if they could be brought back to the construction site.

In a few days, if they hurried, they would be in Biskra, which was much closer than Tozeur and the same distance away as Nefta, neither of which could have provided the same reinforcements. Besides, by heading toward Biskra, it was possible they might meet Pointar.

"Well," remarked the engineer, "what would be the point of defending the work that's been finished if we don't have enough hands to restore it? The important thing is to find out under what circumstances the workers were driven out and where they took refuge when they fled from Goléah."

"Of course," added Lieutenant Villette, "but there's no one here who can give us that information. Perhaps, if we scoured the countryside, we'd find a few natives who could tell us what happened—if they wanted to."

"In any case," continued Captain Hardigan, "it's now out of the question to continue our exploration of the Melrir. We have to decide whether to go on to Biskra or back to Gabès."

Mr. de Schaller was in a quandary. A situation had arisen that could not have been foreseen. The urgent need now was to repair the canal as soon as possible and take steps to protect it from any future attack. But how could he think about doing that before setting out to look for the work party, whose absence at the second canal had caused him such grave concern?

What had prompted the natives to disrupt the construction work had no doubt been their concern over the imminent flooding of the Algerian chotts. And who could say whether there might not be a general uprising of all the tribes in the Djerid, and whether security could ever be established over this four-hundred-kilometer stretch between the end of the Melrir and the Gabès ridge?

"Whatever we decide to do," said Captain Hardigan, "let's make camp here for the night and start out again tomorrow."

That was the wisest course of action. After such a tiring march under a blazing sky, an overnight halt was called for. Orders were given to pitch the tents, position the convoy, turn the horses out to pasture at the oasis, and post watch as usual. The detachment did not appear to be in any danger. The attack on the construction site must have taken place several days earlier. The Goléah oasis and its surroundings seemed completely deserted.

While the engineer and the two officers were engaged in this conversation, the sergeant and two spahis headed toward the interior of the oasis, accompanied by Ace-of-Hearts. The dog kept poking his nose into the grass as he went along, but did not seem to notice anything unusual. Suddenly he stopped and raised his head, like a pointer.

Had Ace-of-Hearts scented some game animal running through the woods? Or some predator—a lion or a panther—ready to pounce?

The sergeant understood what the intelligent animal meant by the way he barked.

"There are some prowlers over there," he said. "Now, if we could just nab one of them . . ."

Ace-of-Hearts was ready to rush ahead, but his master held him back. If there was a native coming from that direction, they did not want to frighten him away. But he must surely have heard the dog barking . . . perhaps he was not trying to hide.

Nicol was not left long in doubt. An Arab was coming through the trees, looking this way and that, not at all concerned about being seen. As soon as he saw the three men, he walked calmly up to them.

He was about thirty or thirty-five years old, dressed like the workers of southern Algeria who are hired wherever there happens to be work, or at harvest time. Nicol said to himself that this meeting might prove useful to his captain. He had already made up his mind to take the Arab to him, willingly or not, when the man walked up to him and asked, "Are there any Frenchmen here?"

"Yes," replied the sergeant, "a detachment of spahis."

The Arab said simply, "Take me to the commanding officer."

With Ace-of-Hearts running ahead and growling in a low voice, and the two spahis walking behind, Nicol retraced his steps to the edge of the oasis. The Arab showed no inclination to run away.

As he came through the last row of trees, Lieutenant Villette spotted him and shouted, "At last, here's someone!"

"Well," said the captain, "Nicol has struck it lucky. He's met someone."

"So he has," added Mr. de Schaller. "Perhaps this man can tell us . . ."

A moment later, the Arab was with the engineer, and the spahis were clustered around their officers.

Nicol reported how he had come to meet the man. The Arab had been wandering through the woods and had approached the sergeant and his comrades as soon as he saw them. Nicol considered it his duty, however, to add that he thought there was something suspicious about the newcomer, which he ought to bring to his superiors' attention. The captain began at once to interrogate the unbidden visitor.

"Who are you?" he asked in French.

The Arab replied fairly accurately, in the same language, "I'm from Tozeur."

"Your name?"

"Mézaki."

"Where were you coming from?"

"From over there, from El Zéribet."

It was the name of an Algerian oasis located some forty-five kilometers from the chott, on a wadi of the same name.

"And for what purpose were you coming here?"

"To see what was going on."

"Why?" interrupted Mr. de Schaller. "Did you once work for the company?"

"Yes, a long time ago. For many years I was a guard at the

Mézaki questioned by Captain Hardigan

construction site here. So Mr. Pointar took me on as soon as he arrived."

Yes, that was the name of the official from the Ministry of Public Works assigned to the company, the one who had been expected to bring the team of workmen from Biskra and whose absence was causing the engineer so much concern. Finally, he was going to have some news of them!

"And I know you well, Mr. Engineer," added the Arab, "because I've seen you more than once, when you used to come to this part of the country."

There was no reason to doubt what Mézaki said. He was one of the many Arabs whom the company had previously employed to dig the canal between the Rharsa and the Melrir and whom agents of the new Sahara Sea Company were now making every effort to recruit. He was a strong man, with the calm expression on his face that is typical of his people, but with a keen and fiery look in his dark eyes.

"Well, where are your friends who were supposed to arrive at the construction site?" asked Mr. de Schaller.

"Over there, toward Zéribet," replied the native, extending his arm northward. "There are about a hundred of them at the Gizeb oasis."

"And why did they leave? Was their camp attacked?"

"Yes, by a band of Berbers."

These Berbers, or people of Berber origin, occupy the land of Icham, bounded by the Touat to the north, Timbuktu to the south, the Niger to the west, and the Fezzan to the east. They include many tribes—Arzchers, Ahaggars, Mahingas, Thagimas— and they are almost always at war with the Arabs, especially with the Algerian Chaambas, their deadliest enemies.

Mézaki gave an account of what had happened at the construction site about a week earlier.

Several hundred nomads, stirred up by their chieftains, had set upon the workers just as they arrived at the site. Once merchant ships on the Sahara Sea began to take control of all the domestic commerce in Algeria and Tunisia, they would not be able to continue their trade as caravan guides. So all the tribes had made a pact, when they saw the work beginning again, to destroy the canal that would bring water from the Gulf of Gabès. Pointar's group was not strong enough to resist an unexpected attack. The workers had been driven away almost at once and had escaped being massacred only by fleeing to the northern part of the Djerid. Because they considered it too dangerous to return to the Rharsa and from there to the oases of Nefta and Tozeur, since the attackers could cut off their escape, they had sought refuge in the direction of Zéribet. After they left, the no-madic plunderers and their accomplices had destroyed the con-struction site, burned the oasis, and destroyed the work on the canal that was already finished. Once the trench had been filled in, the embankment leveled, and the canal's entry to the Melrir completely blocked, the nomads disappeared as suddenly as they had come. There was no doubt that the second canal, between the Rharsa and the Melrir, would be exposed to similar attacks if it were not guarded by a sufficiently strong force.

"Yes," said the engineer, after the Arab had finished his ac-count, "it's important for the military authorities to take mea-sures to protect the building sites when work resumes. After that, the Sahara Sea will be able to defend itself without any help."

Captain Hardigan continued questioning Mézaki.

"How many men were there in that gang of brigands?"

"About four or five hundred," replied the Arab.

"Do you know which way they went?"

"They went south," declared Mézaki.

"And are people not saying that the Tuareg had a hand in this affair?"

"No, only the Berbers."

"Hadjar hasn't been seen in this part of the country?"

"How could he be?" replied Mézaki. "He was captured three months ago and is now a prisoner in the bordj at Gabès."

The Arab knew nothing, then, about Hadjar's escape. They would not be able to find out from him whether the fugitive had been seen in the region again. But he would be able to tell them something about Pointar's workmen, and when the engineer asked him about that, Mézaki replied, "I've already told you, they ran off to the north, toward Zéribet."

"And Pointar, is he with them?" asked Mr. de Schaller.

"He hasn't left them," replied the Arab, "and the foremen are there too."

"Where are they right now?"

"At the Gizeb oasis."

"Is that far from here?"

"About twenty kilometers from the Melrir."

"And could you go and let them know that we're at the Goléah construction site with a few spahis?" asked Captain Hardigan.

"I can, if you want me to," replied Mézaki, "but perhaps, if I go there alone, Mr. Pointar might hesitate . . ."

"We'll talk about it," concluded the captain. He had some food given to the Arab, who seemed to be in great need of nourishment and rest.

The engineer and the two officers stepped aside to confer.

They saw no reason whatsoever to suspect the veracity of this Arab, who obviously knew Pointar and had also recognized Mr. de Schaller. They had no doubt that he was one of the workmen hired to work on that section of the canal.

Under the circumstances, the most urgent priority was to find Pointar and to combine the two expeditions. Then, too, the military commander at Biskra, who had been alerted, would be asked to send reinforcements, and the teams might be put to work again.

"As I told you before," said the engineer, "after the chotts have been flooded there will be nothing more to fear. But above all, we have to reopen the canal, and for that we have to bring back the missing workmen."

There was nothing more to fear from the gang of Berbers, who, according to Mézaki, had withdrawn to the southwest from the Melrir. There was no longer any danger at Kilometer 347, and the wisest course would be to set up camp there and wait for the workmen to return. Lieutenant Villette, Sergeant Nicol, and all available men would go with Mézaki to the oasis of Gizeb, where he assured them they would find Pointar and his work party. In this region, traveled by many caravans and therefore exposed to attacks by bandits, it was only a reasonable precaution. By leaving the following day at sunup, the lieutenant expected to reach the oasis during the morning, leave again in the afternoon, and be back at the construction site before nightfall. Pointar would probably come back with the officer, who would provide a horse for him, and the workmen would follow by short marches. If they could leave the next day, they would all be back on location within forty-eight hours, and the work would resume immediately. The exploratory trip around the Melrir was temporarily canceled.

These were the decisions agreed on by the engineer and Captain Hardigan. Mézaki had no objections and heartily approved of sending Lieutenant Villette and some spahis to the oasis of Gizeb. He assured them that the workmen would have no hesitation in returning to the work site as soon as they knew the engineer and the captain were there. Then a decision could be made whether it would be appropriate to send a strong detachment of Maghzen from Biskra to guard the construction site until the day when water from the gulf began pouring into the Melrir.

xi ✦ A Twelve-Hour Expedition

Lieutenant Villette and his men left camp at seven in the morning. There was every indication that it would be a hot, sultry day, with the likelihood of a thunder storm, one of those meteorological phenomena that often attack the plains of the Djerid. But there was no time to lose, and Mr. de Schaller insisted, quite rightly, that they had to find Pointar and his crew.

The sergeant, of course, was riding Giddup, and Ace-of-Hearts was with them.

Before their departure, the spahis had packed their horses with enough provisions for the day, and even if they did not get as far as Zéribet, they would be sure of finding food at the oasis of Gizeb.

While Lieutenant Villette was away, the engineer and Captain Hardigan would begin to organize the camp with the help of Corporal Pistache, Mr. François, the four spahis who were not part of Lieutenant Villette's escort, and the wagon drivers. The pastures in the oasis were well supplied with grass and watered by a little wadi that emptied into the chott.

Lieutenant Villette's expedition was expected to take only about twelve hours. The distance from Kilometer 347 to Gizeb was not more than twenty kilometers. Without pushing the horses too hard, they could cover that distance during the morning. Then, after a two-hour rest, they would have the afternoon to return with the workers and Pointar, the superintendent of the construction site.

Mézaki had been given a horse, and it was obvious that, like all Arabs, he was a good rider. He trotted along in the lead, near the lieutenant and the sergeant, and headed northeast as soon as they had left the oasis behind.

A vast plain stretched as far as the eye could see, with sparse clumps of trees here and there, and a small stream flowing through it. It was the Algerian outtâ in all its aridity. Only a few yellowish tufts of driss emerged from the overheated soil, where the grains of sand sparkled like jewels in the sun's rays.

This part of the Djerid was completely empty. There were no caravans traveling across it on their way to some large town in the Sahara, such as Ouargla or Touggourt at the edge of the desert. No herds of animals came to plunge into the waters of the wadi, as Ace-of-Hearts did, under the envious gaze of Giddup, who watched him leaping about, dripping wet.

The little troop was traveling up the left bank of the stream. In reply to the officer's question, Mézaki answered, "Yes, we'll follow the wadi as far as the oasis of Gizeb. It runs right through it."

"Is there anyone living in the oasis?"

"No," replied the Arab. "When we left the village of Zéribet, we had to bring food with us, because there was none left at the Goléah construction site."

"That means," said Lieutenant Villette, "that Pointar, your leader, must have intended to go back to the section of the canal where the engineer had arranged to meet him."

"That's right," agreed Mézaki, "and I came to see whether the Berbers had left or not."

"You're sure we'll find the work party at Gizeb?"

"Yes, right where I left them, where Pointar was supposed to wait for me. If we ride a little faster, we'll be there in two hours."

As the sergeant pointed out, it was not really possible to go any faster in that overpowering heat. In any case, even at a moderate pace, they would reach the oasis by noon, and after a few hours' rest the lieutenant would be back at Goléah before nightfall.

As the sun climbed higher into the sky through the steamy mists of the horizon, the heat was growing more and more intense, and the air they breathed soon began to burn their lungs.

"By all the devils, sir," the sergeant kept repeating, "I don't think I've ever been so hot since I became an African! We're breathing in fire, and if we drank water it would start to boil in our stomachs. I wish we could do like Ace-of-Hearts and get some relief by sticking out our tongues. Look at him there, with his long tongue hanging down to his chest."

"Please do, Sergeant," said the lieutenant with a smile. "It's not authorized by army regulations, but go ahead."

"Ouf! That would just make me hotter," replied Nicol. "We'd be better off to keep our mouths shut and not breathe—if we could!"

"There's sure to be a storm before the end of the day," remarked the lieutenant.

"I think so," replied Mézaki, who, being native to the region, suffered less from the extreme temperatures so common in the desert. "Perhaps," he added, "we'll get to Gizeb first, and wait in the shelter of the oasis until the storm is over."

"Let's hope so," said the lieutenant. "The heavy clouds are just beginning to gather in the north, and so far there isn't a breath of wind."

"Well, sir," observed the sergeant, "these African storms don't really need any wind. They travel along under their own power, like the steamboats going from Marseilles to Tunis. You'd think they had an engine in their bellies."

Regardless of the heat and the weariness that it would cause, Lieutenant Villette quickened the pace. He was in a hurry to finish that leg of the journey—about twenty kilometers—without stopping on the shelterless plain. He hoped to stay ahead of the storm, which could then catch up to them during their stop at Gizeb. His spahis would rest there and renew their energy with the food they had brought in their haversacks. About four o'clock in the afternoon, after the fierce midday heat had subsided, they would set out again and be back at the main camp before dark.

However, the horses suffered so much during that part of the journey that their riders could not keep them going at a trot. The threatening storm made the air unbreathable. The thick, heavy clouds, which might have sheltered them from the sun, rose extremely slowly—the lieutenant would certainly have reached the oasis long before they had covered the sky. Beyond the horizon, they were not yet giving off their electrical charges and there was no thunder rolling in the distance.

On and on they went over the sun-baked plain. It was still deserted, and looked as if it would be so forever.

"Hey, wog," the sergeant repeatedly asked the guide, "aren't we ever going to see your cursed oasis? You say it's over there, among those clouds. But will we see it before they start dumping rain on us?"

"Are you sure you're taking us in the right direction?" Lieutenant Villette asked Mézaki.

"I'm sure," replied the Arab. "We can't possibly get lost. All we have to do is follow the wadi as far as Gizeb."

"We should be able to see it now. There's nothing blocking our view," remarked the officer.

"There it is," replied Mézaki, stretching his hand toward the horizon.

Sure enough, a few clumps of trees stood out about a league away. They were the first trees of the oasis, and one good gallop would have brought the little troop to the edge of it. But it was out of the question to ask the horses to gallop. Even Giddup, for all his endurance, dragged himself along with such an effort that he might have deserved the name "Backup."

It was nearly eleven o'clock when the lieutenant reached the edge of the oasis.

It seemed rather surprising that the little troop had not been spotted when it was still far off on the plain by the head of the construction site and his men, who, according to Mézaki, were supposed to be waiting at Gizeb. When the lieutenant commented on this, the Arab feigned surprise. "Aren't they still there?"

"No, and why aren't they?" asked the officer.

"That's just what I'm trying to figure out," declared Mézaki. "They were still there yesterday. Perhaps they may have taken shelter from the storm in the middle of the oasis. But I'll be able to find them all right."

"In the meantime, sir," said the sergeant, "I think it would be a good idea to let the men catch their breath."

"Halt!" commanded the officer.

A hundred paces away was the entrance to a sort of clearing surrounded by tall palm trees, where the horses could rest. There was no fear that they would wander off, and there was an abundance of water for them in the wadi that ran along one side of the clearing before turning to the northeast and going around the oasis toward Zéribet.

After seeing to their horses, the riders attended to their own needs and ate their share of the only meal they would have at Gizeb.

Meanwhile, Mézaki and the sergeant, with Ace-of-Hearts leading the way, had walked a few hundred yards along the right bank of the wadi. According to the Arab, Pointar's crew must have set up camp nearby, waiting for him to come back.

"And this is exactly where you left your friends?"

"Right here," replied Mézaki. "We had been at Gizeb for a few days and, unless they were forced to go back to Zéribet . . ."

"What the devil!" exclaimed Nicol. "I hope we don't have to drag ourselves that far!"

"I hope not," replied Mézaki. "Mr. Pointar can't be far away."

"Anyway," said the sergeant, "let's get back to camp. The lieutenant will worry if we're away too long. Let's go and eat. Afterward we'll take a look through the oasis, and if the work party is still there, we're sure to find them."

Turning to his dog, he asked, "Don't you smell anything, Ace-of-Hearts?"

The animal straightened up as his master repeated, "Look around, look around," then began simply prancing about, giving no indication that he had found any kind of trail. His mouth opened in a long yawn, whose meaning the sergeant could not mistake.

"All right, I understand. You're starving to death and you'd like to have a bite to eat. So would I. My stomach is down to my heels and soon I'll be walking on it. All the same, I'm surprised that Ace-of-Hearts didn't find some trace of Pointar and his men if they're camped near here."

He and the Arab retraced their steps along the bank of the wadi. When they reported to Lieutenant Villette, he seemed no less surprised than Nicol had been.

"Are you sure you didn't make a mistake?" he asked Mézaki.

"Yes, I'm sure. I followed the same route coming here from what you call Kilometer 347 as I took going there."

"And this is the Gizeb oasis, is it?"

"Yes, it's Gizeb. I followed the wadi that runs down toward the Melrir. I couldn't have made a mistake."

"Then where can Pointar and his work party be?"

"They must be in some other part of the woods. I can't understand why they would have gone back to Zéribet."

"In an hour," decided Lieutenant Villette, "we'll search the oasis."

Mézaki went over to his backpack, took out the food he had brought, then sat down by himself beside the wadi and began to eat.

The lieutenant and the sergeant, sitting with their backs against a date palm, ate their meal together, while the dog waited for the morsels his master tossed him.

"It's very strange, though," said Nicol again, "that we haven't noticed anyone yet, or come across any sign of a camp."

"And Ace-of-Hearts didn't smell anything?" asked the officer.

"Nothing."

"Tell me, Nicol," continued the lieutenant, glancing in the direction of the Arab, "would there be any reason to suspect this Mézaki?"

"Well, sir, all we know about him and where he came from is what he told us himself. I made no secret of the fact that I didn't trust him at first, but so far, I haven't noticed any reason not to trust him. Besides, what good would it do him to trick us? And why would he have brought us to Gizeb if Pointar and his men have never set foot here? With these devilish wogs, you're never sure, I know. But after all, he came to us of his own accord when we arrived at Goléah. There's no doubt he recognized the engineer as someone he'd seen before. There's every reason to believe he's one of the Arabs who used to work for the company."

Nicol's line of reasoning seemed logical, on the whole, and Lieutenant Villette let him go on talking. And yet, it did appear strange, to say the least, to find the Gizeb oasis deserted when the Arab had assured them that a large number of workmen were gathered there. If Pointar had been there only the day before with part of his work force, waiting for Mézaki, why had he not been on the lookout for him to return? Why had he not come to meet the little group of spahis, since he would surely have seen them when they were still a long way off? And if he had been forced to move farther back into the woods, why? Was it credible to suppose that he had gone back to Zéribet? If he had, would the lieutenant have to continue his reconnaissance that far? No, definitely not. Now that he had ascertained that Pointar and his work party were not there, the only thing for him to do was to go back to the engineer and Captain Hardigan as soon as possible. It was not a time for hesitation. Regardless of how his expedition to Gizeb turned out, he would be back at the main camp that same evening.

It was half past one when Lieutenant Villette, rested and refreshed, got to his feet again. He studied the sky, which was becoming more overcast, and said to the Arab, "I'm going to take a look through the oasis before we go back. You'll be our guide."

"At your service," replied Mézaki, ready to start.

"Sergeant," added the officer, "take two of our men and come with us. The others will wait here."

"Right away, sir," replied Nicol, motioning to two spahis to come forward.

Ace-of-Hearts, of course, did not need to be told to follow his master.

Walking ahead of the officer and his companions, Mézaki headed north. This meant going away from the wadi, but on the way back they would come down along its left bank. In that way they would have explored the entire oasis. It was not more than twenty-five or thirty hectares in extent, and since no tribes had ever settled there permanently, it was nothing more than a stopping point for caravans traveling from Biskra to the coast.

The lieutenant and his guide rode on for half an hour in the same direction. The canopy of trees was not dense enough to shut out the sky, where great clouds of vapor were rolling along and had now reached the zenith. There were already dull rumblings of thunder on the horizon, and a few distant flashes of lightning slashed through the northern sky.

When he reached the far side of the oasis, the lieutenant stopped. Ahead of him stretched the desert, yellowish, silent, and deserted. If the work party had left Gizeb, where Mézaki claimed to have left them the day before, they must have been far away by this time, whether Pointar had headed for Zéribet or for Nefta. But he had to make sure they were not camped in some other part of the oasis, unlikely as that seemed, and he continued the search back toward the wadi.

For another hour the officer and his men moved among the trees without finding any trace of a campsite. The Arab seemed very surprised. To the quizzical looks directed at him, he always gave the same reply: "They were there just yesterday, the leader and the others. It was Pointar who sent me to Goléah. They must have left since this morning."

"Left for where? Where do you think?"

"Maybe for the construction site."

"But we would have met them as we were coming, wouldn't we?"

"No, not if they didn't travel along the wadi."

"But why would they have taken a different route than ours?"

Mézaki had no answer.

It was nearly four o'clock when the officer got back to the place where they had halted. His search had been fruitless. The dog had found no trail to follow. It certainly seemed that no one, neither the work party nor a caravan, had been at the oasis for a long time.

The sergeant could not repress a thought that had been lurking in his mind. He walked up to the Arab, looked him straight in the eye, and said, "All right, wog, have you been deceiving us?"

Mézaki stared straight back at the sergeant without lowering his eyes and shrugged his shoulders in such a scornful gesture that Nicol would have seized him by the throat if Lieutenant Villette had not held him back.

"That's enough, Nicol," he said. "We're going back to Goléah, and Mézaki will follow us."

"Guarded by two of our men."

"I'm ready," said the Arab coolly. His eyes flashed with anger for an instant, then resumed their usual calm.

The horses had grazed their fill in the pasture and quenched their thirst in the water of the wadi, and were now ready to undertake the return trip from Gizeb to the Melrir. The little group would certainly be back before nightfall.

Searching for Pointar and his work party

It was twenty to five by his watch when the lieutenant gave the signal to leave. The sergeant stationed himself near him, and the Arab fell in between two spahis who would not take their eyes off him. It should be mentioned that Nicol's comrades now shared his suspicion of Mézaki, and there is no doubt that the officer felt the same mistrust, although he preferred not to make his feelings obvious. He was in a hurry to get back to the engineer and Captain Hardigan. They would decide then what steps to take, since the work party could not be put back on the job the next day.

The horses moved along quickly, obviously agitated by the storm that was about to burst over them. The electrical tension was extreme, and the clouds now stretched from one horizon to the other. Flashes of lightning criss-crossed the sky and the thunder rumbled with the terrible claps heard only in the desert, where there is nothing to send back an echo. But there was still not the slightest breath of wind nor drop of rain. The burning atmosphere was stifling, and their lungs were scorched by the heat.

Still, if they made a great effort, and if the weather did not deteriorate, Lieutenant Villette and his men would get back to their base without being too far behind schedule. Their greatest fear was that the storm might become more violent. The wind might spring up, followed by rain, and where would they find shelter in this arid plain, without a tree in sight?

It was important to get back to Kilometer 347 as soon as possible, but try as they might, the horses could not keep up the pace demanded by their riders. Sometimes they stopped as if their feet were hobbled, despite the spurs which drew blood from their flanks. Soon the men began to feel helpless too, and in no condition to cover the last kilometers of their journey. The sturdy Giddup was exhausted. At every step, his master was afraid he might collapse on the overheated sand.

By six o'clock in the evening, however, thanks to the lieutenant's encouragement and prodding, three-quarters of the distance had been covered. If the sun, now very low on the western horizon, had not been veiled by a thick bank of clouds, the salt deposits of Chott Melrir might have been seen glittering a league away. At the tip of the chott they could dimly make out the clumps of trees of the oasis. Assuming that it would take another hour to get there, the little group would have reached the first line of trees before nightfall.

"Courage, my friends," the officer kept repeating. "One last effort."

But, hardy though his men were, he knew the time was coming when disorder would set in among his little troop. A number of horsemen were already lagging behind, and he was forced to wait for them to catch up.

It was their hope that the storm would take some other form than simply flashes of lightning followed by rolling thunder—if only there were wind to make the air more breathable, and if the huge masses of clouds could only condense into rain! There was not enough air, and their lungs had great difficulty functioning in such a stifling atmosphere.

At last the wind sprang up, but with all the violence generated by the extreme electrical tension in the air. The irresistible gusts criss-crossed the parched soil, creating whirlwinds. Along with the claps of thunder, a deafeningly shrill whistling sound now arose. Undampened by the rain, the dust covering the ground was whipped into an immense twister, spinning with incredible speed under the influence of the electricity in the air and creating a powerful funnel of air. The shrieks of birds could be heard as they were sucked into this whirlwind from which even the strongest could not break free.

The horses were right in the path of this whirlwind, which seized and scattered them, and several riders were soon knocked from their saddles. No one could see or hear anyone else, or communicate in any way. The whirlwind engulfed everything as it made its way toward the southern plains of the Djerid.

Under these conditions, Lieutenant Villette could not tell what route he was following. It seemed likely that he and his men had been driven toward the chott, but farther away from the encampment. Fortunately, the rain began to fall in torrents. Gusts of wind dispersed the whirlwind in the already deepening gloom.

The little group was now scattered and had to be brought together again with great difficulty. By the glow of the lightning flashes, the lieutenant had noticed that the oasis was not more than about a kilometer to the southeast.

Finally, after repeated calls in the short periods of calm, men and horses were reunited. Suddenly the sergeant exclaimed, "Where's the wog?"

The two spahis responsible for guarding Mézaki could not answer. They had no idea what had become of him, since they had been driven violently apart when they were caught up in the whirlwind.

"The scoundrel! He's escaped!" the sergeant repeated. "He's escaped, and taken his horse—or rather our horse—with him. He's tricked us!"

The officer, deep in thought, said nothing.

Almost at once, they heard a furious barking, and before Nicol could stop him, the dog sprang forward, headed for the chott in great bounds, and disappeared.

"Here, Ace-of-Hearts, come here!" cried the sergeant, deeply worried.

But the dog either did not hear him or did not want to hear him, and soon disappeared into the darkness.

Perhaps Ace-of-Hearts had set out on Mézaki's trail, and that was an effort Nicol could not have asked of his horse, which, like the others, was utterly exhausted.

Lieutenant Villette now began to wonder whether something had gone wrong, and whether the engineer, Captain Hardigan, and the others who had stayed at Goléah, while he was on his way to Gizeb, were in danger. The Arab's unexplained disappearance made any theory plausible. The detachment, as Nicol suspected, had been dealing with a traitor.[1]

"Back to the camp," ordered Lieutenant Villette, "as fast as we can."

The storm was still raging. Although the wind had died down, the rain fell more and more heavily, carving out many wide potholes in the ground. It was practically pitch black, even though the sun had barely disappeared below the horizon. Continuing toward the oasis would be very difficult, and there was no fire to indicate the position of the camp.

And yet, that was a precaution the engineer would not have

overlooked, to ensure the lieutenant's return. There was no shortage of fuel, since there was an abundance of dead wood in the oasis. Despite the wind and rain, they could have kept a campfire going whose light would have been visible from quite a distance, and the little group could not have been more than half a kilometer away.

These were the fears that tormented Lieutenant Villette, and the sergeant confided to his officer that he shared those same fears.

"Let's keep going," replied the lieutenant, "and hope to God that we get there in time."

As it turned out, the direction they had followed was not exactly accurate, and the little group reached the chott at a point to the left of the oasis. They had to come back eastward along the northern shore, and it was at least half past eight when they finally halted at the far end of the Melrir.

Still no one had appeared, despite the spahis' repeated shouts announcing their return.

A few minutes later, the lieutenant reached the clearing where the wagons and tents should have been. There was still no one to be seen—neither Mr. de Schaller, nor the captain, nor the corporal, nor any of the men who had stayed behind with them.

They called and fired their rifles, but heard no answer. They set fire to a few resinous branches, which shed their pale light through the clumps of trees.

There were no tents, and the wagons had been ransacked and broken. The mules that pulled them, the horses belonging to Captain Hardigan and his friends . . . everything was gone!

Clearly, the camp had been attacked. There was no doubt that Mézaki had come to them only to ensure the success of this new attack at the same place, by drawing Lieutenant Villette and his men off in the direction of Gizeb.

Needless to say, the Arab had not returned. As for Ace-of-Hearts, the sergeant called him in vain. And as the hours of the night went by, the faithful dog still did not come back to the camp at Goléah.

xii ➤ The Mystery Is Solved

After Lieutenant Villette left for the oasis of Gizeb, the engineer began making arrangements for what might prove to be a long stay.

It had not occurred to anyone to suspect Mézaki. No one doubted that Lieutenant Villette would bring him back that same evening, along with Pointar and a number of workmen.

Only ten men stayed behind at Kilometer 347 — Mr. de Schaller, Captain Hardigan, Corporal Pistache, Mr. François, four spahis, and the two wagon drivers. They all went to work at once to set up camp at the edge of the oasis, not far from the construction site. The wagons were brought there, the material unloaded, and the tents set up as usual. The drivers and spahis found pasture for the horses, where they would have an abundance of fodder. There was enough food on hand to supply the detachment for several days, and it seemed likely that when Pointar returned with his foremen and workers, he would bring everything they needed, which they could easily have procured in the village of Zéribet.

They were also counting on getting help in the nearest villages — Nefta, Tozeur, and La Hammâ. Once the construction work was under way, the local inhabitants would not be able to stop the vast project begun by Roudaire and carried on by his successors.

Since it was important to make sure from the outset that the supplies for the construction site at Kilometer 347 could be replenished, the engineer and Captain Hardigan agreed that messengers should be sent to Nefta or Tozeur. They chose the two wagon drivers, who knew the route intimately, since they had often traveled it with caravans. They were two Tunisians in whom they could have complete confidence. By leaving at dawn the next day on their own horses, they would soon come to a village that could send food to the Melrir a few days later. They would carry two letters with them, one from the engineer to a high-ranking employee of the company and one from Captain Hardigan to the military commandant at Tozeur.

After they had finished their morning meal in the tent, under the shade of the outer trees of the oasis, Mr. de Schaller said to the captain, "Now, my dear Hardigan, suppose we let Pistache, Mr. François, and our men go on to the final construction site. I'd like to get a more exact idea of the repairs that need to be done on this last section of the canal."

He walked along its whole length, estimating the quantity of rubble that had been thrown into it.

"Those natives must really have come in great numbers," he remarked to his friend. "I can understand why Pointar and his men couldn't hold out against them."

"But once the workers had been driven away, how did these Arabs, Tuareg, or whatever manage to do so much damage to the work and throw so much debris into the canal, even if they did come in force? It must have taken them a long time, which is exactly the opposite of what Mézaki told us."

"The only explanation I can think of," replied Mr. de Schaller, "is that they didn't have to dig anything. They just had to fill it in by pulling the banks down into the canal bed. Nothing was there but sand, and with material that Pointar and his men must have left behind in their hasty flight, and perhaps with material left from before, the job was much easier than I would have thought."

"In that case," said Captain Hardigan, "about forty-eight hours would have been enough."

"I think so," replied the engineer, "and my estimate is that the repairs can be completed in two weeks at the most."

"That's good news," said the captain, "but there's one precaution we absolutely must take. We must guard the canal, in this part of Chott Melrir and everywhere else, until both chotts have been completely flooded. What happened here could happen somewhere else. There's no question that the inhabitants of the Djerid, especially the nomads, have been incited to revolt, that

143

"My estimate is that the repairs can be completed in two weeks."

the tribal chieftains are encouraging them to oppose the creation of an inland sea, and that there's still some danger of an attack. That means the military authorities must be warned. With garrisons at Biskra, Nefta, Tozeur, and Gabès, it won't be hard to maintain an effective surveillance and keep the construction work safe from any further raids."

That was the most urgent priority, and it was important for the governor-general of Algeria and the resident-general of Tunisia to be informed of the situation without delay. They would have to protect the various interests involved in this great undertaking.

It was true, as the engineer had repeatedly assured, that once the Sahara Sea was completed and in use, it could easily be defended. But according to the initial estimate, it would require at least ten years to flood the Rharsa and Melrir depressions—an estimate that had later been reduced by half after a more thorough study of the terrain. It would not be necessary to guard the part of the chotts that were to be flooded, but only the various stations along the two canals. Nevertheless, at two hundred and twenty-seven kilometers for the first canal and eighty for the second, the zone to be defended was still very long, and it would have to be guarded for a long time.

In response to Captain Hardigan's remarks on the subject, the engineer could only repeat what he had already said about the flooding of the chotts: "I still think the soil of the Djerid, in the area between the coast and the Rharsa and Melrir, has some surprises in store for us. It's really nothing but a salty crust, and I know from experience that it undergoes fairly considerable vibrations. It's quite possible that the canal will widen and deepen as the water flows through it. That's what Roudaire was counting on—quite logically—to finish the work.[1] I wouldn't be at all surprised if nature were to collaborate with human genius. The depressions are the dried-up beds of former lakes. Abruptly or gradually, the action of the water will make them deeper than we now expect, and therefore I'm convinced that the flooding can be completed in less time than is generally supposed. Further, as I said before, the Djerid is not immune to certain seismic disturbances, and these movements can only modify it in a way favor-

145

able to our undertaking. But we'll see, my dear captain, we'll see. I'm not pessimistic. I'm an optimist. And what would you say if, within two years—within a year—the Rharsa and Melrir were filled to the brim, with a whole merchant fleet steaming across their surface?"

"I accept your hypotheses, my friend," replied Captain Hardigan, "but whether it takes two years or one to make them a reality, we'll still need enough military support to protect the work and the workers."

"Agreed," concluded Mr. de Schaller. "I share your opinion that surveillance of the entire length of the canal should begin without delay."

Captain Hardigan was planning to get in touch with the military commander at Biskra by special delivery message the very next day, after the workers had come back to the construction site. In the meantime, the presence of his few spahis might be enough to protect that section. Under the circumstances, there was probably no fear of a new attack by the natives.

After they had finished their inspection, the engineer and the captain returned to the encampment, which was still being organized. There was nothing to do now but wait for the lieutenant, who would certainly be back before evening.

One of the most urgent problems, in the expedition's present situation, was that of procuring supplies. Until now, their food had come from the reserves in the two wagons or from what they had bought in the villages and hamlets in this part of the Djerid. There had been no shortage of provisions, either for men or for horses.

At the reestablished construction site at Kilometer 347, however, it would be necessary to obtain supplies on a more regular basis for a stay of several weeks, and so, when Captain Hardigan sent word to the military authorities at the neighboring garrisons, he would also ask that food be sent to him for the entire duration of his stay at the oasis.

At sunrise on that day, April 13, thick vapors were gathering on the horizon. Everything indicated that the morning would be as stifling as the previous afternoon had been. There was no doubt that a very severe storm was brewing to the north.

In reply to Corporal Pistache's comments on that subject, Mr. François declared, "I would not be surprised if we had a bad storm today. Ever since morning, I have been expecting a battle of the elements to break out any minute in this part of the desert."

"Why is that?" asked Pistache.

"You see, Corporal, when I was shaving early this morning, all the bristles of my beard stood up. They were so hard that I had to go over them two or three times with my razor. Something like a little spark shot out from each of them."

"That's odd," replied the corporal, not doubting for an instant the assertion of such a man as Mr. François. Whether or not it was true that this worthy gentleman's hair possessed electrical properties, like a cat's fur, Pistache was quite willing to believe it.

"And this morning?" he asked, looking at his friend's closely shaven face.

"This morning, it was not to be believed! My cheeks, my chin, were all covered with little luminous bristles."

"I wish I'd seen that," replied Pistache.

But even without relying on the meteorological observations of Mr. François, it was certain that a storm was building up in the northeast and the atmosphere was gradually being saturated with electricity.

The heat was becoming overpowering, and after the midday meal the engineer and the captain allowed themselves a long siesta. Even though they were in their tent, which was pitched under the outer trees of the oasis, a fierce heat smothered them, and there was not a breath of wind.

This state of affairs was a constant source of concern to Mr. de Schaller and the captain. The storm had not yet broken out over Chott Sellem, but there was no doubt that its violence was already being felt in the northeast, precisely over the oasis of Gizeb. Lightning began to slash across the sky in that direction, although the thunder was not yet audible. Assuming that, for one reason or another, the lieutenant had not been able to leave before the storm, there was every reason to suppose that he would wait under the shelter of the trees until it was over, even if that meant not getting back to camp until the following day.

Corporal Pistache and Mr. François

"We probably won't see him this evening," remarked Captain Hardigan. "If Villette had left this afternoon around two o'clock, he'd be in sight of the oasis by now."

"Even if it means a day's delay," replied Mr. de Schaller, "our lieutenant would have been wise not to start out when the sky is so threatening. The worst thing of all would be for him and his men to be caught out in the open, where they would find no shelter."

"On that, I fully agree with you," concluded the captain.

The afternoon was wearing on, and there was no sign of the little group's return, not even the barking of Ace-of-Hearts, who would have been leading the way. Now, less than a league away, the sky was constantly lit up by flashes of lightning. The heavy mass of clouds had passed the zenith and was slowly closing in toward the Melrir. Within half an hour the storm would be over the encampment and would then head toward the chott.

Nevertheless, the engineer, Captain Hardigan, the corporal, and two of the spahis stood at the edge of the oasis. Before their eyes stretched the vast plain, whose salty deposits reflected here and there the flashes of lightning.

They stared in vain at the horizon. There was no group of horsemen to be seen in that direction.

"It's certain," said the captain, "that the detachment didn't start out. We shouldn't expect them before tomorrow."

"I think you're right, sir," replied Pistache. "Even after the storm is over, it would be very difficult for them to find their way to Goléah in the dark, once night has fallen."

"Villette is an experienced officer, and we can depend on his judgement. Let's get back to camp. It's going to rain any minute."

They had hardly taken a dozen steps when the corporal stopped. "Listen, sir," he said.

Everyone turned around.

"It seems to me I hear barking. Is the sergeant's dog . . . ?"

They listened intently. No. There was no sound of barking during the periods of calm. Pistache must surely have been mistaken.

Captain Hardigan and his friends headed back toward the encampment through the oasis, where the trees were bending under the fierce wind, and returned to their tents.

A few minutes more, and they would have been attacked by gusts of wind raging in the midst of a torrential downpour.

It was now six o'clock, and the captain made preparations for what seemed likely to be one of the worst nights since the expedition had left Gabès.

Unquestionably, there was every reason to believe that Lieutenant Villette had been delayed by the sudden onset of the severe storm that would force him to stay at the Gizeb oasis until the next day.

All the same, the captain and Mr. de Schaller continued to be apprehensive. It had never even occurred to them to suspect that Mézaki was not one of Pointar's workmen, as he had claimed to be, and that he had concocted a criminal plot against the expedition on its way to the Melrir. But they could not forget the hostility of the nomads and permanent inhabitants of the Djerid, and the growing agitation among the tribes in opposition to the creation of the Sahara Sea. The recent attack on the construction site at Goléah would probably be repeated if work on that section went ahead. Mézaki maintained, of course, that the attackers had withdrawn to the south of the chott after driving away the workmen, but there might be other parties roaming the plain. And if they encountered Lieutenant Villette's detachment, it would be crushed by the sheer weight of numbers.

The engineer and captain reasoned that, all things considered, these fears were probably exaggerated, but they nevertheless continued to be very concerned. Little did they realize that if anyone was in danger, it was not Lieutenant Villette and his men on their way to Gizeb, but Mr. de Schaller and his friends themselves in the oasis!

By about half past six, the storm was raging in full force. A number of trees were struck by lightning, and the engineer's tent was narrowly missed. The rain fell in torrents, and the thousand little streams flowing toward the chott turned the ground of the oasis into a kind of swampy outtâ. At the same time, the wind unleashed a frightful attack. Branches were snapped like twigs and entire palm trees were ripped up by the roots and blown away.

It was now impossible to set foot outside. Fortunately, the horses had been sheltered in time under a large clump of trees capable of withstanding the hurricane. They could be kept there safely, although they were terrified of the storm.

It was a different story with the mules that had been left in the clearing. Terrified by the thunder, they galloped away across the oasis, despite the efforts of their drivers. One of the spahis reported this to Captain Hardigan.

"They must be brought back at all costs," he shouted.

"The two drivers have gone after them," replied the corporal.

"Send two of our men with them," the officer ordered. "If the mules manage to get out of the oasis, they'll be lost. We'll never be able to catch them in the open country."

Despite the strong gusts of wind that lashed the encampment, two of the four spahis hurried off toward the clearing, guided by the occasional shouts of the mule drivers.

Then, although the thunder and lightning continued unabated, the gusts suddenly died down. There was less wind and less rain, but the darkness was intense, and the men could not see each other except during intermittent flashes of lightning.

The engineer and Captain Hardigan left the tent, followed by Mr. François, the corporal, and the two spahis who had stayed behind in camp.

Considering the lateness of the hour and the violence of the storm, which would probably go on for most of the night, Lieutenant Villette's return was definitely not to be expected. He and his men would not start out until the next day, when travel across the Djerid would be feasible.

The captain and his friends were pleasantly surprised, then, to hear a dog barking somewhere off to the north.

There was no mistake this time. A dog was running toward the oasis and approaching rapidly.

"Ace-of-Hearts! That's who it is!" exclaimed the corporal. "I recognize his bark."

"That means Villette isn't far away," added Captain Hardigan.

If, in fact, the faithful animal was leading the detachment, it could not be more than a few hundred yards behind.

At this moment, without warning, a group of about thirty Arabs, who had been stealthily crawling up to the edge of the oasis, suddenly leaped into the encampment! The captain, the engi-

A surprise attack by the Tuareg

neer, the corporal, Mr. François, and the two spahis were immediately surrounded before they knew what was happening, and were seized without being able to defend themselves. Greatly outnumbered, there was very little they could have done, in any case, against this raiding party that had taken them by surprise.

In an instant, the entire encampment was ransacked and the horses were led toward the Melrir.

The prisoners, kept separate, were unable to communicate with each other. They were pushed along toward the surface of the chott, with the dog following their tracks. They were already far away when Lieutenant Villette finally reached the campsite. There, he found no trace of the men he had left that morning, or of the horses, which he assumed had run away during the storm.

xiii ～ The Oasis of Zenfig

The geometrical shape of Chott Melrir, including the Farfaria marshes to the north and other similar depressions to the south, such as Chott Merouan, is roughly that of a right-angled triangle. Its hypotenuse runs from northwest to southeast in an almost straight line from the direction of Tahir-Nassou to a point below the thirty-fourth parallel at the end of the second canal. Its longer southern side, with random ups and downs, runs along that parallel and extends across many secondary chotts. The western and shorter side runs up toward the settlement of Tahir-Nassou, roughly parallel to the Trans-Sahara Railway line, planned as an extension of the Philippeville-Constantine-Batna-Biskra line, whose route was to be altered to avoid having to build a branch line linking it to a port on the new sea, on the shore opposite to where the second canal flows into it.

The width of this large depression (smaller in area, however, than the Djerid and the Fedjedj) measures fifty-five kilometers from the end of the last section of the canal to the proposed port that would be built on the western side at a location to be determined, between the Signal of Chegga and Wadi Ittel. The plan to go on to Meraïer, farther to the south, had apparently been abandoned. Of the total surface area of the Chott Melrir, only six thousand square kilometers—six hundred thousand hectares—could be flooded, since the remainder was higher than the Mediterranean. In fact, including both chotts, the new sea would cover eight thousand square kilometers, and an area of five thousand square kilometers would be above water once the Rharsa and the Melrir had been completely filled.

These areas of dry land would become islands. Within the Melrir they would form a sort of archipelago containing two large islands. The first one, named Hinguiz, would be shaped like a bent rectangle, dividing the chott into two parts at the middle. The other would occupy the far part contained between the two sides of the right angle near Strarie. The smaller islands would lie in parallel lines, mainly towards the southeast. Ships making the dangerous passage through this archipelago would have to pay strict attention to the available hydrographic data in order to minimize the risks.

Within the boundaries of the two chotts to be inundated were several oases, with their date palms and fields, which of course would have to be bought from their owners. As Captain Roudaire had estimated, the purchase price should not exceed five million francs, and it was to be paid by the France-Overseas Company, which expected to recoup that amount from the two and a half million hectares of land and forest granted to it by the government.[1]

One of the largest oases of the Melrir covered an area of three or four square kilometers in the middle of the Hinguiz, facing north. Once flooded, the northern waters of the chott would come up to the edge of the oasis. It was rich in date palms of the finest species, whose fruit, exported by the kafila, is much sought after in the markets of the Djerid. This was the oasis of Zenfig,[2] whose only contact with the main settlements of La Hammâ, Nefta, Tozeur, and Gabès consisted of rare visits by caravans during the harvest season.

Zenfig's tall trees sheltered a population of three or four hundred Tuareg, one of the most troublesome tribes in the Sahara. The houses in the settlement, about a hundred in all, occupied that part of the oasis that would become a seacoast. Near the center and around the exterior were cultivated fields and pastures, which provided food for this tribe and its domestic animals. A wadi (which would eventually become an arm of the new sea), swollen by little streams from the island, supplied the population with water.

The oasis of Zenfig had only occasional dealings with the other oases in the province of Constantine. Only the nomadic Tuareg roaming the desert came there to replenish their food supply. It was a feared and fearsome place, and caravans did their best to stay away from it, but bands from Zenfig often came out to attack them in the neighborhood of the Melrir.

The approaches to the oasis were extremely difficult and dangerous. Along the Hinguiz the bed of the chott was never solid — there were quicksands everywhere in which an entire kafila could be swallowed up. Across these surfaces of Pliocene terrain, consisting of sand mixed with gypsum and salt, there were only a few negotiable footpaths, and these were known only to the local inhabitants. To reach the oasis one had to follow these paths or risk being engulfed in the quagmires. Obviously, the Hinguiz would be easily accessible once the water had covered the soft crust, which offered no firm support to walk on. But since that was exactly what the Tuareg wanted to prevent, this had become the greatest and most violent hotbed of opposition to the Sahara Sea. From Zenfig continuous calls went out for a "holy war" against the foreigners.

Among the various tribes of the Djerid, the tribe of Zenfig held pride of place, and it continued to exercise a strong influence over the confederation. It could extend this influence with impunity, safe from attack in its almost inaccessible retreat. But this predominance would completely disappear on the day when the waters of the Gulf of Gabès filled the chott to the brim and turned the Hinguiz into the central island of the Melrir.

At the oasis of Zenfig the Tuareg tribe had maintained its racial purity. There, too, its customs and traditions had remained unchanged. The men were handsome, grave in appearance, proud in bearing, slow and dignified of step. They all wore a ring of green serpentine, which, if they were to be believed, gave their right arm greater strength. They were brave by nature and had no fear of death. They still wore the ancestral costume consisting of a long, loose-fitting *gandoura* of Sudanese cotton, a white and blue shirt, trousers tied at the bottom, leather sandals, and a fez held onto the head by a kerchief rolled up to form a turban, to which was attached a veil coming down to the mouth, to protect the lips from dust.

The women, beautiful and blue-eyed, with heavy eyebrows and long lashes, left their faces uncovered and wore a veil only in the presence of strangers, out of respect. There was never more than one woman in a Tuareg household, for the tribe, regardless of the precepts of the Koran, did not allow polygamy, although it did allow divorce.

As a result, the Tuareg in this part of the Melrir formed a sort of separate community and did not intermingle with the other tribes of the Djerid. If the chieftains led their followers out of the area, they always did so for some profitable raid, to ransack a caravan or to carry out a reprisal against a rival oasis. These Zenfig Tuareg were truly fearsome pirates, who sometimes carried out their attacks across the plains of lower Tunisia, as far away as the region of Gabès. The military authorities organized expeditions against them, but they hastily took refuge in their remote hiding places deep within the Melrir.

The Tuareg are rather abstemious by nature, eating neither fish nor game, and very little meat, but subsisting on a diet of dates, figs, the berries of the "Salvadora persica," flour, dairy products, and eggs. They do, however, have slaves, or *imrhaδ*, to do the heaviest tasks for them, for they scorn all kinds of work. The marabouts[3] and the amulet vendors have a very strong influence on the Tuareg, especially in that part of the Melrir. It was these fanatics who were preaching revolt against the plan for the Sahara Sea. The Tuareg are also superstitious. They believe in spirits and are afraid of ghosts, so much so that they do not mourn the dead for fear of bringing them back to life, and the name of the deceased dies with him.

Such, in brief, was the Zenfig tribe to which Hadjar belonged. It had always recognized him as its chieftain, until the day when he fell into the hands of Captain Hardigan.

There, too, was the birthplace of his family, all-powerful over the special population of Zenfig and the other tribes of the Melrir. There were many oases on the surface of the chott, at various points on the Hinguiz, and on the vast perimeter of the depression.

In addition to Hadjar, his mother, Djemma, was held in great veneration by the Tuareg tribes. Among the women of Zenfig, this feeling reached the point of adoration. They all shared Djemma's hatred for foreigners: she fanaticized the women, just as her son fanaticized the men. It must be remembered what an influence Djemma had on her son, an influence characteristic of all Tuareg women. They are, moreover, better educated than their husbands and brothers—they can write, whereas the men can scarcely read—and in the schools they are the ones who teach language and grammar. These Tuareg women's opposition to Captain Roudaire's project had never wavered for a single day.

Such was the situation before the Tuareg chieftain was captured. These various tribes of the Melrir, like the one at Zenfig, would be ruined by the flooding of the chotts. They would not be able to continue their piratical trade when there were no more kafila crossing the Djerid between Biskra and Gabès. Further, their hiding places would be easily accessible when ships could approach them and when they were no longer protected by that shifting ground that threatened to engulf horse and rider at every step. It has already been explained how Hadjar was captured after an encounter with Captain Hardigan's cavalry, how he was imprisoned in the fort at Gabès, and how, with the help of his mother, his brother, and his faithful followers Ahmet, Harrig, and Horeb, he had managed to escape the day before a frigate was to take him to Tunis to be tried by a council of war. Once out of prison, Hadjar had successfully crossed the sebkha and chott region and reached the oasis of Zenfig, where Djemma soon joined him.

When the news of Hadjar's capture first reached Zenfig, emotions rose to a fever pitch. How could it be that their Tuareg chieftain, for whom his followers would have given their lives, was in the hands of his implacable enemies? Was there any hope that he might escape? Was he not condemned to death in advance?

His return was greeted, therefore, with tremendous enthusiasm. The fugitive was carried about in triumph. Gunshots were fired on all sides to mark the happy occasion. Everywhere could be heard the beating of *tabel*, or drums, and the sound of *rebaza*, the violins of Tuareg orchestras. In that atmosphere of incredible delirium, a sign from Hadjar would have been enough to send all his followers out to attack the villages of the Djerid.

But Hadjar knew how to restrain the fiery passions of his Tuareg tribe. Faced with the threat of renewed construction, his first priority was to ensure the safety of the oases at the south-west corner of the chott. The foreigners must not be allowed to transform the Melrir into a vast navigable body of water on which ships would sail in every direction. First of all, the work on the canal had to be disrupted.

At the same time, Hadjar learned that the expedition led by Captain Hardigan would make a stop within the next forty-eight hours at the end of the canal, where it would find another expedition coming from the province of Constantine to meet it.

Hence the attack, led by Hadjar himself, against the final section of the canal, which had driven away the company's original workers. Several hundred Tuareg had taken part in it and then headed back to Zenfig, leaving the canal half filled in.

If Mézaki was still there, it was because his leader had left him there; if he had declared that Hadjar had not taken part in the attack on the construction site, that was only to deceive the captain; if he had claimed that the workers had fled to Gizeb, it was to ensure that part of the detachment would be sent there. And if the engineer, the captain, and four of their friends were now Hadjar's prisoners, it was because they had been surprised by about thirty Tuareg positioned near Goléah, under Sohar's command, and had been sent on to the Zenfig oasis before Lieutenant Villette's cavalry could rejoin them.

Along with their six prisoners, the Tuareg had also taken from the campsite the horses belonging to the engineer, the officer, the corporal, and the two spahis. Mr. François, who had traveled in one of the wagons from the time the expedition left Gabès, had no horse. But the horses and camels that had brought the band of Tuareg to the construction site were waiting two hundred yards away.

The prisoners were forced to mount their own steeds. One of the camels was reserved for Mr. François, who had to perch on the animal as best he could. Then the entire troop disappeared into the stormy night, under a fiery sky.

Sergeant Nicol's dog had arrived at the time of the attack, and Sohar let him follow the prisoners, unaware that the detachment was not far behind.

In preparation for the raid organized by Hadjar, the Tuareg

had enough supplies for several days, and two dromedaries, laden with provisions, would keep the band supplied with food until their return. But the journey would be a very arduous one, for the distance between the eastern end of the chott and the Zenfig oasis was some fifty kilometers.

The first stage brought the prisoners to the spot where Sohar had made a stop before attacking the encampment at Goléah. There the Tuareg stopped, taking great care to ensure that Captain Hardigan and his friends could not escape. The latter spent a dreadful night, for the wind continued to gust until nearly morning. Their only shelter was the foliage of a small palm grove, where they huddled together while the Tuareg prowled around them. But although they could not escape, at least they could talk, and the obvious topic of conversation was the unexpected attack of which they were the victims. They had no reason to suppose it was Hadjar's work, but the spirit of revolt running through the tribes of the Djerid, and especially those of the Melrir, explained matters only too well. A few Tuareg chieftains must have found out that a detachment of spahis would be arriving shortly at the construction site. They probably learned from nomads that a company engineer was coming to inspect the contours of the Melrir before the last few strokes of the pick cut through the Gabès ridge.

Captain Hardigan now began to wonder, seriously this time, whether he had been tricked by the Arab they had met the previous evening at Goléah, and he expressed this view to his friends.

"You must be right, sir," said the corporal. "I never trusted that animal."

"But then," remarked the engineer, "what has become of Lieutenant Villette? He won't have found Pointar or any of his workers at the Gizeb oasis."

"Assuming that he went there," replied the captain. "If Mézaki is the traitor we suspect he is, his only aim was to throw Villette and his men off the track and then give them the slip along the way."

"And who knows? He may rejoin the band that attacked us," exclaimed one of the spahis.

"That wouldn't surprise me in the least," declared Pistache.

"When I think about it, if the lieutenant had come along a little earlier—perhaps only fifteen minutes—he would have been in time to charge those wog scoundrels and rescue us."

"True enough," added Mr. François. "The detachment can't have been far away, because we heard a dog barking at about the same time as we were surprised by the Tuareg."

"Ah! Ace-of-Hearts, Ace-of-Hearts!" Corporal Pistache repeated over and over. "Where is he? Did he follow us here, or did he go back to his master and tell him . . . ?"

"Here he is! Here he is!" exclaimed one of the spahis.

It is not hard to imagine what a warm welcome Ace-of-Hearts received. Everyone stroked him, and Pistache gave him a big kiss right on the head.

"Yes, Ace-of-Hearts, yes. It's us. What about the others? And your master, Sergeant Nicol, is he here?"

Ace-of-Hearts would gladly have barked out a meaningful answer, but the corporal kept him quiet. The Tuareg probably thought the dog had been with the captain at the Goléah encampment and had naturally wanted to follow them.

Where would they be taken? To what part of the Djerid? Perhaps to some remote oasis in Chott Melrir, perhaps into the far reaches of the immense Sahara desert.

When morning came, the prisoners were given food, a kind of cake made of couscous and dates packed together, and water to drink from a wadi flowing beside the little grove.

From where they were, they could see out across the chott, with its salt crystals twinkling in the rising sun, but to the west their view was obstructed by the barrier of dunes curving around on that side, making it impossible to see the oasis of Goléah.

Mr. de Schaller, Captain Hardigan, and their friends looked toward the east, perhaps in the hope of seeing the lieutenant coming toward them, but in vain.

"After all," repeated the officer, "there's no question that Villette reached Goléah last night. When he saw we weren't there and that our campsite was abandoned, why wouldn't he have started out right away to look for us?"

"Unless he was attacked himself, when he was going back to the Gizeb oasis," suggested the engineer.

"Yes, yes, anything is possible—especially with that Mézaki. Ah! If I ever get my hands on him, I hope I'll grow claws, so I can rip the hide off that scoundrel."

At that point, Sohar gave the order to move. Captain Hardigan went up to him and asked, "What do you want of us?"

Sohar made no reply.

"Where are you taking us?"

Sohar's only response was the abrupt command, "Mount your horses."

There was nothing to do but to obey. To make matters worse, Mr. François had not been able to shave that morning.

Suddenly the corporal burst out in great indignation, "There he is! There he is!" Every eye turned toward the person Pistache was pointing out to his companions.

It was Mézaki. After leading the detachment as far as Gizeb, he had disappeared and rejoined Sohar's band during the night.

"I have nothing to say to that villain," declared Captain Hardigan, turning his back on Mézaki, who was staring at him insolently.

Mr. François expressed his opinion in these terms: "This Tuareg certainly does not appear to be a very commendable person."

"You can say that again!" replied Pistache, addressing Mr. François for the first time with the familiar "tu." The latter, correct as ever, made a point of not taking offense.

The previous day's storm was followed by clear weather. Since there was not a cloud in the sky, nor a breath of wind on the surface of the chott, traveling was very difficult. There was not a single oasis to be seen in that part of the desert, and the group found no trees to shelter them until they reached the edge of the Hinguiz.

Sohar kept them moving. He was in a hurry to get back to Zenfig, where his brother was waiting for him. The prisoners still had no reason to suppose that they had fallen into the hands of Hadjar. What Captain Hardigan and Mr. de Schaller thought, with some justification, was that this latest attack had not been launched for the purpose of looting the camp at Goléah, which was not worth the effort involved, but as an act of reprisal on the part of the tribes of the Melrir. Who could say whether the cap-

Sohar arriving at Zenfig with his prisoners

tain and his friends might not pay with their freedom, or even their lives, for the proposed Sahara Sea?

That first day, they traveled in two stages and covered in all some twenty-five kilometers. The heat had not been completely overwhelming, since the weather was not stormy, but it was very intense all the same. The one to suffer most during the march was no doubt Mr. François, perched on the back of a dromedary. He was not accustomed to being shaken around on top of this kind of steed, and the animal trotted along so relentlessly that he had to be tied on to prevent him from falling off.

The night went by quietly, the silence broken only by the loud roars of wild beasts prowling over the surface of the chott.

During the first few stages of the journey, Sohar had to follow the paths he was familiar with, in order not to sink into the quagmires. But the next day their route lay across the Hinguiz, where the ground was solid.

Traveling conditions on April 15 were better than they had been the previous day, and toward evening Sohar arrived at the oasis of Zenfig with his prisoners.

What was their surprise to find that their worst fears were realized, and that they were in the presence of Hadjar!

xiv 〜 Prisoners

The building to which Sohar's prisoners were taken was the former bordj of the village. For a number of years now it had been falling into disrepair. Its crumbling walls ringed the top of a knoll on the northern edge of the oasis. This stronghold was an ordinary fort that had been used in the past by the Tuareg of Zenfig during the great intertribal battles fought in the Djerid, but after peace had been restored, no one had bothered to repair it or maintain it in good condition.

A *jour*, a stone wall, served as the defensive perimeter around this fort. And above it rose a *jouma'ah*, a sort of minaret that had lost its uppermost point and from which there was an unobstructed view in all directions.

Dilapidated though it was, the bordj nevertheless contained a few areas fit for human habitation. Adjoining an interior courtyard were two or three rooms with no furniture or curtains, separated by thick walls. They could provide shelter against the gusts of summer and the cold of winter.

There the engineer, Captain Hardigan, Corporal Pistache, Mr. François, and the two spahis were taken as soon as they reached Zenfig.

Hadjar had not spoken a single word to them, and Sohar, who had brought them to the bordj escorted by a dozen Tuareg, refused to answer any of their questions.

Needless to say, during the attack on the campsite, Captain Hardigan and his companions had had no chance to arm themselves with their sabres, revolvers, and rifles. They were, moreover, searched and robbed of the little money they had on their persons, and Mr. François was righteously indignant when the rascals relieved him of his razor.

After Sohar had left them alone, the captain and the engineer made it their first priority to explore the bordj.

"When one is shut up in a prison," remarked Mr. de Schaller, "the first thing to do is to have a good look around."

"And the second," added Captain Hardigan, "is to escape."

They therefore examined the inner courtyard, in the middle of which stood the minaret, and they realized that it would be impossible to scale the twenty-foot walls surrounding it. They found no openings in the wall, as there were in the outside sour next to the sentinel's walkway. A single doorway, opening onto this walkway, gave access to the central courtyard, but Sohar had closed it behind him, and its heavy doors, reinforced with iron strapping, could not be broken down. There was no way out except through that doorway, and it seemed likely that the approaches to the bordj would be kept under close surveillance.

Night had fallen, a night that the prisoners would spend in total darkness. They had not been able to obtain a light of any kind, nor any food. During the first hours, they waited in vain for food to be brought to them, and water too, for they were parched with thirst. The door remained shut.

The prisoners had reconnoitered the courtyard in the fading light of dusk, and now they reassembled, oppressed by gloomy thoughts, in one of the adjacent rooms, where they made their beds on bundles of dried esparto grass.

During their brief conversation, the corporal asked, "Are those scoundrels going to let us starve to death?"

No, there was no fear of that. Before the last leg of the journey, ten kilometers from Zenfig, the band of Tuareg had made a halt and the prisoners had had their share of the provisions carried by the dromedaries. By evening, Captain Hardigan and his companions would certainly have been glad of something to eat, but their hunger would not become unbearable until the next day, if they did not get food by daybreak.

"Let's try to sleep," suggested the engineer.

"And dream that we're sitting at a table covered with food," added the corporal. "Chops, a stuffed goose, salad."

"Don't stop there, corporal," urged Mr. François. "Just think how much we would enjoy a good bacon soup."[1]

The bordj *prison at Zenfig*

But what were Hadjar's intentions with regard to his prisoners? He had certainly recognized Captain Hardigan. Would he not want to punish him, now that he had him in his power? Would he not have him put to death, and his companions as well?

"I don't think so," declared Mr. de Schaller. "It isn't likely that our lives are in danger. On the contrary, it's in the Tuareg's best interests to keep us as hostages for some future occasion. In order to prevent the work on the canal from being completed, we can assume that Hadjar and the Tuareg will resume their attacks on the construction site if the company's workers return to Kilometer 347. Hadjar may fail in his next attempt, or fall into the hands of the authorities again, and this time he'd be held so securely that he could never escape. So it's a good thing for him that we're still in his power. If the day came when Hadjar was in danger of being imprisoned again, he could simply say, 'My life and those of my friends for the lives of my prisoners.' It would be a proposal that the authorities could not ignore. In my opinion, that day is not far off, for news of Hadjar's daring twofold attack must be well known by now, and he will soon be facing the troops, *maghzen,* and *goums,* sent to rescue us."

"You may be right," replied Captain Hardigan, "but don't forget that Hadjar has a well-established reputation as a vindictive and cruel man. It isn't in his nature to reason the way we do. He has a personal score to settle."

"A score to settle with you in particular, sir," remarked Corporal Pistache, "because it was you who nabbed him a few weeks ago."

"So I did, Corporal, and I'm surprised, now that he's recognized me and knows who I am, that he didn't resort right away to some act of violence. But we'll see. One thing we're sure of is that we're his prisoners, and that we know as little about Villette and Pointar's fate as they know about ours. And having said that, my dear de Schaller, I'm not about to become the price of Hadjar's freedom or the trophy for his thieving life.

"So we must escape, at all costs, and when I think the time is right, I'll move heaven and earth to get out of here. As far as I'm concerned, I want to get back to my friends a free man, not part of a prisoner exchange. I also want to save my life for the day when I come face to face, revolver or sword in hand, with the brigand who took us by surprise and captured us."

While Captain Hardigan and Mr. de Schaller were mulling over plans for escape, Pistache and Mr. François, however firmly resolved they were to follow their leaders, were counting more heavily on help from outside, and perhaps even on the intelligence of their friend Ace-of-Hearts.

As mentioned, Ace-of-Hearts had followed the prisoners from the time of their capture as far as Zenfig, and the Tuareg had made no attempt to drive him away. But when Captain Hardigan and his companions were taken to the bordj, the faithful animal was not allowed to go with them. Was that intentional? It would have been hard to say for sure, but there was no question that they were all sorry not to have the dog with them. And yet, even if he had been there, how could he have helped them, no matter how intelligent and devoted he was?

"You never know. You never know," Corporal Pistache kept repeating during his conversation with Mr. François. "Dogs have instincts that men don't have. If we could talk to Ace-of-Hearts about his master Nicol, about his friend Giddup, perhaps he'd set out on his own to find them. Of course, if we can't get out of this cursed courtyard, Ace-of-Hearts wouldn't be able to get out either. All the same, I wish he was here. I only hope those brutes don't hurt him."

Mr. François simply shook his head without answering and rubbed his hands over his chin and cheeks, where the stubble was beginning to grow.

After waiting in vain for food to be brought to them, there was nothing the prisoners could do but get some badly needed rest. They stretched out on the bundles of esparto grass and eventually all managed to fall sleep. After a rather uncomfortable night, they woke up at the crack of dawn.

"Since we had no supper last night," Mr. François pointed out, logically enough, "does that mean we will go without breakfast this morning?"

"That would be unfortunate. In fact, it would be deplorable," replied Corporal Pistache, with a yawn that threatened to dislocate his jaw, not from sleepiness this time, but from hunger.

The prisoners did not have to wait long for an answer to this question. An hour later Ahmet and a dozen Tuareg came into the courtyard and set down some of the same cake as they had brought the night before, cold meat, and dates, enough to last six people for a day. Several pitchers held a good supply of water, drawn from the wadi that flowed through the oasis of Zenfig.

Once again, Captain Hardigan tried to find out what fate the Tuareg chieftain had in store for them. He put the question to Ahmet.

Like Sohar the evening before, Ahmet did not deign to answer. No doubt he had orders to that effect, and he left the courtyard without speaking a single word. Three days went by, with no change in the situation. To escape from the bordj by scaling the high walls was impossible without a ladder. Perhaps, if they had been able to get over the walls under cover of darkness, Captain Hardigan and his companions might have been able to escape through the oasis. The bordj did not seem to be closely watched on the outside, and there was no sound of footsteps on the sentinel's walkway either by day or by night. And what would have been the point, after all, since the walls were an insurmountable obstacle and the door of the courtyard could not be broken down?

Since the first day of their imprisonment, Corporal Pistache had had a chance to study the layout of the oasis. After many attempts, during which he risked his neck a hundred times, he had succeeded in climbing the dilapidated stairway and reaching the top of the truncated minaret. From there he had looked through the uppermost apertures, where he could be sure of not being seen and observed the broad panorama that spread out before his eyes.

Below him, around the bordj, lay the village, among the trees of the Zenfig oasis. Farther on, the territory of the Hinguiz stretched for three or four kilometers to the east and to the west. A large number of dwellings, facing north, stood out very white against the dark green. One of them he correctly assumed to be the home of Hadjar because of the number of buildings inside its walls, the activity taking place in front of its door, and the number of standards flapping in the breeze over its entrance.

During the afternoon of April 20, on returning to his observation post at the top of the minaret, the corporal noticed that there was great excitement in the village. People were coming out of their houses, and it seemed that groups of natives were arriving at the oasis from various points of the Hinguiz. These were not commercial caravans, because they had no dromedaries or other beasts of burden with them.

Who knows? Perhaps Hadjar had convened an important meeting that day in Zenfig. A large crowd soon filled the main square.

When he saw what was happening, the corporal said to himself that his captain ought to be informed, and called to him.

Captain Hardigan promptly joined Pistache in the confined space at the top of the minaret, although it required a strenuous effort to pull himself up beside him.

It was clear that some kind of conference involving hundreds of Tuareg was taking place in Zenfig at that very moment. From the top of the tower they heard shouts and saw gestures, and this hubbub continued until the arrival of a person, followed by a man and a woman, who came out of the house that the corporal had indicated as probably belonging to the Tuareg chieftain.

"It's Hadjar!" exclaimed Captain Hardigan. "It's him! I recognize him!"

"Right you are, sir," replied Pistache. "I recognize him too."

It was indeed Hadjar, with his mother Djemma and his brother Sohar. They were greeted with applause as soon as they walked out into the square.

Then there was silence. Surrounded by the crowd, Hadjar began to speak, and for an hour, sometimes interrupted by enthusiastic outbursts, he harangued the assembled natives. Neither the captain nor the corporal could hear what he was saying. There was more shouting when the meeting ended, and Hadjar went back into his house, while the village returned to its usual calm.

Captain Hardigan and Pistache climbed at once back down to the courtyard and told their companions what they had observed.

"I suspect," said the engineer, "that this meeting was held to protest the flooding of the chotts, and that it will no doubt be followed by a new attack."

"I think so too," declared Captain Hardigan. "It could mean that Pointar has moved back to the Goléah section."

"Unless it has to do with us," said Corporal Pistache. "Maybe all those scoundrels have gathered to see the prisoners being massacred."

A long silence followed this remark. The captain and the engineer exchanged a glance that betrayed their secret thoughts. Were there not grounds for fearing that the Tuareg chieftain had decided to carry out reprisals, that he wanted to make an example by means of a public execution, and that various tribes from the Hinguiz had been invited to Zenfig for that reason? And how could the prisoners keep on hoping that help might arrive, either from Biskra or from Goléah, since Lieutenant Villette could not know where they had been taken, or what tribe had captured them?

Before coming down from the minaret, Captain Hardigan and the corporal had taken one last look over the part of the Melrir that spread out before them. To the north and to the south it was deserted, as was also the portion stretching to the east and west on both sides of the Hinguiz, which would become an island after the chott was flooded. Over the vast depression, there was not a caravan to be seen. As for Lieutenant Villette's detachment, even assuming that his search had brought him toward Zenfig, what could his few men have done against the whole village?

There was nothing to do but wait and see, and how anxiously they waited! Would the door of the bordj open at any moment to admit Hadjar and his men?

Would it be possible to put up any resistance, if the Tuareg chieftain had them dragged out to the square to be put to death? And if it did not happen today, might it not happen tomorrow?

The day slowly went by, however, and nothing changed. The scanty provisions that had been left in the courtyard in the morning were adequate, and when evening came they stretched out on the bundles of esparto grass in the room where they had spent the previous nights.

About half an hour later they heard a noise outside. Was it

some Tuareg going back up along the sentinel's walkway? Was the door about to open? Was Hadjar sending for the prisoners?

The corporal got up immediately and, pressing his ear to the door, he listened.

What he heard was not the sound of footsteps, but a kind of dull, plaintive barking. A dog was prowling around the outside wall.

"Ace-of-Hearts! It's him! It's him!" shouted Pistache.

Lying down beside the threshold, he called out over and over, "Ace-of-Hearts! Ace-of-Hearts! Good dog!"

The animal recognized the corporal's voice, just as it would have recognized the voice of his master, Nicol, and replied with more half-restrained barks.

"Yes, it's us, Ace-of-Hearts, we're here!" repeated Pistache. "Ah! If you could only find the sergeant and his old brother, your friend Giddup—Giddup, do you understand?—and tell them where we're being held."

Captain Hardigan and the others came over to the door. If only they could have used the dog to communicate with their friends, perhaps by attaching a note to his collar. Who knows? The faithful animal might have been able to find the lieutenant simply by instinct. And once Villette knew where his comrades were, he would take steps to free them.

In any case, Ace-of-Hearts must not be found on the sentinel's walk at the door of the bordj. The corporal said to him again, "Off you go, there's a good dog, off you go."

Ace-of-Hearts must have understood, for he barked a good-bye and departed.

The next day, food was brought to them early in the morning, as it had been the day before, and it seemed likely that there would be no change in the prisoners' situation that day.

The dog did not return the following night. At least Pistache did not hear him, although he was listening. He wondered whether the poor creature might have come to harm, and whether they would ever see him again.

Nothing of importance happened during the next two days, and no new signs of excitement were observed in the village.

About eleven o'clock on April 24, Captain Hardigan, watching from the top of the minaret, noticed something going on in Zenfig, like horses shuffling around, accompanied by an unusual noise of weapons. At the same time, the whole population moved en masse to the main square, toward which a large number of horsemen were riding.

Was this the day when Captain Hardigan and his comrades would be brought before Hadjar?

No, once again it was a false alarm. On the contrary, all indications were that the Tuareg chieftain was about to leave. In the middle of the square, mounted on his horse, he was inspecting about a hundred of his tribesmen, also on horseback.

Half an hour later, Hadjar took his place at the head of the troop and they galloped out of the village, heading toward the eastern end of the Hinguiz.

The captain immediately came down to the courtyard and told his friends what had happened.

"It must be an expedition to attack Goléah, where the work has probably started up again," said the engineer.

"Who knows? Hadjar may meet Villette and his detachment," remarked the captain.

"Yes, anything is possible, but it's not certain," replied the corporal. "What is certain is that, with Hadjar and his rogues out of the village, now is the time to escape."

"What do you mean?" asked one of the spahis.

Yes, how could they take advantage of this sudden opportunity? Were not the walls of the fort still impregnable? Could they break open the door, which was solidly locked from the outside? And besides, who did they think might rescue them?

But help would indeed come.

During the following night, as he done once before, Ace-of-Hearts barked softly, and scratched the ground near the door.

Guided by his instinct, Ace-of-Hearts had discovered an opening under that part of the wall, a hole half-filled with earth, leading from one side to the other.

Suddenly, to the corporal's surprise, he emerged into the courtyard.

Yes! Ace-of-Hearts was beside him, leaping and barking. He had some difficulty in getting the brave animal to calm down.

Captain Hardigan, Mr. de Schaller, and the others came rushing out of the room and followed the dog, who went back to the hole through which he had just come.

There they found the opening of a narrow tunnel. By removing a few stones and a little earth, they could make it large enough for a man to slip through.

"This is a lucky break," exclaimed Pistache.

It was indeed, and unexpected as well. They would have to make the most of it that very night, before Hadjar returned to Zenfig.

Passing through the village and the oasis would present serious difficulties, however. How could the fugitives find their way in complete darkness? Would they not run the risk of meeting someone, perhaps even Hadjar's band? And how could they travel the fifty kilometers between them and Goléah without provisions, with nothing to eat except the fruit and roots growing in the oasis?

But none of them even thought of these dangers. Without an instant's hesitation, they began their escape, following the dog to the hole, through which he was the first to disappear.

"Go ahead," said the officer to Pistache.

"After you, sir," replied the corporal.

Precautions had to be taken to ensure that the wall did not collapse. When that was done, the prisoners reached the sentinel's walk in about ten minutes.

It was a dark, cloudy, starless night. Captain Hardigan and his friends would not have known which way to go if the dog had not been there to guide them. All they had to do was trust the animal's intelligence. They met no one in the area immediately adjacent to the bordj and slid down the slope to the edge of the first trees.

It was now eleven o'clock at night. Silence reigned in the village and there was no light coming through the open windows.

Walking with muffled steps, the fugitives made their way through the trees and reached the edge of the oasis without encountering anyone.

Just then, a man carrying a lighted lantern appeared in front of them.

Ace-of-Hearts leaped upon him and seized his throat.

Recognition was instantaneous on both sides.

It was Mézaki! He was on his way back to his house on that side of the village.

Before he had time to cry out, the dog leaped upon him and seized his throat in his powerful jaws. Mézaki fell to the ground, dead. "Well done, Ace-of-Hearts!" said the corporal. The captain and his comrades would have nothing more to fear from that scoundrel, now lying lifeless at their feet. Quickening their pace, they followed the edge of the Hinguiz and headed for the eastern part of the Melrir.

xv ≈ On the Run

Following their escape, it was only after careful consideration that Captain Hardigan had made the decision to head east. True, in the opposite direction, a little beyond the western edge of the Melrir, lay the well-traveled path to Touggourt, where the Trans-Sahara Railway ran. From there, under ordinary circumstances, it would have been easy to reach Biskra in safety. But he was not familiar with that part of the chott, since he had come from the east, from Goléah to Zenfig. To go west across the Hinguiz not only meant traveling over unknown territory but also risking an encounter with the men posted by Hadjar to watch for troops coming from Biskra. Besides, the distance between Zenfig and the end of the canal was about the same. The workmen might have come back to the construction site in strength, and if they reached Goléah they might join forces with Lieutenant Villette's detachment, which was probably carrying out a search in that part of the Djerid. Last of all, this was the direction in which Ace-of-Hearts had rushed off across the oasis, and, as the corporal thought, he had "his own reasons for doing that," and it surely made sense to rely on the dog's wisdom.

"Sir," he said to the captain, "all we have to do is follow him. He'll make no mistake. Besides, he can see as well by night as by day. I tell you, sir, this is a dog with the eyes of a cat."

"Let's follow him," replied Captain Hardigan.

That was their wisest course. Enveloped in pitch darkness, in the labyrinth of the oasis, the fugitives would have run the risk of wandering aimlessly around the village. Fortunately, with Ace-of-Hearts as their guide, they soon reached the northern edge of the Hinguiz and needed only to follow it to escape.

It was especially important not to stray away from this border, since the surface of the Melrir was dangerous, riddled with quagmires from which it would have been impossible to extricate themselves.[1] The safe paths through them were known only to the Tuareg from Zenfig and the neighboring villages, who worked as guides, and, more often than not, offered their services only in order to loot the caravans.

The fugitives walked quickly, without meeting anyone, until daybreak, when they made a halt in a palm grove. Because of the difficulty of traveling in total darkness, they estimated that they could not have covered more than seven or eight kilometers so far. It was another twenty to the far end of the Hinguiz and as much again, across the chott, to the oasis of Goléah.

At that spot, weary from the night march, Captain Hardigan thought it prudent to rest for an hour. The grove was deserted and the nearest villages, on the southern edge of the future central island, could easily be avoided. As far as the eye could see, there was no sign of Hadjar and his men. They had left Zenfig about fifteen hours ago and were probably far away by now.

Although weariness forced the fugitives to rest for a little while, this would not be sufficient to fully restore them unless they could get some food. They had used up the last of their provisions during their last few hours at the bordj, and there was nothing available except whatever fruit they might gather in the oasis of Hinguiz—dates, berries, and perhaps some edible roots known to Pistache. They all had flint and tinder with them, and these roots, when cooked over a fire of dry wood, would provide a more substantial meal.

There was also reason to hope that Captain Hardigan and his friends would be able to satisfy their thirst as well as their hunger, for there were several wadis running through the Hinguiz. Perhaps Ace-of-Hearts might even help them catch some game birds or animals. But any such possibility would disappear when they set out across the sandy wastes of the chott, the salty terrain where nothing grew except a few inedible clumps of driss.

Since Sohar had brought the prisoners from Goléah to Zenfig in two days, would it take them longer to travel from Zenfig to Goléah? Yes, for two basic reasons. First, they had no horses, and second, it would take time to search out the safe paths through the Melrir.

"It isn't more than about fifty kilometers, all told," the captain pointed out. "By this evening, we'll have covered half of it. After a night's rest we'll start out again, and even if the second half takes twice as long, we'll be within sight of the banks of the canal by the evening of the day after tomorrow."

After their hour-long halt, during which they had nothing to eat but dates, the fugitives followed the edge of the grove, keeping out of sight as much as possible. The sky was overcast, with only a few rays of sunlight filtering through the ragged clouds. Fortunately, the rain, which threatened to fall any minute, was still holding off.

They completed the first leg of the day's journey by noon. There had been no alerts, and they had not met a single native. As for Hadjar and his men, they were probably thirty or forty kilometers to the east by now.

Again they stopped for an hour. There were plenty of dates, and the corporal dug up some roots which they cooked in the ashes. They dined on this meager fare as best they could, and Ace-of-Hearts had to be satisfied with it.

By evening they had covered twenty-five kilometers since leaving Zenfig, and Captain Hardigan stopped at the eastern extremity of the Hinguiz.

They were at the edge of the last oasis. Beyond stretched the vast solitude of the chott, a huge expanse twinkling with salt crystals, where it would be difficult, even dangerous, to proceed without a guide. But the prisoners were finally far away from their prison, and if Ahmet and the others had set out in pursuit, at least they had not yet picked up their track.

They were all badly in need of rest. No matter how important it was for them to reach Goléah as soon as possible, they were forced to spend the night where they were. Besides, it would have been exceedingly unwise to venture out in the darkness over the shifting ground beyond the Hinguiz since they could barely negotiate it in daylight. With no reason to worry about the cold at that time of year and at that latitude, they lay down under a clump of palm trees.

Since it was obviously prudent for one of them to stand watch over the approaches to the encampment, the corporal volunteered to take the first watch, on the understanding that he would be relieved by the two spahis. While his comrades fell into a deep sleep, he stood at his post, accompanied by the faithful Ace-of-Hearts. But scarcely a quarter of an hour had passed before Pistache was overcome by the desire to sleep. Almost unconsciously, he sat down, then stretched out on the ground and closed his eyes in spite of himself.

Fortunately, the faithful Ace-of-Hearts was a better sentinel. Shortly before midnight his low barking awakened the sleepers.

"Wake up! Danger!" shouted the corporal, jumping to his feet.

In an instant Captain Hardigan was beside him.

"Listen, sir," said Pistache.

They could hear a loud disturbance somewhere to the left of the clump of trees, the sound of branches being broken and shrubs being torn up a few hundred meters away.

"Does this mean that the Tuareg from Zenfig are after us and have found our trail?"

There was no doubt that the Tuareg would set out in pursuit as soon as the prisoners' escape had been discovered.

Captain Hardigan listened closely, and he and the corporal came to the same conclusion.

"It's not the Tuareg," he said. "They would have tried to take us by surprise. They wouldn't make all that noise."

"What can it be, then?" asked the engineer.

"Animals, wild animals, prowling around the oasis," said the corporal.

True enough, it was not the Tuareg that threatened the encampment, but something equally dangerous—a lion, or maybe several lions. If they attacked, would it be possible to fight them off, with no means of defense?

The dog was showing signs of extreme agitation. With great difficulty, the corporal held him back, preventing him from barking and rushing toward the spot from which the furious roars were coming.

What was going on? Were the wild animals fighting among themselves, quarreling fiercely over some prey? Had they noticed the fugitives under the clump of trees? Were they about to pounce on them?

181

There were a few moments of profound anxiety. If Captain Hardigan and his comrades had already been discovered, the animals would be on them immediately. It was better to wait where they were and climb up in the trees to avoid being attacked.

The captain gave an order to this effect, but before it could be carried out, the dog escaped from the corporal's hands and disappeared off to the right.

"Here, Ace-of-Hearts, come here!" shouted Pistache.

The animal either did not hear him or did not want to hear him, for it did not come back.

By now the noise and roaring seemed to be getting farther away. It gradually diminished and finally stopped altogether, but Ace-of-Hearts kept on barking and soon reappeared.

"They're gone. Those wild beasts have definitely left," said the captain. "They didn't get wind of our presence. There's nothing to be afraid of now."

"But what's the matter with Ace-of-Hearts?" cried Pistache, stroking the dog and finding his hands wet with blood. "Is he hurt? Did he get clawed when he was out there?"

No, Ace-of-Hearts was not whimpering. He was cavorting about, leaping up and down, dashing off to the right and back again, as if he were trying to get the corporal to follow him in that direction. Pistache would have gone with the dog, but the captain forbade it. "Stay here, Pistache," he ordered. "Let's wait until daybreak, and then we'll see what has to be done."

The corporal obeyed, the men went back to where they had been when the wild animals started roaring, and they all resumed their interrupted sleep.

The fugitives' sleep was not disturbed again, and when they awoke the sun was beginning to spill over the horizon to the east of the Melrir.

Ace-of-Hearts dashed off into the undergrowth, and when he came back this time, his coat showed traces of fresh blood.

"There is surely some injured or dead animal over there," said the engineer. "One of the lions that were fighting among themselves, maybe."

"Too bad that lion isn't very good to eat!" said one of the spahis.

182

"Let's go and have a look," suggested Captain Hardigan.

The dog led the way, barking, and they all followed. About a hundred paces away they found an animal lying in a pool of blood.

It was not a lion, but a large antelope, which the wild beasts had killed, fought over, and then abandoned in their fury.

"Excellent, excellent!" exclaimed the corporal. "We could never have caught an animal like that. It came along just in the nick of time! Now we'll have enough food on hand for our whole trip."

It certainly was a stroke of luck. Now the fugitives would not have to restrict their diet to roots and dates. Pistache and the spahis set to work at once, cutting off the best parts of the antelope, and giving Ace-of-Hearts his share. There were several kilograms of good meat for them to take back to the encampment. They lit a fire, placed a few slices on the glowing coals, and enjoyed a juicy grilled steak.

Everyone's strength began to return after this unexpected meal of meat instead of fruit. When they had eaten their fill, Captain Hardigan gave the order to move on.

"We mustn't waste time," he said. "We're still in danger of being pursued by the Tuareg from Zenfig."

Before leaving their campsite, the fugitives looked very carefully all along the edge of the Hinguiz on the side toward the village. It was deserted, and over the entire expanse of the chott, to the east and to the west, there was not a living creature to be seen. The carnivores and ruminants never ventured into that desolate region, and even the birds avoided flying over it since the oasis of Hinguiz provided them with all the necessities of life that the arid surface of the chott could not.

When Captain Hardigan made a comment to this effect, the engineer quickly replied, "They'll become regular visitors there, at least the sea birds will—gulls, frigate birds, kingfishers—when the Melrir has been turned into a vast lake, with fish and whales from the Mediterranean swimming around below its surface. I can already see naval flotillas and commercial vessels plying the new sea under full sail or a full head of steam."

"While we're waiting for the chott to be flooded, sir," sug-

A large antelope, killed and then abandoned by the wild beasts

gested Corporal Pistache, "my view is that we should take advantage of the fact that it's still dry, and get back to the canal. We might wait a long time for a ship to come and pick us up here."

"True enough," replied Mr. de Schaller, "but I still think the Rharsa and the Melrir will be flooded in less time than anyone thought possible."

"A year at the most," replied the captain with a laugh. "And that would be too long for us. As soon as we've finished our preparations, I'll give the signal to move on."

"Come, Mr. François," said the corporal, "you're going to have to use your legs. I hope you'll soon make a stop in a village that has a barber shop, or we'll end up with beards as long as a goat's!"

"A goat!" muttered Mr. François, who no longer recognized himself when he looked at his reflection in the water of a wadi.

Given the condition the fugitives were in, their preparations were neither long nor elaborate. That morning, however, they were briefly delayed by the necessity of preparing enough food for the two days' march to Goléah. They had nothing available except what was left of the antelope. On their way across the Melrir, where there would be no wood, how could they make a fire? Here, at least, there was no shortage of fuel. The ground was littered with branches broken off by the violent storms that came from the Djerid.

The corporal and the two spahis proceeded to carry out this task, and in half an hour slices of excellent meat had been grilled over the coals. When it had cooled, Pistache divided it into six equal parts and gave a share to each man, who wrapped it in fresh leaves.

It was now seven o'clock in the morning, to judge from the position of the sun over the horizon, where it was rising in a reddish mist that augured a very hot day. This time the captain and his comrades would no longer have the trees of the Hinguiz to shelter them against the burning rays of the sun as they marched.

But there was another, more serious danger. So long as the fugitives were following the edge of the oasis, the risk of being spotted and pursued was greatly reduced, but once they were out in the open, crossing the long expanse of the chott, who could tell whether they might not be seen and reported? If some band of Tuareg happened to come their way, where could they hide to avoid meeting them? And what if Hadjar and his men were to come back toward Zenfig that day or the next? Added to these perils was the difficulty of walking over the shifting terrain of the Melrir, where neither the engineer nor the captain was familiar with the safe paths. Such were the many hazards involved in the twenty-five-kilometer journey between the point of the Hinguiz and the construction site at Goléah.

Captain Hardigan and Mr. de Schaller, after fully considering their alternatives, had decided that it was necessary to risk these terrible dangers. The men were all energetic, vigorous, and capable of making the great effort required. "Let's go!" said the captain. "Yes, let's go, and good luck to us," replied Corporal Pistache.

xvi ≈≈ The *Tell*

I
t was a little after seven o'clock when Captain Hardigan and his friends left the point. Because of the nature of the terrain they were walking on, it was imperative to move with extreme caution. The salt crystals on the surface of the ground made it impossible to tell whether it would support a man's weight or whether at every step they might sink into a quagmire.

On the basis of the soundings taken by Captain Roudaire and those he had taken himself, the engineer was thoroughly familiar with the composition of the terrain at the bottom of the chotts and sebkha. The surface is covered with a salty crust subject to very perceptible vibrations. Below this is a mixture of one-third sand and marl and two-thirds water, which is so fluid that it has no consistency whatever. Sometimes the probes go to a great depth before they touch solid rock. Men and horses can disappear into these semiliquid layers, as if the ground were falling away under them, with no possibility of rescue.

It would have been helpful if the fugitives, on leaving the Hinguiz, had found tracks of Hadjar's passage with his band of Tuareg through this part of the chott. Footprints on the white crust would not have had time to disappear, since there had been neither wind not rain on the eastern end of the Melrir for several days. Simply by following them, they would have avoided straying from the paths, well known to the natives, which led to the oasis of Goléah, the apparent destination of the Tuareg chieftain. But Mr. de Schaller looked for tracks in vain, and they were forced to the conclusion that the Tuareg had not followed the edge of the Hinguiz all the way to the end.

The captain and the engineer led the way as they walked along, preceded by the dog, who acted as their scout. Before committing themselves to one direction or another, they attempted to determine the composition of the ground, but this was difficult because of the layer of salt. Their progress was very slow, and by about eleven o'clock, when they had finished the first leg of their journey, they had not covered more than four or five kilometers. Still, they had to call a halt, in order to rest and eat. There was not an oasis, nor a thicket, nor even a clump of trees, anywhere in sight. A slight rise in the sandy ground, a few hundred paces off, was all that broke the monotony of the plain.

"We have no choice," said Captain Hardigan.

They all headed for the little dune, sat down on the side protected from the sun's rays, and each man took from his pocket a piece of meat. But the corporal searched in vain for a ras, or spring, from which he could draw a little drinking water. There was no wadi flowing through that part of the Melrir, and they had nothing to quench their thirst except the few dates they had picked at the last campsite.

About half past twelve they resumed their march, moving forward wearily and with great difficulty. Captain Hardigan tried as much as possible to keep moving eastward, basing his calculations on the position of the sun, but almost every minute the sand gave way under their feet. The depression was at a very low elevation. After the chott was flooded, its greatest depth—about thirty meters below sea level—would be between the Hinguiz and the mouth of the canal.

The engineer pointed this out, and added, "I'm not surprised that the ground on this side is less stable than anywhere else. During the rainy season, all the runoff from the Melrir must flow into these hollows, and they can never completely harden."

"It's too bad we can't avoid them," remarked the captain, "but we would waste time by going farther north or farther south, and we still wouldn't be sure of finding a better route. We haven't a day to lose. The course we're on will take us to the closest oasis we can reach, so it's best not to alter it."

"There's no doubt about that," declared Mr. de Schaller, "and it's equally certain that Hadjar and his men, if they were going to Kilometer 347, didn't come this way." And indeed, there was nothing to indicate that they had passed by.

What a slow and arduous march it was! And how difficult to stay on the safe paths! Ace-of-Hearts, always in the lead, turned back whenever he felt the white crust give way under him. Then they would have to stop, feel out the terrain, turn to the right or the left, sometimes by as much as fifty meters, and the many detours made their route all the longer. Under these conditions, the second leg of the journey covered no more than a league and a half. When evening came, they stopped, exhausted. But even if they had not been urgently in need of rest, how could they have ventured out on a night march?

It was now five o'clock in the afternoon. Captain Hardigan understood only too well that his friends could go no farther. And yet it was not an ideal spot for making camp at night. Nothing but the level plain. Not even a slight rise of ground to lean against. Not a ras where they could draw a little drinking water. Not even a tuft of driss in these hofra, or hollows, with their accumulation of salt crystals. Overhead, several birds flew by, rapidly crossing this desolate region in order to spend the night in the nearest oasis, several leagues away no doubt, and much too far for the fugitives to reach.

"With all due respect, sir," said the corporal to his commander, "it seems to me that there must be a better spot to make camp than in this place, which even the Tuareg dogs want nothing to do with."

"What do you suggest, Corporal?"

"Look. If I'm not mistaken, isn't that a kind of dune rising up over there, with a few trees on it?"

Motioning with his hand towards the northeast, Pistache indicated a point on the chott not more than three kilometers away.

All eyes turned and looked in that direction. The corporal was right. They saw in the distance one of those little wooded hills known as tells, with three or four trees, very rare in that region, growing on its summit. If Captain Hardigan and his comrades could get to it, they might spend the night under more favorable conditions.

"That's where we must go, at all costs," declared the officer.

"Yes," added Mr. de Schaller, "especially since it won't take us too far out of our way."

189

"Who knows?" said the corporal. "Perhaps, over there, the chott will be easier on our poor feet."

"Come on, friends, one last effort," ordered Captain Hardigan. They all followed him.

But even if the surface of the chott were higher on the other side of the tell, as Pistache had just remarked, and even if the fugitives were to find more solid ground to walk on the next day, such was not the case during the last hour of that leg of their journey.

"I'll never make it!" Mr. François kept repeating.

"Yes, you will!" replied the corporal. "Just hold on to my arm."

They had covered barely two kilometers when the sun began to disappear. The moon, at the beginning of its first quarter, briefly appeared, but it also was rapidly sinking below the horizon. Dusk, already so short in those low latitudes, would soon be followed by profound darkness. It was important to take advantage of the last moments of daylight to reach the tell.

Captain Hardigan, Mr. de Schaller, the corporal, Mr. François, and the two spahis were walking along in single file, slowly and deliberately. The ground was becoming worse and worse. Its crusty surface sank beneath their feet as the sand below gave way and water oozed up through it. They repeatedly found themselves up to their knees in this mire, and had to fight to get free. Mr. François, who had wandered too far from the beaten track, suddenly sank in up to his waist, and would have been completely swallowed up in one of those holes, or "eyes of the sea," if he had not stretched out his arms.

"Help! Help!" he shouted, struggling to save himself.

"Hold on!" Pistache shouted back.

The corporal, who was farther ahead, stopped and turned back to rescue him. Everyone else stopped at the same time. But Ace-of-Hearts was the first to reach the scene. With a few bounds, he reached the unfortunate Mr. François, who, with only his head and shoulders still visible, clung desperately to the neck of the powerful animal.

Eventually the brave fellow managed to extricate himself from the quagmire, dripping wet and covered with marl.

Although it was not a time for making jokes, Pistache quipped,

Mr. François sinking into an "eye of the sea"

"There was nothing to be afraid of, Mr. François. If Ace-of-Hearts hadn't got there ahead of me, I'd have pulled you out by your beard!"

For the next hour, fearful of sinking into treacherous quicksands all around them, the fugitives were forced to crawl across this low-lying stretch of desert. They stayed close together to help each other should the need arise. This concave depression in the surface of the chott resembled a huge basin into which flowed all the underground waters of the area.

Their one hope of safety lay in reaching the tell that Corporal Pistache had pointed out. There the ground would certainly become firm again, especially near the clump of trees on its summit, where they could spend the night in safety.

But it was becoming very difficult to find their way in the darkness. It was barely possible to make out the outline of the tell, and impossible to know whether to turn right or left.

By now Captain Hardigan and his comrades were simply guessing their way, and only luck could keep them on the right path.

At last Ace-of-Hearts, who was their real guide, began barking urgently. The dog seemed to be about a hundred paces to the left, and on higher ground.

"The hill is that way," said the corporal.

"Yes," agreed Mr. de Schaller, "we had wandered away from it."

The dog had obviously found the tell. He had climbed up as far as the trees and was now barking an invitation for them to join him.

And join him they did, but only after more strenuous effort and many dangers. Now the ground began to rise gradually and become more solid. On its surface could be felt a few rough tufts of driss, on which fingers could take hold, and in this way, with Pistache once more giving a helping hand to Mr. François, they all found their way onto the tell.

"Here we are—at last!" exclaimed the corporal, trying to calm Ace-of-Hearts, who was prancing around near him.

It was now after eight o'clock and too dark to see their surroundings. There was nothing to be done but to stretch out under the trees and get a night's rest. But while the corporal, Mr.

François, and the two spahis were soon fast asleep, Captain Hardigan and Mr. de Schaller waited in vain for sleep to come. Too many concerns and worries kept them awake. They were like shipwrecked sailors cast ashore on an uncharted island, not knowing whether they would ever get off it. Would they find negotiable trails at the bottom of the tell? Would they have to venture out again tomorrow onto the shifting ground? And who could say whether the bottom of the chott might not drop still lower as they went on their way to Goléah?

"How far do you estimate we are from Goléah?" Captain Hardigan asked the engineer.

"Twelve or fifteen kilometers."

"We've covered half the distance, then?"

"I think so."

How slowly the hours went by during that night of April 26–27! The engineer and the officer must have envied their comrades, whose weariness plunged them into a sleep so deep that not even a thunderclap would have awakened them. Despite the highly charged atmosphere, no storm had yet broken. Nevertheless, although the breeze had subsided, muffled noises began to disturb the silence.

It was about midnight when these sounds, now growing sharper, first became audible to Captain Hardigan and Mr. de Schaller.

"What's going on?" asked the captain, getting to his feet under the tree against which he had been sitting.

"I'm not quite sure," replied the engineer. "Is it a storm in the distance? No, I think some of these rumblings are coming through the ground."

There was nothing surprising about that. When the chotts were originally being surveyed, Captain Roudaire had noticed that the surface of the Djerid experienced vibrations of considerable magnitude, which interfered with his work on a number of occasions. These vibrations were probably caused by some seismic phenomenon occurring in the lower layers of the earth's surface. There was reason to suspect that a similar disturbance of this type was about to affect this hofra, one of the lowest depressions in the Melrir.[1]

The corporal, Mr. François, and the two spahis were awakened by the underground rumblings, which were growing in intensity.

Just then, Ace-of-Hearts began to show signs of extreme agitation. He went down several times to the foot of the tell, and when he came back up for the last time, he was soaking wet, as if he had just emerged from deep water.

"Yes, it's water—water!" exclaimed the corporal. "And it seems to be sea water! He's not covered with blood, as he was the other night."

Ace-of-Hearts shook himself, splashing water all over Pistache.

The hill, which Captain Hardigan and his men had reached without having to wade, was now surrounded by water deep enough for the dog to dive into.

Had the ground level suddenly dropped, bringing the water from the lower layers up to the surface and transforming the tell into a little island?

How impatiently and apprehensively the fugitives waited for dawn to come! To go back to sleep was impossible. The subterranean disturbances were increasing in intensity, as if Plutonian and Neptunian forces were struggling against each other far below the hollows in the chott, which were gradually undergoing a change. Sometimes the tremors were so violent that the trees bent over, as they would in a heavy storm, and threatened to become uprooted.

At one point, the corporal went down to the bottom of the tell and found water at its base to a depth of two or three feet.

Where was that water coming from? Had the earth tremors pushed it through the subterranean marl and up to the surface of the chott? Had these tremors caused the chott's surface to drop well below the level of the Mediterranean?

These were the questions that Mr. de Schaller kept asking himself. Was it likely that he would be able to answer it when the sun rose once more above the horizon?

As dawn slowly approached, the distant rumblings that seemed to come from the east continued and grew stronger. At regular intervals there were tremors powerful enough to make the tell shudder on its base. The water was now rushing in and crashing against the tell with a sound like that of the surf from a rising tide breaking on the rocks of the seashore.

At one point, while they were all trying to interpret with their ears what their eyes could not see, Captain Hardigan asked, "Is it possible that the Melrir has been filled with water that has risen to the surface from underground?"

"That's highly unlikely," replied Mr. de Schaller, "but I think there's a more plausible explanation."

"And what is that?"

"That water from the gulf has come in from Gabès and flooded this whole section of the Djerid."

"In that case," exclaimed the corporal, "there's only one way out for us now! We'll have to swim for it!"

Day was finally about to break, but the few glimmers of light that appeared to the east of the chott were very pale, as if the horizon were screened by a heavy curtain of fog.

Standing under the trees, they all stared in that direction, waiting for the first light of dawn to show them what their current situation was. But their hopes were soon to be dashed by a stroke of bad luck!

xvii ━━━━ Conclusion

The dune was enveloped in a mist so thick that the first rays of the sun could not dispel it. Visibility was less than four paces, and the branches of the trees were shrouded in the heavy vapor.

"Obviously," exclaimed the corporal, "the devil is mixed up in this."

"I'm inclined to believe you," replied Mr. François.

There was reason to hope, however, that in a few hours, as the sun approached the zenith and shone down more strongly, the mist would finally disappear, and a large part of the Melrir would come into view.

There was nothing to do but wait patiently. Although it was more necessary than ever to conserve their limited provisions, they had to eat something. In fact, there was only enough food left for two days. They quenched their thirst as best they could with the brackish water lying at the base of the tell.

Three hours went by under these conditions. The rumblings had gradually diminished. A brisk breeze was springing up and rattling the branches of the trees, and the thick mass of fog, with help from the sun, would soon dissipate.

At last the wreaths of fog began to clear away around the tell, revealing the skeletons of trees and their branches. "Skeleton" is indeed the right word, for there was nothing there but dead trees—neither fruit nor leaves. Then a gust of wind drove the fog completely away toward the west.

The vast expanse of the Melrir was revealed.

The bottom of the depression had collapsed, and the surface of the chott was partly flooded. The tell was now surrounded by a ring of water some fifty meters wide. On the higher ground beyond, the crystalline plain reappeared. In the hollows, the water reflected back the rays of the sun between the long, sandy plains, which were high enough to stay dry.

Captain Hardigan and the engineer scanned the horizon in every direction. "Some huge seismic phenomenon has definitely just occurred," said Mr. de Schaller. "The bed of the chott has sunk and been flooded by water coming up from under ground."

"Well then," said the captain, "we have to leave right away, before it's impossible to go anywhere."

They were all about to start down from the tell when their eyes met a terrifying spectacle, which held them riveted to the spot.

Half a league to the north, a herd of animals was running at top speed, coming from the northeast. About a hundred wild beasts and ruminants—lions, gazelles, antelopes, wild sheep, buffaloes—were running for their lives toward the western part of the Melrir. They must have been seized by some common terror, which overcame the ferocity of some and the timidity of others. In their extreme panic, they could think only of escaping from the danger that had caused this mass stampede of all the quadrupeds in the Djerid.

"What's going on there?" Corporal Pistache kept repeating.

"Yes," asked Captain Hardigan, "what is it?"

The engineer, to whom this question was addressed, had no answer.

"Are those animals going to head this way?" shouted one of the spahis.

"How can we escape, if they do?" asked another.

By this time, the herd was no more than a kilometer away, and approaching with express-train speed. But apparently the animals, in their wild flight, had not noticed the six men who had taken refuge on the tell. Changing direction, they veered off to the left and finally disappeared in a cloud of dust.

When, on Captain Hardigan's order, his comrades lay down under the trees in order not to be seen, they saw flocks of flamingoes taking flight in the distance and thousands of birds fleeing toward the banks of the Melrir.

"What's this all about?" Corporal Pistache asked again.

By four o'clock in the afternoon the cause of this strange exodus became apparent.

To the east, an expanse of liquid was beginning to spread over the surface of the chott, and the sandy plain was soon entirely covered by a shallow layer of water. The efflorescent salt crystals had gradually disappeared, as far as the eye could see, and the rays of the sun were now reflected back by a vast lake.

"Does this mean that the water from the gulf has entered the Melrir?" asked the captain.

"I'm sure it does," replied the engineer. "Those subterranean rumblings we heard came from an earthquake. There have been huge underground disturbances, causing the bed of the Melrir, and perhaps this whole eastern part of the Djerid, to sink. The sea must have broken through what was left of the Gabès ridge and flooded it all the way to the Melrir."

This explanation was undoubtedly correct. They were experiencing a seismic phenomenon on a scale that they had not yet grasped. As a result of these disturbances, it was possible that the Sahara Sea had come into being all by itself, and was bigger than Captain Roudaire had ever dreamed.

But now another sound, still far off in the distance, filled the air.

This time the sound traveled not through the ground, but through the air, and it grew louder and louder.

Suddenly, to the northeast, a cloud of dust arose, and from this cloud soon emerged a band of horsemen, galloping at top speed, just as the animals had done.

"Hadjar!" exclaimed Captain Hardigan.

Yes, it was the Tuareg chieftain. He and his comrades were riding at breakneck speed to escape a monstrous, swirling wall of water that was rising up behind them and spreading out over the entire breadth of the chott.

Two hours had elapsed since the animals had gone by, and the sun was about to set. In the midst of the growing flood, the tell was now the only hope of safety for Hadjar's band—an island in the middle of this new sea.

Hadjar and the Tuareg, who were not more than a kilometer away, had surely seen it and were heading toward it at a frenzied

Hadjar and the Tuareg engulfed by the flood

gallop. Would they manage to reach it ahead of the wall of water? What would happen then to the fugitives who had, since the evening before, found refuge under this small clump of trees?

But the mountain of water was moving even faster. It was a veritable tidal wave, a succession of foaming billows of irresistible power, and advancing at such speed that the fastest horse could not have outrun it.

Captain Hardigan and his friends now witnessed a terrible sight: the hundred men were suddenly overtaken by the wall of water and disappeared into its foaming flood! The entire jumbled mass of horses and horsemen were swallowed up! The fading twilight revealed nothing but dead bodies, carried along by the enormous wave toward the western end of the Melrir.[1]

When the sun finished its course that day, it set behind a watery horizon.

What a night it was for the fugitives! After being spared an encounter with the wild beasts and then with the Tuareg, they now feared that their sanctuary would be submerged!

It was impossible to leave, and they listened with terror to the sound of breaking surf, as the water rose, little by little, in the total darkness.

It is not hard to imagine what that night was like, with the constant sound of water rolling along before a strong easterly breeze. The air was filled with the cries of countless sea birds, now flying over the surface of the Melrir.

When morning came at last, the rising water seemed to have crested. It had filled the chott to the brim, but had not covered the top of the little hill.

There was nothing on the surface of that vast watery plain. The fugitives' situation seemed desperate. They had no food left to see them through that day, and no way of obtaining any more on their barren island. Escape? But how? Build a raft with the trees and set sail on it? But how could they cut them down? And would they be able to steer such a raft? With the fierce winds that were blowing, they would be powerless to struggle against the currents that would drive them away from the shores of the Melrir.

Captain Hardigan took a long look at the chott. "It won't be easy to get ourselves out of this," he said.

"Well, sir," said Corporal Pistache, "maybe help will arrive. You never know."

The day went by with no change in their predicament. The Melrir had become a lake, and so, no doubt, had the Rharsa. And how far had the flooding extended? Had the banks of the canal been broken down along its entire length?

Had Nefta and other villages been destroyed, either by the earthquake or by the huge wave that had followed it? Had the disaster spread over that whole section of the Djerid, as far as the Gulf of Gabès?

Evening was approaching, however, and Captain Hardigan and his men had nothing left to eat. As they had noticed when they set foot on the tell, there was no fruit hanging from the branches of the trees, nothing but dead wood. Not a single bird, not even one of the flocks of habibis that flew by in the distance, came down to light on their island, not even a starling, which might have brought some relief to a hunger-wracked stomach. There were already a few fish beneath the surface of the new body of water, but Corporal Pistache's attempts to catch them were in vain. And how could they quench their thirst, now that the water was as salty as the sea itself?

About half past seven, just as the last rays of the sun were fading away, Mr. François, who was looking off to the northeast, said, in a completely emotionless tone of voice, "I see smoke."

"Smoke?" exclaimed Corporal Pistache.

"Smoke," repeated Mr. François.

Every eye turned in the direction to which he was pointing.

There was no doubt about it. The wind was definitely blowing smoke in the direction of the tell. It could be seen quite distinctly.

The fugitives were silent, gripped by the fear that the smoke might disappear, that the ship from which it was coming might turn out to sea, away from the tell.

The engineer's explanation had been correct, then. His predictions had come true!

During the night of April 26–27, the waters of the Mediterranean had spread out over the eastern part of the Djerid. There was now a link between the Gulf of Gabès and the Melrir, and a navigable link at that, since a vessel had been able to follow this new seaway across the region of sebkha and chotts, no doubt along the line of the canal.

Twenty-five minutes after the ship's presence had been noted, its smokestack could be seen on the horizon, and then its hull, the hull of the first ship to ply the waters of the new lake.

"Signals!" shouted one of the spahis. "Let's make signals!"

But how could Captain Hardigan signal the presence of the fugitives on the narrow summit of that little island? Was the hill even high enough for the crew to notice it? And the ship they had spotted was still more than two leagues off to the northeast.

To make matters worse, night had now fallen after a short period of twilight, and in the darkness the smoke was soon no longer visible.

The spahi was now beside himself, and began to gesture despairingly and shout, "We're done for!"

"On the contrary," replied Captain Hardigan, "we're saved. Our signals could not have been seen by daylight, but they will be seen at night. Set fire to the trees."

Corporal Pistache positively roared in reply. "Yes, sir! Set fire to the trees. They'll blaze up like matches."

In an instant, someone had struck a light. Fallen branches were piled up at the foot of the tree trunks. A flame shot out, rising to the topmost branches, and bright flashes dispelled the darkness around the island.

"If they don't see our bonfire," exclaimed Pistache, "it will mean that everyone on board that ship is blind."

Within an hour, however, the blaze had died down. All that dead wood had been quickly consumed, and when the last flames went out, no one knew whether the ship had turned toward the tell, for it did not even fire a cannon to announce its presence.

The island was now enveloped in total darkness. The night went on, and no steam whistle screamed, no rumble from a propeller or paddle wheel beating the waters of the chott reached the ears of the fugitives.

"It's there! It's there!" shouted Pistache with the first light of day, while Ace-of-Hearts barked with all his might.

The corporal was not mistaken.

Two miles off, a small vessel flying the French flag was lying at anchor. When the flames had lit up the unknown island, the captain had changed course and steered southwest, but since the island could no longer be seen after the flames went out, he had prudently dropped anchor to wait until morning.

Captain Hardigan and his friends shouted, and soon heard voices shouting back, among which they recognized those of Lieutenant Villette and Sergeant Nicol, who were approaching in a launch.

The ship was the small, steam-powered frigate *Benassir*, from Tunis. It had arrived at Gabès six days earlier, and was the first vessel to strike out boldly onto the newly created sea.

A few minutes later, the launch reached the base of the tell that had been the salvation of the fugitives. Captain Hardigan and the lieutenant embraced warmly, as did the sergeant and Corporal Pistache, while Ace-of-Hearts leaped into the arms of his master. Nicol could hardly recognize Mr. François with his beard and moustache. The latter's first priority, when he got on board the *Benassir*, would be to shave.

Here is what had happened during the previous forty-eight hours.

The entire eastern part of the Djerid, between the gulf and the Melrir, had been transformed by an earthquake, which had broken open the Gabès ridge and caused the ground to sink over an expanse of more than two hundred kilometers. The water from the Gulf of Gabès had rushed into the canal, which was not big enough to contain it, and poured into the region of the sebkha and chotts, flooding not only the whole of the Rharsa but also the vast depression of Fejey-Tris. Fortunately, La Hammâ, Nefta, Tozeur, and other villages located on high ground had not been engulfed. They would henceforth appear on the map as seaports.

The Hinguiz had become a large island in the center of the Melrir. But, although Zenfig had been spared, Hadjar and his band of brigands, overtaken by the tidal wave, had perished to the last man.

As for Lieutenant Villette, he had tried in vain to find Captain Hardigan and his friends. After searching the area around the Melrir in the direction of the construction site at Kilometer 347, where the workers had not reappeared (Pointar's expedition

203

having waited for an escort to be sent out from Biskra), he had gone to Nefta to organize an expedition among the various Tuareg tribes.

There he had met the drivers and the two spahis who, thanks to a lucky turn of events, had escaped their leaders' fate.

Lieutenant Villette was in that town at the time of the earthquake and was still there when the captain of the *Benassir*, which had left Gabès as soon as the flooding made it possible, came to seek information about the Rharsa and the Melrir.

The lieutenant immediately went to see the captain of the frigate, who, when he was made aware of the situation, offered free passage to him and the sergeant. The first priority was to set out in search of Captain Hardigan, Mr. de Schaller, and their friends. And so the *Benassir* steamed through the Rharsa at top speed and into the Melrir, to search through the oases that were still above water and in the Farfaria.

During the second night of his voyage on the Melrir, the captain had seen the bonfire and headed in the direction of the tell. But in those unfamiliar waters, and with only a small crew, he had decided, despite Villette's urging, to wait until morning before approaching the island. Now the fugitives were all on board, safe and sound.

As soon as its new passengers were on board, the frigate headed back to Tozeur, where the captain intended to leave them and send a report to his superiors by the quickest means possible before resuming his voyage of reconnaissance to the farthest reaches of the Melrir.

When Mr. de Schaller and his comrades disembarked at Tozeur, Captain Hardigan was reunited with the men of his detachment. How delighted they were to see him again! Even the long-lost Biskra column was represented by a dispatch via Tunis, in which Pointar, who had had to go back to Biskra with his men, requested new orders. It was there, too, that Giddup, the old brother, saw Ace-of-Hearts again. The expressions of delight exchanged between the two friends defied description.

Around them all swarmed an enthusiastic throng, still excited by all the events surrounding the cataclysm, crowding around the first explorers of the new sea.

Mr. de Schaller and the company agent

Suddenly the engineer came face to face with a stranger who had elbowed his way through the crowd and now bowed very low and said to him, in a strong foreign accent, "Do I have the honor of speaking to Mr. de Schaller in person?"

"Yes, I believe you do."

"In that case, sir, I have the honor of informing you that, by the terms of an official and duly authenticated power of attorney, signed in the presence of a notary, invested with the legality of the president of the court of first instance within the jurisdiction of the head office of the France-Overseas Company and stamped in the margin, at the office of the resident-general of France in Tunis, with the following note: 'Registered folio 200 overleaf, square 12, received 3.75 francs, including tax,' signature illegible, I am the agent of the liquidators of the aforementioned company, with full authority, including the power to negotiate and, if necessary, to compromise—the said powers well and duly ratified. You will not be surprised, sir, if, acting in this capacity and on their behalf, I call on you to give an accounting of the construction begun by the company, which you had entered into an agreement to make use of."[2]

In the joyful exuberance that was gradually overwhelming him, now that he had been reunited with his friends and had seen his work completed in such a fantastic way, this cold, methodical man, so self-controlled in the most difficult situations, became once again, for a moment, the well-known jester of years gone by, the top student of his class, who used to haze with devilish verve the "newbie" students in the École Centrale's courtyard. And there was a note of impudence in his voice when he replied, "Mr. Agent with full authority, let me give you a bit of friendly advice. You would do better to buy shares in the Sahara Sea Company."

As he went on his way, surrounded on all sides by cheers and congratulations, Mr. de Schaller was already working out a cost estimate of the new construction, which would appear in the report he intended to send to the company's directors that very day.

THE END

 Notes

Throughout these notes, each Verne novel will be identified by its most commonly recognized English title. For a listing of the alternate English titles that have been used for each novel, see the "Works of Jules Verne" section in the bibliography.

Introduction

1. The only previous appearance of Verne's *L'Invasion de la mer* in English, discovered by "literary detective" Victor Berch in 1999, was a very loose adaptation published as a serial in the Sunday supplement of the *Boston American* newspaper on August 6 and 13, 1905. Titled "Captain Hardizan [*sic*]: A Stirring Tragedy-Romance" and edited and translated by Oswald Mathew, this story contained seven chapters (Verne's had seventeen) and, in contrast to the original novel, its focus was shifted from the construction of an inland sea in the Algerian Sahara to a rather insipid love story between the heroic captain and a girl named Marie. See Andrew Nash's account of this text in *"Invasion of the Sea: 1905 Translation," Extraordinary Voyages: The Newsletter of the North American Jules Verne Society* 6.1 (Nov. 1999): 1–3.

2. As was the case with many of Jules Verne's novels, *L'Invasion de la mer* was first published in serial format in Hetzel's *Magasin d'Éducation et de Récréation* (Jan. 1–Aug. 1, 1905) and, shortly thereafter, as a book. Although Verne, at age seventy-seven, lived to witness the magazine publication of the first few chapters of this novel, he died on March 24 before the book version appeared in November. As revealed in the last three letters to his editor before his death (the third one accompanied by proofs of the novel), Verne apparently decided on its final title at the last moment:

The title Sahara Sea was only provisional. . . . As for me, I was thinking of something simple like *A New Sea in the Sahara*. We'll discuss all this. . . . (Dec. 7, 1904)

I think the title that I suggested to you, *A New Sea in the Sahara*, is very appropriate and very simple and works the best. (Dec. 8, 1904)

Today I am mailing you two packages, the proofs of *Invasion of the Sea*. If you have the time to return them to me, I'll look at them again. If not, please be sure that the corrections are done well. . . . (Dec. 12, 1904)

These letters are reprinted in Charles-Noël Martin's preface to the 1970 Editions Rencontre version of *L'Invasion de la mer* (x–xii).

3. As recent scholarship has convincingly shown, all of Verne's posthumous novels and anthologies—*Le Phare du bout du monde* (1905, The Lighthouse at the End of the World), *Le Volcan d'or* (1906, The Golden Volcano), *L'Agence Thompson and Co.* (1907, The Thompson Travel Agency), *La Chasse au météore* (1908, The Hunt for the Meteor), *Le Pilote du Danube* (1908, The Danube Pilot), *Les Naufragés du Jonathan* (1910, The Survivors of the Jonathan), *Le Secret du Wilhelm Storitz* (1910, The Secret of Wilhelm Storitz), the short story collection *Hier et demain* (1910, Yesterday and Tomorrow [including the oft-reprinted tales of "In the Year 2889" and "The Eternal Adam"]), and *L'Étonnante aventure de la mission Barsac* (1919, The Amazing Adventure of the Barsac Mission)—were, in part or whole, actually written by Verne's son Michel. For details concerning the modifications to Verne's posthumous works, see the seminal studies by French scholars Piero Gondolo della Riva ("A propos des oeuvres postumes de Jules Verne." *Europe* 595–96 [1978]: 73–82) and Olivier Dumas (*Jules Verne* [Lyon: La Manufacture, 1988]), partially recapped in chapter 39, "Death and Resurrection," in Herbert Lottman's biography, *Jules Verne: An Exploratory Biography* [New York: St. Martin's, 1996]). It should be pointed out that, since 1985, the Société Jules Verne in France, under the leadership of its president, Dumas, has published the "original versions" of many of these novels, taken directly from the author's surviving manuscripts. And a few, such as the Société editions of *Le Volcan d'or* and *En Magellanie* (Verne's original title for *Les Naufragés du Jonathan*), have now become the standard French texts of these posthumous works; they are commonly available today as trade paperbacks (L'Archipel, Gallimard/Folio) in most Parisian bookstores.

4. For a brief overview of the facts versus myths of Verne's life and works, see the introduction to Arthur B. Evans, *Jules Verne Rediscovered: Didacticism and the Scientific Novel* (Westport, Conn.: Greenwood, 1988), 1–5, as well as Evans and Ron Miller, "Jules Verne: Misunderstood Visionary," *Scientific American* (April 1997): 92–97. The latter is available online at http://www.sciam.com/0497issue/0497evans.html.

5. In fact, according to UNESCO's *Index Translationum*, Verne ranks as the fifth most-translated author of all time (after the collective works of Walt Disney Productions, Agatha Christie, the Bible, and Lenin). Throughout the world, more than twenty-seven hundred translations and thirty million copies of Verne's works have appeared in over forty different languages—three times more translations than those of Shakespeare's works and nine times more than those of the next-ranking French author, Antoine de Saint-Exupéry. The *Index Translationum* is available online at www.unesco.org/general/eng/infoserv/db/xtra—form.html.

6. Marc Angenot, "Science Fiction in France before Jules Verne," *Science Fiction Studies* 5.1 (March 1978): 64.

7. See Arthur B. Evans, "Science Fiction in France: A Brief History and Selective Bibliography," *Science Fiction Studies* 16.3 (Nov. 1989): 254–76, 338–65 256–58, and especially Paul Alkon's *Science Fiction Before 1900* (New York: Twayne, 1994), 1–21, 65–100.

8. For additional information on the publishing trends of the 1890s and early 1900s, consult Sam Moskowitz, *Science Fiction by Gaslight* (New York: World, 1968), and Brian Stableford, *Scientific Romance in Britain, 1890–1950* (London: Fourth Estate, 1985).

9. It is interesting to witness Verne's reaction to the growing popularity of his British counterpart H. G. Wells. In 1903 and 1904, during two separate interviews, Verne openly criticized Wells's novels as wholly lacking in scientific verisimilitude:

"We do not proceed in the same manner. It occurs to me that his stories do not repose on very scientific bases. No, there is no rapport between his work and mine. I make use of physics. He invents. I go to the moon in a cannonball discharged from a cannon. Here there is no invention. He goes to the Mars [*sic*] in an airship which he constructs of a metal which does away with the law of gravitation. *Ça c'est très joli*," cried Monsieur Verne in an animated way. "But show me this metal. Let him produce it." (Robert H. Sherard, "Jules Verne Revisited," *T.P.'s Weekly* [Oct. 9, 1903]: 589)

Some of my friends have suggested to me that his work is on somewhat similar lines to my own, but here, I think, they err. I consider him, as a purely imaginative writer, to be deserving of very high praise, but our methods are entirely different. I have always made a point in my romances of basing my so-called inventions upon a groundwork of actual fact, and of using in their construction methods and materials which are not entirely beyond the pale of contemporary engineering skill and knowledge. . . .

The creations of Mr. Wells, on the other hand, belong unreservedly to an age and degree of scientific knowledge far removed from the present, though I will not say entirely beyond the limits of the possible. Not only does he evolve his constructions entirely from the realm of the imagination, but he also evolves the materials of which he builds them. See, for example, his story "The First Men in the Moon." You will remember that here he introduces an entirely new anti-gravitational substance, about whose mode of preparation or actual chemical composition we are not given the slightest clue, nor does our reference to our present scientific knowledge enable us for a moment to predict a method by which such a result might be achieved. (Gordon Jones, "Jules Verne at Home," *Temple Bar* 129 [1904]: 669–70)

10. For a more detailed analysis of the semiotic evolution (didactic to hermeneutic) of this brand of scientific-literary discourse in France, see Arthur B. Evans, "Science Fiction vs. Scientific Fiction in France: From Jules Verne to J.-H. Rosny Aîné," *Science Fiction Studies* 15.1 (1988): 1–11.

11. See Charles-Noël Martin, *La Vie et l'oeuvre de Jules Verne* (Paris: Michel de l'Ormeraie, 1978), 280–81.

12. Brian Taves and Stephen Michaluk Jr., eds., *The Jules Verne Encyclopedia* (Lanham, Md.: Scarecrow, 1996), 16.

13. Walter James Miller, "Foreword," *The Annotated Jules Verne: Twenty Thousand Leagues under the Sea* (New York: Crowell, 1976), ix.

14. See Arthur B. Evans, "Jules Verne and the French Literary Canon," in *Jules Verne: Narratives of Modernity*, ed. Edward J. Smyth (Liverpool: Liverpool University Press, 2000).

15. Marc Angenot, "Jules Verne and French Literary Criticism I," *Science Fiction Studies* 1.1 (1973): 37.

16. One exception to the general poverty of pre-1980 English-language criticism on Verne is Peter Costello's fine monograph, *Jules Verne: Inventor of Science Fiction*, published in 1978.

17. Among the modern retranslations of Verne's *Voyages Extraordinaires* into English, the following are especially noteworthy: Edward Baxter's *Family Without a Name* (Toronto: NC Press, 1982) and *The Fur Country* (Toronto: NC Press, 1987); Jacqueline and Robert Baldick's *From the Earth to the Moon* (New York: Dent, 1970); Robert Baldick's *Journey to the Center of the Earth* (New York: Penguin, 1965); William Butcher's *Journey to the Centre of the Earth* (Oxford: Oxford University Press, 1992), *Around the World in Eighty Days* (Oxford: Oxford University Press, 1995), and *Twenty Thousand Leagues under the Sea* (Oxford: Oxford University Press, 1998); Emanuel Mickel's *Twenty Thousand Leagues under the Sea* (Bloomington: Indiana University Press, 1992); Walter James Miller and Frederick Paul Walter's *Twenty Thousand Leagues under the Sea* (Annapolis, Md.: Naval Institute Press, 1993); and Harold Salemson's *From the Earth to the Moon* and *Around the Moon* (New York: Heritage, 1970).

18. Andrew Martin at Cambridge in 1982 (published as *The Knowledge of Ignorance: From Genesis to Jules Verne* [Cambridge University Press, 1985]), William Butcher at Queen Mary College in 1985 (published as *Verne's Journey to the Centre of the Self* [London: Macmillan, 1990]), and myself at Columbia University in 1985 (published as *Jules Verne Rediscovered* [Westport, Conn.: Greenwood, 1988]).

19. Walter James Miller, "Jules Verne in America: A Translator's Preface," in Verne, *Twenty Thousand Leagues under the Sea* (New York: Washington Square, 1965), vii.

20. Robert H. Sherard, "Jules Verne at Home," *McClure's Magazine* (Jan. 1894), 120–21.

21. For additional information on this recurring dream of creating a "Saharan Sea," consult René Letolle and Hocine Bendjoudi, *Histoires d'une mer au Sahara: Utopies et politique* (Paris: L'Harmattan, 1997). As an indication of the continuing power of this idea even today, see Grove Koger, "The Great Saharan Sea: An Idea Whose Time Has Come?" *Mercator's World* 4.2 (Mar.–Apr. 1999): 18–23.

22. In chapter 4 of *Invasion of the Sea*, Verne cites one source that he used for documenting this novel: Maxime Hélène (pseudonym of Maxime Vuillaume, 1844–1925), "La Mer intérieure d'Algérie," *La Nature* 10.11 (1882): 22–24, 35–38. Other scientific sources probably used by Verne—in addition to general reference books on geography by Élisée Reclus, Vivien de Saint-Martin, Malte-Brun, and Auguste Petermann, which he is known to have consulted regularly—include Henri Duveyrier's published reports to the French Geographical Society and his books on such topics as *Les Touaregs du Nord* (1864), and *La Tunisie* (1881), as well as some works by Louis Figuier, such as *Les Nouvelles Conquêtes de la science* (1885), which features an article entitled "La mer intérieure africaine." An extensive bibliography of materials pertaining to the "Sahara Sea" is contained in Letolle and Bendjoudi, *Histoires d'une mer au Sahara*.

23. Jules Verne, *Hector Servadac*, trans. Ellen E. Frewer (New York: Scribner's, 1906), 71–72, 91. It is interesting to note that at least two other English translations exist for this particular novel: one by Edward Roth (*To the Sun?* and *Off on a Comet!* [Philadelphia: Claxton, Remsen, Haffelfinger, 1877–78]) and one by I. O. Evans (London: Arco, 1965). In the latter, a highly abridged edition, this particular passage was deleted in its entirety. In the former, Roth—who is known for his gratuitous "embroidering" of Verne's original texts—added the following lines:

> . . . evaporated by the fiery action of a Lybian [*sic*] sun. To turn it once more into a sea, therefore, nothing more was necessary than to cut through the narrow isthmus forming the obstruction and thereby restore the communication. To show the feasibility of the project, and probably also to excite more confidence among the shareholders, Lesseps, the famous originator and successful engineer of the Suez Canal, a kindred work, had employed a few hundred men under Captain Roudaire to do the preliminary work of cutting a narrow channel through the rocky peninsula that separated Lake Melghigh from the Gulf of Cabes [*sic*]. (86)

It is obvious that Roth, the American translator, was also well aware of Captain Roudaire's ongoing efforts to create a "Saharan Sea" in Algeria in the late 1870s. And, much like Verne's own extrapolation of history, Roth too assumes that this project would be successfully completed one day.

24. Literary scholars have often discussed the recurring theme of circles, circularity, and circulation in Verne's *Voyages Extraordinaires*. See, for instance, the studies by Marc Angenot, "Jules Verne: The Last Happy Utopianist," in *Science Fiction*, ed. Patrick Parrinder (New York: Longman, 1979), 18–32; Alain Buisine, "Circulations en tous genres," *Europe* 595–96 (1978): 48–56; and Michel Serres, *Jouvences sur Jules Verne* (Paris: Editions de Minuit, 1974).

25. Lottman, *Jules Verne*, 322.

26. For example, Francis Lacassin, in his introduction to a French reprint of *L'Invasion de la mer* (Paris: UGE "10/18," 1978), argues that Verne secretly admired Hadjar, leader of the Tuareg, and actually sympathized

with the plight of his people (11–13). But Georges-Pierre Hourant, in "L'Algérie dans l'oeuvre de Jules Verne," *Bulletin de la Société Jules Verne* 21.82 (Apr.–June 1987): 21–24, strongly disagrees and insists that Verne portrayed the Tuareg as the thieves, murderers, and slave traders they truly were during this historical period.

Chapter I

1. In the French edition, Verne often refers to this bay off the Tunisian coastal city of Gabès as the "Petite-Syrte," derived from its original Latin name, "Sirtis Parva" or "Syrta Minor." Today it is commonly known as the Gulf of Gabès.

2. The Tuareg are a nomadic Berber people of the Sahara region who, according to estimates, currently number more than one million. Their presence in North Africa was first recorded by the Greek historian Herodotus in the fifth century B.C. For thousands of years, their camel caravans (and their raids on caravans) dominated all trans-Saharan trade; the Tuareg sold items of gold and ivory as well as slaves from western Africa to merchants from Europe and the Middle East. Although not Arab, most Tuareg traditionally practice a form of Islam. Women, in contrast to the men, do not wear veils and are highly respected in Tuareg society, where social status depends on matrilineal descent. Throughout the nineteenth century, the fiercely independent Tuareg long resisted European (especially French) colonization efforts in North Africa. They were finally subdued by the French military in the 1870s and 1880s.

3. The chotts are vast, dry salt lakes located in south-central Tunisia and extending hundreds of kilometers west into Algeria.. The four principal chotts of this region are the Chott Fedjedj (also spelled Fedjadj or Fedjej), Chott Djerid (Jerid or Jarid), Chott Rharsa (Gharsa), and Chott Melrir (Melrhir). Together they constitute some eight thousand square kilometers of barren desert (punctuated by an occasional date-palm oasis), stretching from the eastern port city of Gabès on the Tunisian coast to the eastern Algerian town of Biskra. It was in this forbidding land that many desert scenes were filmed for movies such as *Star Wars* and *The English Patient*.

4. The presence of such French military posts, responsible for maintaining law and order throughout this region, reflects the true political situation during this historical period. From its conquest of Algeria in 1830–47 to its eventual annexation of Tunisia as a protectorate in 1881, France and its colonialist governmental policies dominated much of North Africa throughout the nineteenth century. Native Algerians (but not French settlers) were under the strict military rule of a "governor-general"—an appointed French Army officer—until well into the 1880s. Interestingly, during this period the highly romantic (but wholly self-serving) mythology surrounding the French Foreign Legion was also born.

Chapter II

1. Captain Roudaire was neither the first nor the last to propose the creation of an inland sea in a desert area. For example, famous explorer and statesman John C. Fremont (1813–1890) suggested constructing a canal to link the Colorado River with a dry lakebed in southern California (which eventually became the Salton Sea in 1905–7) and, in the late 1870s, the British engineer D. Mackenzie proposed flooding large tracts of desert land in western Morocco from a canal to be built near the port of Tarfaya (see René Letolle and Hocine Bendjoudi, *Histoires d'une mer au Sahara: Utopies et politique* [Paris: L'Harmattan, 1997], 12–13, 217–21). Moreover, even in the late twentieth century, many plans to build canals or pipelines for the creation of inland seas continue to be proposed—consider, for instance, those suggested for the vast Egyptian lowland of Qattara (see www.hydroconsult. se/eia.html) or the Lake Eyre Basin in southern Australia (see www.cs. uwa.edu/~skot/bigschemes/lake_eyre/).

2. A "bey" is the title originally used to designate a provincial governor in the Ottoman Empire. In Tunisia, during its years as a French protectorate (1881–1956), the bey of Tunis was still, in theory, absolute monarch of the country and responsible for all domestic matters. But the appointed French resident-general controlled all questions of foreign policy and finance. In contrast to the much harsher French occupation of Algeria, native Tunisians continued to be subjects of the reigning bey; Islam remained the official religion of the country and Arabic one of its official languages; and confiscation and colonization of native lands was much less prevalent.

3. Verne's original French text misspells Laing's name as "Paing" (a typo no doubt due to the author's failing health and cataract-blurred vision). Alexander Gordon Laing (1793–1826) was a major in the British army and, in addition to his discovery of the headwaters of the Niger, was the first European to cross the Sahara and to visit the ancient African city of Timbuktu, where he soon met his death at the hands of a local Tuareg tribe. In Verne's *Five Weeks in a Balloon*, Samuel Fergusson describes Laing's heroic exploits as follows:

> In 1822, Major Laing explored the entire region of Western Africa adjacent to the British possessions. It was he who discovered the sources of the Niger; and, according to his documents, the spring from which flows this immense river is less than 2 feet across. . . .
>
> . . . Five years later, it was Major Laing who crossed the Sahara, penetrated as far as Timbuktu, and died a few miles above that city, strangled by the Oulad-Shiman, who wanted to force him to convert to Islam. (*Cinq semaines en ballon* [Paris: Livre de poche, 1966], 319)

Although he could not have known (historians did not learn the full details of Laing's fate until the early 1920s), Verne's account of Laing's journey and death are partially in error here: Laing actually died a few miles north of Timbuktu on September 26, 1826 (not 1827), by stabbing and decapitation (not strangulation). But the motive for his murder was indeed religious hatred. According to a reconstructed record of Laing's journey published by the French explorer Bonnel de Mezières in 1912, the Tuareg not only massacred Laing and his companions but also destroyed all Laing's possessions—his scientific observations made during his crossing of the Sahara, the first street map ever made of Timbuktu, copies of rare manuscripts he had consulted, etc.—because he was a Christian "infidel."

4. At the time of his death, Paul-François-Xavier Flatters (1832–1881), a lieutenant-colonel in the French army, was leading a reconnaissance mission to survey the possibility of a Trans-Saharan railway—a project that was abandoned soon after the massacre of the Flatters expedition and not completed until the mid-twentieth century. Jules Verne referred to this unfinished rail line across the sands of the Sahara in his 1886 novel *Clipper of the Clouds* (alternately titled *Robur the Conqueror* or *Around the World in a Flying Machine*):

> During the following hours the air-ship turned to the southwest, crossing the route to El Golea, discovered in 1859 by the intrepid Frenchman, Duveyrier. The darkness was profound. Nothing could be seen of the Trans-Saharan Railway then in course of construction, a long band of iron reaching from Algiers to Timbuctoo, through Laghouat, Gardaia, and finally reaching the Gulf of Guinea. Crossing the Tropic of Cancer, the "Albatross" entered the equatorial regions. (*A Trip Around the World in a Flying Machine* [Chicago: Donahue, n.d.], 112)

5. The Belgian explorer Carl Steinx did not actually exist, and Verne's account of his massacre at the hands of the Tuareg is pure fiction. But, according to Volker Dehs, in an article entitled "Dernières impressions d'Afrique" (*Le Monde*, Dec. 5, 1988, 9), this episode "correspond exactement au massacre réel de Paul Crampel, relaté dans le deuxième chapitre de *Voyage d'études*" ("corresponds exactly to the real massacre of Paul Crampel, recounted in the second chapter of *Study Trip*"). At the time of Verne's death, *Study Trip* was one of his surviving rough-draft manuscripts: approximately four chapters, the beginning of a fifth, and some notes. Verne's son Michel completed the novel, and it was eventually published in serial format in the French newspaper *Le Matin* in 1914—now retitled *Étonnante adventure de la mission Barsac* (The Amazing Adventure of the Barsac Mission). In 1919, it was reprinted by Hachette (who had purchased from Hetzel the rights to publish Verne's works) as the final novel in Verne's *Voyages Extraordinaires*. A reprint of the original manuscript can be found in Jules Verne, *San Carlos, et autres récits inédits* (Paris: Cherche Midi, 1993, 207–60).

Chapter III

1. In many ways a man typical of his times, Jules Verne was not immune to anti-Semitism. The most obvious example—and frequently cited—was

214

his strongly pejorative portrayal of the Jewish merchant Isac [*sic*] Hakhabut in the novel *Hector Servadac* (1877).

2. Such daring escapes from captivity are a common theme throughout Verne's *Voyages Extraordinaires*: for example, that of the enslaved missionary whom Fergusson rescues from a tribe of African savages in *Five Weeks in a Balloon* (1863), Lord Glenarvan and his companions' escape from the Maori cannibals in *In Search of the Castaways* (1867), the balloon getaway of Cyrus Smith and his companions from a military stockade in *The Mysterious Island* (1874), the hero's breakout from the prison of Pisino in *Mathias Sandorf* (1885), and Marcel Bruckmann's courageous dash for freedom after his incarceration in the fortress of Stahlstadt by the evil Herr Schultze in *The Begum's Fortune* (1879), among many others. Of particular note is the prison escape portrayed in the first chapter of *The Steam House* (1880) by the novel's anti-hero and Indian insurrectionist leader Nana Sabib, a character who resembles Hadjar in many ways. In several of Verne's narratives—for example, *Twenty Thousand Leagues under the Sea* (1870), *The Clipper of the Clouds* (1886)—the imprisonment and delayed escape of the protagonists allows the story's plot to unfold. It is not coincidental, therefore, that Verne's *Invasion of the Sea* not only begins with such a captivity/escape episode but also concludes with one: Captain Hardigan and his companions will, themselves, ultimately be captured by Hadjar, and their escape will lead to the dramatic deus ex machina conclusion of the novel.

Chapter IV

1. The depression known today as Chott Djerid was called by the Romans "Palus Tritonis." The Latin word "palus" means "a lowland seasonally covered with water" or "a shallow sea." Since Lake Triton (or Palus Tritonis) was believed by some ancient Greeks to have been the birthplace of the goddess Pallas Athena, Verne may have assumed that it had been named in her honor.

2. Maxime Hélène (pseudonym of Maxime Vuillaume, 1844–1925), "La Mer intérieure d'Algérie," *La Nature* 10.11 (1882): 22–24, 35–38.

3. These criticisms of Roudaire's plan were repeatedly voiced in the French Académie des Sciences by such scientists as the botanists Ernest Cosson and Charles Naudin, the geologist Gabriel-Auguste Daubrée, and others. An account of these discussions can be found under "Géographie" and "Physique du Globe" in the biannual compilations of the *Comptes rendus des séances de l'Académie des Sciences* from this period (available online through the Bibliothèque Nationale): see especially vols. 79 (July–Dec. 1874), 80 (Jan.–June 1875), 85 (July–Dec. 1877), 87 (July–Dec. 1878), 93 (July–Dec.1881), and 94 (Jan.–June 1882).

4. In December 1882, following the French government's refusal to support this project, Ferdinand de Lesseps founded the Société d'Étude de

la Mer Intérieure, a private company whose specific goal was to finalize plans for the creation of this inland sea. This company funded Roudaire's last fact-finding mission to the chotts region in the spring of 1883. It changed its name to the Compagnie française du Sud Tunisien in 1892, and eventually went bankrupt in 1899. The Compagnie franco-étrangère (France-Overseas Company), described here by Verne as having been established by foreign engineers and capitalists for the subsequent realization of this project in the early 1900s, is pure "alternative history" and never truly existed.

5. The French invasion and conquest of Algeria took place in 1830. The fictional setting for Verne's *Invasion of the Sea* is, therefore, around 1930. The patriotic fervor of de Schaller's final words exemplifies the "manifest destiny" outlook that was very typical of European colonialism during the 1880s, 1890s, and early 1900s. And it stands in surprising contrast to the majority of Verne's later novels—for example, *Propeller Island* (1895), *The Purchase of the North Pole* (1889), and *The Village in the Treetops* (1901)—in which the author was highly critical of such nationalistic sabre rattling and the colonialist agendas of the Great Powers.

Chapter V

1. Approximately six million acres. Of course, this immense land grant by the French government to the private "France-Overseas Company" never really took place. But it was an integral part of Roudaire and de Lesseps's original plan. As summarized by the High Commission of the French Ministry of Foreign Affairs in its final report (July 28, 1882) on the viability of this proposed project:

M. Roudaire and M. De Lesseps have again emphasized that the company undertaking these works would do so at their own risk and perils. They would request no financial subsidy from the State, but simply the concession of a zone of approximately two million hectares of undeveloped land on the site of the future sea as well as the concession of the forests in the adjacent Aurès region. The exploitation of these lands and forests, the fisheries and saltworks to be constructed around this inland sea, would provide the principal sources of revenue by which the company would be assured of a return from its investments. In exchange for these concessions, the State would reserve the right to share in the net profits to the company. (Cited in Letolle and Bendjoudi, *Histoires d'une mer au Sahara*, 201; my translation)

The commission's final recommendation was that the project should "not be encouraged." Among its many stated reasons, the commission cited the political and social backlash that would surely result from such a grant, especially in Tunisia (205).

2. The École centrale des arts et manufactures, founded in Paris in 1829,

specialized in the training of civil engineers. The Saint-Simonian glori-
fication of scientists and engineers—a reflection of their growing status as
national heroes in France during the latter half of the nineteenth century—
is a fundamental and well-known element of the majority of Verne's early
Voyages Extraordinaires (see Jean Chesneaux, *Une Lecture politique de Jules
Verne* [Paris: Maspero, 1971]). But in his portrayal of these heroes, Verne
rarely cites the specific universities where they received their training,
preferring instead to emphasize their vast, encyclopedic knowledge. For example, Samuel Fergusson of *Five Weeks in a Balloon* did "serious studies in
hydrography, physics, and mechanics, along with a smattering of botany,
medicine, and astronomy" (*Cinq semaines en ballon* [Paris: Livre de poche,
1966], 5); Captain Nemo of *Twenty Thousand Leagues under the Sea* "studied in
London, Paris, and New York" and became an expert in "mechanics, ballis-
tics, hydrography, meteorology, geography, geology . . . [and] natural history" (*Vingt mille lieues sous les mers* [Paris: Livre de poche, 1966], 135, 107);
and Cyrus Smith of *Mysterious Island* went to an unnamed American "military school," where he became "a microcosm, a compound of every science,
a possessor of all human knowledge" (*L'Île mystérieuse* [Paris: Livre de
poche, 1966] 13, 102). Only in his post-1878 works—where hero-scientists
progressively tend to give way to hero-engineers (and, just as often, villain-
scientists and villain-engineers)—does Verne begin to identify their academic backgrounds. For example, Marcel Bruckmann of *The Begum's Fortune*,
like de Schaller, attended the École centrale (*Les 500 millions de la Bégum* [Paris:
Livre de poche, 1966], 17); Cyprien Méré of *The Southern Star* (*L'Étoile de
Sud* [Paris: Livre de poche, 1967], 2) and Alcide Pierdeux of *The Purchase of
the North Pole* (*Sans dessus dessous* [Paris: Éditions Glénat, 1976], 93) were
both graduates of the École polytechnique; Mathias Sandorf of *Mathias
Sandorf* did his studies at the University of Pesth, the Academy of Sciences
at Presbourg, the Royal School of Mining at Schemnitz (*Mathias Sandorf*
[Paris: Livre de poche, 1967], 30); and Aristobulus Ursiclos of *The Green
Ray* received his advanced degrees from the Universities of Oxford and Ed-
inburgh (*Le Rayon vert* [Paris: Livre de poche, 1968], 64). It might be argued
that this palpable shift in the institutional affiliation of Verne's scientists
(from societies to universities) as well as the parameters of scientific knowledge itself (from broadly interdisciplinary to narrowly applied) reflects the
increasing prestige of university education in Third Republic France and
the progressive specialization in science in general from the mid-nineteenth
century onward. One Vernian scholar has also suggested that these changes
might be due to the influence of education-minded André Laurie, with
whom Verne collaborated on a number of later novels (see Pierre Terrasse,
"Jules Verne et les grandes écoles scientifiques," *Bulletin de la Société Jules
Verne* 12 [1968]: 72–78).

3. As in the majority of Verne's earlier novels, *Invasion* features a triad of
heroic protagonists who represent the three "H's" (head, heart, and hand),
most often portrayed in Verne's works by the brainy scientist, the coura-

geous common man and/or youthful acolyte, and the faithful servant. Examples include Fergusson, Kennedy, and Joe in *Five Weeks in a Balloon*; Aronnax, Ned Land, and Conseil in *Twenty Thousand Leagues under the Sea*; Lidenbrock, Axel, and Hans in *Journey to the Center of the Earth*; and Palmyrin Rosette, Hector Servadac, and Ben-Zouf in *Hector Servadac*, among many others. This tripartite structure of characterization serves not only to facilitate the didactic purpose of Verne's texts—the scientist teaching, the common man acting as a "vox populi" for the reader, and the servant adding a touch of humor to the lesson—but also to reinforce, à la Saint-Simon, the hierarchical social status of these three "classes" of people. Further, such a fictional configuration also exemplifies the typically Vernian ideal of supra-individual teamwork as the necessary prerequisite for accomplishing great deeds, that is, where the "team" constitutes an assemblage of disparate parts working together (like a well-oiled machine) toward a higher purpose. For a more extensive discussion of the ideological subtexts present in Verne's works, consult Arthur B. Evans, *Jules Verne Rediscovered: Didacticism and the Scientific Novel* (Westport, Conn.: Greenwood, 1988), 37–57.

4. A title commonly used for Muslim head priests, or for any Muslim religious leader or chieftain.

5. The École d'application de la cavalerie, a military college located in Saumur, specialized in the training of calvary officers.

6. Munito "the learned dog" was a circus poodle who gained celebrity throughout Europe during the early years of the nineteenth century for his amazing ability to read and write and to play games (cards, dominoes, chess). He performed in London and Paris in 1814–18.

7. Rams, also called *rems*, is a card game with no more than five players. It is similar to poker (five-card hands, chips, etc.), but its goal is to empty one's hand by following suit with the card of the next highest value. For each hand, the winning player is allowed to relinquish one chip. The first player with no chips left wins the game.

8. Verne's obvious fondness for dogs is demonstrated by the important role they play in many novels of his *Voyages Extraordinaires*. Examples include the multitalented Top of *The Mysterious Island* who saves the life of Cyrus Smith and continually helps the castaways during their "robinsonade" on Lincoln Island; the shipwise Duk [*sic*] of *The Adventures of Captain Hatteras*, who, at the outset of their voyage toward the North Pole and in the absence of the captain, commands the *Forward* and is promptly dubbed "Dog-Captain" by its crew; and the taciturn Dingo of *Dick Sands, The Boy Captain*, who reads the alphabet, faithfully protects young Jack, and forever mourns the death of his original master. See A. Pavolini, "Les Chiens dans l'oeuvre de Jules Verne," *Grand Album Jules Verne* (Paris: Hachette, 1982), 22–29. It is not surprising that, during the final decade of his life, some of the last photographs taken of Jules Verne show him accompanied by his dog Follet as they stroll alone through the gardens at his home on rue Charles-Dubois.

218

Chapter VI

1. This humorous critique of scientific progress by Captain Hardigan is fairly common even in Verne's earlier, mostly pro-science *Voyages Extraordinaires*. For instance, in Verne's first novel, *Five Weeks in a Balloon*, Dick Kennedy cautions: "It may prove to be a very unhappy time when industry takes over everything for its own profit. By dint of inventing machines, mankind will end up being devoured by them! I have always envisioned that the last day of the world will be one where some gigantic boiler, heated to three billion atmospheres, shall explode and blow up our globe!" (*Cinq semaines en ballon* [Paris: Livre de poche, 1966], 124). Throughout these works, scientists are often the butt of Verne's tongue-in-cheek humor: for example, Michel Ardan's constant satirical jibes at Barbicane and Nicholl in *From the Earth to the Moon* and *Around the Moon*, Axel's gentle mocking of his obsessive uncle Lidenbrock in *Journey to the Center of the Earth*, Ned Land's not-so-gentle resistance to Conseil's taxonomic instruction in *Twenty Thousand Leagues under the Sea*, and Ben-Zouf's down-to-earth repartee with the pedantic Palmyrin Rosette in *Hector Servadac*. In addition to their other functions in these novels, such "vox populi" characters provide the lay reader with a humanizing counterweight to the sometimes highly technical scientific pedagogy contained in Verne's texts (see Evans, *Jules Verne Rediscovered*, 76–79). Nevertheless, it is quite rare in Verne's earlier works to find engineers—as opposed to scientists—satirized in this manner; note, for example, the author's uniformly positive portrayal of Cyrus Smith in *The Mysterious Island*.

2. The 1882 report of the High Commission of the Ministry of Foreign Affairs (cited in chap. 5, note 1) states that the proposed specifications of Roudaire's original plan would have necessitated *twenty-seven* years before the waters of the Mediterranean would completely fill the new "Sahara Sea," and that Roudaire's later modification of these specifications—for example, widening the initial breach through the Gabès ridge to approximately thirty meters—would still require at least ten years. Careful to maintain at least the semblance of scientific verisimilitude, Verne therefore extrapolates from these figures and describes his fictional France-Overseas Company as having widened the canal even more—to eighty meters—reducing the estimated fill-time to only five years.

Chapter VII

1. It was especially the French botanist Ernest Cosson (1819–1889), member of the Académie des Sciences and a specialist of North African flora, who protested vociferously against Roudaire's "Sahara Sea" project. In 1874, immediately after Roudaire's proposal was first presented, Cosson argued that the increased humidity resulting from this huge body of water

(estimated at twenty-eight billion tons of water per year evaporating into the atmosphere of the region) would do severe damage to the millions of date palms located there. See his "Note sur le projet d'établissement d'une mer intérieure en Algérie," *Comptes rendus des séances de l'Académie des Sciences*, 79 (July–Dec. 1874): 435–42.

Chapter VIII

1. Verne's use of the term "Neptunian" here raises an interesting question: which of the major geological theories pertaining to the origins of the Earth—that is, Neptunism, Catastrophism, or Vulcanism—did Verne support? Neptunists believed that the entire geological makeup of the Earth resulted from deposits left by receding primeval seas that once covered it and that this process occurred over a relatively short period of time (about six thousand years). The German scientist Abraham Werner (1749–1817) was the principal source of this viewpoint in the late 1780s. A similar theory also popular during the early nineteenth century, which was championed by, among others, the French paleontologist Georges Cuvier (1769–1832), was known as Catastrophism. Catastrophists believed that the Earth was created over a few thousand years as the result of six major cataclysms (corresponding to the six "days" of Genesis), the last of which was Noah's flood. This theory dovetailed quite nicely with Neptunism and both, as might be surmised, were well received by biblical scholars and Christian "diluvialists" of the time. In contrast, the Vulcanists—led by the British scientists James Hutton (1726–1797) and, more importantly, Charles Lyell (1779–1875) with his 1831 book *Principles of Geology*—contended that the formation of the Earth's crust was the result of repeated cycles of volcanic upheaval, erosion, and deposition that occurred over millions of years or more. Further, they argued, this geological process was uniform and still ongoing, that is, that the past could be understood in terms of the geological processes of the present. Incidentally, it is known that Charles Darwin (1809–1882), a young friend of Lyell who took Lyell's book on his five-year voyage aboard the *Beagle*, was strongly influenced by the latter's ideas while developing his theory of biological evolution.

As for Verne, his own geological beliefs, at least as expressed in *Invasion of the Sea*, do not seem to have changed much from when he first articulated them in *Journey to the Center of the Earth* (1864). Like Louis Figuier (1819–1894), a much-published populizer of science and technology during the nineteenth century and one of his frequent sources, Verne adhered to what might be called a "modified" Catastrophist/Vulcanist worldview. He believed that the Earth was created through a series of planetary cataclysms, but that these occurred over millions of years. Verne also supported the notions of "directionalism" (i.e., that such geologic activity had decreased as the Earth's interior continued to cool) and "progressionism" (i.e., that biological life steadily increased in complexity to create its supreme species, Man). In this way, Verne reconciled geologic science with religion—God's plan was achieved through the processes of natural law rather than via direct intervention.

2. Before *Invasion of the Sea*, Verne refers to the legendary Atlantis in four different novels: *The Adventures of Captain Hatteras* (1866), *Twenty Thousand Leagues under the Sea* (1870), *The Mysterious Island* (1874), and *The Headstrong Turk* (1883). Incidentally, despite its inclusion in the 1959 Disney film version of *Journey to the Center of the Earth*, Atlantis was never mentioned in Verne's original novel of 1864. The visit to the ruins of Atlantis in *Twenty Thousand Leagues under the Sea* remains, by far, Verne's most developed treatment of this theme (Oxford: Oxford University Press, 1998, 253–62). In this novel, Professor Aronnax identifies the location of this submerged continent at approximately 16° 17′ longitude by 33° 22′ latitude (410).

3. The sudden eruption of Krakatoa on August 26, 1883 ranks as one of the greatest natural disasters in recorded history. The explosion of this island volcano, located in Indonesia between Java and Sumatra, was supposedly heard more than three thousand miles away, and its resulting tidal waves (some over a hundred feet in height) killed more than thirty-six thousand people in the region.

4. Another indication of Verne's entropy-based Catastrophist philosophy.

5. It is somewhat ironic that this (very obvious) foreshadowing is attributed to de Schaller, the engineer who had earlier offered, in precise scientific fashion, estimates of the time required for the chotts to fill and become the Sahara Sea.

Chapter IX

1. Constantine, an important Algerian city from which this northeastern province takes its name, is known as the "Venice of the Mountains" because it is perched on a mountaintop and surrounded by deep gorges. Following the French invasion of Algeria in 1830, it served as a nearly impregnable stronghold for Islamic rebels, who surrendered only in 1837 after a lengthy siege. Therefore, it might appear as somewhat incongruous that Verne's French-Overseas Company would wish to use this province as a base of operations for its creation of a Sahara Sea. But Roudaire and de Lesseps's original plan, as mentioned, called for the French government to "concede" vast tracts of forested lands in the southern part of this province along the Aurès mountain range, far from the city of Constantine itself. From this fertile region, just north of the Chott Melrir, they hoped to obtain the necessary supplies to complete their final section of the canal.

Chapter X

1. Of course, neither the Trans-Sahara Railway nor the Sahara Sea would be created as Verne had predicted, and Roudaire's name would never be so commemorated either in Tunisia or in Algeria. De Lesseps, after Roudaire's death in 1885, did manage to win from the French government a concession of some 1,500 hectares near the Wadi Melah and the Gulf of Gabès (at the site of the origin of the proposed canal), where he planned to build a port to be baptized Port Roudaire. But the project was soon abandoned for lack of funds (see Letolle and Bendjoudi, *Histoires d'une mer au Sahara*, 112).

Chapter XI

1. The heroes are betrayed and find themselves in mortal danger because of the treachery of a scheming traitor in their midst. This is a common theme throughout all of Verne's *Voyages Extraordinaires*, but it seems especially prevalent in his later works: for example, Negoro in *Dick Sands, The Boy Captain* (1878), Torrès in *The Jangada* (1881), Sarcany and Carpena in *Mathias Sandorf* (1885), Len Burker in *Mistress Branican* (1891), and Flig Balt in *The Kip Brothers* (1902). In an earlier novel, *In Search of the Castaways* (1867), the traitor Ayrton is marooned on a deserted island for his crimes, but he is subsequently rescued and rehabilitated by Cyrus Smith in *The Mysterious Island* (1875). In contrast, most traitors in Verne's later novels suffer singularly violent deaths: Negoro is torn apart by the dog whose master he had murdered years before, Torrès is slashed open during a machete duel and falls into the Amazon, Sarcany and Carpena are blown to bits when the island on which they are imprisoned explodes, Len Burker is shot through the heart after slaying his wife in a fit of rage, and the pirate Flig Balt is killed in a gun battle with the British navy. It might be argued that Verne's growing pessimism—clearly evident in many of his later works—was also coupled with a harsher sense of justice, where vengeance and "eye-for-an-eye" retribution (often satisfied via divine intervention) were more frequently portrayed as the appropriate punishment for heinous crimes.

Chapter XII

1. As summarized by Maxime Hélène, Roudaire's estimates of the "erosive" power of the water, which would serve both to enlarge the canals and to accelerate the flooding of the chotts, were a key part of the latter's engineering plan: "To widen the canal, M. Roudaire is planning to use the enor-

mous volumes of water which will be flowing into the floodable chotts . . . like what occurred in the reshaping of the riverbed of the Meuse near Hock von Holland where, in two years and over a distance of 5 kilometers, the water widened it from 120 to 200 meters and deepened it from 3 to 10 meters" ("La Mer intérieure d'Algérie," 35). Unfortunately, the High Commission of the Ministry of Foreign Affairs appointed to study the feasibility of Roudaire's plan were not convinced. In their 1882 report to the President of France, they stated:

> The proposed excavation by water erosion has raised several serious objections. This procedure . . . cannot be validated by experience. Those rare instances where the reshaping of a riverbed was carried out by the flow of the water itself are not applicable to the operation being proposed here. . . . The flowing water will perhaps assist somewhat in the digging of the canal, thereby reducing the costs of this task, but by how much? This cannot be predicted and, accordingly, should not be considered as a factor. (Quoted in Letolle and Bendjoudi, *Histoires d'une mer au Sahara*, 199).

Chapter XIII

1. In his preface to the 1978 French reprint of Verne's *L'Invasion de la mer*, Francis Lacassin makes the following observation about this governmental land grant:

> In other words, each one of these 2,500,000 hectares of land—graciously given away by the French government just as easily as it had "acquired" them from the North African people—ended up costing the Sahara Sea Company about two francs apiece. Jules Verne thus invites the reader to infer how one man's joy is another man's sorrow: it is clear that "civilizing missions" do not always go unrewarded. (13)

Lacassin argues that, hidden between the lines of this ostensibly procolonization novel, Jules Verne actually admires and empathizes with Hadjar and the Tuareg people whom Lacassin calls the "oppressed majority" (12–13).

In contrast, Georges-Pierre Hourant, in an article entitled "L'Algérie dans l'oeuvre de Jules Verne" published in the *Bulletin de la Société Jules Verne* in 1987, disagrees with Lacassin's interpretation and maintains that Verne viewed Hadjar and his tribe as pure criminals motivated only by greed:

> In truth, Verne's portrayal of the Tuareg as marvelous horsemen and a proud and fatalistic people does not prevent him from identifying as the prime motive of their rebellion the desire to protect their deplorable right to be pillagers of caravans and slave-traders. . . . These nomad tribes try to indoctrinate their sedentary countrymen, exploiting their fears and gullibility with the aid of the worst sort of "fanatics." . . . And events of

the story itself demonstrate their guilt: Hadjar and his men are ultimately swallowed up by the sea. . . . (38–39)

2. Zenfig is a purely fictional oasis and village, invented by Verne to be the hidden desert stronghold of Hadjar and his tribe.

3. A marabout is a Muslim holy man believed to possess supernatural power. The word is also used to designate the tomb or shrine of such a man.

Chapter XIV

1. Verne's seeming obsession with food, evident in several episodes of this novel, is in fact omnipresent throughout all of his *Voyages Extraordinaires*, and it constitutes one of the central organizing themes of his fictional epistemology. In the words of Andrew Martin:

Rabelais would envy and Flaubert disdain the extravagant heterogeneity, the exoticism, the sheer indiscriminateness of the infinitely various diets prescribed in the polyphagous novels of Jules Verne. It would be difficult to name any other writer whose textual menu extends not only to such delicacies as elephant's tongue (and feet), kangaroo's tail and seaweed, but also to assorted organs and limbs subtracted from walrus, polar bear, and armadillo. . . . [T]he *Voyages* compose a gastronomic guide to the globe, an alimentary atlas. . . . Considered with respect to their structural position in the economy of the text, the meals distributed throughout the *Voyages* are remarkable for their regularity and frequency. . . . [H]is writing proceeds demonstrably from the premise of a nutritive epistemology: consciousness is conceived on the model of the digestive system as an apparatus dedicated to the automatic internalization of external objects. Thus diet, no less than travel (the two are effectively inseparable), furnishes an organizing metaphor in the Voyages to the accumulation of knowledge. Nutrition and cognition, the two major activities on the Vernian voyage, are serviced by an identical vocabulary and coupled by a unitary philosophy. (*The Knowledge of Ignorance from Cervantes to Jules Verne* [Cambridge: Cambridge University Press, 1985], 123–29)

Chapter XV

1. Such potentially lethal quagmires in the chott region of the desert were described by Maxime Hélène as follows:

[T]he terrain is far from being uniformly solid. The Arabs themselves do not adventure into it without the greatest of care, and they tell a thousand gloomy tales about the entombment of entire caravans who were foolhardy enough to stray from the narrow path that serves as the road across the sebkha. An Arab writer of the eleventh century, Moula Ahmed, reports that a caravan of a thousand camels was once swallowed up when the first camel of the column mistakenly wandered from the path and all the others followed it into the abyss. "It is a strange place, this sebkha," says Moula Ahmed, "where the night is without stars. They hide behind the mountains. The wind blows deafeningly from all sides at once and, to make the traveler lose his way, it throws sand into his face. . . ." M. Roudaire reports that, during his fact-finding missions to the region, he often sank up to his knees in the salty sand. Sending a probe very deep into several of these holes, which the natives call "eyes of the sea," he was unable to find solid ground. A horseman of his party, stumbling into one of these chasms of the sebkha, disappeared along with his mount; his comrades joined together twenty ramrods from their rifles in a vain attempt to locate the poor man, but the sands had swallowed him up and there was no trace of him. ("La Mer intérieure d'Algérie," 35)

Hélène's account of this tragic event may be somewhat exaggerated. According to the published reports of Henri Duveyrier, the government's geographer who accompanied Roudaire during his first expedition to the region in 1875, the spahi in question was indeed rescued, albeit in the nick of time:

The clay and viscous sand sometimes form, there as in some areas of the Chott Es-Selâm, certain holes, *bormas*, or quicksand pits in which both horses and riders could be swallowed up. Captain Roudaire and I nearly witnessed an accident of this sort happen to a spahi. He had great difficulty in saving himself and his horse when he began to submerge, and we would not have been able to rescue him if he had continued sinking. (Cited in Letolle and Bendjoudi, *Histoires d'une mer au Sahara*, 49–50)

Chapter XVI

1. Seismic tremors in the region of Tunisia and eastern Algeria were — and continue to be — a relatively common occurrence. Not only were they briefly mentioned by Captain Roudaire during his expeditions there in 1875 and 1876, but they were also described in two other sources that Verne most likely consulted when writing *Invasion of the Sea*: the July 23, 1881, issue of the French periodical *La Nature* (the same magazine in which Maxime Hélène later published his article on the Sahara Sea, mentioned by Verne in chapter 4) and the *Comptes rendus des séances de l'Académie des Sciences* of July 1881. Both give details of a particularly severe earthquake that took place near Gabès during the week of June 10–17, 1881. It is highly possible that these two news bulletins — together with the widespread public discussions of Roudaire's proposed Sahara Sea project during the years immedi-

ately preceding (as outlined in the introduction)—served as the twofold historical "inspiration" for this novel.

Chapter XVII

1. The illustrator Léon Benett's depiction of this violent scene—a Delacroix-like rendering strongly reminiscent of the Red Sea crashing in on the pharaoh's army as they pursued Moses and the fleeing Israelites—is perhaps one of his finest works. Léon Benett (1839–1917) was the most prolific illustrator of Verne's *Voyages Extraordinaires*: he was responsible for almost *half* of the sixty-plus novels in this series, nearly two thousand illustrations. A good friend of both Verne and Hetzel, his real name was Benet (with one "t"), but he added another "t" so that his name would not resemble the French word for a simpleton. In addition to his artwork for Verne's *Voyages Extraordinaires*, Benett also illustrated books by Hugo, Erkmann-Chatrian, Tolstoy, André Laurie, and Camille Flammarion, among many others. See Arthur B. Evans, "The Illustrators of Jules Verne's *Voyages Extraordinaires*," *Science Fiction Studies* 25.2 (July 1998): 241–70.

2. Throughout the *Voyages Extraordinaires* but especially in his later works, Verne frequently satirizes pedantic, affected, and/or jargon-filled speech. Note, for example, the following passage of quintessentially hyperbolic legalese in his novel *Propeller Island* (1895, also known as *The Floating Island*):

"I have the honour to acquaint his Excellency the Governor of Floating Island, at this moment in a hundred and seventy-seven degrees thirteen minutes east of the meridian of Greenwich, and in sixteen degrees fifty-four minutes south latitude, that during the night of the 31st of December and the 1st of January, the steamer *Glen*, of Glasgow, of three thousand five hundred tons, laden with wheat, indigo, rice, and wine, a cargo of considerable value, was run into by Floating Island, belonging to the Floating Island Company, Limited, whose offices are at Madeleine Bay, Lower California, United States of America, although the steamer was showing the regulation lights, a white at the foremast, green at the starboard side, and red at the port side, and that having got clear after the collision she was met with the next morning thirty-five miles from the scene of the disaster, ready to sink on account of a gap in her port side, and that she did sink after fortunately putting her captain, his officers and crew on board the *Herald*, Her Britannic Majesty's cruiser of the first-class under the flag of Rear-Admiral Sir Edward Collinson, who reports the fact to his Excellency Governor Cyrus Bikerstaff, requesting him to acknowledge the responsibility of the Floating Island Company, Limited, under the guarantee of the inhabitants of the said Floating Island, in favour of the owners of the said *Glen*, the value of which in hull, engines, and cargo amounts to the sum of twelve hundred thousand pounds sterling, that is six millions of dollars, which sum should be paid into the hands of the said Admiral Sir Edward Collinson, or in default he will forcibly proceed against the said Floating Island."

One long sentence of about three hundred words, cut up with commas, but without a single full-stop! *(Floating Island* [London: Sampson, Low, 1896], 229–30)

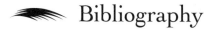 # Bibliography

WORKS OF JULES VERNE

All works were published in Paris by J. Hetzel unless otherwise indicated. Most novels by Verne were first published in serial format in Hetzel's *Magasin d'Éducation et de Récréation*, then as octodecimo books (normally unillustrated), and finally as octavo illustrated "luxury" editions in red and gold. The date given is that of the first book publication. Many entries have been gleaned from the excellent bibliographical studies of Volker Dehs and Jean-Michel Margot, François Raymond, Olivier Dumas, Edward Gallagher, Judith A. Mistichelli, and John A. Van Eerde, and especially those of Piero Gondolo della Riva and Brian Taves and Stephen Michaluk Jr.

Works in the Series *Voyages Extraordinaires* (Extraordinary Voyages)

Note: Those novels marked by an asterisk were published after Jules Verne's death in 1905. It is important to understand that most of these post-1905 works were either substantially revamped or, in some cases, almost totally written by Jules Verne's son, Michel. For each novel listed, information about its first English-language edition is provided (date of publication, publisher, and translator) as well as the alternate English titles sometimes used. Also included are recommendations about the translation quality of certain English-language editions.

Cinq semaines en ballon (1863, illus. Edouard Riou and Henri de Montaut). *Five Weeks in a Balloon* (1869, New York: Appleton, trans. William Lackland). Recommended: translation by William Lackland. Not recommended: Chapman & Hall edition (rpt. 1995, Sutton "Pocket Classics"), the Routledge edition (rpt. 1911, Parke), and translations by Arthur Chambers (1926, Dutton; rpt. 1996, Wordsworth Classics) and by I. O. Evans (1958, Hanison).
Voyage au centre de la terre (1864, illus. Edouard Riou). *A Journey to the Centre of the Earth* (1871, Griffith & Farran, translator unknown). Alternate titles: *A Journey to the Interior of the Earth, Journey to the Center of the Earth.* Recommended: translations by Robert Baldick (1965, Penguin, *Journey*

to the Center of the Earth) and by William Butcher (1992, Oxford, *Journey to the Centre of the Earth*). Not recommended: all reprints of the Griffith & Farran ("Hardwigg") edition, which begin "Looking back to all that has occurred to me since that eventful day . . ." (1965, Airmont; 1986, Signet Classics; 1992, Tor; among many others).

De la terre à la lune (1865, illus. Henri de Montaut). *From the Earth to the Moon* (1867, Gage, translator unknown). Alternate titles: *From the Earth to the Moon Direct, in Ninety-Seven Hours Twenty Minutes, The Baltimore Gun Club, The American Gun Club, The Moon Voyage*. Recommended: translations by Harold Salemson (1970, Heritage, *From the Earth to the Moon*) and by Walter James Miller (1978, Crowell, *The Annotated Jules Verne: From the Earth to the Moon*). Not recommended: translations by Louis Mercier and Eleanor King (1873, Sampson Low, *From the Earth to the Moon Direct, in Ninety-Seven Hours Twenty Minutes*; rpt. 1967, Airmont; 1983, Avenel; among many others), by Edward Roth (1874, King and Baird, *The Baltimore Gun Club*; rpt. 1962, Dover), and by Lowell Bair (1967, Bantam, *From the Earth to the Moon*).

Voyages et aventures du capitaine Hatteras (1866, illus. Edouard Riou and Henri de Montaut). *At the North Pole* and *The Desert of Ice* (1874–75, Osgood, translator unknown). Alternate titles: *The English at the North Pole* and *The Field of Ice, The Voyages and Adventures of Captain Hatteras, The Adventures of Captain Hatteras*. Recommended: Osgood edition (rpt. 1976, Aeonian).

Les Enfants du capitaine Grant (1867–68, illus. Edouard Riou). *In Search of the Castaways* (1873, Lippincott, translator unknown). Alternate titles: *The Mysterious Document/On the Track/Among the Cannibals, The Castaways; or A Voyage Around the World, Captain Grant's Children*. Recommended: None.

Vingt mille lieues sous les mers (1869–70, illus. Edouard Riou and Alphonse-Marie de Neuville). *Twenty Thousand Leagues Under the Seas* (1872, Sampson Low, trans. Louis Mercier). Alternate titles: *Twenty Thousand Leagues under the Sea, 20,000 Leagues under the Sea, At the Bottom of the Deep, Deep Sea*. Recommended: translations by Walter James Miller and Frederick Paul Walter (1993, Naval Institute Press, *Jules Verne's Twenty Thousand Leagues under the Sea*) and by William Butcher (1998, Oxford, *Twenty Thousand Leagues under the Seas*). Not recommended: translation by Louis Mercier cited above (rpt. 1963, Airmont; 1981, Castle; 1995, Tor; among many others) and the I. O. Evans "Fitzroy Edition" translation (1960, Arco).

Autour de la lune (1870, illus. Émile-Antoine Bayard and Alphonse-Marie de Neuville). *Round the Moon* (1873, Sampson Low, trans. Louis Mercier and Eleanor King). Alternate titles: *All Around the Moon, Around the Moon, A Moon Voyage*. Recommended: translations by Jacqueline and Robert Baldick (1970, Dent, *Around the Moon*) and by Harold Salemson (1970, Heritage, *Around the Moon*). Not recommended: translations by Louis

Mercier and Eleanor King (cited above) and by Edward Roth (1874, Catholic, *All Around the Moon*; rpt. 1962, Dover).

Une Ville flottante (1871, illus. Jules-Descartes Férat). *A Floating City* (1874, Sampson Low, translator unknown). Alternate title: *The Floating City*. Recommended: translation by Henry Frith (1876, Routledge, *The Floating City*).

Aventures de trois Russes et de trois Anglais (1872, illus. Jules-Descartes Férat). *Meridiana: The Adventures of Three Englishmen and Three Russians in South Africa* (1872, Sampson Low, translator Ellen E. Frewer). Alternate titles: *Adventures of Three Englishmen and Three Russians in Southern Africa, Aventures in the Land of the Behemoth, Measuring a Meridian*. Recommended: translation by Henry Frith (1877, Routledge, *Adventures of Three Englishmen and Three Russians in Southern Africa*). Not recommended: Shepard edition (1874, translator unknown, *Adventures in the Land of the Behemoth*).

Le Pays des fourrures (1873, illus. Jules-Descartes Férat and Alfred Quesnay de Beaurepaire). *The Fur Country* (1873, Sampson Low, trans. N. D'Anvers). Alternate title: *Sun in Eclipse/Through the Behring Strait*. Recommended: translation by Edward Baxter (1987, NC Press, *The Fur Country*).

Le Tour du monde en quatre-vingts jours (1873, illus. Alphonse-Marie de Neuville and Léon Benett). *A Tour of the World in Eighty Days* (1873, Osgood, trans. George M. Towle). Alternate titles: *The Tour of the World in Eighty Days, Around the World in Eighty Days, Around the World in 80 Days, Round the World in Eighty Days*. Recommended: translation by William Butcher (1995, Oxford, *Around the World in Eighty Days*). Not recommended: translations by Lewis Mercier (1962, Collier/Doubleday) and by K. E. Lichtenecker (1965, Hamlyn).

Le Docteur Ox (1874, illus. Lorenz Froelich, Théophile Schuler, Émile-Antoine Bayard, Adrien Marie, Edmond Yon, Antoine Bertrand). *Doctor Ox* (1874, Osgood, trans. George M. Towle). Short story collection. Alternate titles: *From the Clouds to the Mountains, A Fancy of Doctor Ox, Dr. Ox and Other Stories, Dr. Ox's Experiment and Other Stories, A Winter amid the Ice and Other Stories, A Winter amid the Ice and Other Thrilling Tales*. Collection contains the following short stories and nonfiction: "Une Fantaisie du docteur Ox" (Doctor Ox), "Maître Zacharius" (Master Zacharius), "Un Hivernage dans les glaces" (A Winter amid the Ice), "Un Drame dans les airs" (A Drama in the Air), and "Quarantième ascension du Mont-Blanc" (Fortieth French Ascent of Mont Blanc, written by Verne's brother, Paul). Recommended: Osgood edition, translation by Towle. Not recommended: translation by Abby L. Alger (1874, Gill, From the Clouds to the Mountains).

L'Île mystérieuse (1874–75, illus. Jules-Descartes Férat). *The Mysterious Island: Dropped from the Clouds/The Abandoned/The Secret of the Island* (1875, Sampson Low, trans. W. H. G. Kingston). Alternate titles: *The Mysterious Island: Dropped from the Clouds/Marooned/Secret of the Island*,

Mysterious Island. Recommended: translation by Sidney Kravitz (forthcoming in 2001 from Wesleyan University Press).

Le Chancellor (1875, illus. Edouard Riou and Jules-Descartes Férat). *The Wreck of the Chancellor* (1875, Osgood, trans. George M. Towle), *The Survivors of the Chancellor, The Chancellor*. Recommended: translation by Towle.

Michel Strogoff (1876, illus. Jules-Descartes Férat). *Michael Strogoff* (1876, Leslie, trans. E. G. Walraven), *Michael Strogoff: From Moscow to Irkoutsk, Michael Strogoff, or the Russian Courier, Michael Strogoff, or the Courier of the Czar*. Recommended: translation by Kingston as "revised" by Julius Chambers (1876, Sampson Low).

Hector Servadac (1877, illus. Paul Philippoteaux). *Hector Servadac* (1877, Sampson Low, trans. Ellen E. Frewer). Alternate titles: *To the Sun? and Off on a Comet!, Hector Servadac: Travels and Adventures Through the Solar System, Anomalous Phenomena/Homward Bound, Astounding Adventures Among the Comets*. Recommended: Frewer translation cited above. Not recommended: translations by Edward Roth (1877–78, Claxton et al., *To the Sun? and Off on a Comet!*; rpt. 1960, Dover) and by I. O. Evans (1965, *Anomalous Phenomena/Homeward Bound*).

Les Indes noires (1877, illus. Jules-Descartes Férat). *The Black Indies* (1877, Munro, translator unknown). Alternate titles: *The Child of the Cavern, The Underground City, Black Diamonds*. Recommended: Munro edition cited above.

Un Capitaine de quinze ans (1878, illus. Henri Meyer). *Dick Sand; or a Captain at Fifteen* (1878, Munro, translator unknown). Alternate titles: *Dick Sands, The Boy Captain; A Fifteen Year Old Captain; Captain at Fifteen*. Recommended: Munro edition cited above. Not recommended: translation by Forlag (1976, Abelard-Schuman, *Captain at Fifteen*).

Les Cinq Cents millions de la Bégum (1879, illus. Léon Benett). *The Five Hundred Millions of the Begum* (1879, Munro, translator unknown). Alternate titles: *The Begum's Fortune, The 500 Millions of the Begum*. Recommended: Munro edition cited above.

Les Tribulations d'un Chinois en Chine (1879, illus. Léon Benett). *The Tribulations of a Chinaman in China* (1879, Lee & Shepard, trans. Virginia Champlin [Grace Virginia Lord]). Alternate titles: *The Tribulations of a Chinese Gentleman, The Tribulations of a Chinaman*. Recommended: translation by Champlin cited above.

La Maison à vapeur (1880, illus. Léon Benett). *The Steam House, or a Trip across Northern India* (1880, Munro, trans. James Cotterell). Alternate titles: *The Steam House, The Demon of Cawnpore/Tigers and Traitors*. Recommended: translation by Agnes D. Kingston (1880, Sampson Low, *The Steam House*).

La Jangada (1881, illus. Léon Benett and Edouard Riou). *The Jangada, or 800 Leagues over the Amazon* (1881, Munro, trans. James Cotterell). Alternate titles: *The Giant Raft, The Jangada, The Giant Raft: Down the*

Amazon/The Cryptogram. Recommended: translation by W. J. Gordon (1881–82, Sampson Low, *The Giant Raft*). Not recommended: I. O. Evans "Fitzroy Edition" translation (1967, Arco, *Down the Amazon/The Cryptogram*).

L'École des Robinsons (1882, illus. Léon Benett). *Robinson's School* (1883, Munro, trans. James Cotterell). Alternate titles: *Godfrey Morgan: A California Mystery, The School for Crusoes*. Recommended: translation by Cotterell cited above.

Le Rayon vert (1882, illus. Léon Benett). *The Green Ray* (1883, Sampson Low, trans. Mary de Hautville).

Kéraban-le-têtu (1883, illus. Léon Benett). *The Headstrong Turk* (1883–84, Munro, trans. James Cotterell). Alternate titles: *Kéraban the Inflexible: The Captain of the Guidara/Scarpante, the Spy*. Recommended: translation by Cotterell cited above.

L'Étoile du sud (1884, illus. Léon Benett). *The Southern Star* (1885, Munro, translator unknown). Alternate titles: *The Vanished Diamond: A Tale of South Africa, The Southern Star Mystery*. Recommended: Munro edition cited above.

L'Archipel en feu (1884, illus. Léon Benett). *Archipelago on Fire* (1885, Munro, translator unknown). Alternate title: *The Archipelago on Fire*. Recommended: Munro edition cited above.

Mathias Sandorf (1885, illus. Léon Benett). *Mathias Sandorf* (1885, Munro, translator unknown).

L'Épave du Cynthia (1885, illus. George Roux). *Waif of the "Cynthia"* (1885, Munro, translator unknown). Alternate title: *Salvage from the Cynthia*. Recommended: Munro edition cited above.

Robur-le-conquérant (1886, illus. Léon Benett). *Robur the Conqueror* (1887, Munro, translator unknown). Alternate titles: *The Clipper of the Clouds, A Trip Round the World in a Flying Machine*. Recommended: Sampson Low edition (1887, translator unknown, *The Clipper of the Clouds*).

Un Billet de loterie (1886, illus. George Roux). *Ticket No. "9672"* (1886, Munro, trans. Laura E. Kendall). Alternate title: *The Lottery Ticket*. Recommended: translation by Kendall.

Nord contre Sud (1887, illus. Léon Benett). *Texar's Vengeance, or North Versus South* (1887, Munro, translator unknown). Alternate titles: *Texar's Revenge; or, North Against South, North Against South: A Tale of the American Civil War, North Against South: Burbank the Northerner/Texar the Southerner*. Recommended: Munro edition cited above.

Le Chemin de France (1887, illus. George Roux). *The Flight to France, or The Memoirs of a Dragoon* (1888, Sampson Low, translator unknown).

Deux ans de vacances (1888, illus. Léon Benett). *A Two Year's Vacation* (1889, Munro, translator unknown). Alternate titles: *Adrift in the Pacific, Adrift in the Pacific/Second Year Ashore, Two Years' Holiday, A Long Vacation*. Recommended: Munro edition cited above. Not recommended: translation by Olga Marx (1967, Holt, Rinehart & Winston, *A Long Vacation*).

Famille-sans-nom (1889, illus. Georges Tiret-Bognet). *A Family without a
Name* (1889, Munro, Lovell, translator unknown). Alternate titles: *A
Family without a Name: Leader of the Resistance/Into the Abyss, Family without
a Name*. Recommended: translation by Edward Baxter (1982, NC Press,
Family without a Name).

Sans dessus dessous (1889, illus. George Roux). *The Purchase of the North Pole*
(1890, Sampson Low, translator unknown). Alternate title: *Topsy-Turvy*.
Recommended: Sampson Low edition cited above.

César Cascabel (1890, illus. George Roux). *Caesar Cascabel* (1890, Cassell,
trans. A. Estoclet). Alternate title: *The Travelling Circus/The Show on Ice*.
Recommended: translation by Estoclet cited above.

Mistress Branican (1891, illus. Léon Benett). *Mistress Branican* (1891, Cassell,
trans. A. Estoclet). Alternate titles: *Mystery of the Franklin, The Wreck of
the Franklin*. Recommended: translation by Estoclet cited above.

Le Château des Carpathes (1892, illus. Léon Benett). *The Castle of the
Carpathians* (1893, Sampson Low, translator unknown). Alternate title:
Carpathian Castle. Recommended: Sampson Low edition cited above.

Claudius Bombarnac (1893, illus. Léon Benett). *The Special Correspondent, or the
Adventures of Claudius Bombarnac* (1894, Lovell, translator unknown).
Alternate title: *Claudius Bombarnac* (same translation).

P'tit-Bonhomme (1893, illus. Léon Benett). *Foundling Mick* (1895, Sampson
Low, translator unknown).

Mirifiques aventures de Maître Antifer (1894, illus. George Roux). *Captain
Antifer* (1895, Sampson Low, translator unknown).

L'Île à hélice (1895, illus. Léon Benett). *The Floating Island* (1896, Sampson
Low, trans. W. J. Gordon; rpt. 1990, Kegan Paul). Alternate title:
Propeller Island. Recommended: none.

Face au drapeau (1896, illus. Léon Benett). *Facing the Flag* (1897, Neely,
translator unknown). Alternate titles: *For the Flag, Simon Hart: A Strange
Story of Science and the Sea*. Recommended: Neely edition cited above.

Clovis Dardentor (1896, illus. Léon Benett). *Clovis Dardentor* (1897, Sampson
Low, translator unknown).

Le Sphinx des glaces (1897, illus. George Roux). *An Antarctic Mystery* (1898,
Sampson Low, trans. Mrs. Cashel Hoey). Alternate titles: *The Sphinx of the
Ice, An Antarctic Mystery*. Recommended: translation by Hoey cited above.
Not recommended: Basil Ashmore "Fitzroy Edition" translation (1961,
Arco, *The Mystery of Arthur Gordon Pym by Edgar Allan Poe and Jules Verne*).

Le Superbe Orénoque (1898, illus. George Roux). *The Mighty Orinoco*. No
published English translation yet available.

Le Testament d'un excentrique (1899, illus. George Roux). *The Will of an Eccentric*
(1900, Sampson Low, translator unknown).

Seconde patrie (1900, illus. George Roux). *Their Island Home/The Castaways of
the Flag* (1923, Sampson Low, trans. Cranstoun Metcalfe).

Le Village aérien (1901, illus. George Roux). *The Village in the Treetops* (1964,
"Fitzroy Edition," Arco, trans. I. O. Evans).

Les Histoires de Jean-Marie Cabidoulin (1901, illus. George Roux). *The Sea Serpent: The Yarns of Jean Marie Cabidoulin* (1967, "Fitzroy Edition," Arco, trans. I. O. Evans).

Les Frères Kip (1902, illus. George Roux). *The Kip Brothers*. No published English translation yet available.

Bourses de voyage (1903, illus. Léon Benett). *Travel Scholarships*. No published English translation yet available.

Un Drame en Livonie (1904, illus. Léon Benett). *A Drama in Livonia* (1967, "Fitzroy Edition," Arco, trans. I. O. Evans).

Maître du monde (1904, illus. George Roux). *The Master of the World* (1911, Parke, translator unknown). Recommended: translation by Cranstoun Metcalfe (1914, Sampson Low). Not recommended: Parke edition cited above.

L'Invasion de la mer (1905, illus. Benett). *Invasion of the Sea* (2001, Wesleyan University Press, trans. Edward Baxter).

*Le Phare du bout du monde (1905, illus. George Roux). *The Lighthouse at the Edge of the World* (1923, Sampson Low, trans. Cranstoun Metcalfe).

*Le Volcan d'or (1906, illus. George Roux). *The Golden Volcano: The Claim on the Forty Mile Creek/Flood and Famine* (1962, "Fitzroy Edition," Arco, trans. I. O. Evans).

*L'Agence Thompson and Co. (1907, illus. Léon Benett). *The Thompson Travel Agency: Package Holiday/End of the Journey* (1965, "Fitzroy Edition," Arco, trans. I. O. Evans).

*La Chasse au météore (1908, illus. George Roux). *The Chase of the Golden Meteor* (1909, Grant Richards, trans. Frederick Lawton). Alternate title: *The Hunt for the Meteor*.

*Le Pilote du Danube (1908, illus. George Roux). *The Danube Pilote* (1967, "Fitzroy Edition," Arco, trans. I. O. Evans).

*Les Naufragés du Jonathan (1909, illus. George Roux). *The Survivors of the Jonathan: The Masterless Man/The Unwilling Dictator* (1962, "Fitzroy Edition," Arco, trans. I. O. Evans).

*Le Secret de Wilhelm Storitz (1910, illus. George Roux). *The Secret of Wilhelm Storitz* (1963, "Fitzroy Edition," Arco, trans. I. O. Evans).

*Hier et demain (1910, illus. Léon Benett, George Roux, Félicien Myrbach-Rheinfeld). *Yesterday and Tomorrow* (1965, "Fitzroy Edition,"Arco, trans. I. O. Evans). Short story collection. Original French collection contains the following short stories: "La Famille Raton" (The Rat Family), "M. Ré-Dièze et Mlle Mi-Bémol" (Mr. Ray Sharp and Miss Me Flat), "La Destinée de Jean Morénas" (The Fate of Jean Morénas), "Le Humbug" (The Humbug), "Au XXIXeme siècle: La Journée d'un journaliste américain en 2889" (In the Twenty-Ninth Century: The Diary of an American Journalist in 2889) and "L'Eternel Adam" (The Eternal Adam). The 1965 Arco English translation does not contain the same stories as the original French edition: "La Famille Raton" (The Rat Family) and "Le Humbug" (The Humbug) were deleted and replaced

with "Une ville idéale" ("An Ideal City"), "Dix heures de chasse" ("Ten
    Hours Hunting"), "Frritt-Flacc" ("Frritt-Flacc"), and
    "Gil Braltar" ("Gil Braltar").
*L'Étonnante aventure de la mission Barsac (Hachette, 1919, illus. George
    Roux). *The Barsac Mission: Into the Niger Bend/The City in the Sahara* (1960,
    "Fitzroy Edition," Arco, trans. I. O. Evans).

Novellas and Short Stories

Note: In the octavo illustrated editions of Verne's *Voyages Extraordinaires*,
some novels were supplemented with a novella or a short story that had often
been previously published in a periodical journal (e.g., *Musée des familles*) or a
newspaper (e.g., *Le Figaro*). Only two short story collections were published
as part of the *Voyages Extraordinaires*—*Le Docteur Ox* (Doctor Ox) and *Hier et
demain* (Yesterday and Tomorrow)—and most of the stories contained
therein also had appeared earlier. The latter collection was published only after Verne's death in 1905, and many of the short stories in it were either
significantly revamped or entirely written by Jules Verne's son, Michel.

"Un Drame au Mexique. Les premiers navires de la marine mexicaine"
    (1876, illus. Jules-Descartes Férat) with *Michel Strogoff*. First published
    as "L'Amérique du Sud. Études historiques. Les premiers navires de
    la marine mexicaine" in the *Musée des familles* (July 1851, illus. Eugène
    Forest, Alexandre de Bar): 304–12. "The Mutineers: A Romance of
    Mexico" with *Michel Strogoff, the Courier of the Czar* (1877, Sampson
    Low, trans. W. G. Kingston). Alternate titles: "A Drama in Mexico,"
    "The Mutineers, or A Tragedy in Mexico," "The Mutineers."
"Un Drame dans les airs" (1874, illus. Émile-Antoine Bayard) in *Le Docteur
    Ox*. First published as "La science en famille. Un voyage en ballon"
    in the *Musée de familles* (Aug. 1851, illus. Alexandre de Bar): 329–36. "A
    Voyage in a Balloon" in *Sartain's Union Magazine of Literature and Art*
    (May 1852, trans. Anne T. Wilbur): 389–95. Alternate titles: "A Drama
    in the Air," "Balloon Journey," "A Drama in Mid-Air." This Verne story
    was the first one translated into English.
"Martin Paz" (1875, illus. Jules-Descartes Férat) with *Le Chancellor*. First
    published as "L'Amérique du Sud. Moeurs péruviennes. Martin Paz,
    nouvelle historique" in the *Musée des familles* (July–Aug.1852, illus.
    Eugène Forest, Émile Berton): 301–13, 321–35. "Martin Paz" in *The
    Survivors of the Chancellor; and Martin Paz* (1876, Sampson Low, trans.
    Ellen E. Frewer). Alternate title: "The Pearl of Lima."
"Maître Zacharius" (1874, illus. Théophile Schuler) in *Le Docteur Ox*.
    First published as "Maître Zacharius, ou l'horloger qui avait perdu son
    âme. Tradition genevoise" in the *Musée des familles* (Apr.–May 1854,
    illus. Alexandre de Bar, Gustave Janet): 193–200, 225–31. "Master

Zacharius" in *Dr. Ox and Other Stories* (1874, Osgood, trans. George M.
Towle). Alternate titles: "Master Zachary," "The Watch's Soul."

"Un Hivernage dans les glaces" (1874, illus. Adrien Marie) in *Le Docteur
Ox*. First published in the *Musée des familles* (Apr.–May 1855, illus. Jean-
Antoine de Beauce): 161–72, 209–20. "Winter in the Ice" in *Dr. Ox
and Other Stories* (1874, Osgood, trans. George M. Towle). Alternate
titles: "A Winter amid the Ice," "A Winter among the Ice-Fields," "Winter
on Ice."

"Le Comte de Chanteleine." Published as "Le Comte de Chanteleine.
Épisode de la révolution" in the *Musée des familles* (Oct.–Nov. 1864, illus.
Edmond Morin, Alexandre de Bar, Jean-Valentin Foulquier): 1–15,
37–51. No English translation available.

"Les Forceurs de blocus" (1871, illus. Jules-Descartes Férat) with *Une Ville
flottante*. First published in the *Musée des familles* (Oct.–Nov. 1865, illus.
Léon Morel-Fatio, Evrémond Bérard, Fréderic Lixe, Jean-Valentin
Foulquier): 17–21, 35–47. "The Blockade Runners" in *The Floating City,
and the Blockade Runners* (1874, Sampson Low, translator unknown).

"Le Docteur Ox" (1874, illus. Lorenz Froelich) in *Le Docteur Ox*. First
published in the *Musée des familles* (Mar.–May 1872, illus. Ulysse Parent,
Alexandre de Bar): 65–74, 99–107, 133–41. "Doctor Ox's Experiment"
in *Dr. Ox and Other Stories* (1874, Osgood, trans. George M. Towle).
Alternate titles: "A Fancy of Doctor Ox," "Dr. Ox," "Dr. Ox's Hobby."

"Les Révoltés de la Bounty" (1879, illus. S. Drée) with *Les CinqCents
millions de la Bégum*. First published in the *Magasin d'Éducation et de
Récréation* (Oct.–Dec. 1879, illus. S. Drée): 193–98, 225–30, 257–63.
"The Mutineers of the Bounty" in *The Begum's Fortune, with an account of
The Mutineers of the Bounty* (1880, Sampson Low, trans. W. H. G.
Kingston).

"Dix heures en chasse" (1882, illus. Gédéon Baril) with *Le Rayon vert*. First
published in the *Journal d'Amiens, Moniteur de la Somme* (Dec. 19–20,
1881): 2–3. "Ten Hours Hunting" in *Yesterday and Tomorrow* (1965, Arco,
trans. I. O. Evans).

"Frritt-Flacc" (1886, illus. George Roux) with *Un Billet de loterie*. First
published in *Le Figaro illustré* (1884–85): 6–7. "Dr. Trifulgas:
A Fantastic Tale" in *Strand Magazine* 4 (July–Dec. 1892, translator
unknown): 53–57. Alternate titles: "Fritt-Flacc," "The Ordeal of
Dr. Trifulgas," "Fweeee–Spash!"

"Gil Braltar" (1887, illus. George Roux) with *Le Chemin de France*.
"Gilbraltar" (1938, Hurd and Walling, trans. Ernest H. De Gay).

"Un Express de l'avenir." Written by Verne's son, Michel, and first
published in *Le Figaro* (September 1, 1888). Translated and published
(under his father's name) as "An Express of the Future" in *Strand
Magazine* 10 (July–Dec. 1895): 638–40.

"La Journée d'un journaliste américain en 2889" (1910, illus. George
Roux) in *Hier et demain*. Written by Verne's son Michel and first

published in English (under his father's name) as "In the Year 2889" in *The Forum* 6 (Sept. 1888–Feb. 1889, illus. George Roux): 662–77. Later modified by Jules Verne and published as "La Journée d'un journaliste américain en 2890" in *Mémoires de l'Académie d'Amiens* 37 (1890): 348–70. The latter version was then published as "Au XIXe siècle: La Journée d'un journaliste américain en 2889" in *Hier et demain* (Paris: Hetzel, 1910). It was translated and reprinted as "In the Twenty-Ninth Century: The Diary of an American Journalist in 2889" in *Yesterday and Tomorrow* (1965, Arco, trans. I. O. Evans).

"La Famille Raton" (1910, illus. Félicien Myrbach-Rheinfeld) in *Hier et demain*. First published as "Aventures de la famille Raton. Conte de fées" in *Le Figaro illustré* (Jan. 1891): 1–12. *Adventures of the Rat Family*, trans. Evelyn Copeland (1993, Oxford).

"La Destinée de Jean Morénas" (1910, illus. Léon Benett) in *Hier et demain*. Written by Verne's son, Michel, from his father's unpublished short story "Pierre-Jean" (see under "Rediscovered Works"). "The Fate of Jean Morénas" in *Yesterday and Tomorrow* (1965, Arco, trans. I. O. Evans).

"Le Humbug" (1910, illus. George Roux) in *Hier et demain*. "Humbug, The American Way of Life" (1991, Acadian, trans. William Butcher) and "The Humbug" in *The Jules Verne Encyclopedia*, ed. Brian Taves and Stephen Michaluk Jr. (1996, Scarecrow, trans. Edward Baxter).

"Monsieur Ré-Dièze et Mademoiselle Mi-Bémol" (1910, illus. George Roux) in *Hier et demain*. First published in *Le Figaro illustré* (Dec. 25, 1893): 221–28. "Mr. Ray Sharp and Miss Me Flat" [*sic*] in *Yesterday and Tomorrow* (1965, Arco, trans. I. O. Evans).

"L'Eternel Adam" (1910, illus. Léon Benett) in *Hier et demain*. Written by Verne's son, Michel, from his father's unfinished short story "Edom" (see under "Rediscovered Works") and first published in *La Revue de Paris* (Oct. 1, 1910): 449–84. "Eternal Adam" in *Saturn* 1.1 (March 1957, trans. Willis T. Bradley): 76–112.

Rediscovered Works: Unpublished Early Novels, Short Stories, and Original Manuscripts

Un Prêtre en 1835 (A Priest in 1835, written 1846–47). Published as *Un Prêtre en 1839* (1992, Cherche Midi, illus. Jacques Tardi).

"Jédédias Jamet" (Jedediah Jamet, written 1847). Published in *San Carlos et autres récits inédits*, 177–206 (1993, Cherche Midi, illus. Tardi).

"Pierre-Jean" (written ca.1852). Published as "Pierre-Jean" in Olivier Dumas, *Jules Verne*, 205–34 (1988, La Manufacture). Original manuscript of "La Destinée de Jean Morénas."

"Le Siège de Rome" (The Siege of Rome, written ca.1853). Published as

"Le Siège de Rome" in *San Carlos et autres récits inédits*, 81–146 (1993, Cherche Midi, illus. Jacques Tardi).

"Le Mariage de Monsieur Anselme des Tilleuls" (The Marriage of M. Anselme des Tilleuls, written ca.1855). Published as "Le Mariage de M. Anselme des Tilleuls. Souvenirs d'un élève de huitième" (1991, Olifant, illus. Gérard Bregnat) and as "Le Mariage de M. Anselme des Tilleuls. Souvenirs d'un élève de huitième" in *San Carlos et autres récits inédits*, 47–80 (1993, Cherche Midi, illus. Jacques Tardi).

"San Carlos" (San Carlos, written ca. 1856). Published as "San Carlos" in *San Carlos et autres récits inédits*, 147–76 (1993, Cherche Midi, illus. Jacques Tardi).

Voyage en Angleterre et en Ecosse—Voyage à reculons (written 1859–60). Published as *Voyage à reculons en Angleterre et en Ecosse* (1989, Cherche Midi). Translated by William Butcher as *Backwards to Britain* (1992, Chambers).

Paris au XXe siècle (written 1863). Published as *Paris au XXe siècle* (1994, Hachette, illus. François Schuiten). Translated by Richard Howard as *Paris in the Twentieth Century* (1996, Random House, illus. Anders Wenngren).

L'Oncle Robinson (Uncle Robinson, written 1870–71). Published as *L'Oncle Robinson* (1991, Cherche Midi). Original manuscript of *L'Île mystérieuse*.

Le Beau Danube jaune (The Beautiful Yellow Danube, written 1896–97). Published as *Le Beau Danube jaune* (1988, Société Jules Verne). Original manuscript of *Le Pilote du Danube*.

En Magellanie—Au Bout du monde (In the Magellanes—At the End of the World, written 1896–99). Published as *En Magellanie* (1987, Société Jules Verne). Original manuscript of *Les Naufragés du Jonathan*.

Le Volcan d'or—Le Klondyke (The Golden Volcano—The Klondyke, written 1899–1900). Published as *Le Volcan d'or*. Version originale (1989, Société Jules Verne). Original manuscript of *Le Volcan d'or*.

Le Secret de Wilhelm Storitz—L'Invisible, L'Invisible fiancée, Le Secret de Storitz (The Secret of Wilhelm Storitz, written 1901). Published as *Le Secret de Wilhelm Storitz* (1985, Société Jules Verne). Original manuscript of *Le Secret de Wilhelm Storitz*.

La Chasse au Météore—Le Bolide (The Hunt for the Meteor—The Bolide, written 1901). Published as *La Chasse au météore. Version originale* (1986) and as *La Chasse au Météore (Version originale) Suivi de Edom* (1994, Société Jules Verne, illus. George Roux). Original manuscript of *La Chasse au météore*.

"Voyage d'études" (Study Trip, written in 1903–4). Unfinished manuscript, completed and published by Michel Verne as *L'Étonnante aventure de la mission Barsac* (1919). Original version published in *San Carlos et autres récits inédits*, 207–60 (1993, Cherche Midi, illus. Jacques Tardi).

"Edom." (Edom, written in 1903–5). Unfinished manuscript, rewritten

and published in *Hier et demain* by Michel Verne as "L'Eternel Adam."
Original version published in the *Bulletin de la Société Jules Verne* 100
(1991): 21–48.

Theater Plays and Operettas (Performed or Published)

Les Pailles rompues (Broken Straws, 1849). First performed at the Théâtre
Historique on June 12, 1850. Published by Beck (Paris) in 1850.

Monna Lisa (Mona Lisa, 1852). Published posthumously in *Jules Verne*, ed.
Pierre-André Touttain, 1974.

Les Châteaux en Californie (Castles in California, 1852). Published in the
Musée des familles, September 1852.

Le Colin-Maillard (Blind Man's Bluff, 1852). First performed at the Théâtre
Lyrique on April 21, 1853. Published by Michel Lévy (Paris) in 1853.

Les Compagnons de la Marjolaine (The Companions of the Marjolaine, 1853).
First performed at the Théâtre Lyrique on June 6, 1855. Published
by Michel Lévy (Paris) in 1855.

Monsieur de Chimpanzé (Mister Chimpanze, 1857). First performed at the
Bouffes-Parisiennes on February 8, 1858. Published in the *Bulletin de la
Société Jules Verne* 57 (1981).

L'Auberge des Ardennes (The Ardennes Inn, 1859). First performed at the
Théâtre Lyrique on September 1, 1860. Published by Michel Lévy
(Paris) in 1860.

Onze jours de siège (Eleven Days of Siege, 1854–60). First performed at the
Théâtre du Vaudeville on June 1, 1861. Published by Michel Lévy
(Paris) in 1861.

Un Neveu d'Amérique, ou les Deux Frontignac (A Nephew from America, or the
Two Frontignacs, 1872). First performed at the Théâtre Cluny on April 17,
1873. Published by Hetzel (Paris) in 1873.

Le Tour du monde en quatre-vingts jours (Around the World in Eighty Days,
1874). First performed at the Théâtre de la Porte Saint-Martin,
November, 1874. Published in *Les Voyages au théâtre* by Jules Verne and
Adolphe d'Ennery (Paris, J. Hetzel, 1881).

Les Enfants du capitaine Grant (The Children of Captain Grant, 1878). First
performed at the Théâtre de la Porte Saint-Martin on December 26,
1878. Published in *Les Voyages au théâtre* by Jules Verne and Adolphe
d'Ennery (Paris, J. Hetzel, 1881).

Michel Strogoff (Michael Strogoff, 1880). First performed at the Théâtre de
Châtelet on November 17, 1880. Published in *Les Voyages au théâtre* by
Jules Verne and Adolphe d'Ennery (Paris, J. Hetzel, 1881).

Voyage à travers l'impossible (Journey through the Impossible, 1882). First
performed at the Théâtre de la Porte Saint-Martin on November 25,
1882. Published by Jean-Jacques Pauvert (Paris) in 1981.

Kéraban-le-têtu (Keraban the Stubborn, 1883). First performed at La Gaîté-
Lyrique on September 3, 1883. Published in the *Bulletin de la Société Jules
Verne* 85–86 (1988).

Poetry and Song Lyrics

Collected in *Poésies inédites*, ed. Christian Robin (1989, Cherche Midi) and
in *Textes oubliés*, ed. Francis Lacassin (1979, "10/18").

Literary Criticism, Nonfiction, Speeches, et al.

"A propos du 'Géant'" (Concerning the "Giant"). *Musée des familles*
(Dec.1863): 92–93. Rpt. in *Textes oubliés*, ed. Francis Lacassin (1979,
"10/18").
"Edgard Poë [*sic*] et ses oeuvres" (Edgar Poe and his Works). *Musée des
familles* (Apr. 1864): 193–208. Rpt. in *Textes oubliés*, ed. Francis Lacassin
(1979, "10/18"). Translated by I. O. Evans as "The Leader of the Cult of
the Unusual" in *The Edgar Allan Poe Scrapbook*, ed. Peter Haining (1978,
Schocken).
Géographie illustrée de la France et de ses colonies (Illustrated Geography of
France and Its Colonies, 1866, illus. Edouard Riou and Hubert
Clerget), coauthored with Théophile Lavallée.
"Une Ville idéale" (An Ideal City). *Mémoires de l'Académie des sciences, belles-
lettres, et arts d'Amiens* vol. 22 (1874–75): 347–78. Rpt. in *Textes oubliés*,
ed. Francis Lacassin (1979, "10/18"). Translated by I. O. Evans as "An
Ideal City" and included in *Yesterday and Tomorrow* (1965, Arco).
*Histoire des grands voyages et des grands voyageurs: Découverte de la terre (1878),
Les Grands navigateurs du XVIIIeme siècle* (1879, illus. Léon Benett, Paul
Philippoteaux), and *Les Voyageurs du XIXeme siècle* (1880). Translated by
Dora Leigh as *The Exploration of the World: Famous Travels and Travellers,
The Great Navigators of the Eighteenth Century, The Exploration of the World*
(1879, Scribners).
"The Story of My Boyhood." *The Youth's Companion* (Apr. 9, 1891): 221.
Verne's original autobiographical essay, "Souvenirs d'enfance et de
jeunesse" (Memories of Childhood and Youth), was published in French
for the first time in *Jules Verne*, ed. Pierre-André Touttain (1974, Cahiers
de l'Herne).
"Discours de distribution des prix au Lycée de Jeunes Filles d'Amiens"
(July 29, 1893). Rpt. in *Textes oubliés*, ed. Francis Lacassin (1979,
"10/18"). Translated by I. O. Evans as "The Future for Women: An
Address by Jules Verne," in *The Jules Verne Companion*, ed. Peter
Haining (1978, Souvenir).

"Future of the Submarine." *Popular Mechanics* 6 (June 1904): 629–31.
"Solution of Mind Problems by the Imagination." *Hearst's International Cosmopolitan* (Oct. 1928): 95, 132. Written in 1903.

Interviews

Belloc, Marie A. "Jules Verne at Home." *Strand Magazine* (Feb. 1895): 207–13.

Compère, Daniel, and Jean-Michel Margot. *Entretiens avec Jules Verne 1873–1905*. Geneva: Slatkine, 1998.

De Amicis, Edmondo. "A Visit to Jules Verne and Victorien Sardou." *Chautauquan* (Mar. 1897): 702–7.

Jones, Gordon. "Jules Verne at Home." *Temple Bar* 129 (1904): 664–70.

Sherard, Robert H. "Jules Verne at Home." *McClure's Magazine* (Jan. 1894): 115–24.

_____. "Jules Verne Revisited." *T.P.'s Weekly* (Oct. 9, 1903): 589.

Correspondence and Other Autobiographical Writings

Bottin, André. "Lettres inédites de Jules Verne au lieutenant colonel Hennebert." *Bulletin de la Société Jules Verne* 18 (1971): 36–44.

Dumas, Olivier, Piero Gondolo della Riva, and Volker Dehs. *Correspondance inédite de Jules Verne et de Pierre-Jules Hetzel (1863–1886)*. Vol. 1: *(1863–1874)*. Geneva: Slatkine, 1999. Additional volumes forthcoming.

Martin, Charles-Noël. *La Vie et l'oeuvre de Jules Verne*. Paris: Michel de l'Ormeraie, 1978.

Parménie, A. "Huit lettres de Jules Verne à son éditeur P.-J. Hetzel." *Arts et Lettres* 15 (1949): 102–7.

Parménie, A. and C. Bonnier de la Chapelle. *Histoire d'un éditeur et de ses auteurs, P.-J. Hetzel (Stahl)*. Paris: Albin Michel, 1953.

Turiello, Mario. "Lettre de Jules Verne à un jeune Italien." *Bulletin de la Société Jules Verne* 1 (1936): 158–61.

Verne, Jules. "Correspondance." *Bulletin de la Société Jules Verne* 49 (1979): 31–34

_____. "Correspondance avec Fernando Ricci," *Europe* 613 (1980): 137–38.

_____. "Correspondance avec Mario Turiello." *Europe* 613 (1980): 108–35.

_____. "Deux lettres à Louis-Jules Hetzel." In *Jules Verne*, ed. P.-A. Touttain, 73–74. Paris: Cahiers de l'Herne, 1974.

_____. "Deux lettres inédites." *Bulletin de la Société Jules Verne* 48 (1978): 253–54.

_____. "Jules Verne: 63 lettres." *Bulletin de la Société Jules Verne* 11–13 (1938): 47–129.

_____. "Lettre à Nadar." *L'Arc* 29 (1966): 83.

_____. "Lettres à Nadar." In *Jules Verne*, ed. P.-A. Touttain, 76–80. Paris: Cahiers de l'Herne, 1974.

_____. "Lettre à Paul, à propos de Turpin." In *Jules Verne*, ed. P.-A. Touttain, 81–82. Paris: Cahiers de l'Herne, 1974.

_____. "Lettres diverses." *Europe* 613 (1980): 143–51.

_____. "Quelques lettres." *Livres de France* 6 (May–June 1955): 13–15.

_____. "Sept lettres à sa famille et à divers correspondants." In *Jules Verne*, ed. P.-A. Touttain, 63–70. Paris: Cahiers de l'Herne, 1974.

_____. "Souvenirs d'Enfance et de Jeunesse." In *Jules Verne*, ed. P.-A. Touttain, 57–62. Paris: Cahiers de l'Herne, 1974.

_____. "Spécial Lettres No. 1." *Bulletin de la Société Jules Verne* 65–66 (1983): 4–50.

_____. "Spécial Lettres No. 2." *Bulletin de la Société Jules Verne* 69 (1984): 3–25.

_____. "Spécial Lettres No. 3." *Bulletin de la Société Jules Verne* 78 (1986): 3–52.

_____. "Spécial Lettres No. 4." *Bulletin de la Société Jules Verne* 83 (1987): 4–27.

_____. "Spécial Lettres No. 5." *Bulletin de la Société Jules Verne* 88 (1988): 8–18.

_____. "Spécial Lettres No. 6." *Bulletin de la Société Jules Verne* 94 (1990): 10–33.

_____. "Trente-six lettres inédites." *Bulletin de la Société Jules Verne* 68 (1983): 4–50.

_____. "Vingt-deux lettres de Jules Verne à son frère Paul." *Bulletin de la Société Jules Verne* 69 (1984): 3–25.

SECONDARY SOURCES ON JULES VERNE AND HIS WORKS

Bibliographies and Bibliographical Studies

Angenot, Marc. "Jules Verne and French Literary Criticism I." *Science Fiction Studies* 1.1 (1973): 33–37.

_____. "Jules Verne and French Literary Criticism II." *Science Fiction Studies* 1.2 (1973): 46–49.

Butcher, William. "Jules and Michel Verne." In *Critical Bibliography of French Literature: The Nineteenth Century*, ed. David Baguley, 923–40. Syracuse: Syracuse University Press, 1994.

Compère, Daniel. "Le Monde des études verniennes." *Magazine Littéraire* 119 (1976): 27–29.

Decré, Françoise. *Catalogue du fonds Jules Verne*. Nantes: Bibliothèque
Municipale, 1978. Updated by Colette Gaillois in *Catalogue du fonds Jules
Verne (1978–1983)*. Nantes: Bibliothèque Municipale, 1984.

Dumas, Olivier, et al. "Bibliographie des oeuvres de Jules Verne." *Bulletin
de la Société Jules Verne* 1 (1967): 7–12. Additions and updates: *BSJV* 2
(1967): 11–15; *BSJV* 3 (1967): 13; *BSJV* 4 (1967): 15–16. Rpt. in
Dumas, *Jules Verne*, 160–67. Lyon: La Manufacture, 1988.

Gallagher, Edward J., Judith A. Mistichelli, and John A. Van Eerde. *Jules
Verne: A Primary and Secondary Bibliography*. Boston: G. K. Hall, 1980.

Gondolo della Riva, Piero. *Bibliographie analytique de toutes les oeuvres de Jules
Verne*. Vols. 1 and 2. Paris: Société Jules Verne, 1977 and 1985.

Margot, Jean-Michel. *Bibliographie documentaire sur Jules Verne*. Amiens:
Centre de Documentation Jule Verne, 1989.

Raymond, François, and Daniel Compère. *Le Développement des études sur
Jules Verne*. Paris: Minard, Archives des Lettres Modernes, 1976.

Biographies

Allott, Kenneth. *Jules Verne*. London: Crescent Press, 1940.

Allotte de la Fuÿe, Marguerite. *Jules Verne, sa vie, son oeuvre*. Paris: Simon
Kra, 1928. Published in English as *Jules Verne*, trans. Erik de Mauny.
London: Staples, 1954.

Avrane, Patrick. *Jules Verne*. Paris: Stock, 1997.

Born, Franz. *The Man Who Invented the Future: Jules Verne*. New York:
Prentice-Hall, 1963.

Clarétie, Jules. *Jules Verne*. Paris: A. Quantin, 1883.

Costello, Peter. *Jules Verne: Inventor of Science Fiction*. London: Hodder and
Stroughton, 1978.

Dehs, Volker. *Jules Verne*. Hamburg: Rowohlt, 1986.

Dekiss, Jean-Paul. *Jules Verne, L'enchanteur*. Paris: Editions du Félin, 1999.

Dumas, Olivier. *Jules Verne*. Lyon: La Manufacture, 1988.

Jules-Verne, Jean. *Jules Verne*. Paris: Hachette, 1973. Published in English as
Jules Verne: A Biography, trans. Roger Greaves. New York: Taplinger, 1976.

Lemire, Charles. *Jules Verne*. Paris: Berger-Levrault, 1908.

Lottman, Herbert R. *Jules Verne: An Exploratory Biography*. New York:
St. Martin's Press, 1996. Published in French as *Jules Verne*, trans.
Marianne Véron. Paris: Flammarion, 1996.

Lynch, Lawrence. *Jules Verne*. New York: Twayne, 1992.

Martin, Charles-Noël. *La Vie et l'oeuvre de Jules Verne*. Paris: Michel de
l'Ormeraie, 1978.

Robien, Gilles de. *Jules Verne, le rêveur incompris*. Neuilly-sur-Seine: Michel
Lafon, 2000.

Soriano, Mark. *Jules Verne*. Paris: Julliard, 1978.

Teeters, Peggy. *Jules Verne: The Man Who Invented Tomorrow*. New York: Walter, 1992.

General Critical Studies

Alkon, Paul. *Science Fiction before 1900*. New York: Twayne, 1994.

Angenot, Marc. "Jules Verne: The Last Happy Utopianist." In *Science Fiction: A Critical Guide*, ed. Patrick Parrinder, 18–32. New York: Longman, 1979.

———. "Science Fiction in France before Verne." *Science Fiction Studies* 5.1 (Mar. 1978): 58–66.

L'Arc 29 (1966). Special issue devoted to Jules Verne.

Arts et Lettres 15 (1949). Special issue devoted to Jules Verne.

Barthes, Roland. "Nautilus et Bateau Ivre." In *Mythologies*, 90–92. Paris: Seuil, 1957, 1970. Published in English as "The Nautilus and the Drunken Boat," trans. A. Lavers, in Barthes, *Mythologies*, 65–67. New York: Hill and Wang, 1972.

———. "Par où commencer?" *Poétique* 1 (1970): 3–9. Rpt. in his *Nouveaux essais critiques*, 145–51. Paris: Seuil, 1972.

Bellemin-Noël, Jean. "Analectures de Jules Verne." *Critique* 26 (1970): 692–704.

Berri, Kenneth. "Les *Cinq cents millions de la Bégum* ou la technologie de la fable." *Stanford French Review* 3 (1979): 29–40.

Boia, Lucien. "Un Ecrivain original: Michel Verne." *Bulletin de la Société Jules Verne* 70 (1984): 90–95.

Bradbury, Ray. "The Ardent Blasphemers." Foreword to Jules Verne, *Twenty Thousand Leagues under the Sea*, trans. Anthony Bonner, 1–12. New York: Bantam Books, 1962.

Bridenne, Jean-Jacques. *La Littérature française d'imagination scientifique*. Lausanne: Dassonville, 1950.

Buisine, Alain. "Circulations en tous genres." *Europe* 595–96 (1978): 48–56.

———. "Repères, marques, gisements: à propos de la robinsonnade vernienne." *Revue des Lettres Modernes* 523–529 (Apr.–June 1978). Special issue devoted to Jules Verne.

Bulletin de la Société Jules Verne (1967–2000). Edited by Olivier Dumas. The official publication of the Jules Verne Society and one of the best sources for up-to-date and reliable information on Jules Verne.

Butcher, William. "Crevettes de l'air et baleines volantes." *La Nouvelle Revue Maritime* 386–87 (May–June 1984): 35–40.

———. "Graphes et graphie." In *Regards sur la théorie des graphes*, 177–82. Lausanne: Presses polytechniques romandes, 1980.

———. "Long-Lost Manuscript." *Modern Language Review* 93.4 (Oct. 1998): 961–71.

_____. "La Poésie de l'arborescence chez Verne." *Studi Francesi* 104 (1992): 261–67.

_____. "Le Sens de *L'Eternel Adam*." *Bulletin de la Société Jules Verne* 58 (1981): 73–81.

_____. "Le Verbe et la chair, ou l'emploi du temps." In *Jules Verne 4: Texte, image, spectacle*, ed. François Raymond, 125–48. Paris: Minard, 1983.

_____. *Verne's Journey to the Center of the Self: Space and Time in the Voyages Extraordinaires*. London and New York: Macmillan and St. Martin's, 1990.

Butor, Michel. "Homage to Jules Verne." Trans. John Coleman. *New Statesman*, July 15, 1966, 94.

_____. "Le Point suprême et l'âge d'or à travers quelques oeuvres de Jules Verne." *Arts et Lettres* 15 (1949): 3–31. Rpt. in Michel Butor, *Répertoire I*, 130–62. Paris: Editions de Minuit, 1960.

Cahiers du Centre d'études verniennes et du Musée Jules Verne (1981–). Edited by Christian Robin. The official journal of the Jules Verne Archives, located in Nantes.

Carrouges, Michel. "Le Mythe de Vulcain chez Jules Verne." *Arts et Lettres* 15 (1949): 32–48.

Chambers, Ross. "Cultural and Ideological Determinations in Narrative: A Note on Jules Verne's *Cinq Cents millions de la Bégum*." *L'Esprit créateur* 21 (fall 1981): 69–78.

Chesneaux, Jean. "L'Invention linguistique chez Jules Verne." In *Langues et techniques, Nature et Société 1*, ed. J. M. C. Thomas et Lucien Bernot, 345–51. Paris: Klincksieck, 1972.

_____. *Une Lecture politique de Jules Verne*. Paris: Maspero, 1971. Published in English as *The Political and Social Ideas of Jules Verne*, trans. Thomas Wikeley. London: Thames and Hudson, 1972.

Compère, Daniel. *Approche de l'île chez Jules Verne*. Paris: Lettres Modernes, 1977.

_____. "Le Bas des pages." *Bulletin de la Société Jules Verne* 68 (1983): 147–53.

_____. *Jules Verne écrivain*. Genève: Droz, 1991.

_____. *Jules Verne: parcours d'une oeuvre*. Amiens: Encrage, 1996.

_____. "Poétique de la carte." *Bulletin de la Société Jules Verne* 50 (1979): 69–74.

_____. *Un Voyage imaginaire de Jules Verne: Voyage au Centre de la Terre*. Paris: Lettres Modernes, 1977.

Compère, Daniel, and Volker Dehs. "Tashinar and Co. Introduction à une étude des mots inventés dans l'oeuvre de Jules Verne." *Bulletin de la Société Jules Verne* 67 (1983): 107–11.

Costello, Peter. *Jules Verne: Inventor of Science Fiction*. London: Hodder and Stoughton, 1978.

Davy, Jacques. "A Propos de l'antropophagie chez Jules Verne." *Cahiers du Centre d'études verniennes et du Musée Jules Verne* 1 (1981): 15–23.

Diesbach, Ghislain de. *Le Tour de Jules Verne en quatre-vingts livres*. Paris: Julliard, 1969.

Dumas, Olivier. "La main du fils dans l'oeuvre du père." *Bulletin de la Société Jules Verne* 82 (1987): 21–24.

Escaich, René. *Voyage au monde de Jules Verne*. Paris: Plantin, 1955.

Europe 33 (1955). Special issue devoted to Jules Verne.

Europe 595–96 (1978). Special issue devoted to Jules Verne.

Evans, Arthur B. "The Extraordinary Libraries of Jules Verne." *L'Esprit créateur* 28 (1988): 75–86.

_____. "Le Franglais vernien (père et fils)." In *Modernités de Jules Verne*, ed. Jean Bessière, 87–105. Paris: PUF, 1988.

_____. "The Illustrators of Jules Verne's *Voyages Extraordinaires*." *Science Fiction Studies* 25.2 (July 1998): 241–70.

_____. "Jules Verne and the French Literary Canon." In *Jules Verne: Narratives of Modernity*, ed. Edmund J. Smyth, 11–39. Liverpool: Liverpool University Press, 2000.

_____. "Jules Verne et la persistence rétinienne." *Cahiers du centre d'études verniennes et du Musée Jules Verne* 13 (1996): 11–17.

_____. "Jules Verne, visionnaire incompris." *Pour la Science* 236 (June 1997): 94–101.

_____. *Jules Verne Rediscovered: Didacticism and the Scientific Novel*. Westport, Conn.: Greenwood, 1988.

_____. "Literary Intertexts in Jules Verne's *Voyages Extraordinaires*." *Science Fiction Studies* 23.2 (July 1996): 171–87.

_____. "The 'New' Jules Verne." *Science Fiction Studies* 22.1 (Mar. 1995): 35–46.

_____. "Science Fiction in France: A Brief History and Selective Bibliography." *Science Fiction Studies* 16.3 (Nov. 1989): 254–76, 338–65.

_____. "Science Fiction vs. Scientific Fiction in France: From Jules Verne to J.-H. Rosny Aîné." *Science Fiction Studies* 15.1 (1988): 1–11.

_____. "Vehicular Utopias of Jules Verne." In *Transformations of Utopia*, ed. George Slusser et al., 99–108. New York: AMS Press, 1999.

Evans, Arthur B., and Ron Miller. "Jules Verne: Misunderstood Visionary." *Scientific American* (Apr. 1997): 92–97. Available online at http://www.sciam.com/0497issue/0497evans.html.

Evans, I. O. *Jules Verne and His Works*. London: Arco, 1965.

_____. "Jules Verne et le lecteur anglais." *Bulletin de la Société Jules Verne* 6 (1937): 36.

Foucault, Michel. "L'Arrière-fable." *L Arc* 29 (1966): 5–13. Published in English as "Behind the Fable," trans. Pierre A. Walker, *Critical Texts* 5 (1988): 1–5; also as "Behind the Fable," trans. Robert Hurley, in *Aesthetics, Method, and Epistemology*, ed. J. Faubion, 137–45. New York: New Press, 1998.

Frank, Bernard. *Jules Verne et ses Voyages*. Paris: Flammarion, 1941.

Gilli, Yves, Florent Montaclair, and Sylvie Petit. *Le Naufrage dans l'oeuvre de Jules Verne*. Paris: Harmattan, 1998.

Gondolo della Riva, Piero. "A propos des oeuvres posthumes de Jules Verne." *Europe* 595–96 (1978): 73–82.

———. "A propos d'une nouvelle." In *Jules Verne,* ed. Pierre-André Touttain, 284–85. Paris: Cahiers de l'Herne, 1974.

Haining, Peter. *The Jules Verne Companion.* London: Souvenir, 1978.

Huet, Marie-Hélène. *L'Histoire des Voyages Extraordinaires.* Paris: Minard, 1973.

Jensen, William B. "Captain Nemo's Battery: Chemistry and the Science Fiction of Jules Verne." *The Chemical Intelligencer* (Apr. 1997): 23–32.

Jules Verne et les sciences humaines. Paris: UGE, "10/18," 1979.

Jules Verne—filiations, rencontres, influences. Colloque d'Amiens II. Paris: Minard, 1980.

Ketterer, David. "Fathoming *20,000 Leagues under the Sea.*" In *The Stellar Gauge: Essays on Science Fiction Writers,* 7–24. Carlton, Australia: Nostrillia Press, 1981.

Klein, Gérard. "Pour lire Verne (I)." *Fiction* 197 (1970): 137–43.

———. "Pour lire Verne (II)." *Fiction* 198 (1970): 143–52.

Lacassin, Francis. "Du Pavillion noir au Québec libre." *Magazine Littéraire* 119 (1976): 22–26.

———. *Passagers clandestins.* Paris: UGE, "10/18," 1979.

———, ed. *Textes oubliés.* Paris: UGE, "10/18," 1979.

Lengrand, Claude. *Dictionnaire des "Voyages Extraordinaires" de Jules Verne: Cahier Jules Verne, I.* Amiens: Encrage, 1998.

Livres de France 5 (1955). Special issue devoted to Jules Verne.

Macherey, Pierre. "Jules Verne ou le récit en défaut." In *Pour une théorie de la production littéraire.* Paris: Maspero, 1966. 183–266. Published in English as "The Faulty Narrative," in Macherey, *A Theory of Literary Production,* trans. G. Wall, 159–240. London: Routledge & Kegan Paul, 1978.

Magazine littéraire 119 (December 1976). Special issue devoted to Jules Verne.

Martin, Andrew. "Chez Jules: Nutrition and Cognition in the Novels of Jules Verne." *French Studies* 37 (Jan. 1983): 47–58.

———. "The Entropy of Bazacian Tropes in the Scientific Fictions of Jules Verne." *Modern Language Review* 77 (Jan. 1982): 51–62.

———. *The Knowledge of Ignorance from Cervantes to Jules Verne.* Cambridge: Cambridge University Press, 1985.

———. *The Mask of the Prophet: The Extraordinary Fictions of Jules Verne.* Oxford: Clarendon, 1990.

Miller, Ron. *Extraordinary Voyages: A Reader's Guide to the Works of Jules Verne.* Fredericksburg, Va.: Black Cat, 1994.

Miller, Walter James. *The Annotated Jules Verne: From the Earth to the Moon.* New York: Crowell, 1978.

———. *The Annotated Jules Verne: Twenty Thousand Leagues under the Sea.* New York: Crowell, 1976.

———. "Jules Verne in America: A Translator's Preface." In Jules Verne,

Twenty Thousand Leagues under the Sea, trans. Walter James Miller, vii–xxii. New York: Washington Square, 1965.

Modernités de Jules Verne. Edited by Jean Bessière. Paris: PUF, 1988.

Moré, Marcel. *Nouvelles Explorations de Jules Verne*. Paris: NRF, 1963.

_____. *Le Très Curieux Jules Verne*. Paris: NRF, 1960.

Moskowitz, Sam, ed. *Science Fiction by Gaslight*. Cleveland: World, 1968.

Noiray, Jacques. *Le Romancier et la machine: l'image de la machine dans le roman français (1850–1900)*. Paris: José Corti, 1982.

Nouvelles recherches sur Jules Verne et le voyage. Colloque d'Amiens I. Paris: Minard, 1978.

Pourvoyeur, Robert. "De l'invention des mots chez Jules Verne." *Bulletin de la Société Jules Verne* 25 (1973): 19–24.

Raymond, François, ed. *Jules Verne 1: Le Tour du monde*. Paris: Minard, 1976.

_____. *Jules Verne 2: L'Ecriture vernienne*. Paris: Minard, 1978.

_____. *Jules Verne 3: Machines et imaginaire*. Paris: Minard, 1980.

_____. *Jules Verne 4: Texte, image, spectacle*. Paris: Minard, 1983.

_____. *Jules Verne 5: Emergences du fantastique*. Paris: Minard, 1987.

_____. *Jules Verne 6: La Science en question*. Paris: Minard, 1992.

_____. "Jules Verne ou le mouvement perpetuel." *Subsidia Pataphysica* 8 (1969): 21–52.

Renzi, Thomas C. *Jules Verne on Film: A Filmography of the Cinematic Adaptations of His Works, 1902 through 1997*. Jefferson, N.C.: McFarland, 1998.

Revue Jules Verne (1996–99). Edited by Jean-Paul Dekiss. Amiens: Centre de documentation Jules Verne.

Robin, Christian. *Un Monde connu et inconnu*. Nantes: Centre universitaire de recherches verniennes, 1978.

_____, ed. *Textes et langages X: Jules Verne*. Nantes: Université de Nantes, 1984.

Rose, Mark. "Jules Verne: Journey to the Center of Science Fiction." In *Coordinates: Placing Science Fiction*, ed. George E. Slusser, 31–41. Carbondale: Southern Illinois University Press, 1983.

_____. "Filling the Void: Verne, Wells, and Lem." *Science Fiction Studies* 8.2 (1981): 121–42.

Serres, Michel. "India (The Black and the Archipelago) on Fire." *Substance* 8 (1974): 49–60.

_____. *Jouvences sur Jules Verne*. Paris: Editions de Minuit, 1974.

_____. "Le Savoir, la guerre, et le sacrifice." *Critique* 367 (Dec. 1977): 1067–77.

Slusser, George E. "The Perils of Experiment: Jules Verne and the American Lone Genius." *Extrapolation* 40.2 (1999): 101–15.

Smyth, Edmund J., ed. *Jules Verne: Narratives of Modernity*. Liverpool: Liverpool University Press, 2000.

Stableford, Brian. *Scientific Romance in Britain, 1890–1950*. London: Fourth Estate, 1985.

Suvin, Darko. "Communication in Quantified Space: The Utopian
    Liberalism of Jules Verne's Fiction." *Clio*, 4 (1974): 51–71. Rpt. in
    Suvin, *Metamorphoses of Science Fiction*, 147–63. New Haven: Yale
    University Press, 1979.
Taves, Brian, and Stephen Michaluk Jr. *The Jules Verne Encyclopedia.*
    Lanham, Md.: Scarecrow, 1996.
Touttain, Pierre-André, ed. *Jules Verne*. Paris: Cahiers de l'Herne, 1974.
Unwin, Timothy. *Jules Verne: Le Tour du monde en quatre-vingts jours*. Glasgow:
    Glasgow University Press, 1992.
Vierne, Simone. "Hetzel et Jules Verne, ou l'invention d'un auteur." In
    Europe 619–20 (1980): 53–63.
_____. *Jules Verne, mythe et modernité*. Paris: PUF, 1989.
_____. *Jules Verne et le roman initiatique*. Paris: Sirac, 1973.
_____. *Jules Verne, une vie, une oeuvre*. Paris: Ballard, 1986.

Materials Relating to Jules Verne's *Invasion of the Sea*

Hélène, Maxime (pseudonym of Maxime Vuillaume). "La Mer intérieure
    d'Algerie." *La Nature* 10.11 (1882): 22–24, 35–38. Cited by Jules Verne
    as one of his sources for *L'Invasion de la mer* (see introduction in this
    volume).
Hourant, Georges-Pierre. "L'Algérie dans l'oeuvre de Jules Verne." *Bulletin
    de la Société Jules Verne* 21.82 (Apr.–June 1987): 21–24.
Lacassin, Francis. "Jules Verne et les majorités opprimées. In Jules Verne,
    L'Invasion de la mer, 9–13. Paris: UGE, "10/18," 1978.
Letolle, René, and Hocine Bendjoudi. *Histoires d'une mer au Sahara: Utopies et
    politique*. Paris: L'Harmattan, 1997.
Martin, Charles-Noël. "Préface." In Jules Verne, *"Adventures de Trois Russes
    et de Trois Anglais" et "L'Invasion de la mer,"* 7–13. Lausanne: Rencontre,
    1970.
Nash, Andrew. *"Invasion of the Sea:* 1905 Translation." *Extraordinary Voyages:
    The Newsletter of the North American Jules Verne Society* 6.1 (Nov. 1999):
    1–3.

Jules Gabriel Verne

A BIOGRAPHY

Jules Gabriel Verne was born on February 8, 1828, to a middle-class family in the port city of Nantes, France. His mother, Sophie, née Allotte de la Fuÿe, was the daughter of a prominent family of shipowners, and his father, Pierre Verne, was an attorney and the son of a Provins magistrate. Jules was the eldest of five children. In addition to his three sisters—Anna, Mathilde, and Marie—he had a younger brother, Paul, to whom he was very close. Paul eventually became a naval engineer.

As a child and young man, Jules was a relatively conscientious student. Although far from the top of his class, he apparently did win awards for meritorious performance in geography, music, and Greek and Latin, and he easily passed his *baccalauréat* in 1846. But his true passion was the sea. The shipyard docks of nearby Île Feydeau and the bustling commerce of the Nantes harbor never failed to spark Jules's youthful imagination with visions of far-off lands and exotic peoples. Legend has it that he once ran off to sea as a cabin boy aboard a schooner bound for the Indies, but his father managed to intercept the ship before it reached the open sea and retrieved his wayward son. According to this story, Jules (probably after a good thrashing) promised his parents that he would travel henceforth only in his dreams. Although this charming tale was most likely invented by Verne's familial biographer Marguerite Allotte de la Fuÿe, it nevertheless exemplifies the author's lifelong love for the sea and his yearnings for adventure-filled journeys to distant ports of call.

Young Jules also loved machines. During an interview toward the end of his life, he reminisced about his early formative years: "While I was quite a lad, I used to adore watching machines at work. My father had a country-house at Chantenay, at the mouth of the Loire, and near the government factory at Indret. I never went to Chantenay without entering the factory and standing for hours watching the machines.... This penchant has remained with me all my life, and today I have still as much pleasure in watching a steam-engine or a fine locomotive at work as I have in contemplating a picture by Raphael or Corregio" (Robert H. Sherard, "Jules Verne at Home," *McClure's Magazine* [Jan. 1984]: 118).

Intending that Jules follow in his footsteps as a lawyer, Pierre Verne sent him to Paris in 1848 to study law. The correspondence between father and son during the ensuing ten years shows that Jules took his studies seriously, completing his law degree in just two years. But his letters home also

Jules Verne (anonymous engraving, c. 1880)

make quite it clear that Jules had discovered a new passion—literature. Inspired by authors such as Victor Hugo, Alfred de Vigny, and Théophile Gautier and introduced (via family contacts on his mother's side) into several high-society Parisian literary circles, the young Romantic Verne began to write. From 1847 to 1862, he composed poetry, wrote several plays and a novel entitled *Un Prêtre en 1839* (unpublished during his lifetime), and penned a variety of short stories that he published in the popular French journal *Musée des familles* to supplement his meager income: "Les Premiers navires de la marine mexicaine " (1851), "Un Voyage en ballon" (1851), "Martin Paz" (1852), "Maître Zacharius" (1854), and "Un Hivernage dans les glaces" (1855). Some of his plays were performed in local Parisian theaters: *Les Pailles rompues* (1850), *Le Colin-Maillard* (1853), *Les Compagnons de la Marjolaine* (1855), *Monsieur de Chimpanzé* (1858), *L'Auberge des Ardennes* (1860), and *Onze jours de siège* (1861). During this period, Verne also became close friends with Alexandre Dumas père and Dumas fils and, through the former's intervention, eventually became the secretary of the Théâtre Lyrique in 1852.

In 1857 Verne married Honorine Morel née de Viane, a twenty-six-year-old widow with two daughters. Taking advantage of his new father-in-law's contacts in Paris and a monetary wedding gift from Pierre Verne, Jules decided to discontinue his work at the Théâtre Lyrique and to take a full-time job as *agent de change* at the Paris Stock Market with the firm Eggly & Cie. He spent his early mornings at home writing (at a desk with two drawers—one for his plays, the other for his scientific essays) and most of his days at the Bourse de Paris doing business and associating with a number of other young stockbrokers who had interests similar to his own.

When not busy writing or working at the stock exchange, Verne spent the rest of his time either visiting his old theater friends (he took trips with Aristide Hignard to Scotland and England in 1859 and to Norway and Denmark in 1862—the former resulting in a travelogue called *Voyage en Angleterre et en Écosse*) or at the Bibliothèque Nationale, collecting scientific and historical news items and copying them onto notecards for future use—a work habit he would continue throughout his life. As at least one biographer has noted, the long weekend sessions he spent in the reading rooms of the library may well have been partly motivated by a simple desire for peace and quiet: in 1861 Verne's son Michel had just been born and greatly annoyed his father with his incessant crying.

It was during this time that Verne first conceived of writing a new type of novel called a *roman de la science*. It would incorporate the large amounts of scientific material that Verne accumulated in his library research, as well as that gleaned from essays in the *Musée des familles* and other journals to which he himself occasionally contributed. It would combine scientific exploration and discovery with action and adventure and be patterned on the novels of Walter Scott, James Fenimore Cooper, and Edgar Allan Poe. The latter's works in particular, which had recently been translated into French by Charles Baudelaire in 1856, strongly interested Verne for their unusual mixture of scientific reasoning and the fantastic (he later wrote his only piece of literary criticism on Poe in 1864). Verne's efforts eventually crystallized into a rough draft of a novel-length narrative, which he tentatively entitled *Un Voyage en l'air* (A Voyage through the Air).

In September 1862, Verne was introduced to Pierre-Jules Hetzel through a common friend of the publisher and Alexandre Dumas père. Verne promptly asked Hetzel if he would consider reviewing for publication the rough draft of his novel—a manuscript that, according to his wife, the author had very nearly destroyed a few weeks earlier after his rejection by another publishing house. Hetzel agreed to the request, seeing in this narrative the potential for an ideal "fit" with his new family-oriented magazine, the *Magasin d'Education et de Récréation*. A few days later, Verne and Hetzel began what would prove to be a highly successful author-publisher collaboration. It lasted for more than forty years and resulted in over sixty "scientific novels" collectively called the *Voyages Extraordinaires—Voyages dans les mondes connus et inconnus* (The Extraordinary Voyages—Journeys in Known and Unknown Worlds).

Shortly after the publication and immediate commercial success of Verne's first novel in 1863—now retitled *Cinq semaines en ballon, Voyage de découvertes en Afrique par trois Anglais* (Five Weeks in a Balloon, Voyage of Discovery in Africa by Three Englishmen)—Hetzel offered the young writer a ten-year contract for at least two works per year of the same sort. Not long after, Verne quit his job at the stock market and began to write full-time.

Following Verne's historic meeting with Hetzel, the remainder of his life and works can be divided into three distinct periods. 1862–1886, 1886–1905, and 1905–1925.

The first, from 1862 to 1886, might be termed Verne's "Hetzel period." During this time he wrote his most popular *Voyages Extraordinaires*, settled permanently with his family in Amiens, purchased a yacht, collaborated on theater adaptations of several of his novels with Adolphe d'Ennery, and ultimately gained both fame and fortune.

Other notable events in Verne's life during this period include:
  —Hetzel's rejection of his second novel, *Paris au XXe siècle* in 1863 as well as an early draft of *L'Île mystérieuse* (called *L'Oncle Robinson*) in 1865.
  —the publication of his nonfiction books *Géographie de la France et de ses colonies* (1866, coauthored with Théophile Lavallée) and the three-volume *Histoire des grands voyages et des grands voyageurs* (1878–80).
  —the unparalleled success of the novels *Voyage au centre de la terre* (1864), *De la terre à la lune* (1865) and *Autour de la lune* (1870), *Vingt mille lieues sous les mers* (1870), *Le Tour du monde en quatre-vingts jours* (1873), and *Michel Strogoff* (1876), among others.
  —a brief trip to America in 1867 on the *Great Eastern*, accompanied

by his brother Paul, and visits to New York and Niagara Falls—
subsequently fictionalized in his novel *La Ville flottante* (1871).

—received the *Légion d'honneur* just before the outbreak of the Franco-
Prussian War in 1870.

—the death of his father, Pierre Verne, on November 3, 1871.

—the purchase of his third yacht, the *Saint-Michel III*, in which he sailed
to Lisbon and Algiers in 1878, to Norway, Ireland, and Scotland
in 1879–80, to Holland, Denmark, Germany, and the Baltics in 1881,
and to Portugal, Algeria, Tunisia, and Italy in 1884 (and, while
in Italy, was supposedly invited to a private audience with Pope Leo
XIII).

—in 1879, the publication of *Le Cinq cents millions de la Bégum* (in
collaboration with Paschal Grousset, a.k.a. André Laurie), Verne's
only utopia/dystopia, which featured his first "mad scientist," Herr
Schultze.

—in 1882, he moved to a new, larger home at 2 rue Charles-Dubois,
Amiens—the famous house with the circular tower, which is today
the headquarters of the Centre de Documentation Jules Verne
d'Amiens.

The second phase, from 1886 to 1905, might be called Verne's "post-Hetzel
period." During this time, Verne worked with Hetzel's son, Louis-Jules,
who succeeded his father as manager and principal editor of the Hetzel
publishing house. Verne also entered into politics: he was elected to the mu-
nicipal council of Amiens in 1888, a post he would occupy for fifteen years.
But this period is especially notable because of a gradual change in the ideological tone of his *Voyages Extraordinaires*. In these later works, the Saint-
Simonian pro-science optimism is largely absent, replaced by a growing pessimism about the true value of progress. The omnipresent scientific didacticism, a trademark of Verne's *roman scientifique*, is more frequently muted and
supplemented by romantic melodrama, pathos, and tragedy. And the leit-
motif of the triumphant exploration and conquest of nature, which seemed
to undergird most of Verne's earlier novels, is now often abandoned—
replaced by an increased focus on politics, social issues, and human morality. This dramatic change of focus in Verne's later works appears to parallel
certain personal adversities experienced by the author during this period of
his life. For example:

—serious problems with his rebellious son Michel (e.g., repeated
bankruptcies, costly amorous escapades, divorce from his first wife,
difficulties with the law, etc.).

—severe financial worries, forcing Verne to sell his beloved yacht in
1886.

—the successive deaths of three individuals who were very close to him:
his longtime friend Mme Duchène in 1885, his editor Hetzel in 1886,
and his mother in 1887.

—an attack at gunpoint on March 9, 1886, by his mentally disturbed nephew Gaston; Verne was shot in the lower leg and remained partially crippled for the rest of his life.

Verne's personal correspondence from this period also reflects his growing pessimism. In a letter dated December 21, 1886, to Hetzel fils, Verne confides: "As for the rest, I have now entered into the blackest part of my life." A few years later in 1894, the author tells his brother Paul: "All that remains to me are these intellectual distractions. . . . My character is profoundly changed and I have received blows from which I'll never recover."

Whatever the underlying reasons may have been for this change—the absence of Hetzel père's editorial supervision, Verne's awareness of certain disturbing trends in the world at large (e.g., the growth of imperialism and the military-industrial complex), or the sudden flood of tragedies in his personal life—it is evident that many of Verne's post-1886 *Voyages Extraordinaires* tend to portray both scientists and scientific innovation with a heavy dose of cynicism and/or biting satire. And, in contrast to the intrepid "go where no man has gone before" scientific explorations that characterized most of his earlier and most popular works, the later novels now often foreground, in whole or in part, a broad range of political, social, and moral concerns: the potential dangers of technology in *Sans dessus dessous* (1889), *Face au drapeau* (1896), and *Maître du monde* (1904), the cruel oppression of the Québécois in Canada in *Famille-sans-nom* (1889), the evils of ignorance and superstition in *Le Château des Carpathes* (1892), the intolerable living conditions in orphanages in *P'tit-Bonhomme* (1893), the malevolent influence of religious missionaries on South Sea island cultures in *L'Île à hélice* (1895), the imminent extinction of whales in *Le Sphinx des glaces* (1897), the environmental damage caused by the oil industry in *Le Testament d'un excentrique* (1899), and the slaughter of elephants for their ivory in *Le Village aérien* (1901), among many others.

During his last years, despite increasingly poor health (arthritis, cataracts, diabetes, and severe gastrointestinal problems) and continuing family squabbles because of his son Michel, Verne continued diligently to write two to three novels per year. But, with a drawer full of nearly completed manuscripts in his desk, he suddenly fell seriously ill in early March 1905, a few weeks after his seventy-seventh birthday. He told his wife Honorine to gather the family around him, and he died quietly on March 24, 1905. He was buried on March 28 in the cemetery of La Madeleine in Amiens. Two years later, an elaborate marble sculpture by Albert Roze was placed over his grave, depicting the author rising from his tomb and stretching his hand toward the sky.

The third and final phase of the Jules Verne story, following the author's death and extending from 1905 to 1919, might well be called the "Verne fils period." During these years Verne's posthumous works were published, but most of them were substantially modified—and, in some instances, entirely authored—by his son Michel.

In early May 1905, Michel, as executor of his father's estate, published in the Parisian newspapers *Le Figaro* and *Le Temps* a complete list of Jules Verne's surviving manuscripts: eight novels (titled and untitled, in various stages of completion), sixteen plays, several short stories (two unpublished), a travelogue of his early trip to England and Scotland, and an assortment of historical sketches, notes, etc. Hetzel fils immediately agreed to publish six of the novels that were originally intended to be part of the *Voyages Extraordinaires* as well as Verne's short stories, which were grouped in the collection published in 1910 as *Hier et demain*. Another remaining novel in the series, *L'Étonnante Aventure de la mission Barsac*, was published first in serial format in the newspaper *Le Matin* and later as a book by the publishing company Hachette—who had bought the rights to Verne's works from Hetzel fils in 1914.

In recent years, these posthumous works have become the topic of heated controversy among Verne scholars: how much and in what ways did Michel alter these texts prior to their publication? After a close examination of the available manuscripts (now housed in the Centre d'études verniennes in Nantes) by Piero Gondolo della Riva, Olivier Dumas, and other respected Vernian researchers, it now seems indisputable that Michel had a much greater hand in the composition of Jules Verne's posthumous works than had ever been suspected:

—*Le Volcan d'or* (1906): fourteen chapters by Jules; four more chapters added by Michel as well as four new characters.

—*L'Agence Thompson and Co.* (1907): in all probability, almost entirely written by Michel.

—*La Chasse au météore* (1908): seventeen chapters by Jules; four added by Michel.

—*Le Pilote du Danube* (1908): sixteen chapters by Jules; three added by Michel as well as at least one new character and a new title.

—*Les Naufragés du Jonathan* (1909): sixteen chapters by Jules; fifteen added by Michel as well as many new characters, episodes, and a new title.

—*Le Secret de Wilhelm Storitz* (1910): rewritten by Michel to take place in the eighteenth century instead of at the end of the nineteenth; a different conclusion is also added.

—*Hier et demain* (1910): most of the short stories appearing in this collection were substantially altered by Michel; one of them, "Au XXIXe siècle: la Journée d'un journaliste américain en 2889," is attributable to Michel almost wholly, and another, "L'Eternel Adam," is most probably by him as well.

—*L'Etonnante aventure de la mission Barsac* (1919): this supposedly "final" novel of the *Voyage Extraordinaires* was written entirely by Michel from his father's notes for a novel to be called *Voyages d'études*.

Scholarly reaction to Michel's rewrites of his father's manuscripts has been mixed. Some have called Michel's intervention in Verne's posthumous works an inexcusable betrayal of trust and a financially motivated scam that dealt a damaging blow to the overall integrity of Verne's *Voyages Extraordinaires*. In an attempt to set the record straight, from 1985 through the early 1990s, the Société Jules Verne in France arranged for the publication of Verne's orginal manuscripts of several of these works. Other scholars, in contrast, have pointed out that Jules Verne encouraged Michel to publish his own fiction under his father's illustrious name; that during the final decade of his life when his eyesight was rapidly failing, Jules often asked Michel to "collaborate" with him (as secretary-typist) to help bring several of his later novels to publication; and that Michel's sometimes radical modifications of Verne's posthumous works served, more often than not, to improve their readability—an enhancement that would assuredly have received his father's wholehearted approval. The debate continues to this day.

With Michel's death in 1925, the final chapter of Verne's literary legacy was (for better or worse) complete. Ironically, in April of the following year, a pulp magazine called *Amazing Stories* first appeared on American newsstands. It published tales of a supposedly new species of literature dubbed "scientification"—defined by its publisher Hugo Gernsback as a "Jules Verne, H. G. Wells, and Edgar Allan Poe type of story"—and its title page featured a drawing of Verne's tomb as the magazine's logo. The popularity of *Amazing Stories* and its many pulp progeny such as *Science Wonder Stories* and *Astounding Stories* was both immediate and long-lasting. As the term "scientification" evolved into "science fiction," the new genre began to flourish as never before. And the legend of Jules Verne as its patron saint, as the putative "Father of Science Fiction," soon became firmly rooted in American cultural folklore.

Library of Congress Cataloging-in-Publication Data
Verne, Jules, 1828–1905.
  [Invasion de la mer. English]
  Invasion of the sea / Jules Verne ; translated by Edward T. Baxter ;
edited by Arthur B. Evans ; introduction and critical material by
Arthur B. Evans.
      p. cm.
  Includes bibliographical references.
  ISBN 0-8195-6465-6 (cloth : alk. paper) — ISBN 0-8195-6558-X
(paper : alk. paper)
    I. Baxter, Edward II. Evans, Arthur B. III. Title.
PQ2469.I5 E5 2001
843'.8—dc21   2001043515